To Tempt an Heiress

By Susanna Craig

To Tempt an Heiress
To Kiss a Thief

Published by Kensington Publishing Corp.

To Tempt an Heiress

Susanna Craig

LYRICAL PRESS
Kensington Publishing Corp.
www.kensingtonbooks.com

LYRICAL PRESS BOOKS are published by

Kensington Publishing Corp.
119 West 40th Street
New York, NY 10018

All Kensington titles, imprints, and distributed lines are available at special quantity discounts for bulk purchases for sales promotion, premiums, fund-raising, educational, or institutional use.

Special book excerpts or customized printings can also be created to fit specific needs. For details, write or phone the office of the Kensington Sales Manager: Kensington Publishing Corp., 119 West 40th Street, New York, NY 10018. Attn. Sales Department. Phone: 1-800-221-2647.

Lyrical Press and Lyrical Press logo Reg. U.S. Pat. & TM Off.

First Electronic Edition: December 2016
eISBN-13: 978-1-60183-617-5
eISBN-10: 1-60183-617-1

First Print Edition: December 2016
ISBN-13: 978-1-60183-618-2
ISBN-10: 1-60183-618-X

Printed in the United States of America

To my husband,
who showed me that love at first sight,
triumph over adversity, and happily-ever-after
aren't just for stories.

ACKNOWLEDGMENTS

Thank you to all the folks at Kensington who help bring my books into the world, especially my editor, Esi Sogah, whose enthusiasm for this project helped to carry me through it.

My friend and first reader, Amy, advocated on behalf of these characters many times. Without her encouragement, their story might never have been told.

Finally, my husband, a historian of colonial British America, helped immensely with a number of details, and if the job of "romance novelist's research assistant" wasn't *quite* what he'd imagined it would be, he never complained. I hope he, and my readers, will forgive me for occasionally bending historical realities to serve the interests of romantic fiction.

Chapter 1

Captain Andrew Corrvan would never claim to have always acted on the right side of the law, but there were crimes even he would not stoop to commit.

Kidnapping was one of them.

This conversation ought to have been taking place in some dark dockside alley, not in the sun-dappled sitting room of the little stone house occupied by the plantation manager at Harper's Hill. Andrew had never met the man before today, although he knew him by reputation. Throughout Antigua, Edward Cary was talked of by those who knew him, and by many more who didn't, as a fool. As best Andrew had been able to work out, he had earned the epithet for being sober, honest, and humane—a string of adjectives rarely, if ever, applied to overseers on West Indian sugar plantations.

As the afternoon's exchange suggested, however, even a paragon of virtue could be corrupted by a villainous place. Why else would Cary be attempting to arrange the abduction of a wealthy young woman?

"So, the talk of valuable cargo was just a ruse to lure me here?" Andrew asked.

"Not at all," Cary insisted with a shake of his head. "Between her father's private fortune, which she has already inherited, and Harper's Hill"—he swept his arm in a gesture that took in the plantation around them—"which she will inherit on her grandfather's death, Miss Holderin is worth in excess of one hundred thousand pounds."

Despite himself, Andrew let a low whistle escape between his teeth. The chit would be valuable cargo indeed. "And how do you benefit from sending her four thousand miles away?"

"I don't," Cary said, and behind that rough-voiced admission and the mournful expression that accompanied it, lay a wealth of meaning. So the man had taken a fancy to his employer's granddaughter, had he? "She has always been like a younger sister to me," he insisted; somehow Andrew managed to contain his scoff. "When Thomas Holderin was on his deathbed, I gave him my solemn oath I would do all in my power to look after his daughter."

"And now you wish to be rid of the obligation."

"I *wish*—" he began heatedly. But apparently deciding his own wishes were beside the point, he changed course and said instead, "I believe she will be safer in England."

"Then book her passage on the next packet to London." Andrew thumped his battered tricorn against his palm, preparatory to placing it on his head and taking his leave. At his feet, his shaggy gray dog rose and gave an eager wag of his tail, bored with all the talk and ready to be on his way.

"If I could, I would. I have tried many times to reason with her. But Miss Holderin is . . . reluctant to leave Antigua. She believes she is more than a match for the dangers the island presents." Cary turned toward the window. "She is wrong."

Andrew followed the other man's gaze. Fertile fields, lush forest, and just a glimpse of the turquoise waters of the Caribbean Sea where they touched a cerulean sky. It would have been difficult to imagine a less threatening landscape, but Andrew knew well that appearances could deceive. The dangers here were legion.

"Why me?" Andrew asked after a moment, folding his arms across his chest and fixing the other man with a hard stare. "Do you know the sort of man I am?"

Unexpectedly, Cary met Andrew's gaze with an adamant one of his own. "I do. You are said to be a ruthless, money-hungry black-guard."

Andrew tipped his chin in satisfied agreement. He had spent ten years cultivating that reputation.

"But of course, the sort of man you are *said* to be might not be entirely accurate, I suppose," Cary continued, steepling his fingers and tilting his head to the side. "Your crew tells a slightly different story, Captain."

Despite himself, Andrew shifted slightly. The movement might have gone unobserved if not for the dog, whose ears pricked up, as if awaiting some command.

One corner of Cary's mouth curled upward as he glanced at the mongrel. "Most of the sailors on your ship were admirably tight-lipped, rest assured," he said. "But then I happened to make the acquaintance of a fellow called Madcombe. New to your crew, I believe."

Andrew jerked his chin in affirmation. There was no denying Timmy Madcombe was a talker. He might have told Cary anything, and probably had.

"He seemed most grateful to find himself aboard a ship captained by what he called a 'r'al gent,' you will be pleased to know. 'Good grub, a fair share, an' no lashin's, neither,'" Cary added, mimicking Timmy's voice—right down to the boyish crack. "If that proves true, such a style of shipboard management would make you rather unusual among your set." This time, Andrew was careful not to move, offering neither acknowledgment nor denial. Still, Cary seemed to read something in him. He nodded knowingly. "Yes. Madcombe's story, and the vehemence with which the rest of your crew attempted to keep him from telling it, made me wonder whether you are quite as ruthless as you wish to seem."

"If you are willing to take the word of that green boy, you must be desperate, indeed," Andrew said, pushing back against Cary's probing.

"I am." Cary flicked his gaze up and down, taking in every detail of Andrew's appearance. "Desperate enough to hope that in some ways at least, you are as ruthless as you look—despite any assurances I may have received to the contrary. For it will take a ruthless man to succeed."

"I take it Miss Holderin's is not the only resistance I can expect to encounter if I take her away."

"Hers will be formidable," Cary warned. "Do not underestimate it. You may be required to use some rather creative measures to get her aboard your ship."

Creative measures? A sudden sweat prickled along Andrew's spine. Nothing about this situation sat well with him.

A welcome breath of wind stirred the draperies behind him, drawing cooler, sweetly scented air through the house, scattering some papers across the desk beside which Cary stood. "But I will confess, her opposition is not my primary concern," he continued. "As you might imagine, an heiress of Miss Holderin's magnitude receives a great deal of attention—unwelcome attention—from prospective suitors. And one of them is not content to accept her refusal."

"If she's turned the man down, what of it?" Andrew dismissed the supposed menace with a shrug. "He can't bloody well drag her down the aisle, bound and gagged."

"Can he not?" Cary asked. Absently, he neatened the stack of papers disordered by the breeze, weighting them with a green baize ledger, never raising his eyes from the desk. "I wish I shared your certainty about the matter. But we live on the very edge of what might be considered civilized society, Captain, and Lord Nathaniel Delamere has lived the sort of life that has put a great many influential men in his thrall. Men who would be willing to look the other way if some injustice were done. Planters. Merchants." At last he lifted his gaze. "Even a clergyman or two."

"There's something rather odd about your determination to go against Miss Holderin's express wishes in order to keep another man from doing the same," Andrew pointed out.

By the expression on Cary's face, Andrew guessed the irony had not been lost on him. "If she learns what I've done, she will never forgive the betrayal—I know that. But Delamere will stop at nothing to get his hands on Harper's Hill and Thomas Holderin's fortune. And once he has what he wants, what will become of her? She will not listen to reason. What ought I to do?"

The question hung on the air between them for a long moment.

"A desperate man. A dangerous voyage. And an heiress who doesn't want either one." Andrew ticked off each item on his fingertips. Perhaps it was her plantation manager from whom Miss Holderin most needed to be saved. "I thank you for the consideration, but I think I'll pass. Find another ship to do your dirty work, Cary."

"Would you have me trust her with just anyone? I have reason to believe you're a man of honor. Besides," he added frankly, "yours is the last private vessel in the harbor over which Delamere has no hold. You are my best hope, Captain Corrvan."

But Andrew had learned long ago not to be swayed by another's tale of woe. "London is not on the *Fair Colleen*'s route," he said, moving toward the door and motioning the dog to follow.

Before he could take more than a step or two, there was a knock at the door. "Put down that musty old ledger, Edward," a feminine voice rang out in the corridor. "Angel's Cove is beckoning. I can ask Mari to pack us a—oh!"

Startled by the intrusion, the dog charged toward the door, barking furiously. The woman dropped the book she had been carrying and let out an inhuman screech of alarm. Suddenly, the once-quiet sitting room was a flurry of activity: a flash of brown hair, more shrieks, and two snarling leaps into the air.

"Sit!" Andrew grasped the dog's collar to enforce the order.

Stepping past him, Cary shouted, "Stop that racket, you little devil."

More defiant screeches, another brown blur, and Andrew at last sorted out the source of both the noise and the confusion: a little monkey, who had been driven up the wall by the unexpected greeting and now clung to the curtain rod, taunting the dog. The shaggy gray mutt strained against Andrew's hold, trying to lunge at the unfamiliar animal, and Cary's brow was knit in a fierce frown.

On the floor sat the woman, perhaps two- or three-and-twenty, her heart-shaped face framed by red-gold curls that tumbled down her back in inviting disarray, barely contained by her broad-brimmed straw hat. She was emphatically *not* screeching. That had been the monkey.

No, the woman was laughing.

Once she had recovered her breath, she scrambled to her feet without waiting for an offer of assistance from either man and instead held out her hand to the monkey. "Come, Jasper. Mind your manners."

When Jasper refused with a mocking grin and a vigorous shake of his head, the woman shrugged and turned toward Andrew. "My apologies. He doesn't respond well to being startled. But you couldn't know that, could you?" she said in a hearty voice, ruffling the dog's shaggy gray ears once her hand had been sniffed and approved. "What a brave boy . . . Does he have a name?"

Then her fingers met Andrew's in the dog's rough fur, and with a gasp of surprise, she jerked her hand away.

She glanced upward, and Andrew, who was still bent over the dog, found himself just inches from the most startling eyes he had ever seen. A swirling mixture of blue and green and gray for which there was no name.

He straightened abruptly and tugged the dog a respectable distance away. "Caliban."

"Caliban?" she echoed, wiping her hands down the skirt of her brownish-green dress, which was already smudged with dusty handprints.

"After the half-man, half-beast in—"

"In *The Tempest*," she finished. Something that was not quite a smile lurked about her lips, and her blue-green eyes twinkled. "By Mr. Shakespeare."

"It seemed a fitting name for such a mongrel," Andrew said with a glance at the dog's feathery tail where it thumped against the floorboards. Since when was Caliban's affection to be won with a mere pat on the head?

When he turned back to face the woman, he found his own appearance an object of similar scrutiny. "And you are?" she asked.

"Captain Andrew Corrvan." Edward Cary inserted himself between them and completed the introductions. "Miss Tempest Holderin."

"Tempest?" Unable to keep the note of disbelief from creeping into his voice, Andrew still managed a bow. Although he had cast aside most other hallmarks of a gentleman's upbringing, too many years of training had made that particular gesture automatic.

Cary's explanation was predictably measured. "Her father was . . . unconventional."

"A lover of Shakespeare," Tempest Holderin corrected. Her eyes flashed, and at once he realized why their unusual hue looked so hauntingly familiar to him. They were eyes in which a man might easily drown, the precise shade of the sea before a storm.

Perhaps Thomas Holderin had known what he was about, after all.

"The two are hardly mutually exclusive," Andrew remarked, a part of him hoping she would rise to the challenge in his words. "No matter how much your father might have enjoyed the Bard, you cannot deny that the more conventional choice would have been to name you after a character from one of Shakespeare's plays, rather than the play itself."

"Perhaps he felt 'Caliban' wouldn't suit," she shot back, lifting her pointed chin.

Andrew fought the temptation to smile. "I was referring, of course, to 'Miranda.'"

His familiarity with the play seemed to surprise her. "'O brave new world, that has such people in 't!'" She quoted Miranda's famous line, the moment at which the sheltered heroine of *The Tempest* first glimpses a handsome young man. But she spoke it with the sort of half sigh more befitting the character's world-weary father, Prospero. "No, 'Miranda' would never have done, I assure you. I am not so naïve as she. Particularly where men are concerned," she added, not quite under her breath.

"If you'll excuse us, Tempest." Cary seemed to find little amusement in the exchange. "The captain and I have a matter of urgent business to discuss."

"Business? Excellent," she declared, standing firm. "I've been meaning to ask you about Dr. Murray's report on Regis's leg. And have you heard from Mr. Whelan? I know the harvest is almost upon us, but I won't have people put to work in the mill if there's danger of it collapsing."

"Murray called here this morning and pronounced Regis's wound almost healed," Cary told her. "No sign of infection. And I intend to follow up with Whelan tomorrow. You know I have no wish for anyone to come to harm."

"Of course not, Edward," she said, softening. "But you've been so dreadfully busy since Mr. Fairfax left us. Why, sometimes I think I ought to have forbidden him to leave."

"We are not all so susceptible to the stamp of your foot, my dear." Cary's lips were stretched in a forced smile. "Besides, although his head seemed sound enough, I always suspected Fairfax's heart—or a piece of it, anyway—lay in England."

Miss Holderin made no comment on Cary's sentimental twaddle, but her expression said all that was needed. "Why won't you let me help? I might speak to Mr. Whelan," she suggested, shifting the subject.

"You will do no such thing."

Andrew expected her to pout in response to Cary's flat refusal, but he was quickly disabused. Tempest Holderin looked quite accustomed to hearing such commands, if not accustomed to obeying them. A frown creased her brow, but Cary did not relent. Although far from immune to those eyes, it seemed he had at least learned to judge the difference between squall and hurricane. "It is not safe for a young woman to go about English Harbour unattended."

"You cannot expect me to sit idly by and—"

"Idly?" Cary looked her up and down. "Somehow, I doubt you have been idle. Is that chalk dust I see on your skirt?" At her somewhat abashed nod, he shook his head. "How many times have I told you—?"

"Not to teach them? It's only letters and numbers, Edward. What harm can it do?" she argued as she attempted to brush the evidence from her dress.

"In these days, with rumors of an uprising on everyone's lips? It would do a great deal of harm if you are caught—both to them and to you."

"Then I won't get caught." Failing in the attempt to improve the dress's appearance, she straightened and clicked her tongue to the little brown monkey. "Come, Jasper. It seems we're interrupting." Cautiously, the monkey made its way down the drapery and onto her shoulder. Caliban strained against Andrew's hold and snapped at the air in one desperate, final attempt to catch his tiny tormentor.

"A pleasure to meet you, Caliban," she said with a smile for the dog. "And you, too, Captain."

"Wait."

With his free hand Andrew swept up the book she had dropped, a thin leather-bound volume that looked not old, but well-read. Nodding her thanks, she stretched out her hand so he could lay it on her palm.

"What are you reading?" he asked instead, lifting the cover with his thumb.

"Something really very horrid, you may be sure," she answered as she tried to snatch the book from his grasp before he saw.

"A gothic tale?" He tightened his fingertips around the book's spine, refusing to relinquish it. "Are you a devotee of Mrs. Radcliffe's, then?"

"Not particularly." She wrenched the book from his hand and tucked it against her bosom. "If you must know, this is Miss Wollstonecraft."

"Ah." Even a man who had spent years roaming the Atlantic could not remain ignorant of the controversy surrounding Miss Wollstonecraft and her books, with their support of the revolution in France and outspoken demands for women's rights. So Miss Holderin was a radical? It was of a piece with the rest of what he had heard.

And none of it inclined him toward Edward Cary's mad scheme. Six weeks at sea with a bluestocking who spouted Wollstonecraft? Not if he could help it. " 'Really very horrid,' indeed," he murmured.

Evidently suspecting she was being mocked, she parted her lips to reply. Before words could slip past them, Edward interjected. "Go home, Tempest," he urged, walking with her toward the doorway, his hand resting at the small of her back. The gesture might have been permitted under the guise of brotherly affection, but to Andrew it looked more like staking a claim. "I'll join you for supper, if I may."

The offer of his company seemed to mollify her somewhat. "Like old times. I'll have Mari make one of your favorites. But you won't forget about the mill?"

"I won't forget."

The monkey shot one leering grin behind him as they left, sending Caliban into another flurry of barks and forcing Andrew to squat beside him to contain him.

"Hush, Cal," he murmured, his heart not in the command.

"I haven't much patience for Jasper either, old boy," Cary acknowledged when he reentered the room, casting the dog a sympathetic look. "But that little monkey is a long way from home. A sailor on a slave ship captured him in Africa, intending him for a pet," he explained to Andrew, who was rising to his feet. "When Tempest saw how cruelly the animal was being treated, she rescued him. It's what the Holderins do," he added, almost as an afterthought.

With such a fortune at her disposal, Andrew had imagined the sugar princess would prove pampered and elegant and probably cruel. He had not anticipated a chalk-streaked dress, radical sympathies, and a monkey. Tempest Holderin was not the sort of woman who ran away from trouble—she ran toward it with open arms. He had been wrong. And Edward Cary was wrong. She didn't need to be rescued from this Lord Nathaniel character.

She needed to be rescued from herself.

Cary returned to the desk and riffled through the stack of papers he had set to rights mere moments ago. Selecting one sheet, he dipped a pen. "Name your price."

Andrew shook his head. He had not been to England—*home*, some would say, although it would never be so to him—in more than ten years. A man in Cary's position could never offer enough to send him back now. "I draw the line at kidnapping."

Undeterred, Cary scratched something on the paper. "Then think of it as a rescue."

But if abduction was not Andrew's game, neither was salvation. For much of his life, in fact, he had been bent on destruction instead.

And whatever amount Cary offered, the encounter with Miss Holderin left him even more determined to refuse it. Oh, she was tempting in her way, it was true, with that riot of red curls and those stormy eyes.

That, he feared, was the problem.

"Half now," Cary said, thrusting the note toward him. "The rest upon her safe delivery to her grandfather in Yorkshire."

Reluctantly, Andrew took it, at the same time raising his free hand to his eyes, some part of him hoping he could rub them hard enough to erase the afternoon entirely—hard enough, at least, to render the figures on the paper an illegible blur.

He must have been staring at the number longer than he realized, for Caliban gave a troubled sort of whimper and nudged his wet nose against his hand, confused by his master's unusual stillness. The paper trembled.

He could not begin to imagine where Edward Cary could have acquired such a sum. Was he somehow stealing from Miss Holderin's personal fortune to subsidize her abduction? For his own part, it still would not have been enough. But harder, much harder, to refuse it on behalf of his crew. Certainly Bewick and some of the others would be glad enough to glimpse old London town once more.

"Well?" Cary prompted.

The man had persuaded himself that he needed someone who was willing to break the rules, to save a woman who seemed quite indifferent to them herself.

Had he fully considered what might happen between his Tempest and such a man?

"Six weeks at sea. She will be ruined, you know."

A muscle ticked along Cary's jaw. "Only her reputation, I trust. And far more than that could be lost if she stays," he added, sounding resigned.

Andrew's fingers curled around the paper, crumpling it into a tight ball. Against his better judgment, he jerked his chin in a single nod. "I'll do it."

Chapter 2

What would Miss Wollstonecraft do?

It was a question Tempest asked herself often, particularly in moments such as these. She knew Miss Wollstonecraft faced a great deal of opposition from the world for her ideas about women's rights, but she felt certain the author must never have met anyone quite like Edward Cary, someone who might agree with every principle her books espoused and then some, but who was nonetheless determined to swaddle certain women in cotton wool to keep them from harm. It was infuriating really, these constant reminders that Edward, who had known her almost forever, did not believe she was capable of taking care of herself. It had been one thing when they were children, but now that she was nearly three-and-twenty . . .

Her musings were interrupted by the sound of booted feet thundering down the steps of Edward's house. Reluctant to face either Edward or his guest, she ducked around the corner, almost colliding with the stable boy, Hector. He stood in the shade, holding the bridle of Captain Corrvan's hired mount, a magnificent bay gelding that defied the reputation of McGinty's Livery for supplying only sway-backed mares.

The horse shied and tried to toss his head but Hector's firm grip kept him in line, restricting him to a noisy snort of displeasure at Tempest's unanticipated arrival. Thankfully, Jasper did not shriek or even chatter. Instead, he clambered onto Hector's shoulder and began to search the boy's pocket for lumps of sugar. Returning the boy's grin, Tempest felt the horse's hot breath as she slipped almost beneath his nose.

At a man's shout, Hector led the horse forward, and Tempest chanced a peek after them. Man of the sea he might be, but Captain

Corrvan looked equally at home with horseflesh as he took the reins and ran one steadying hand along the bay's quivering flank.

Edward was nowhere to be seen. The exchange between the two men must have wrapped up more quickly than Edward had anticipated. It was unlike him not to show his guest out. Had the meeting ended as he had wanted?

People did not generally get the upper hand of Edward Cary, a fact for which she was genuinely grateful. His oversight kept Harper's Hill running smoothly—better, even, than it had been managed when her father had been alive. Without Edward, her father's dream, and her own, might have collapsed around them.

But at the moment, her frustration with him made her hope, rather selfishly, that Captain Corrvan had refused to do Edward's bidding.

Not that she felt any great need to see the sardonic captain satisfied, either.

While she watched, he offered Hector a coin for the care of his mount. He did not toss the money into the air for the pleasure of watching the boy scrabble in the dirt for it, as so many men would have done—if they had thought to give a slave anything at all.

Then, in a seemingly effortless motion, he swung one long leg over the saddle and wheeled the bay about. Caliban, who had been nosing something in the scrub, followed without being called. In a spray of gravel and crushed seashells, the threesome swept down the drive.

As Captain Corrvan disappeared from sight, Tempest jerked herself out of the shadows. Hector still stared after horse and rider, wide-eyed, and she feared her own face wore a similar expression of awe. What would Edward say if he caught her gawking after the captain like some green girl? Once upon a time, he would have laughed at her, but in the last year or so he had turned into such a stick in the mud.

Oh, she hoped Edward's absence and Captain Corrvan's dramatic departure meant that their business had concluded in mutual dissatisfaction, neither side getting what it wanted. That would just suit her mood.

With a self-satisfied nod, she set off toward the main house, choosing to ignore the fact that her destination smacked of compliance with Edward's earlier command—for really, where else was there to go?

As she climbed the north-facing steps of a dual staircase leading to a wide veranda, she could hear footsteps on the other side, echoing her own. Probably Edward, come to give her another scold. "Haven't you made your point already?" she asked as she reached the top and could at last see who was coming from the south.

But it was not Edward.

"I beg your pardon?" Although he was nearly fifty, Lord Nathaniel Delamere trotted up the remaining steps with the sprightliness of a far younger man, his crimson chintz duster swirling around his ankles. He bowed when he met Tempest at the door.

"Forgive me, my lord," she said with an answering curtsy as the door swung inward, opened by unseen hands. "I thought you were someone else."

As he ushered her inside, she glimpsed the displeasure that flitted across his face. "Now, Tempest, I thought we were agreed?"

On the occasion of his first proposal of marriage, he had asked— no, *ordered* was the better word—that she give up the formal title. But what alternative was there? With a shudder she recalled how, as a child, she had called the man "Uncle Nate." Any pretense of a familial bond between them had long since been abandoned.

As she untied her broad-brimmed bonnet and laid it on a table beside a lavish arrangement of hibiscus flowers, the movement startled a gecko camouflaged in the greenery. With a flick of its tail, it scooted down the wall and across the floor, where it met its fate beneath the heel of Lord Nathaniel's boot.

"Pestilential creatures," he muttered, as Jubal, the ancient butler, stepped out of the shadows and stooped with rheumatic stiffness to clean up the mess. "May we speak privately?" he asked, indicating the doorway to their left.

Papa had always called it the receiving room, although it was neither so grand nor so formal as such a name implied. The furnishings were dark, heavy, English. But no one entering the room would imagine themselves in England. A wall of tall windows let onto the veranda, and they stood open now, their gauzy draperies swaying in the salty-sweet breeze.

As soon as they had crossed the threshold, Tempest turned to face Lord Nathaniel. "What is it you wish to discuss?" She remained standing, hoping to avoid the sort of pleasantries that might prolong the visit.

But when he stepped closer, so that they were almost touching, she longed suddenly for the relative protection of a chair. "I think you know, Tempest," he said, reaching for her hand.

He was not an unhandsome man, despite his years. His dark hair had only just begun to silver at the temples. On occasion, Tempest forced herself to acknowledge how easily she might have been taken in by him, if she had not known what she knew.

"If you have come to renew your offer, sir," she began, but her words were interrupted by Lord Nathaniel's discovery that his way to her heart was blocked by the book she still held.

Prying it from her grasp, he glanced down at the blue leather boards. A cursory glance at the contents of the pages between them caused him to throw the volume aside with an oath. "Your father was a fool to have indulged such nonsense."

Tempest watched as the book landed, facedown and open, and slid across the floor, stopped at last by the unforgiving corner of the stiff rattan mat that took the place of a wool rug. In the stillness, she heard something tear.

"How dare you?" she demanded, moving to retrieve it.

But the fingers that had at first sought her own now wrapped themselves in a vise-like grip around her upper arm. "You will not speak to me in that insolent way." His dark eyes flashed, and for a moment, she almost feared he was going to strike her. But then, as he studied her face, his expression shifted and softened, though his grip did not. "Ah, my dear, you are the very image of your lovely mother, although regrettably sharp-tongued—proof that it does not become a young lady to spend all her time giving orders. Your father would not have wanted you to bear the burden of running this plantation alone, Tempest. Else he would not have asked me to keep an eye on you."

Papa had said it, it was true, although his words had come so near the end, Tempest felt certain they had been meant for another, someone only her dying father had been able to see.

"I am not alone," she insisted, refusing to give him the satisfaction of struggling to get free. "I have Edward."

Lord Nathaniel's lips curved upward at the corners, but no one who saw the expression would have mistaken it for a smile. "I have reason to believe that Mr. Cary's . . . inefficiencies in the running of Harper's Hill will not be allowed to continue much longer."

With Tempest's support, Edward had done everything in his power to supply adequate food and clothing and shelter for the plantation's slaves. He had hired a physician to care for them. He refused to whip them, or allow another to do so in his place.

Inefficiencies, Lord Nathaniel called those small acts of mercy, and she supposed in most people's eyes they were. Other planters maximized profits by treating their slaves worse than beasts, starving them, lashing them, using them up and then replacing them when they soon died. Sir Barton's income had undoubtedly been reduced over the years by first her father's and now Edward's unusual management. But so far as she knew, he had never complained—perhaps had never even noticed.

Tempest had the sinking feeling all that was about to change.

"I took the liberty of writing to your grandfather about my concerns," Lord Nathaniel continued, his expression just shy of smug. "Perhaps you would like to see his reply?"

Without releasing her, he reached inside his coat and withdrew a folded letter. The worn paper and broken seal suggested he had been carrying it there for some days. Willing her fingers not to tremble, Tempest took it from him.

> *My Lord—*
> *I thank you most sincerely for your last. As the mail packet leaves in an hour, I have no time for more than a note in reply. In the morning, I travel to Crosslands and will consult my solicitor there. Expect formal word that Mr. Cary has been removed from his post, forthwith. In my absence, I shall rely on you to choose a suitable successor.*
> *Hastily,*
> *B. Harper, Bt.*

As she refolded the note and returned it to him, Tempest managed to hold her tongue even as her mind raced. The letter was undated. How long ago had Lord Nathaniel written? And when had this reply come? Her grandfather was a notoriously poor correspondent. In twenty-three years, she had had one letter from him, on the occasion of her father's death. In it, he had acknowledged that he was now her guardian, but he had not invited her to come to him—to say nothing of coming to her, to Antigua, where he had never been, despite his extensive holdings on the island. He had offered a few pat words of comfort, and promised to write again. But he had not. What ought she to expect now? The letter bearing his solicitor's orders might arrive within the month. Or never.

And if it did come? Oh, that did not bear thinking of. Edward gone. The people of Harper's Hill at the mercy of some tyrant. She half-wondered whether Lord Nathaniel might not take on the job of overseer himself. It required no stretch of imagination to picture him with a cowhide in his hand.

"Why would you do this?"

"I could not allow him to continue to take advantage of your grand-father's generous nature," he replied. "Why, the damage he might do—nay, has already done to your inheritance . . ." With a melancholy shake of his head, he at last released her arm.

She had always known it was about her fortune. Men had been clamoring after it for four long years, before the life had even left her father's eyes.

But she had made a promise to Papa, and she meant to keep it. She fought the impulse to rub the place where Lord Nathaniel's fingers had been. He was simply going to have to learn to take *no* for an answer.

"It is . . . kind of you to take such an interest in something that does not concern you in the slightest, my lord."

"Tempest," he chided, a deceptively gentle note in his voice. "You must believe that I value your future happiness, my dear. What must I do to show you how much?" He raised one hand, and despite her resolve to stay firm in the face of his threats, Tempest flinched. With a knowing smile, he tucked one wayward curl behind her ear before skating cool fingertips along her cheekbone to rest against her lips. "Say you'll marry me and I'll let Cary keep his post."

She could not open her mouth to speak without seeming to kiss the fingers he held there. So she shook her head instead, a gesture that unfortunately seemed to provide him almost as much pleasure.

"Ah, Tempest. You do seem to enjoy making a man work to earn a *yes* from you," he murmured, leaning closer. His fingers slipped lower, pinching her chin between knuckle and thumb and forcing her head upward to meet his gaze. "But never doubt that I shall continue to rise to the challenge of your disobedience. In the end, I will have my way." Thrusting her away from him, he turned and strode from the house.

As soon as the door had closed behind him, she snatched up her book from the floor, then raced into the hall and up the stairs to her bedchamber. Omeah was already within. Tempest laid the broken and battered volume on her dressing table, studying the place where the stitching had ripped and the quires had pulled away from the binding. Most of the damage could be repaired. All but one page, which was torn almost in half.

With the tip of one finger, she traced the jagged line now running through the words her father had written, in a shaky, spidery hand she could hardly recognize as his.

> *For my daughter, that she may ever be a <u>rational</u> <u>creature</u>.*
> *Thos. Holderin, 1792.*

The book was the product of those passionate early days of the revolution, when all the talk had been of the French "Rights of Man." Mary Wollstonecraft had bravely stepped forward to speak of the rights of women—"rational creatures," she insisted, who were capable of thinking for themselves and making sensible choices. Women were expected to act according to the dictates of their hearts. Miss Wollstonecraft simply wanted them to use their heads as well.

Those words of wisdom had been one of the last gifts her father had been able to give, and it was a gift Tempest was determined to repay.

Omeah bent over her shoulder and clucked. "How'd that happen, missy?"

"Lord Nathaniel," she whispered.

"That man think nothin' of hurtin' others." She paused and laid her black fingers over Tempest's pale ones. "Maybe it time t' make sure he don' do the like t' you."

Tempest pulled her eyes away from the book and focused on Omeah's frown. "What are you saying?"

The woman dipped her hand into the pocket of her snowy apron, pulled forth a stack of folded papers, and held it out to Tempest. "Jubal ask me t' give you the post."

Wordlessly, Tempest sorted through the pile. Unfamiliar hands. Hands she knew too well. An invitation to a ball in St. John's from a planter who hoped to promote a match with his son. Two offers to go out riding after church on Sunday. And the fifth proposal of marriage in as many days from a man named Gillingham, who owned a public house in English Harbour but apparently hoped for something better.

"You think I ought to accept one of them, do you, Omeah?"

Omeah shrugged.

"Make one of them my master—and yours?" she pressed. "Give some man the right to send Mr. Edward away, put your Hector to work in the cane fields, flog Jubal for the way he polishes the silver, and warm Mari's bed on the odd days, perhaps?"

They both knew it was not an exaggerated picture of a planter's prerogative, but Omeah straightened her spine and stood her ground nonetheless. "Him be worse."

She was right, of course. Lord Nathaniel was worse, and Tempest knew it.

He had not always been the man he was now—or at least, if he had been, he had hid it well. Oh, he had always drunk too much and had a wicked tongue, but in the West Indies, those were hardly vices. It was only since her father's death that his capacity for brutality and baseness had begun to show itself. If Papa had known the man's true nature, he would never have befriended him.

And he certainly would never have wanted his daughter to marry such a man.

Not even to save Edward, whom he had loved as a son.

Hot tears welled in her eyes, rendering Mr. Gillingham's business-like penmanship a blur. Blinking them away, she forced herself to focus on something else, and her wandering gaze fell on the still-open book.

Head over heart, head over heart—again and again, Miss Wollstonecraft urged women to value reason over emotion. Papa had been all heart. *Soft*, other planters had called him. So Tempest had tried to be the rational one. Oh, she still felt things, felt them deeply. Not for nothing had she been named after something as wild and unpredictable as a tropical storm. But she could not afford to cherish any romantic notions, particularly ones that stood in the way of her duty.

"I don't want a husband, Omeah," she reminded the companion of her childhood.

According to Miss Wollstonecraft, marriage was a state of slavery for women—and Tempest knew something of slavery. If she married, she would sacrifice all control over everything she would one day inherit. "We don't need anyone else to keep Harper's Hill running smoothly," she insisted, not for the first time, "and my staying single and independent is the best way to keep us all safe."

But she had to admit there were days when it seemed that all the determination in the world would not be enough to ensure her freedom and the freedom of those she loved. With a cry of frustration, she tossed both hands in the air. Her suitors' letters fluttered upward and then pelted onto the floor like a plague of locusts dropping from the sky.

There simply had to be a way to drive them off—starting with Lord Nathaniel.

If only she could count on her grandfather's support. She could write, contradict the lies he had been told. But even if her letter arrived in time, her words would likely have little effect. She doubted he would listen to her even if they were standing face-to-face. Not, of course, that she had any intention of leaving Antigua.

Desperate, suddenly, for a breath of air, she kicked the letters aside and stepped through the window and onto the upper veranda, heedless of the sun or the coarsening wind, focused only on the vista before her. From this height, she could see much of the plantation: the neat rows of slave quarters with provision plots between them; sugarcane grown taller than any man and ripening to a deep yellow-green; the sheltered blue waters of Angel's Cove in the distance.

What would happen to all of it if Edward were no longer here to keep everything running as it should?

It was not enough to refuse to marry. It was not enough to go into those little cabins bearing ladylike offerings of food or a poultice, or even to go in carrying chalk and a slate. If Lord Nathaniel succeeded in removing her most stalwart supporter, she was going to have to find a way to run Harper's Hill on her own.

And she could start by meeting with Mr. Whelan in Edward's place, she thought as she watched the windmill turn listlessly despite the stiff breeze.

A small step, perhaps. But maybe, just maybe, if the men on this island began to see her as a woman of business, they would cease to think of her as a bride.

"Omeah," she said, turning away from the window, feeling the wind tangle the wayward curls that clung to her neck, "ask Jubal to order the pony cart. I'm going to English Harbour."

The whirling in her mind must have shown itself on her face. "What you thinkin' of, missy?" Omeah settled her hands on her ample hips.

"A way to keep us free."

Based on Omeah's upraised brow, the answer failed to satisfy. "How so?"

"I think," Tempest replied, stepping on rather than over the pile of letters as she crossed the floor, "these worthy gentlemen need to see who is in charge."

"Who's goin' with you?"

"No one."

Omeah shook her head. "No, missy. Better you stay home." She waved a hand at the discarded and trampled post. "These here men come 'round, after while."

"There's really no danger," Tempest declared with a bit more boldness than she really felt.

"English Harbour ain't no place for you. 'Specially not alone."

Striking as it did the exact same note as Edward's warning had, Omeah's words fell on deaf ears.

As a girl she had gone frequently to English Harbour with her father, watching the loading of sugar, the unloading of slaves. It was there he had first entrusted her with his dream. She knew the narrow cobbled streets would be crawling with sailors, from the rough men who manned the slavers to the uniformed dandies of His Majesty's Navy. But in the course of a lifetime spent on the island, she had learned how to recognize—and avoid—their ilk.

Take that Captain Corrvan, for instance. If he were a character in a novel, his appearance would surely be described as "piratical," with those sharp green eyes and dark good looks. Salt-stained clothes, scuffed boots, and a week's growth of black beard shadowing his jaw certainly helped him look the part.

But in her world, pirates were not merely the romantic product of some authoress's overheated imagination. They did not generally discuss Shakespeare or bow like gentlemen or formulate opinions on the philosophy of Mary Wollstonecraft. More important, Edward Cary did not do business with them.

Captain Corrvan was no pirate, only playing at one, and what was there to fear from such a man, really? Coarse language? Insulting leers? She endured as much from Lord Nathaniel in her own home.

It was not as if someone was going to abduct her from the street in broad daylight.

She would go to English Harbour, conduct her business, and be home in time for supper. And if her behavior elicited a few more raised brows, so much the better. She could stand up to Edward's inevitable disapproval if it meant that George Gillingham and the rest would consider her a less suitable bride.

Tempest peered into the looking glass as she settled a fresh bonnet on her head. Under ordinary circumstances, she would put up her hair and change into a clean dress before going out. But today, she wanted to be seen as she really was: a woman who didn't give a fig for such frivolities. A woman bent on charting her own course.

Beside her reflection, she caught a glimpse of her old nurse's face. "Oh, Omeah, don't worry so," she said, turning to give the woman a quick embrace. "How much trouble could I possibly get into in just a few hours' time?"

Chapter 3

The conversation at Harper's Hill had led Andrew on a quest for a dark, quiet hole-in-the-wall, somewhere he could get drunk enough to forget that he had agreed to take Tempest Holderin away on the turn of the tide.

The King's Arse, or whatever the sorry little pub called itself, was certainly dark enough. A hundred years of grime covering one small window was an effective antidote to the blinding late-afternoon sun. By contrast with the crowded street, the air inside the pub felt blessedly cool. The ale wasn't the worst he had had. And the place was definitely quiet.

Too quiet.

By his feet, Caliban lay with his head on his paws, eyes closed but ears alert. At his right elbow sat Mr. Bewick, quartermaster of the *Fair Colleen*, staring silently into his untouched mug. To Bewick's other side, Timmy Madcombe wore the queasy, closemouthed grimace of a boy who had just quaffed an illicit pint and feared its imminent return.

On the far side of the pub sat the only other customers: a pair of men huddled together in whispered conversation. One was a dark-haired fellow of middle age, wearing a long red coat; the other was clad mostly in black. Andrew could hear nothing that passed between them. Once, the man in red murmured something and spread his hands, palms up, before him. On the little finger of his right hand, a gold signet ring winked in the half light. The other man had laughed.

Nothing about the two or their behavior should have attracted Andrew's particular notice. Yet it had, and he could not shake the suspicion that there was something sinister in their talk.

Or was it merely his own guilty conscience that made him think it? After all, he was the one meant to be plotting the abduction of an heiress.

Despairing of the peace he had sought, Andrew pushed away from the table and was preparing to rise when a crash and a shout from the far table sent his hand automatically to his boot and the slender dagger he kept secreted there. Caliban leapt to attention. When Andrew turned, the blade hidden in his palm, the man in red was shaking wet hair from his eyes and swiping foam from the ruined sleeve of his coat. A battered, empty tray wobbled in an erratic circle before coming to rest, and once-full tankards now lay impotently on their sides, littering the table and the floor. Beneath the men's feet, a puddle of ale was spreading.

The dark-clothed man, untouched by the accident, struggled to mask a sly smile of amusement, but the other man stood, his face growing as red as his coat. When he spoke, Andrew could hear every word quite clearly, although his voice was still eerily quiet.

"You little shit," he hissed, grabbing the serving boy by the throat. The boy's eyes rolled in fear, large and white in his black face. A scrawny lad of perhaps eight, he must have been almost outweighed by the tray he'd been carrying.

With a shove, the man pushed the boy down to the ale-slick floor. One swift kick kept the lad from trying to crawl and slither away, and when his hands slipped from beneath him, the man seized his advantage, toeing him over and then pinning him supine, with the sole of his boot pressed against that narrow chest. The boy wheezed once, and then ceased to struggle.

"Hey, now," muttered Timmy, his sympathy with the boy's predicament driven by his own youth and experiences. Caliban's hackles rose and Bewick started to his feet, but Andrew waved them all into silence, hoping the two men would not take notice and decide to start a brawl. He liked his odds against a pair of drunken louts, but he would rather avoid the fight entirely if he could.

When he turned back to the other table, he saw the man in red fumbling with the buttons of his fall. "Shower me with that piss your master tries to pass off as ale, will you, boy? Let's just see how you like it."

The boy squirmed, twisting his face away from the expected fouling, but the man simply leaned more heavily onto the foot that pinned his victim in place. Still, the child did not cry out.

"Enough." Andrew took one long step toward the man. At well over six feet tall, he had ended more than one fight just by standing up.

But the man in red seemed to be too caught up in his twisted plan to exact revenge to be mindful of his own safety. He tore his eyes from his victim only long enough to growl, "Bugger off."

Laying one hand against the stranger's shoulder, Andrew repeated his command. "Enough, I said. Let the boy go."

"And if I don't?"

With his left hand, Andrew laid his knife against the man's side, careful to keep the movement hidden from the others. "If that worm you're hiding in your breeches makes an appearance," he said, speaking low enough that only the man in red could hear, "I'll serve it up to you instead." Andrew turned his wrist slightly, pressing the tip of his blade into the space between two ribs, so that the man might suffer from no illusions about either his ability or his willingness to do what he said, and more.

The man's back arched away from the knife and he sent one dark, desperate look at his companion, who seemed frozen in his helplessness, unwilling to step in where he was so clearly outmatched.

After a long moment of dreadful silence, in which the only sounds were a low, rumbling growl from Caliban and the pattering of ale as it dripped off the edge of the table onto the flagstones, Andrew heard the telltale creak of leather. His opponent shifted his weight onto his other leg and lifted his boot from the boy's chest.

The boy tried to scramble to his feet but fell back, his face awash with pain. He had bruises, certainly, perhaps even a cracked rib. But Andrew guessed him likely to recover.

"You're captain of that ship called the *Fair Colleen*, ain't you?" the lad rasped.

"Aye."

"The *Fair Colleen*? Odd name for a merchant vessel," said the man in red. "I suppose her owner had an itch for some Irish whore."

Caliban, who understood English better than most men seemed to expect, charged from his spot beneath the table, teeth bared and hackles raised. The man flailed out with one booted foot, as if to ward off the dog with a kick.

"I wouldn't," Andrew said softly, twisting the knife just enough that it pricked the fabric of the red coat, but not quite enough to draw a brighter drop of crimson from the man's side. Slowly the man lifted both hands in a gesture of surrender. "And though I shouldn't, I'll forgive the insult. The *Colleen* was my father's ship, and he named her for my mother." Sheathing the knife, Andrew shoved the man toward his dumbstruck companion.

"You'll answer for this, you son of a bitch." The man in red ground out the threat with a scowl rendered somewhat less menacing by the fact that his breeches drooped around his knees. Snatching them up, he motioned for his friend to follow him from the pub.

Andrew stretched out a hand to help the boy rise and saw scars ringing the small wrists that peeped from beneath tattered sleeves. "What's your name?"

"Mas'r Gillingham calls me Caesar."

"I see. And the man in red?"

With fear in his eyes, Caesar darted a glance toward the back door of the pub. "Lord Somethin'. De—De—"

"Delamere?" Andrew suggested. The boy nodded.

"Who's that?" Bewick asked, surprised by his captain's recognition of the name.

"No one," Andrew snapped, cutting short the older man's speculation.

No one . . . Just a man who took obvious pleasure in the abuse of the innocent and powerless. Who hoped to have the ownership of an extraordinarily valuable plantation one day. Whose influence extended beyond local merchants and passing sailors to the highest levels of society in Antigua.

The man who meant to tame Miss Tempest Holderin.

"And the other fellow?"

Caesar shrugged. "Don' know his name. A church man, Mas'r Gillingham say."

A clergyman. And clearly in Delamere's thrall. It seemed Cary had been right to worry, after all.

Quickly, Andrew considered the very limited options before them. The first question was what do with the boy. Rescue from one tyrant would not spare him a flogging from another; when his master saw the mess that had been made, punishment would surely be forthcoming.

"Fancy a change of scenery, Caesar?"

"How's that, sir?"

"I could use a cabin boy aboard the *Colleen*," Andrew said, ignoring the warning shake of Bewick's gray head.

"Leave Mas'r Gillingham?" Some of the brightness in Caesar's dark eyes began to return.

"I imagine he'll be glad enough to part with such a clumsy lad," Andrew replied with a half smile, laying his palm on the boy's dark, curly head.

"Aye. Fer a price," Bewick confirmed, and then spat. The boy looked from one man to the other.

"Then we'll pay it," Andrew declared, fishing in his pocket for a few coins and tossing them into the puddle of ale on the floor. "Consider yourself free. Now, can you walk?"

When Caesar nodded, Caliban bounded forward to lick the child's face. The boy laughed, grimaced against the sharp stab of pain it caused, then finally gave up and laughed again, wrapping one arm around the dog's shaggy neck and the other about his own injured ribs. Some of the tension ebbed from Andrew's shoulders as he looked on. No lasting physical harm had been done, it seemed.

"Mr. Bewick," he said, turning toward the quartermaster, "you and young Madcombe take the boy to the ship. Try not to attract any attention. Caliban and I will meet you there, after I've made certain neither Mr. Gillingham nor his lordship have decided to interfere in our plans."

"An' then what?" Bewick asked, raising one skeptical brow.

"We sail."

"Where to, if'n you don' mind me askin'?"

Andrew hesitated a moment longer than should have been necessary. "London."

Timmy's eyes widened, but Bewick only crossed his arms before his chest. "Lon'on?"

"Aye."

He had already ordered the ship to be provisioned for the six weeks' journey. The only question now was whether he meant to take Tempest Holderin along.

The encounter with Delamere had given him proof of the truth of Cary's words. It had also shown him how dangerous it would be to get embroiled in their affairs. This kidnapping—or rescue, or whatever one called it—was a risky business indeed, and while Andrew had taken many risks in his life, the benefit to him had always been clear. What did he stand to gain in this case? Or, more accurately, what did he stand to lose?

"But before we leave Antigua, we must stop at a little slip called Angel's Cove, in the northeast corner of the island. We've some valuable cargo to take aboard there."

Bewick studied Andrew's expression without revealing anything in his own. "As you wish," he finally said. "Cap'n."

In another moment the threesome was shuffling toward the door.

Frustrating did not begin to describe it.

"Why do you refuse to speak seriously about the matter, Mr. Whelan?" Tempest asked, struggling to keep her voice calm and businesslike.

"'Tisn't a matter to be discussed with a lady, Miss Holderin," explained the architect as he dug in his ear with his little finger and then inspected what he had mined. "Besides, you haven't the authority to order work at Harper's Hill. Only Mr. Cary can do that."

"But he has already hired your company to fix the mill," Tempest explained, forcing herself not to look away as he wiped the finger clean on his sleeve. "I am merely here to see that the work is completed in a timely fashion."

"Gets done when it gets done, miss. Difficult job, and I haven't got but two masons right now."

"I realize, of course, that skilled slaves are in high demand," she began.

Mr. Whelan nodded. "Desperate hard to teach those savages how to lay stone properly. The devil's in 'em when it comes to hard work."

At the familiar complaint, her jaw tightened. "Perhaps you'd find free labor more willing to learn."

"Free—?" Whelan gave a snort of derision. "Best not to worry your pretty head about it, miss. Have Cary come down tomorrow. He and I can talk sense."

"Talk sense! My pretty—!" The disjointed words exploded from her with such energy that they brought her to her feet, forcing Whelan to rise as well, albeit much more slowly. "I will thank you, sir, to recollect that Harper's Hill will be mine one day. Then I will be the one making decisions about such matters—and the tradesmen with whom we do business."

Skepticism lined the man's weathered face. "Not the way I hear tell it. Good day, Miss Holderin."

She wanted to know what Whelan meant by such a remark, but not enough to listen to his answer. Whirling on one heel, she marched from his office, further disgruntled when the door clicked quietly closed behind her.

Across the street, however, another door slammed with exactly the sort of rattle and crash she craved. The noise made her look up with interest, but the sight that greeted her eyes was far less satisfying. Lord Nathaniel was striding away from Mr. Gillingham's pub.

She shrank out of sight, pulling herself into the shadow of the awning that ran along the row of shopfronts. But he never glanced her way as he parted from his companion, Reverend Goodacre. Instead, Lord Nathaniel turned toward the harbor, tugging his waistcoat into place over his breeches, setting his clothing to rights. As he disappeared down another alley, she could see dark streaks of damp down the back of his red duster.

Before she could even begin to speculate about what had happened inside to dishevel him so, three more people left through a side door: two sailors and Mr. Gillingham's potboy, Caesar.

The child looked . . . frightened? Injured? She couldn't quite decide. Nor could she imagine why two strangers would be dragging him away.

No, that was not true. She *could* imagine. She had heard stories, the kind to which she had been warned never to listen. They might be taking him away to use him. Abuse him. And then sell him to someone else.

Swallowing the bile that rose in her throat, she clutched her reticule against her skirts so it would not betray her with a jingle and set off after them. When Caesar's steps lagged, one sailor put an arm around the boy to urge him along, but their progress was curiously unhurried. Tempest stayed just a few paces behind as they made their roundabout way to the waterfront.

The scents and sounds of the harbor rose like a cloud as they approached the water, dead fish and raw sugar mingling in a heavy sweetness that could not quite mask the stench of decay. On the docks, men, mostly black, shouted and spoke in a welter of languages, almost none of them English.

She watched the three climb into a rowboat and make for a ship anchored in the deep water of the harbor, the two sailors pulling at the oars while the boy huddled in the prow. As the boat slipped through the shallows, she considered what she could do to save him.

"Missy Hold'rin?"

The voice belonged to Darius, the foreman at the warehouse where the produce of Harper's Hill was usually stored. A smile of greeting split his jet-black face, but his eyes darted uncertainly past her. "Is Mas'r Edward here with you?"

"No," she said, returning his smile. "There was something I needed at one of the shops in town, and I didn't like to bother him."

Darius was not to be so easily put off. "Omeah here, then? You never come alone, missy?"

"It's not I you should worry about, Darius," she insisted, shifting his attention to the rowboat, now a speck in the distance. "Those sailors have taken that boy!"

"He yours?"

"Mine?" Tempest scrambled for an explanation that might lead to the desired solution. "Yes, of course. He's a—a new houseboy. Yes. I brought him with me to—to carry my packages. And those men snatched him away. Can you help me get him back?"

"Go after 'em?" Darius looked deeply suspicious of the proposal. "Like to be twenty, thirty men on that ship, missy. Best we call for help."

"Oh, there isn't time! Just take me out there, and I'll speak to them," she pleaded.

Darius hesitated. He clearly did not want to disobey the orders of a white woman, but he also no doubt realized that putting her in danger was equally likely to earn him a whipping. If something happened to her, even Edward, who never raised a hand to anyone, would be unlikely to intervene on his behalf.

Hating to put Darius in an untenable position, but unwilling to see the boy come to harm, Tempest knew she had to act. "I'm sorry," she whispered as she dropped her reticule, jumped off the dock onto one of the flat-bottomed lighters, and lifted the heavy pole to push off.

"Missy, wait!" he shouted after her, but the raft was already skimming across the harbor.

It was harder to steer than she had ever guessed while watching the men work from the shore, and she had not gotten very far before her arms and shoulders ached with the effort. When she at last drew abreast of the ship, the rowboat had been pulled up to the ship's railing and not a soul was in sight. But there was still a makeshift ladder dangling over the ship's side, and with only a moment's hesitation, she grabbed the heavy rope with both hands and pulled herself upward, through an empty gun bay, bumping her head against the frame of the narrow opening as she did so and knocking her bonnet into the water.

As her eyes grew accustomed to the dimness, she could make out a little of what was around her. The ship was slight compared to most of the West India merchantmen, agile, built for speed. She peered down into the dark, stifling hold. The ship wasn't used to haul slaves—her nose had already told her that, and the absence of stocks and chains confirmed it. Instead of bodies, there were barrels and crates of supplies. Gunpowder. Ballast. But very little in the way of cargo. Perhaps it simply hadn't been loaded yet?

She creeped cautiously around, ignoring her headache, wondering where to look for one terrified little boy. From above came rumbles and shouts. The crew was at work, doing what, she could not be sure. She would have to risk exploring the other decks, though, if she expected to find Caesar. Stepping into the square of light at the bottom of a wooden ladder, she looked up.

A handsome brown face was looking down. "Well, well, what have we here?" An educated voice. But not English.

With three quick steps he was down the ladder and standing beside her. Tempest did not try to run, since there was nowhere for her to go. "I demand to see the captain of this vessel," she said with as much dignity as she could muster.

The man inspected her with a curious eye. "And I'm quite sure he'll want to see you. Up you get." He gestured with his chin for her to ascend the ladder and followed close behind, touching her only when they arrived on the uppermost deck and her feet would no longer obey her command.

Men of every shade and a range of ages stopped whatever task had employed them and turned to look as he propelled her toward the rear of the ship with one strong hand on her elbow. When they reached the short flight of steps that led down into the captain's cabin, he preceded her, rapping against the door with the knuckles of one hand.

"Enter," came the muffled command.

He opened the door and stepped through. "It would seem we've a stowaway, Cap'n," the man said before motioning to her. "Come along, then."

Heart pounding, she descended to the doorway. What she could see of the cabin's interior looked neat and surprisingly spacious. The captains of merchant vessels were a fairly gentlemanly set, as a rule. Perhaps she had nothing to fear. She would tell him what she had witnessed, demand Caesar's return, and then ask him to escort them back to shore. No doubt he would be happy to be rid of her.

"Sir," she began, stepping over the threshold, "I—"

The captain was standing at a table in the center of the room, his dark head bent over the chart spread out before him. Her heart, which just a moment ago had threatened to leap from her chest, stopped beating. Or so it seemed, at least. She could not see his face yet. But she knew.

Oh, she knew.

At the sound of her voice, she saw him stiffen, then slowly raise his head. "Welcome aboard, Miss Holderin," said Captain Andrew Corrvan, fixing her with his pale green eyes.

Chapter 4

He was not yet sure he would call it a stroke of good fortune. Admittedly, she had saved him a great deal of trouble. But for all that *she* had come to *him*, the sugar princess radiated fury.

"That will be all, Mr. Ford," he said to the ship's carpenter, who was looking from one to the other, amusement twinkling in his dark eyes.

Caliban trotted forward and sat down beside her, nuzzling against her hand, asking to be petted. When she winced at the contact, Andrew came around to the front of the table and took her hand in his, turning the palm upward to his gaze. To his surprise, she did not resist.

Blisters. What looked like rope burns. And dirt.

He dropped her hand and leaned back against the table's edge, crossing his legs at the ankle and surveying her from head to toe. Good Lord, but she was filthy, her face and dress streaked with grime and sweat, her hair a tangled mess, and no bonnet to be seen.

"Mr. Ford," he called before the man was out of earshot.

"Yes, sir?"

"Ask Mr. Beals to come up when he's finished."

"Very good, Cap'n."

"I am not at liberty to wait for this Mr. Beals," she said primly when the door closed behind Ford.

"Oh?" Andrew folded his arms across his chest, fighting a smile. Did she never back down? "Just where were you planning to go, Miss Holderin?"

"Home, of course," she answered with a defiant tilt of her chin. "After I get what I came for."

"And what would that be?"

"A boy called Caesar."

Her answer ought not to have surprised him, but it did.

"I saw two men carry him away from the King's Arms," she explained. "They forced him on board this ship, no doubt for some less-than-savory purpose. And I intend to put a stop to it."

Uncrossing his legs, he levered away from the table and took one step closer to her. "Don't assume his life was more savory at Mr. Gillingham's establishment than it will be aboard my ship," he said, more irritated by her insinuation than he should have been.

Her mouth popped open to retort, but before she could speak the cabin floor shivered and seemed to shift beneath their feet.

"Are we . . . moving?" she asked, stretching onto her toes to scan the view from the windows behind him.

As if the answer to her question were not already obvious, the ship gave a great lurch and threw her off balance. She stumbled forward, landing with her head on his shoulder, her breasts against his ribs, and her skirts tangled about his legs. Reflexively, his arms came around her, steadying her, drawing her to him.

For the merest fraction of a moment, she did not protest. Shock, he supposed. Or perhaps fatigue. He could not imagine how she had managed to get from the docks to the ship without assistance. But before he had time to marvel at her combination of strength and softness, she was pushing herself upright, pushing away from him.

It was undoubtedly the smartest thing she had done all day.

"Yes, we're under sail," he confirmed, as she looked daggers at him.

"I demand to be set ashore this instant," she said, setting her feet apart so the ship's motion would not catch her off guard again. "With the boy."

Andrew glanced behind him at the receding view of English Harbour. "Can't be done, I'm afraid."

"Wh-wh-where are you taking me?" she spluttered, the barest hint of anxiety now creeping into her voice.

"As luck would have it, I've just given orders to make for the north side of the island," he told her. At her skeptical glance, he stepped away from the table and motioned to the charts spread across it. "See for yourself."

She stepped forward and peered down at the map, tracing one finger along the route he had marked out. "Why, there's Angel's Cove."

"Aye."

A frown wrinkled her brow. "I would think a merchant ship's captain would conduct his business in the docks."

"Not all of it," he said, locking her gaze until she looked away.

"So you will take me home."

It was not exactly a question, so he evaded it. "It grows late. I won't risk my ship, slipping into unknown waters after dark. We'll have to wait until morning to make landfall now." He felt a twinge of guilt for deceiving her. But she would learn the truth soon enough. And he would arrange to be out of earshot when she did.

"I couldn't possibly stay on board overnight."

"I'm afraid you'll have to," he replied with a half smile. "Unless you fancy swimming to shore."

"I can, you know," she insisted, drawing herself up. "Swim."

A forbidden image rose in his mind, of a water sprite with red-gold curls and stormy eyes, emerging from the sea clad only in a clinging wet shift . . .

But the fantasy evaporated when she added, "Edward taught me."

Cary was the very last person of whom he wished to be reminded right now. "I wouldn't recommend it, all the same," he snapped, dismissing the heat in his voice as annoyance. "Ship's surgeon, Mr. Beals, will be here soon to look at those hands. And I'll send up some food and hot water too."

"You'll see that Caesar is well taken care of?"

"I already have," he assured her, although he could see by the look in her eyes that she distrusted his claim. No doubt she would attempt to check on things as soon as she had the chance. God knew where one of his crew might find her next. "You're safest here. Rest."

"I'm not a child, Captain Corrvan," she pointed out, quite unnecessarily. "And I am not accustomed to being ordered about like one."

"Well, Miss Holderin, you've found your way onto my ship. I give the orders here," he said as he turned toward the door, snapping his fingers to bring Caliban to his side. "And when I give orders, they are obeyed."

Caliban, however, remained firmly planted at Tempest's feet. Emboldened, she gave a sly smile. "Always, Captain Corrvan?"

With a black look for her and a muttered oath for the dog, he ducked under the lintel, then fished a key from the pocket of his waistcoat and locked his cabin door behind him.

* * *

"Of all the—" She was at the door in three quick steps, but still too late to keep herself from being locked in. Twice she slapped her palm against the door, demanding release, but she soon stopped, finding the act far more injurious to her battered hands than to the unforgiving wood. Anyway, Captain Corrvan was probably at the other end of the ship by now, and who among his crew would defy him in order to set her free?

With an eye to possible routes of escape, she made her way slowly around the cabin. Caliban, already familiar with the territory, quickly grew bored with the project and curled up under the table, releasing his breath with a *whoosh* as he laid his head on his paws.

There were two rooms, the great room and a smaller chamber, hardly bigger than the bed it housed. Both were bright and airy, thanks to a row of square windows across the rear of the ship. Although they opened, going through one would get her nothing but wet, as she discovered when she peered out, for there were no footholds to be seen. The lines of the ship curved downward toward the keel and disappeared into the foamy wake.

Other than the door, then, the only remaining openings in the cabin's tight walls were two gun bays, one on either side—useless to her, because she hadn't the strength to move the guns—and a skylight above the table whose frame she could just brush with her fingertips while standing on a chair.

She was well and truly stuck there until morning.

Unless this Mr. Beals could be brought to see her side of things? Or whoever brought her food and water? Surely there would be an opportunity to free herself from this temporary prison.

Clambering off the chair, she examined the larger room more thoroughly. Its furnishings were rather sparse: two chairs and the table at which Captain Corrvan had been standing when she entered; beneath the window, two leather-topped benches built into the wall, and between them, a small, disorganized desk, cluttered with papers held in place by some instrument for navigation she could not name; and finally, a bookcase with a wire-fronted door over each shelf, designed to keep the contents in place if the sea grew rough.

Deciding that the bookcase offered the most potential to appease her curiosity—since the sea chest in the next room was locked—she sat down on the bench nearest it and lifted one of the little doors. Every shelf was so tightly packed and stacked with books that selecting one volume might cause the remainder to tumble like a poorly mortised brick wall. She ran her finger along their spines, muttering over their titles: a volume of poetry beside a book on navigation, the travelogue of a famous explorer beside a popular work of sentimental fiction. She remembered what he had said about the works of Mrs. Radcliffe. So, the captain really did read novels?

Carefully, she eased a few leather-bound volumes from the spots into which they had been wedged. Some—a geometry text, a Latin grammar—were clearly schoolbooks, his name written inside the cover in boyish copperplate. Others were evidently of more recent acquisition. With her fingertip she traced the thick strokes of his pen. *A. Corrvan.* Darker, bolder, sharper—suggestive of the man he had become.

Last on the shelf was a much older book, its boards worn, its pages tattered. *Compleat Works of Wm. Shakespeare,* she read on the spine in embossed letters that had once been outlined in gilt. He had written his name on its flyleaf too, in the schoolboy script. Above it, in faded brown ink was written *Alastor Mitchel, 1732.*

The edition was familiar to her, and she found it more than a little unsettling to discover that Andrew Corrvan had something, anything, in common with her father. But she knew the captain had read *The Tempest* at some point, and really, what had she expected to find? A well-thumbed copy of *A Gentleman's Guide to Piracy?*

At first glance, the great room of the captain's cabin had struck her as an elegantly masculine space, with its wool carpet and polished dark wood. But while it might be a space befitting a gentleman, the man to whom it belonged strained the edges of that polite label. The coarse clothes that hung from the hard lines of his body made it unapologetically clear he was a man who labored for a living. Yet something in his voice and his demeanor hinted that he had not been raised to do so. It was as if the captain's loyalties were somehow divided between the rough and the refined, the sea and some other world entirely.

Curling up her legs beneath her on the bench, she laid the Shakespeare aside. She could not remember ever having felt so tired. With a sigh to match the dog's, she leaned her cheek against the cool glass and from beneath drooping eyelids watched English Harbour fade from view. How many hours until dawn, until she could return to Harper's Hill?

While propelling the lighter across the harbor, she had hardly noticed her discomfort, bent as she was on saving Caesar. But sometime since then, the mixture of fury and fear that had driven her onward had drained away, leaving only exhaustion—tinged with remorse—in its wake. A truly rational creature would not have acted so impulsively and gotten herself into this predicament. She had not succeeded in rescuing the boy, only in endangering herself. Or at least, in endangering her reputation.

Since she meant never to marry, she had rarely spared much concern for her reputation. The less desirable she was in suitors' eyes, the better. But the recent discovery that Lord Nathaniel had been telling tales to her grandfather gave her pause. What might happen if news of this little adventure reached Sir Barton's ears and made him decide she was unfit to inherit the plantation? It would mean the destruction of all her dreams.

She could only reassure herself with the knowledge that, if all went according to plan, she would be home again before almost anyone discovered she had been gone.

Unless, of course, they were not really headed toward Angel's Cove. What reason had she to trust anything Captain Corrvan said to her?

Oh, at least let the boy be all right! Surely he had no reason to lie about that . . .

She awoke to a rap on the door, the rattle of the latch, and an unfamiliar voice calling, "Miss Holderin?" By the time she sat up, a man with a balding head, portly build, and horn-rimmed glasses was crossing the threshold, a young man—really, a boy—following at his heels.

"Miss Holderin? I'm Geoffrey Beals, ship's surgeon. And this lad is Timmy Madcombe."

Caliban emerged from beneath the table, offering a wag of greeting to the visitors.

"You old rascal," Mr. Beals said as he squatted near the door to scratch the dog's ears. "What are you doing here? Cal gener'ly sticks pretty close to the cap'n," he explained, pulling himself upright and looking at Tempest, who had not risen from the bench.

At a loss to explain the bond between her and the dog, she merely lifted her shoulders—and then winced from the twinge of pain even that slight movement caused.

"There now," Mr. Beals said, noticing her discomfort. "Timmy, put those things down." The boy, struggling to juggle the weight of a tray, a steaming ewer of water, and another bundle besides, looked relieved by the order. Dropping the bundle in a chair, he set the water on the floor and then placed the tray carefully on the table.

Despite her uncertainty, Tempest's stomach rumbled when she spied the food: soup, bread, cheese, and tea.

The surgeon must have heard the sound. "Go on, then. Eat," he told her as he opened his bag and began to spread the tools of his trade across the table.

She needed surprisingly little encouragement. Rising from her place by the window, she made her way across the room and took a seat at the table. Although the state of her hands made it impossible to hold the spoon properly, she managed to get most of the soup in her mouth, mopping up the last of it with a piece of bread pinched between the very tips of her fingers. The boy, Timmy, watched from the shadows near the door, eyes wide, as she ate.

"Mr. Madcombe," the surgeon barked, when he had followed Tempest's gaze, "that will be all." The boy nodded and scampered out the door, leaving it ajar. Before she had a chance to consider how she might put his oversight to good use, Caliban rose and lay down across the opening, blocking her path. "You'll have to forgive the boy," Mr. Beals said. "Like as not, he hasn't ever seen a lady before."

As she brushed a few crumbs and a tangled strand of hair away from her mouth with the back of one hand, she was tempted to suggest he still hadn't. Tempest was no stranger to scrapes. Usually, however, they were not of the physical variety. Even without the aid of a mirror, she could guess how wild she looked.

Seemingly reading the direction of her thoughts, Mr. Beals rubbed his palms together and said, "Now, let's get you cleaned up."

He reached up to light a pierced tin lamp that hung from the ceiling over the table. It cast a speckled glow around the room. When had it gotten so dark? She glanced behind her, but the windows showed nothing but her own blurry reflection and the outline of Mr. Beals lifting the ewer of steaming water onto the table. When she turned back, he was untying the bundle Timmy had dropped into a chair, revealing clean squares of linen and a roll of bandages.

With gentle hands, he dipped a corner of linen into the water and began to sponge off her face, probing a tender welt at the edge of her hairline, where she had bumped her head climbing into the ship.

"You'll have the headache in the morning, if you don't already," he proclaimed. "Let's see your hands." Reluctantly, she uncurled her fingers and held them out for his inspection. When she stiffened in anticipation of his touch, he muttered, "Tsk-tsk."

Rising from his chair, he stepped past her to one of the cupboards in the wall near the desk and removed a crystal decanter and a glass. After he had poured one scant measure, he put the stopper in the bottle and brought the glass to her. "This'll help. But be careful," he advised as he handed it to her. "T'ain't likely you're much used to this."

"Brandy?" She raised the faceted glass and sniffed.

"Irish whiskey. Cap'n's personal favorite," he added with a wink.

That was no recommendation as far as she was concerned, and she knew she ought to have refused. But she could not help but hope that whatever Mr. Beals had poured had the promised power to blur and blunt the edge of her pain. So, as she had seen Edward do once or twice, and Lord Nathaniel do all too often, she flicked her wrist and tossed the golden liquid down her throat.

The effort it cost to suppress the ensuing cough brought tears to her eyes, but when they had cleared, she saw that she had earned Mr. Beals's grudging admiration. He did not, however, offer to pour her another tot.

With what she hoped was a steady hand, she set the empty glass just inside the raised edge of the polished tabletop, one of those shipboard conveniences that kept items from sliding where they shouldn't.

Caliban was studying her with his head tilted to one side, as if the whiskey had had some visible effect he could assess. In truth, it probably had. She could feel its warmth spreading through her, pinking her cheeks.

"Irish," she murmured to herself.

"Aye," nodded Mr. Beals. "Born and bred."

She knew few Irishmen, and those with whom she was familiar— overseers, drivers—were valued for their violent temperaments. Certainly none of them spoke in a soft, cultured voice that betrayed just a hint of a lilt.

"And the rest of the crew?"

"Well, now, we're what you might call a mixed bag," he said with a laugh as he sat down beside her again and lifted her right hand toward the light. "Mr. Bewick, t' quartermaster, is a Londoner. Fleming, the boatswain, is a Scot, o' course. Young Madcombe's an orphan. Come aboard the *Colleen* last month in Kingston."

"The *Colleen*?"

"That's the ship you're on. The *Fair Colleen*, to give 'er her proper due. Irish name. Means 'lovely lass' or some such falderal."

Lovely lass? Had Captain Corrvan named the ship? And if so, had he been thinking of a particular "lovely lass" at the time? Tamping out a spark of curiosity that verged inexplicably on jealousy, she asked instead, "What of you, Mr. Beals?"

"Oh, I was raised in a little village in the West Country. Haverhythe, by name. Got family there still—a younger brother. My pa cut me out for a baker's boy, but my heart was for the sea. So he 'prenticed me to a Bristol surgeon instead and . . . here I am."

She knew there must be a wealth of stories in that brief pause, and she sensed Mr. Beals would be only too happy to tell them, but she didn't press, other than to ask, "Have you been surgeon aboard the *Fair Colleen* long, then?"

As if the calculation required some effort, Beals rubbed one finger behind his right ear, dislodging his spectacles. "Oh, eight years. Give or take."

Was that a lot of time for a surgeon to stay with one ship, or a little? She had no guide by which to measure. "So, you know the captain well, then?" Could the man be coaxed into revealing something more useful than Andrew Corrvan's Celtic roots?

"Well enough, I guess you'd say." Suspicion began to cloud his features. "Only Mr. Bewick and a handful of t' others been here longer."

"And Mr . . . .um . . . ?" It was better to keep the surgeon talking, both to maintain the flow of information and to prevent her from thinking about her hands. "The one who found me?"

"Ford," he supplied as he finished work on one hand and started on the other. "Ship's carpenter."

"A slave, I suppose."

"Naw," Beals protested, shaking his head. Then a pause, accompanied by an expression that was almost sly. "Leastways, not Cap'n's."

"He's a runaway, you mean? Or stolen?" she added, thinking of Caesar. When Beals did not answer, she pressed further. "What about the boy who came aboard just before I did? I saw two men take him from his place and bring him here. Did they harm him?"

"Someone did," he said, a rumble of anger in his voice. "He says Cap'n saved his life, an' then Bewick and young Madcombe brought him here."

"Madcombe?" she repeated. "The lad who just left?"

"Aye."

In her memory Caesar had been dragged away by two hulking giants. The discovery that one of them had, in fact, been very little older than Caesar himself gave her pause. Perhaps she *had* misunderstood the situation.

"You can ask the boy for the particulars when he's on his feet again in a few days," Beals suggested.

"I—I won't be here. Captain Corrvan is putting me ashore in the morning."

Beals gave a little grunt of surprise as he daubed salve onto her palm. "That right?"

"And I hoped to take the child with me."

"That's between you and the cap'n, I reckon. The boy seemed right excited about going to sea. Now," he said as he tied off the second bandage and then pushed back from the table, "to bed with you, missy."

Tempest glanced down at her tightly laced boots, her filthy dress, and lastly her hands, now bandaged to the tips of her fingers and perfectly useless. The slightest sigh escaped her lips. She hated nothing so much as having to ask for help. Well, she would simply sleep fully clothed tonight. Under the circumstances, it was probably the wisest course of action.

But Mr. Beals had recognized her difficulty. "Here," he said, kneeling at her feet and drawing off her boots, then putting a hand beneath her elbow to help her to rise. "Turn about," he motioned, reaching to unfasten her dress. When she hesitated, he laughed. "You've naught to fear from ol' Geoff, miss. It'd take more than stockings and a shift to turn this gray head."

Not so very *gray*, she wanted to say. She had been revising her initial estimate of the man's age steadily downward over the course of their conversation. But she let him assist her because she had little choice. Besides, he was a medical man, even if his female patients were likely few and far between. Once she could step out of her dress, however, she darted to the relative security of the small, shadowy bedchamber. "I thank you, Mr. Beals," she called after him.

"Think nothing of it," he said with a gallant little bow.

She closed the door between the two rooms and heard Mr. Beals leave a few moments later, locking the outer door behind him. She was too tired even to be disappointed by the sound of the key turning in the latch.

As she elbowed her way into the bed, collapsing gratefully onto the pillow, the scent of sandalwood and sea air—Captain Corrvan's scent—rose from the linens. From the edge of sleep, a question niggled at her.

Where was he spending this night?

Chapter 5

A narrow seam of pale pink edged the western horizon, making the sky over Angel's Cove appear blacker yet. Even after all these years, the speed of a Caribbean sunset still surprised him. A moment ago it had been full daylight. In another moment, it would be night.

Why had they come this way? Not because he intended to take Tempest Holderin back where she belonged, although the better part of him knew he ought. Yet he hesitated to order Bewick to make for open water instead, as if keeping a stretch of coastline in sight could make Andrew somehow less complicit in this strange affair.

Waves slapped the hull as the tide rose, and he could hear the occasional creak and groan from the rigging, but otherwise, all around him lay in eerie silence, a sure sign the whole crew, even the men off duty, were as awake and alert as he. As if to prove his suspicion right, Bewick soundlessly approached his side, the scent of his tobacco the only indication that Andrew was no longer alone.

After a long moment, the other man spoke. "Seems that dustup in the harbor attracted a bit o' notice, Cap'n," the quartermaster mumbled around his pipe.

"I wouldn't worry, Mr. Bewick," Andrew said, refusing to look in the direction he had indicated. "I'd like to see even His Majesty's finest catch the *Colleen* with a dinghy."

"Naw," Bewick concurred dismissively. But he held out his spyglass and directed Andrew's attention aft. Fog rose from the water in ghostly ribbons, making shapes where there were none and disguising those that were. A breath of air rippled through the mist, giving him a glimpse of a hulking shadow that lay just beyond his view. No dinghy, this.

"It's the *Justice*, if I don't miss my guess," Bewick said, naming a schooner whose reputation was well known to Andrew and most every man on his crew.

Damn.

If Captain Stratton and the *Justice* had business in these waters, it could not be honest business. Was Cary smuggling goods out of Angel's Cove? That would certainly explain how he had been able to offer Andrew such a sizable sum without dipping into his employer's coffers.

The wind was heightening. Out of habit, he glanced down, looking for Caliban, whose nose was the most reliable instrument he knew. But the dog was nowhere in sight. And then he remembered. He would be spending the night closeted with Tempest Holderin. "Lucky mutt."

"What's that, sir?" Bewick asked, his voice still low.

"Full sail, Mr. Bewick," came Andrew's curt order, in place of an explanation.

Bewick hesitated, an uncharacteristic gesture reminiscent of Andrew's first months at sea. "What o' the—?" The quartermaster shot one nervous glance toward the captain's cabin and seemed to lose the courage needed to finish that question. "What o' the cargo at Angel's Cove?"

Andrew's lips twitched. "We'll have to sail on without it. I don't fancy meeting the *Justice* in the shallows." The ship's jagged outline was still wreathed in darkness and fog.

The older man raised one shaggy brow. "Make for Lon'on without even a load? 'Tain't like you to stand a loss, Cap'n."

Too late, Andrew wanted to retort, but he bit back the words. "The men will get paid, Mr. Bewick. Surely you know me well enough by now."

"Aye. Well enough to know you don't mean to let Stratton slip out from under your nose again."

Could he really let go of this golden opportunity he had been handed? It felt rather like fate to see the *Justice* here, now, after so many years of searching. Every man on his crew would expect him to engage Stratton. How would he look them in the eye if he refused?

But there was a woman on his ship now. And a child—two, if he counted Timmy Madcombe, which he almost certainly should. None of them had signed on to hunt down and kill Stratton. How dare he risk more innocent lives? He would be no better than Stratton, then.

Reaching into his coat, Andrew withdrew a battered silver flask, his thumb brushing over the worn engraving of his father's initials. As if it were the answer he had been waiting for, Bewick gave a curt nod and signaled silently to the rest of the crew. The ship sprang to life once again—all except Andrew, who remained anchored at the railing, wondering whether the *Justice* would follow.

He lifted the flask to his lips and allowed a single swallow to sear its way down his throat.

Was it wrong to hope that Stratton would give him no choice but to open fire?

Waking abruptly in a familiar tangle of bed linens and sunshine, Tempest forgot at first to be alarmed. But as she blinked the sleep from her eyes and less familiar objects began to take shape—a heavy sea chest, unshuttered windows, a shaggy gray dog—she remembered in a rush that she was aboard the *Fair Colleen*.

And realized almost immediately thereafter that if Captain Corrvan had done as he had promised, she should already be ashore.

She twisted around in the bed, but the row of square windows behind her revealed nothing but shimmering turquoise water. And that, of course, was to be expected, since she was looking out the back of the ship. Angel's Cove no doubt lay before them.

Hearing one of her jailers rattling his keys, she sprang from the bed and looked around for her dress, but there was no sign of it. Mr. Beals must have taken it away. Well, she did not intend to allow a little thing like the lack of a dress to keep her from making a bid for freedom. With clumsy fingers, she pried open one of the tall doors in the cabinet at the foot of the bed, which, as yesterday's search had revealed, contained Captain Corrvan's clothes. Pulling his greatcoat from a peg, she jerked it around her shoulders, heedless of her tender hands.

And just in time, for in the next moment, the cabin door swung open and Timmy Madcombe stepped inside. Caliban greeted him with a polite but impatient wag of his tail.

"Mr. Beals told me to bring your breakfast, miss," he said, tipping his head in the direction of a small tray he balanced on one hand.

Somehow the tray of food held considerably less appeal this morning, although its contents were remarkably similar to last evening's supper tray: dry bread, some sort of hearty soup, and coffee. As Caliban pushed past the boy and into the open, Tempest waved a hand toward the table where the empty tray sat. "Thank you, Timmy. You and Mr. Beals have been most kind. But I suppose I shan't be aboard long enough to require breakfast," she said, averting her gaze from the food as Timmy carried it past, although the odors lingered.

"If you say so, miss," was Timmy's only reply, accompanied by a furious blush as he tried to avoid looking at her.

Captain Corrvan's coat was long enough to cover a multitude of sins, but her bare feet still peeped from beneath its hem, and if she took a step, she would surely offer curious eyes a view of her shift where the coat opened, front and back.

"Please tell Captain Corrvan I'd like to speak to him at the first opportunity," she said, mustering all the authority she could, "so that I may know when I can expect to be put ashore."

"Yes, miss," the boy said as he turned to go.

"How long will it take you to fetch him?"

"Fetch who, miss?" he asked, a look of genuine puzzlement on his face.

Tempest squared her shoulders and tried to keep the exasperation from her voice. "Captain Corrvan."

"Cap'n is on watch," he explained patiently, as if she were the child. "Just begun. Mr. Bewick'll relieve him at next bell. That's four hours," he added in an edifying tone. "I'll tell him what you said, though. I s'pect he'll come down right after mess."

"Right after . . . ?" Despite herself, her voice rose to a squeak. "I believe you've misunderstood, Timmy. I need to speak to Captain Corrvan *immediately*. Please tell him so."

With wide eyes, Timmy nodded. "I'll tell him, miss. But he won't leave his post. If it's an urgent matter, I s'pose you could go to him."

"Very well," Tempest replied, taking two mincing steps toward the cabin door. "Lead the way."

"I, er . . . that is, I don't think . . ." he began sheepishly, but at her frown, he gave a curt nod and shifted course. "Yes, miss."

A few steps behind Timmy Madcombe, Tempest ascended the short flight of stairs to the aft deck, emerging into a world quite apart from her first impression of the *Fair Colleen*. A ship at sea was quite a different place to a ship in harbor, it seemed. Without the stout handrail, she might have been knocked off her feet by the wind that swept across the deck, tangling her hair and threatening exposure even when she stood still. And the noise! Her head and heart pounded with the unfamiliar shouts and songs of a dozen men at work at various tasks around the ship, the creaking and cracking of sails and ropes and wood, and the steady *dhrub-dhrub-dhrub* of the water against the hull as they sliced through the sea like a scythe through cane.

As she struggled to get her bearings, she located Captain Corrvan, his white shirt rippling like a flag in the stiff breeze. He was standing near, but not at, the ship's wheel. Another man's hands actually guided the ship, and the discovery only increased her outrage. Surely he might have spared a moment to have come to her, if that were the case. Besides, she was not entirely confident in her ability to cross the deck with aplomb. Neither her knees nor her eyes seemed to want to work with their usual efficiency, and she feared if she looked down at her feet to set them where they ought to go, she would have a great deal of trouble to raise either of them again.

A good half-dozen paces ahead, Timmy at last paused to look back. With a grin, he returned to her side, holding out one arm with surprising gallantry. "Never fear, miss. Happens to us all. To hear Mr. Bewick tell it, even the cap'n—" He broke off when Tempest stumbled. "You'll get your sea legs after a bit. Why, on my first voyage, I was sicker'n two dogs tied together, beggin' your pardon, but since then I ain't hardly—" This time, the flow of words was halted by a feeble wave of Tempest's hand.

Oh God. The boy must stop talking. *And moving. If everything around her would be still for* just one moment, *she might avoid—*

But in the end, she could *not* avoid it. Nausea rolled upward, stinging her throat, and though she tried valiantly to fight the inevitable, in another moment the contents of last night's supper tray were spattering the mid-deck, narrowly missing Andrew Corrvan's boots.

He cast a gaze over her that might have been pitying, although very little registered in Tempest's mind beyond the awful sensation that it was only a matter of time until she vomited again.

"Have you never been to sea, Miss Holderin?" he asked, as he stepped nimbly over the mess and led her to a seat on an upturned crate.

She shook her head, then realized belatedly that such a movement was likely to lead to another disaster. Clenching her jaw, she replied instead through barely parted lips, "I fail to understand why I am at sea *now*, Captain Corrvan."

He crouched beside her and pointed, inviting her to sight along his outstretched arm. "See that ship to starboard?"

She could see nothing but an endless span of blue: blue sky, blue sea, darker in some places, lighter in others. "I'm sorry, no."

Or perhaps there *was* nothing to see. She turned toward him, noting with some surprise the fine lines at the corners of his catlike eyes—the mark not of old age, for she very much doubted he was even thirty, but of one who had spent years squinting across the open water. It seemed an oddly intimate thing to notice about a person.

She returned her gaze to the horizon, discovering—as he had no doubt known she would—that focusing on the far-off line between sky and sea somehow calmed the riot behind her eyes and in her stomach. "I don't see a ship," she admitted. "Nor do I see Angel's Cove."

"We're a fair ways off the coast now, I'm afraid. Slipped away at sunset to avoid an entanglement with that ship you don't see, the *Justice. Swift Justice*, some call her. 'Lazarus' Stratton, captain. So named because he was once raised from the dead."

"Is he a—a privateer?" she asked.

"Ah, well. That's not for me to say." Captain Corrvan shrugged, one corner of his mouth lifting slightly at her polite euphemism. "I leave those fine distinctions to the authorities. But I'd rather not meet him in the dark. Or the shallows." Rising, he moved a short way off to lean against some piece of rigging, his eyes still focused on the unseen ship. "Mr. Madcombe, fetch Miss Holderin a cup of Greaves's special tea."

"Aye, Cap'n," the boy replied, scampering off.

"I don't want tea," Tempest insisted, still not trusting her stomach enough to unclench her jaw farther than it took to grind out a few words. "I want to know when you'll be returning me to Antigua."

"You're seasick, Miss Holderin," he declared, turning his gaze from the water at last. "It happens to the best of us—even those with names that would seem to defy any such weakness where the water is concerned," he added with a sardonic smile. "Why, the only man I've known to avoid it entirely is Mr. Bewick, the *Colleen*'s quartermaster. And that's only because he sprang fully formed from a ship's figurehead, I do believe."

"Modeled after Zeus, I suppose?" she forced out in the lightest tone she could manage. She would not give in, not to the sea nor to Captain Corrvan.

His answering smile held both surprise and approval, the identical expression to the one he had been wearing when she quoted Shakespeare. "More likely one of Zeus's wives. We men of the sea like to carry a lady with us. For luck."

"I thought women were believed to bring bad luck aboard ships?" she countered. The words were coming more easily now, although she still did not trust herself to stand.

"Flesh-and-blood ones, yes. For obvious reasons." His eyes swept over her in that assessing fashion that was growing annoyingly familiar, and this time, she felt an answering tremor stir somewhere deep within her, which she quickly dismissed as queasiness.

Then she realized that his gaze had shifted to the mess on the middeck, and heat flared in her chest and her cheeks. "I *am* sorry," she ground out, the tightness in her jaw having less to do now with the state of her stomach.

"It's nothing, Miss Holderin," he said with a wave of his hand that she would have called dismissive. But his crew must have read the gesture somewhat differently, for in another moment, a seaman was on the scene with mop and bucket, making short work of her disgrace.

And then Timmy was at her side with a steaming mug full of some noxious brew that was most certainly *not* tea. She was on the point of refusing it when she caught the gleam in Captain Corrvan's green eyes. Never one to back down from a challenge—even an unspoken one—she snaked one arm free of the captain's coat to accept the cup and swallowed the bitter beverage in short, scalding gulps. In a few moments, she was oddly disappointed to discover he had been right about its healing properties. She did feel better.

Better enough that she tried too soon to push to her feet and found herself somehow—she could never afterward say *exactly* how—on her back on the deck, looking up first into a merciless blue sky and then into Captain Corrvan's mercilessly handsome face.

"I'd advise you to keep your seat," he said.

She shook her head—another dreadful mistake. The sound of her hair scrubbing against the deck was earsplitting. "No," she managed to whisper. "I wish to return to my—er, *your*—that is, the cabin. To rest."

"You'll do better in the fresh air, I assure you."

She pressed her lips together and dared one quick negative.

"Very well," he sighed. A mocking sigh, she felt certain. And then he was leaning over her, lifting her in arms that were every bit as strong as she might have suspected, and carrying her back down the short flight of stairs to the quarterdeck. Not cradling her in his arms, against his chest, as if she were some precious cargo. But slung over his shoulder, like a sack of grain. Probably with her backside in full view of every sailor on the ship. Out of nowhere, Caliban appeared at his heels, laughing up at her with a wide, doggy grin.

Rather than struggle and humiliate herself further, she chose to close her eyes and pretend this was not happening. She did not open them again until she felt herself being dropped ignominiously onto the captain's rumpled bed.

"You will wake me, will you not?" she murmured from its shockingly comfortable depths. "When we land at Angel's Cove?"

His reply seemed to come from a long way off, although she knew he was leaning over her. She could smell the salty spiciness of his skin. "We won't be landing at Angel's Cove."

Fighting against the haze that threatened to envelop her, she struggled to prop herself up on one elbow and swallowed against the feeling that rose in her throat, equal parts nausea and fear. "Did you say . . . '*won't*'?"

"That is what I was trying to tell you, Miss Holderin," he said matter-of-factly as he eased her back against the pillow and tucked the sheets around her. "Thanks to the *Justice*, we've had to sail on."

The pillow was a siren's song, calling to her aching head. But wasn't there a question she should ask before she slept? She felt certain there was. If only . . . *Ah, yes.* There it was, floating past like a bit of flotsam on a gentle wave. She plucked it up. "Thail on?" she slurred.

"On," he reiterated as her eyes drifted closed. "To London."

Chapter 6

Surely, in death, people were not subjected to the shrill notes of an Irish jig being whistled by someone incapable of carrying a tune.

So, she was not dead, then.

Pity.

Cracking one eyelid just enough to sort out the sound from its maker, she was assaulted first by the airy brightness of the room and a mere moment later by a smooth, wet tongue.

"Caliban," she croaked, trying to restrain the animal's affection and finding, to her chagrin, that she was too weak to do so.

Her brain and teeth felt equally fuzzy, but she managed to struggle first into a sitting position and then standing. The fact that she was still wearing only her shift gave her momentary pause, but that god-awful sound from the next room was not going to stop itself. Tugging a sheet free of the bed, she wrapped it tightly around her body and marched into the great room on regrettably wobbly legs.

Captain Corrvan was seated at the large table, whistling as he wrote in some sort of ledger. He did not immediately look up from his work. The ebony waves of his hair fell forward, obscuring his eyes, though they did nothing to soften the angular planes of his face.

When it was obvious that he meant to ignore her, she said with as much hauteur as she could manage, "How dare you violate my privacy in this ungentlemanly fashion."

His sharp green gaze was immediately upon her, looking far more amused than surprised. "Awake at last, are we? Well, this *is* my cabin. And I'm no gentleman."

"I never!" She knew she was blushing, a curse of her complexion, but she kept her spine ramrod-straight.

"A pity, Miss Holderin," he said with a laugh, coming at last to his feet. His dark head almost brushed the ceiling.

"Just what was in that 'tea' you gave me? How long have I been asleep? Did you—did you—?" For all her bravery, she could not muster the courage to put an accusation into words.

"Violate *you*?" he suggested. If she had imagined his expression sardonic before, the look he gave her now made her realize she had only just tapped the deep vein of mordant humor that ran through his soul. "Would that have been before or after you vomited in my sea chest?"

"I couldn't have," she whispered in a voice that lacked all conviction.

A cocked brow. "No?"

Mortification rolled over her in a wave almost as powerful as the seasickness had been. Anything might have happened in the hours . . . or days . . . since he had carried—oh God, *carried*—her to bed. Everything was a blur. She seemed to remember Mr. Beals bending over her, murmuring something . . . She pulled the sheet more tightly around her body and discovered what she ought to have noticed first. The bandages were gone. And her hands were mostly healed.

"How long?" she demanded, still staring at the pink flesh of her palms.

"Oh, call it a week."

Shock jerked her chin upright again. "A *week*? First, you take me prisoner—"

"I seem to recall that you climbed aboard this ship under your own power, Miss Holderin," he countered.

"Not with any intention of sailing across the Atlantic, as you well know," she tossed back. But the accusation earned little more reaction than a careless shrug. "So you *drugged* me with that so-called tea—"

With those words, she seemed to have crossed some invisible line. "In ten years at sea I've found nothing more effective against the scourge of seasickness," he said, stepping closer. "Greaves's brew quiets the stomach and calms the head. As the best recourse is often rest until one has adjusted to the sea, and you seemed—forgive me—unlikely to listen to that sage advice, I ordered something I knew would ensure it. Now, if young Madcombe neglected to convey to Greaves that the patient in question weighed, oh"—he paused to look her up and down—"eight stone, and not twice that, certainly *I* cannot be held responsible for the error. And in any case, you seem well enough now."

His explanation made some sense, but it did very little to mollify her. "Yes. I *am* well now. And I demand that you take me back to Antigua."

"Not possible." Stepping around the corner of the table, he brushed past her on his way to the door. She sputtered out a protest, but he merely held up his hand in reply, his face a carefully schooled blank. "When you're ready, come on deck and I'll explain. Here are some clothes," he said, lifting a small bundle from the floor, "and you'll find tooth powder and a, um, hairbrush in the top of the chest of drawers."

"But," she exclaimed as she took the bundle from him, "these are boys' clothes."

His lips twitched in a sort of smile. "None of the crew would confess to keeping ladies' garments in their sea chests."

She could find no humor in the situation. "What became of the dress I was wearing when I came aboard?"

"If I had to guess, Miss Holderin, given its condition, one of the deckhands claimed it for polishing the brasses." Then he bowed his head in that unexpectedly proper way of his and motioned to Caliban to follow him from the room. This time the dog heeded orders.

With a sigh, Tempest walked back into the bedroom and freshened up as best she could with the dregs of the washbasin, then turned her attention to the garments that had been supplied. In truth she was no stranger to wearing boys' clothes on occasion. She kept a few items that had once belonged to Edward for . . . oh, *emergencies*, one might call them. And as emergencies went, being kidnapped and held prisoner aboard a ship at sea would seem to qualify.

Once she had pulled the shirt over her head, she sat down to shimmy into the breeches. Over all, she donned a long waistcoat of scratchy wool. The clothes were ill-fitting and inelegant, but the greater freedom of movement could not be denied.

Lastly, she pulled open the drawer he had indicated. Inside, a clever mechanism pushed a mirror upward as the drawer slid out—at an angle suited for a much taller person, it was true, but she would make do. She glanced at her image, expecting wan and delicate. She was greeted instead by a Gorgon.

And true to form, when faced with her reflection, the Gorgon froze in stony horror.

She was pale, yes. But then, she was always pale. Except for her left cheek, which was still red where it had been creased by the pillow. And her eyes, which were bloodshot and ringed with circles so dark they might have been mistaken for bruises, suggesting the captain had not entirely exaggerated how ill she had been.

Worst of all, though, was her hair. A tangled mess under the best of conditions, now it looked as if—well, it looked as if she had stood in a salt-damp wind, rolled about on the deck of a ship, and then slept in a sweaty heap for a se'ennight.

No wonder Captain Corrvan had looked so wry. Violate her? It was a miracle he had not laughed in her face.

With a will and a wince, she took the brush to the worst of the snarls. Before she had managed a single pass, however, bristles had broken and her wrist was trembling with fatigue. She thought longingly of the daring new short crop described in the latest London magazines. *If only she could . . .*

She glanced down at her clothing. Well, why not?

At the cost of a few more bristles, she jerked the brush from her hair, laid it aside, and set out for the great room, the captain's desk, and, hopefully, a decent pair of shears.

"And the, uh . . . er, the, uh, topsail . . ." As the boatswain stared over Andrew's shoulder with widening eyes and what looked for all the world like a blush, the ginger-haired Scot's jaw grew slack and let his words slip free from their moorings.

"A problem, Mr. Fleming?"

"No, sir! That is, well . . ." *Definitely a blush.* The man's head nodded forward. "See for yourself."

Andrew forced himself to turn, although he knew full well what, or rather whom, he would find.

He was nonetheless unprepared for how she looked.

Tempest Holderin had emerged from below wearing Timmy Madcombe's shore clothes, as he had expected. What he had *not* expected were her freshly, and rather haphazardly, shorn locks. By rights, she ought to have resembled a deck swab—or the boy who wielded it. Instead she looked like a sprite or a fairy, something from one of the tales his gran had once delighted in telling him, stories of the wee folks who lived in the glades and the glens. *"They can do a body good or ill, as they choose,"* she had always warned him.

But there was little doubt in his mind about the sort of sorcery to which he had made the mistake of subjecting himself.

"Miss Holderin." He stepped forward, abandoning Fleming, who seemed to have forgotten all about the ship's rigging in any case.

"Captain," she said when she had drawn close enough to him that she could reply without shouting. Her hands were crossed behind her back and she moved now with a quiet confidence that drove from his mind all thought of her earlier disastrous appearance on deck. "What could I offer that would entice you into taking me back?"

Under sail, the *Colleen* was not a quiet place, but in that moment, it seemed as if total silence had fallen: not a sound from the ship or the air or the water. Just the heated roar of blood in his ears. Without meaning to, he wet his lips. "Pray, what did you have in mind, Miss Holderin?"

"Why, money, of course," she answered with the merest hint of a smile. "I'm fully prepared to match what others have already offered." And with that, she brought her hands forward. In one of them, she held a slip of printed paper. A bank draft. Signed by Edward Cary.

Damn and damn.

"You went through my desk."

"I was looking for scissors."

"Which you found," he observed, unnecessarily.

"Mmm." She sounded as if she had not heard him. Her eyes were still focused on the bank draft. "Why did Edward give you this?"

"As a sort of bonus," Andrew explained smoothly. "He had cargo to be moved and he had run into difficulty finding someone willing to take it."

"What sort of cargo?"

"*Human* cargo, Miss Holderin." Why not let her believe the worst of him? People usually did. And no one would be served if she imagined him a better man than he was.

"Not slaves," she declared, her voice tight with shock.

"No," he agreed, folding his arms across his chest. "*You.* I was to take you to England. Whether you were willing to go or not."

"I see." Her short curls bobbed in a slight nod of acknowledgment. "He had often suggested I leave, but . . ."

"For your own safety, as I understand it." He did not know why he rose to Cary's defense, except that he was beginning to sympathize with the man's dilemma. Her slight stature and general heedlessness of danger roused a primal, protective instinct in a man. So much so that he found himself tempted to give in to that urge and ignore the voice of good sense, which recommended putting as much distance between the two of them as possible.

"Harper's Hill is my *home*, Captain Corrvan," she said, waving off his words, as if his point were irrelevant. "I do not wish to leave it. I *cannot* leave it. If I do, God knows what sort of authority over its management others will attempt to claim, or what will be done in my family's name."

"I was under the impression you found Cary a satisfactory manager."

"I did," she said, a heavy emphasis falling on the last word.

Then she let the bank draft fly.

Fortunately, Andrew had two advantages on his side: long arms and light winds. Snatching the paper with the tips of his fingers as it whirled past him, he kept it from her grasp long enough to tuck it into the waist of his trousers. *Let her look for it there.* "Get to work!" he shouted to his crew, conscious suddenly of having attracted an audience. "Even if I wanted to take you back to Antigua," he said, a prospect that grew ever more appealing, "I cannot."

She had the temerity to roll her eyes.

Wordlessly, Andrew drew his perspective glass from his jerkin and handed it to her. One look at the *Justice*, still lurking to starboard, and she would understand the fix they were in. So far the winds had not been in their favor. Why Stratton hadn't attacked already remained a mystery to him. It was almost as if he had some reason not to.

Her slender hands encircled the shining brass cylinder and then she hesitated, as if considering the varied uses to which the heavy instrument could be put. With a slight grimace and a toss of her head, she lifted the glass to her eye. Although she obviously struggled first to locate the other ship, then to bring it into focus, she refused to ask for his assistance, a foolish sort of stubbornness he could not help but admire.

Then she saw. And she gasped. Her hands trembled. "No." It was a quiet prayer, little more than a breath. He caught the spyglass as it slipped from her grasp. "It can't be."

"I assure you, it is," he demurred, reluctantly lifting the glass to his own eye. Since Bewick had first spotted the *Justice* off the cove, Andrew had refused to take a clearer look at the other ship. Stratton already had a place in his nightmares.

With a practiced eye, he swept the deck, counting the guns, assessing the crew. Stratton himself was at the wheel. And beside him—

It was Andrew's turn to freeze and to fight the tremor that rose in his own hand. Lowering the glass, he squinted across the distance instead, as if the instrument were not to be trusted, as if it were little more than a child's toy, rendering a kaleidoscope of shapes and colors.

But it was not the glass, of course. He had seen what he had seen. He had seen what *she* had seen.

On the deck of the *Justice*, his red duster swirling about his ankles, stood Lord Nathaniel Delamere, a spyglass raised to his own eye. And he was looking right at them.

When Andrew entered his cabin a short while later, Tempest was sitting curled atop one of the leather benches, staring out over the water, one breeches-clad knee drawn up to her chest. Caliban, who had followed her when she flew from the mid-deck, sat beside her, his head in her lap.

At first, neither dog nor woman seemed to remark Andrew's arrival, but after a moment, Tempest turned and spoke to him. "You *must* take me back, Captain Corrvan. I have a duty to the people of Harper's Hill. A duty that does *not* include running away from my problems and leaving those people vulnerable to the machinations of others."

Did others mistake it for courage, this bravado that hardened her voice and lifted her chin? Had Cary himself been misled by it? Andrew could see the uncertainty in her blue-green eyes.

"Lord Nathaniel Delamere, you mean." When he spoke the name, her body jerked as if she were suppressing a shudder. "Cary told me the man has proposed marriage."

She nodded, the movement stiff with the stubborn set of her jaw, as if prepared to issue another refusal.

He found himself wondering whether she knew enough to understand how afraid she ought to be. There were many men who liked authority, who wanted power, and the better part of them sometimes abused it, he had little doubt. But the men who wanted to dominate, who enjoyed punishing and humiliating, who craved another's total and abject submission—ah, theirs was a special sort of sickness, one whose telltale symptoms could sometimes be hidden from innocent eyes.

The question was, after a lifetime spent in the West Indies, just how innocent was Tempest Holderin?

"You might forestall him by marrying another, you know," he pointed out, pulling a chair away from the table and easing into its depths. The leather protested softly. "With that fortune of yours, your suitors must be legion. Surely one among their number is eligible."

"That has proven a surprisingly popular suggestion of late. And I cannot help but wonder which one I ought to choose," she said, lifting her hands in an exaggerated shrug of indecision and then ticking off her choices on her fingers. "The son of a local planter, sent to England as a boy, who knows nothing of Antigua and has no intention to fulfill his responsibility to his plantation by living on it? Or perhaps an earnest publican would be a better choice?"

"Not Gillingham?" he said, recalling the identity of Caesar's former owner.

Her hands fell and the mocking expression left her face. "How do you know that name?"

"I stopped in his fine establishment for a drink. That's how I came to meet . . . Caesar," he explained, deciding at the last moment not to mention the run-in with Delamere, knowing an account of the man's behavior would only fuel Tempest's insistence that they return to English Harbour. "What about Cary?" he suggested. "There's a man who seems ideal for your purposes."

"Edward?" She snorted. "Impossible. Why, we're as much brother and sister as anything. He's been a part of our family for twenty years, since the day Papa and I found him on the docks and brought him home."

That, then, was what Cary had meant when he had said the Holderins rescued lost souls . . . It was on the tip of Andrew's tongue to point out he felt quite certain Cary had long since outgrown their supposed sibling ties, but in the end, he resisted that devilish impulse. "You've named three men—four, if one counts"—he paused and jerked his head in the general direction of the *Justice* rather than say Delamere's name again—"who are, for one reason or another, ineligible. But surely there are others to whom you can have no objection?" She shook her head with surprising vehemence. "Why are you so desperate to avoid marriage, Miss Holderin? I'm given to understand many women find the state desirable. Has reading Miss Wollstonecraft given you such a thorough disgust for the institution, then?"

Her lips twitched with annoyance, but in the end, she humored his question. "Exactly what is it you imagine marriage offers a woman, Captain Corrvan?"

He had never thought much about it before, but surely it could not be too difficult to muster a respectable list of benefits. "A home. Economic security."

"I have those things already—as I think you well know. I realize there are some who find the notion of making one's home on the fringes of the empire most unsettling—"

"*Improper*, even," he suggested, lifting one brow. "For a lady."

"But I did not think a man of the sea would prove susceptible to such nonsense," she continued as if he had not interrupted. "Harper's Hill is my home, my only home, and I do not wish to leave it. As to economic security, when my grandfather dies, the plantation will be mine, and I feel quite confident of its ability to provide me with a comfortable life."

But of course she did. West Indian plantations produced sugar under the most inhumane conditions imaginable to satisfy an all-too-human craving for sweets. And for that, the planters enjoyed extravagant wealth. Regardless of the gossip that swirled around English Harbour about Cary's unusual management of Harper's Hill, he suspected things were far from idyllic there; otherwise, she would not be so rich.

He did not pursue the point, however, preferring for the moment to provoke her in other ways. "What about . . . affection?" His voice deepened as he hesitated over the last word, although he had not entirely meant it as a euphemism. "Or love?"

She laughed, but there was very little humor in the sound. "Oh, Captain, even if I *were* susceptible to such sentiment, the men vying for my hand are not interested in my personal charms—as you yourself pointed out."

"I suppose you are far too rational to believe in love, in any case."

Something about his words seemed to unsettle her, but she recovered quickly. "Too rational? Can one be any such thing?" she asked.

"In any case, it is because of love that I insist on returning to Antigua. It is because of love that I refuse to marry."

"So you *love* Harper's Hill," he scoffed. He had not expected her to revel in that sort of sentimentality.

"I love its people," she corrected. "And as soon as I am legally able to do so, I intend to prove it in the best way I can. Once the plantation is mine, I will set them free."

Everything about Tempest Holderin bespoke the rash energy of a reformer, so her intentions did not exactly surprise him. His own antipathy toward the institution of slavery aside, however, he knew very well how unusual such beliefs were, and how such an act would be met by others in the West Indies. He could not help but ask her, "Why?"

Shock widened her blue-green eyes. "If you can ask that question, sir, then I cannot expect any answer I give to be satisfactory. Slavery is a great evil," she stated in an assured, pompous sort of tone, as if she were some Methodist preacher shouting from the pulpit, "born of greed and a mistaken belief that some people deserve to be ground beneath the heel of others—"

"Ah, of course." He cut across her, taking some of the wind from her sails. "*Liberté, égalité, fraternité,* and all that," he cried in mocking imitation of a revolutionary. "Just don't forget the sugar for your tea."

"Surely you believe—"

"I *believe* nothing, Miss Holderin. I *know* that men are capable of unspeakable cruelty toward one another, and have been acting on those base impulses since the beginning of time. If you imagine that your grand gesture will change anything—"

"It will change *something*," she countered. "For the people of Harper's Hill, at least."

"And what will become of them when they are free?" he asked, doubting she had thought her decision through. "Will you send them back to Africa? Surely you must know they will only be captured and sold again."

"Freedom, Captain Corrvan, means they will decide for themselves, in the end. But I hope they will stay at Harper's Hill. I intend to offer them fair wages for their work."

"Your profits will be destroyed," he pointed out.

She shrugged, in the way only a spoiled heiress could. "I'm given to understand that many large English estates are run profitably on a similar system."

"Aye," he acknowledged. "Raising sheep, not sugar. And you have not really answered my question, you know. Why are you so determined to do this mad thing?"

"Because my dear papa wished it," she said simply. "With his dying breath. And I love my father, too—*loved*, people seem to expect me to say, as if my feelings were somehow diminished by his death. In his life, he did all he could for my grandfather's slaves, but the most important thing he could not do. Once Harper's Hill is mine, I can."

"Unless you are wed before you inherit." In which case her husband would control the property, both the plantation and its people. Good God, no wonder Delamere and the others were determined to push her into marriage before she was given the chance to throw all that money away.

"And so, I refuse to marry. Just as I refuse to leave."

With an air of finality, she folded her arms across her chest, as if she were a barrister who had just made an unassailable argument. Disturbed by the movement, Caliban left his comfortable nest and slunk over to Andrew, nudging against his hand to be petted. The dog's rough gray fur was warm where it had lain against her thighs.

Andrew understood the deep desire to ensure that a beloved father's dream had not died with him. Perhaps better than she could imagine. And for that reason, he knew precisely how difficult it would prove to weaken her resolve. "Cary seemed to believe that you would be protected from Delamere if you were in England," he ventured. He still dreaded the prospect of taking Tempest Holderin on a voyage she did not want to make. Nothing had changed in that regard. But they had come too far to turn back now—in more ways than one.

This time she did not roll her eyes at the suggestion, although it was clear she was tempted. "And did he say why?"

"Not precisely, no," he admitted, looking back at her. "But I take it that the power Delamere enjoys in Antigua is at least partly a product of the environment, so by removing you from that environment . . ."

She nodded her understanding. "Certainly, he has thrived in a place where the laws may be bent or broken to one's will, a place where men seem to prove particularly vulnerable to blackmail. Or bribery," she added with a twitch of her lips. "But don't you see? That is precisely why I must stay. What damage might he do at Harper's Hill while I am not there to protect it?"

"Cary remains. Will he not protect your grandfather's interests?"

"As he has protected mine?"

That was a challenge he could not counter. For the briefest moment, he could not even meet her gaze. "What authority has Delamere to do anything with the plantation?" he at last asked instead.

"My grandfather and Lord Nathaniel are old friends. Did Edward not also mention that? Lord Nathaniel already has a great deal more authority at Harper's Hill than I would like, I am afraid. On the very day we left, he showed me a letter from my grandfather, intimating that he would soon be granted even more."

Andrew tried and failed to imagine the grounds for friendship between the dissipated son of a nobleman and an elderly baronet. "What sort of a man is your grandfather?"

"I do not know. I have never met him. Like too many planters, he is an absentee." Her voice dripped with disdain. "I have always thought it shameful to care so little for something for which one is responsible."

Andrew forced himself to remember that her words had not been directed at him, though they cut rather near the bone.

"After my parents married, Papa offered to go to Antigua and take over the plantation's management," she explained. "My grandfather accepted the arrangement—until his daughter died here. He blamed my father for her death, of course, and after that, he wanted even less to do with the place. That was twenty years ago. I do not see how Edward can feel certain that I would be better off in England, with him. My grandfather's health is said to be poor, and his communication with Harper's Hill has always been sporadic at best. How can Edward claim to know anything about the man or his wishes?"

Andrew dropped his gaze to the charts littering the table. He was losing this fight. It was time to change tactics. Rising, he stepped closer to her. "Then perhaps you should consider that every minute Delamere spends at sea is a minute the people of Harper's Hill are spared." He waited. Let the words sink in. "If you truly want to help them, then you must do what countless young women have done over the ages. Lead your suitor on a merry dance." At her baffled expression, he gestured toward the window behind her and the water beyond. "Away from Antigua. Across the Atlantic."

He did not add that, by sailing toward London with the precious cargo Stratton seemed to seek, Andrew would also be able to lure the *Justice* into the open water she generally avoided. The advantage at last would be the *Colleen*'s, and Andrew could—if he chose—seize the opportunity for vengeance with both hands.

In a small voice, Tempest asked, "What if he gets to England first and goes to my grandfather—?"

What if Stratton outsailed him again, as he had before? "I will make sure that does not happen," Andrew swore, although he had never been one to make promises—to say nothing of keeping them.

Still looking out the window, she whispered, "What if he *doesn't* follow?"

"He will." Delamere had the instincts of a predator. If she ran, he would chase her. Of that, Andrew had no doubt.

"To London." On her lips, it was the name of a mystical place, found only in storybooks.

Reflected sunlight limned her profile: the gentle curve of her jaw, the translucence of her skin, the sunrise shimmer of her hair. Hers was a pale, radiant beauty, like an eggshell held up to a candle's flame, or a spider's web touched with dew at dawn. Fragile.

Without conscious thought, his left hand rose, his fingertips eager to trace the highlighted features of her face. But before he reached her, she turned slightly to face him. Her close-cropped curls made her wide eyes look even larger. As her gaze locked with his, he was reminded that the true beauty of delicate things sometimes lay in their unexpected strength.

Tempest.

He could not be sure which he named—the woman, or the storm-clouded depths of her eyes. In this moment, they were one and the same.

Her throat worked. "I suppose I haven't much choice, have I?"

"No."

And with that monosyllable he condemned himself to spending an eternity at sea with her. Forty days, give or take.

And forty nights.

Once, on a schoolboy dare, he had asked the rector what the people on the ark did all day, in such cramped confines, surrounded by all those animals no doubt giving in to their animal natures, what with being so perfectly paired and all. He had been soundly thrashed for his insolence—or had it been sacrilege? In any case, the rector had refused to answer the question.

Nevertheless, Andrew had had a good idea then, and a better one now, how a man and a woman, trapped together for six weeks, might be tempted to pass the time. Which was why he never allowed women aboard his ship.

His hand dropped.

"Do you know, Captain Corrvan, I half-expected you to suggest I might save myself by marrying *you*," she said. If she had seen the movement of his arm, she gave no indication.

"I can promise you that such a thought never crossed my mind," he answered with a small smile and shake of his head. "I am a man ill-suited to such responsibilities."

Her brows knit together in a slight frown as she glanced around the cabin. He might have expected such a reaction, given the pride with which she wore her own sense of duty. "But you must have a great deal of responsibility as captain of this ship."

More than he had imagined when he left home. Less than he had avoided by leaving.

"I leave all the hard work to Mr. Bewick." Twisting his mouth into something he hoped might be mistaken for a wry grin, he turned and walked to the door.

For once, Caliban followed without being called.

Chapter 7

Captain Corrvan did not lock the door behind him, but Tempest took little comfort in the omission. As they were now many miles from land, she obviously no longer posed a flight risk. Even if the cabin door had been standing wide open, she would have been no closer to getting home.

But that did not mean she was going to stop trying.

Oh, she was willing to admit that Captain Corrvan was right about one thing: Her departure had offered the unexpected benefit of drawing Lord Nathaniel away from Antigua. But as far as she was concerned, leaving Harper's Hill was too steep a price to pay for that small reward—even aside from the exorbitant sum Edward had given the captain.

Oh, Edward. Edward. She had known him all her life, loved him as a brother, trusted him as much she had ever trusted anyone. And *this*, she thought, looking around the confines of the cabin, was how he had repaid that trust. How could Captain Corrvan imagine she might marry a man who had betrayed her so spectacularly?

With Lord Nathaniel on one side of her, and the wide expanse of the Atlantic on the other, she was truly caught between the devil and the deep blue sea. In the past, those words had been nothing more than a familiar saying. A way of dramatizing the impossibility of a choice.

Now, however, she was living it.

It was even more disconcerting to wonder whether she would recognize the devil when she saw him. She had grown accustomed to thinking of Lord Nathaniel as the very devil incarnate. But mightn't the devil as likely be dangerously attractive? It required no great stretch of imagination to think he might also speak with a soft Irish lilt.

How much had Edward truly known about the man he had hired to take her away? What if he had been misled or misinformed? How strange to think that she might be the one aboard a pirate ship, from which Lord Nathaniel was trying to rescue her, dubious though such a "rescue" would prove to be.

No, she didn't really think it could be that, but something about Stratton and the *Justice* had made Captain Corrvan nervous, even before he had realized who else was aboard the other ship. Was there some history between the two? Did Captain Corrvan have something to hide?

Her search of the captain's quarters had uncovered intimate things. Personal things. But nothing that helped her know Andrew Corrvan better. Nothing that helped her choose between thinking of him as her kidnapper and thinking of him as her rescuer.

She wished she could simply *not* think of him at all. But that was proving nigh on impossible.

If only she had truly become the rational creature her father had wanted her to be, she surely would not have felt anything like attraction to a man she ought to despise. From that moment in Edward's sitting room, however, when both she and Captain Corrvan had reached for the dog and their hands had met, she had felt there was *something* between them.

A few moments ago, she had sensed as much as seen that he had been about to touch her, had been about to brush his finger across her cheek or through her curls. She feared he might attempt to do it again.

Worse, she feared she might let him.

It was rather a novel experience to be thinking of a man's attentions in terms of what she might accept or deny. For four years, she had been saying "no," and really, had anyone ever listened? Half a dozen men were still determined to marry her, despite her refusals. Lord Nathaniel's touch had left bruises more than once. Even Edward had behaved with an odd sort of possessiveness now and again—and look where that had gotten her.

Twice since coming aboard his ship, she had found herself in Andrew Corrvan's arms: once when she had almost fallen, and once when she had been ill. He might have imagined she would be willing enough to end up there again—or he might have been indifferent to her unwillingness. She was, after all, entirely within his power. But he had stretched out a hand with the intention of touching her, and then had stopped himself from doing so. Would a kidnapper, a villain, a rogue have done that?

It was not precisely that she trusted him. She knew better than to trust anyone here.

But it was something to realize she did not fear him, either.

Rising, she brushed her palms down the front of the blue worsted waistcoat, smoothing it over curves it had never been designed to cover. Enough. If the captain was going to allow her to move freely about the ship now, she needed to use that freedom to her advantage, for it might be taken away at any moment. Any one of the members of the *Fair Colleen*'s crew might prove able, even eager, to provide useful information where Captain Corrvan was concerned.

Just because circumstances had come together—and Edward had conspired—to force her to leave Antigua, that did not mean she had to go quietly to England. Or even go at all. If necessary, could she not use all her considerable charms, or at least her considerable wealth, to persuade some of the sailors to go against their captain and turn back?

Much depended on the crew's loyalty, and whether their captain was the sort of man to inspire it. It felt as if they were all engaged in some quest. Had these men thrown in their lot with his willingly, or were they, like she, unwitting participants on this risky journey and thus prone to rebel?

To answer that question, she needed to find out what drove Andrew Corrvan.

She decided to begin her inquiries with Mr. Beals. The years the surgeon had spent in Captain Corrvan's company meant he was likely to have the knowledge she sought. And his talkative nature meant he was even more likely to share it.

As luck would have it, she did not even have to leave the captain's quarters. Mr. Beals came to her. "How's my prettiest patient?" he called as he entered with a knock and a friendly smile.

"Well, thank you," she answered honestly.

From the doorway, Beals looked her up and down, taking in her unusual dress. Even as she fumbled for an explanation, he nodded in approval. "It shows good sense, I think. Very practical. Now, let's see those hands."

When he had pronounced them healed, he next looked at her eyes and asked about her appetite, then declared himself satisfied with her progress. "Why, I shall have to come up with another excuse for calling on you now, Miss Holderin."

"No excuse needed, Mr. Beals," she insisted. "It is always pleasant to have someone to talk to."

The surgeon made a little noise of agreement but nonetheless turned as if planning to depart, prompting Tempest to move quickly between him and the door. "I've been thinking about what you told me that first night, Mr. Beals," she said, glancing about the cabin as if recollecting the occasion fondly. "Eight years aboard this ship. What wonderful stories you must have to tell."

Pride swelled his chest. "I fancy I do have a few."

"I hope you'll share some with me when you have the time," she said. "I fear it's going to be rather dull for me, being stuck in this cabin for the next few weeks."

"Well, now, I suppose I could . . ." he began as she gently coaxed him to a seat at the table. "'Course, more'n a few of 'em aren't fit for a young lady's ears," he cautioned.

From somewhere, she mustered a titter. "What a pity. Perhaps you could arrange to tell those to someone else while I eavesdrop," she suggested teasingly, and as she had hoped, he laughed, settled into his chair, and had soon launched easily into some escapade involving the boatswain Mr. Fleming, a tar bucket, and a goat.

It was not hard to laugh at such a tale, which was succeeded by another of equal good humor told at the quartermaster Mr. Bewick's expense. While she was still wiping her eyes, she asked, rather breathlessly, "Haven't you any about Captain Corrvan?"

"Oh, a fair few," he acknowledged. But there was a sort of reserve in his manner now, and no story was immediately forthcoming.

"I was just wondering about the sort of man he is. I really hadn't bargained on this trip, you see," she said, averting her gaze, "and to find oneself quite at the mercy of strangers . . ."

"You've naught to fear here, miss."

"Fear?" she echoed, as if the thought had never crossed her mind. "Certainly not. The captain has such a gentlemanly air about him," she suggested, but the observation earned her only a nod of agreement. "I was wondering, in particular," she said at last, hoping she would not be punished for her impatience, "what you know of the history between Captain Corrvan and this ship that's following us, the *Justice*."

The friendly light left Mr. Beals's eyes, as if someone had shuttered a pair of windows. "Why do you ask, miss?"

"Oh, just curious," she began, but Beals clearly saw through that lie, prompting a more honest reply than she had intended to give. "You see . . ." *I've been betrayed by one I loved as a brother. And I don't know when I'll see my home again . . .* "Captain Corrvan accepted an enormous sum of money to deliver some valuable cargo to England."

To her surprise, Beals nodded. "Aye. He's promised us all our fair share."

It was how sailors were usually paid, of course, each man getting a portion of the profits, according to his rank. But somehow she had not expected Captain Corrvan to divide even his ill-gotten gains. Then again, wasn't there some old proverb about honor among thieves? "By coming aboard after Caesar, I inadvertently played into the hands of the person who paid him. *I* am the valuable cargo, Mr. Beals."

His eyebrows shot above the rims of his glasses.

"And there's a man aboard the *Justice* who knows it, a man who wishes me nothing but ill. I can't help but wonder . . ."

"What, miss?" he prompted.

"Whether Captain Corrvan means to deliver me to him," she finished at last. Gravely, Mr. Beals shook his head. "Is it so impossible to believe that your captain has entered into another bargain, a more lucrative one yet? Might he not intend to make an exchange—my life for a fortune in gold?"

"I won't believe it of him, leastways."

"He is always forthcoming to you and the rest of the crew, then?" she pressed. "Has never held back something you ought to have known?" Beals shifted in his chair and she knew she had touched very near an old wound, one that was imperfectly healed. "Some deal in which you ought to have shared, perhaps?"

But money, it seemed, was not the nature of Captain Corrvan's particular offense. Beals shook his head more sharply this time. "Never, miss. No man on this crew has aught to complain of, an' they're all better off than they were." The more agitated he became, the more his West Country accent broke through. "But it ain't money what drives him."

"Oh, of course not," Tempest scoffed. "It never is."

"Why, he only ever went after Stratton because his father—"

She leaned forward in order that she might not miss a word of his story, but the movement unfortunately alerted Mr. Beals to his near blunder. "It's not my story to tell," he insisted after he had pulled himself back from the brink of telling it. "But I can say this: Cap'n Corrvan would sooner scuttle the *Colleen* with his own two hands than help out Stratton and his band of pirates. No matter what he was paid."

His earnestness was surprisingly persuasive. But her curiosity was still unappeased. And whatever the source of the bad blood between Andrew Corrvan and Captain Stratton, she did not relish the prospect of being caught in the middle of their feud.

Mr. Beals had risen from the table and walked closer to the door as he spoke. "Before you go," she called after him, "you did promise I might visit Caesar. He is well?"

"Like naught was ever wrong wit' 'im," the surgeon said with a warmer smile. "I'll say that you asked after 'im and see what can't be arranged."

"And Mr. Beals?" His hand hesitated on the door latch. "Forgive me for asking so many questions," she said. "I hope I haven't given offense."

"Naw," he said, opening the cabin door. "Perfectly understandable that you'd be curious, under the circumstances. But if you want to know more, you'll have to ask t' cap'n direct."

"Of course," she agreed, despite having no intention of doing so. She was formulating another plan.

Early the next morning, she ventured out onto the deck once more. A handful of sailors were busy at varied tasks. At the helm stood a weathered-looking man of middle age, his eyes focused on the far horizon. Mr. Bewick, she presumed. Captain Corrvan was nowhere in sight.

Setting out on what she hoped would be mistaken for a morning stroll to take the air, she passed the quartermaster with a nod. Farther along, she met two seamen mending sails under the supervision of the Scottish boatswain.

"Good morning, Mr. Fleming," she began. "Am I disturbing you?"

One of the other sailors snorted. "That'll do, Hackett," Fleming said sharply before stepping away and motioning for Tempest to follow.

"What is it you wanted, Miss Holderin?"

A sudden gust made her borrowed shirt billow away from her skin, and she was suddenly grateful to have been deprived of her muslin dress, which would have revealed a great deal more than the shape of her arms. The wind filled the sails, too—those of them that were up, that is. A goodly number of them remained tightly furled.

"Would we not travel faster with more sails, Mr. Fleming?" she asked, hoping her curiosity would sound innocent. "I thought speed was of the essence."

It almost felt as if they were not really trying to get away from the *Justice*. She twisted surreptitiously to glance behind them, but as had been the case before, she could see nothing but water.

"Cap'n's orders," Fleming told her.

She might have predicted that would be everyone's favorite reply, whatever her question.

"Now, then, I'd advise you to return to your quarters, miss," he continued. "'Tisna wise for you to be out and about."

Her lips parted in a would-be scold. Under no circumstances did she intend to spend the next weeks locked away like the cargo in the hold. He and the other men were going to have to accustom themselves to her presence.

But Mr. Fleming had already returned to his post.

So someone didn't want her poking her nose into things, eh? That meant there must be something more than Captain Corrvan's past to hide. And she was determined to uncover it. Only then could she know whether she dared to trust him at all.

Which was why, a few days later, it came to pass that Timmy Madcombe found her near the seamen's quarters on a lower deck.

He started as he closed a door behind him. Tempest just caught a glimpse of the room's interior: rows of berths stacked one above the other, most filled with unidentifiable, snoring heaps. "Can I help you, miss?"

"Why, Timmy." He had not been her first choice to interrogate, since she doubted the boy had been aboard the ship long enough to know anything useful. But despite his shyness in her presence, he had a reputation among the crew for being something of a chatterbox, and beggars could not be choosers. She flashed a smile and then corrected herself. "Er, Mr. Madcombe, I suppose I'm to say. I'm still not accustomed to these shipboard conventions."

A frown of uncertainty wrinkled his brow. "As you wish, ma'am—er, *miss*."

"I'm glad of a chance to say thank you for the loan of your clothes."

He glanced at her nervously, blushing to the roots of his hair. "'Tweren't nothin', miss." A pause. "Are you . . . looking for something?"

"Oh, just acquainting myself with the ship. Is that a problem?" Another smile, but this one might have crossed the border into simpering, for it actually drove Timmy backward a step.

"No, o' course not," he insisted, bumping hard against the wall. "It's only . . . well, sailors aren't used to having ladies about, miss. If you choose to wander about, you might hear—or see—something you'd rather not."

Ah, *now* she was getting somewhere. She widened her eyes and wished she could summon a blush at will. "Oh my. I didn't think of that . . . Is there some illicit cargo aboard?" she asked, lowering her voice to a whisper.

"Ill-icit?" He shaped the word uncertainly and at last shook his head when he could not puzzle out its meaning. "Dunno, miss. I just thought you might not like to hear the men swearing and such. They takes care not to do it so much above," he explained with a jerk of his head to indicate the upper deck, "fearin' you might be by. But it gets awful rough down here, sometimes."

"Oh." She could not keep the disappointment from her voice. "Yes, of course. I thought you meant that Captain Corrvan had undertaken something illegal. You'd know, wouldn't you, if something weren't quite right?"

"Miss?"

"I mean, you seem like such an honest young man," she flattered. "You'd resist, I suppose, if you were asked to do something that was wrong."

"'Tain't likely," he insisted, and she was left to wonder whether it was the illegal activity or the resistance to it he found improbable. "Now if you'll excuse me, miss. I'm due on watch."

So it went, for the better part of a week. Deep suspicion of her questions. Half answers given to them, at best. No information about Andrew Corrvan's past. Only tantalizing glimpses of his present.

One evening her supper tray had been brought by none other than Caesar, who had been put to work alongside Greaves in the galley and showed some promising culinary skills. The boy seemed both well and happy, and he readily confirmed that he owed the captain his life for saving him not from his master's cruelties, although there had been plenty of those, but from the violence of an angry customer.

Andrew Corrvan was willing to subvert the law, it seemed, but not quite—or at least, not only—in the ways she had at first imagined.

This new revelation about his character was confirmed the next afternoon when she almost stumbled over the carpenter, Mr. Ford, repairing a section of railing, damaged by a barrel of gunpowder that had broken loose of its ropes and almost rolled overboard. Although the air was cool, he was bareheaded and bare-chested and sweating from the exertion of his task.

As soon as he realized she was standing there, he grunted and reached for his shirt, pulling it swiftly over his head. But not before she glimpsed the maze of jagged scars across his back, remnants of a flogging that must nearly have cost him his life.

"Pardon, miss," he said, but he did not sound apologetic. He could tell that she had seen.

After a moment, he returned to his work, apparently deciding that she didn't mean to move on. "That must require a great deal of skill," she said as she watched him.

"A fair bit," Ford acknowledged without looking up.

"I was . . . wondering when you joined the crew of the *Fair Colleen*, Mr. Ford." While she wanted desperately to find someone able to reveal something about Stratton and the *Justice*, another part of her prayed that his answer would be a recent date, more recent at least than those scars. Neither sailors nor slaves were strangers to the lash, but she found herself hoping that those scars had been gained on land, not at sea. Not under Captain Corrvan's watch.

"Why do you ask, miss?"

Tempest's eyes darted around the deck. Prior to coming aboard this ship, uncertainty had been an unfamiliar feeling to her, but it was growing more familiar by the day. "Just—curious, I suppose you could say."

"Curious?" he echoed.

Tempest hesitated. "Truthfully, I'm trying to learn something about the ship that's following us. Rumor has it, there's some history between its captain and ours."

She expected to be told once again to ask Captain Corrvan, but this time, her question was rewarded only with silence.

"I came aboard two years ago," he answered at last, fingering the blade of the tool in his hands. "In the Barbados."

"Is that where you learned to do such fine work?"

"No, miss." Dusting off his hands, he at last rose and stood before her. "I hail from Charleston. My *master*"—the word was spat from his lips with such vehemence, she would not have needed to have seen the scars to know what kind of man his master had been; by Ford's light complexion, she could also guess the relationship between the two had been one of blood, and not just bondage—"had me trained for a carpenter. Loaned me out. Took what I earned. Didn't seem right, so I ran. Twice. And when he couldn't persuade me not to do it again, he decided to send me to his plantation in the Barbados and teach me a lesson I wouldn't forget."

It would have been kinder, Tempest thought, to have killed him outright. But his master had obviously not been interested in kindness.

"That's where I met the captain and decided to go to sea instead," Ford concluded.

"I see." She remembered something Mr. Beals had told her. "So, you're a freeman now?"

His eyes narrowed. "If I'm not, it soon won't matter. Captain says we're for England, and I've been told there are no slaves there."

"That's right," Tempest agreed. Her father had once explained the intricacies of Lord Mansfield's rulings to her; no man could be a slave on English soil. Realizing Ford had told her much more than he should have, if not precisely what she had asked, she excused herself and returned to the cabin, feeling a stab of something like guilt when she considered that her bid to change the *Fair Colleen*'s destination might result in changing Mr. Ford's, and perhaps Caesar's, lives for the worse.

Over dinner, she paused to take stock of what more than a week's worth of effort had gained her. She now knew every nook and cranny of the *Fair Colleen*—or the *Colleen*, as the men all insisted on calling the ship, as if her fairness were somehow in question. Every port she'd heard named had been a West Indian port, and it sounded as if the transatlantic voyage was a rarity. In general, though, the crew behaved as if they were content. Captain Corrvan seemed to be well-liked by his men. He dined in the galley. Played cards with the ship's officers. Even volunteered for night watch.

And twice, at least, he had helped a slave escape from his master—an unthinkable crime in Tempest's world, if not her worldview.

So what did it all add up to? And what did Captain Stratton have to do with any of it?

With every day that passed, home slipped farther away. She needed to decide now whether she was willing to sail on, or whether she meant to find some way to resist. Everything seemed to hinge on the character of the man captaining this vessel. But if Andrew Corrvan's past actions were to have any influence on her decision, then she was going to have to do whatever it took to find out what she wanted to know about him.

Contrary to everyone's insistence that only the captain himself could answer her questions, she felt certain one other person on this ship knew the truth. And that man was Mr. Bewick, the taciturn quartermaster of whom the whole crew seemed slightly afraid.

Tempest pushed away from the table and stood. Tonight, it was time to be brave.

Chapter 8

"How's that new cabin boy workin' out for you, Cap'n?" With narrowed eyes, Fleming pretended to focus on his hand as he spoke.

Andrew knew instantly he was not being asked about Caesar. "I'm out," he said, slapping down his cards.

Ford and Beals looked up from their own hands, surprised by the abrupt end to their game.

But Andrew could not listen quietly to another ribald comment on the pleasing effect of Timmy Madcombe's breeches on Tempest Holderin's arse.

What kind of fool traipsed about a ship in boys' clothes, asking treacherous questions?

And what kind of captain allowed it?

The kind of fool, he supposed, who wanted answers—and the kind of captain who wondered who might supply them.

"Now, Cap'n," Fleming began, trying to placate him but unable entirely to wipe the smirk from his freckled face, "I didna mean—"

But Andrew had had enough. The boatswain's small cabin felt like a cage, and he needed to be free of it at once. "I'll send Mr. Bewick down to finish my hand," he said as he pushed away from the table and stood. "Good night, gentlemen."

"G'night, sir," the others called after him as he ducked through the doorway and walked along the passageway to the ladder nearest the helm. Before the top of his head had passed through the opening to the upper deck, he could hear voices. If he tilted his head, he could see the quartermaster's back, and young Madcombe's narrower frame alongside.

"I wanted to thank you for the part you played in rescuing Caesar from that horrible establishment." He could only just make out Tempest's voice above the noises of the ship.

A grunt of acknowledgment from Bewick, not quite audible, but visible by the lift of his shoulders. "Is there somethin' you require, miss?"

"As a matter of a fact, yes." A long pause followed. "Answers. Mr. Beals hinted there was bad blood between Captain Corrvan and the captain of the *Justice*. Is it true?"

Nothing subtle about this one. Well, she'd never get anything out of Bewick.

"You'd have t' ask the cap'n, miss."

"A fine idea." He could hear the indignation in her voice. "If I ever saw him."

"Night watch," Timmy explained in uncharacteristically tight-lipped fashion.

Bewick gave the boy a nod of support. It seemed the man was coming around to Andrew's suggestion that he train Timmy to the helm. Then, "Off t' bed wit' you, lad," the quartermaster ordered gently.

Expecting any moment to be discovered by the boy as he descended, Andrew listened for footsteps and relaxed only when he heard them shuffle away to the stairs in the prow. And then silence. The muscles in his calf began to ache, and he hitched himself higher on the rung, wondering whether she had left, too.

"Aye, it's true," he heard Bewick admit softly. "But Geoff shouldn'ta said awt."

Andrew froze, waiting.

"What happened?"

"Twenty years ago, Stratton tried his damnedest—beggin' yer pardon, miss—to sink the *Colleen*. Almost succeeded."

"Twenty years ago? But Captain Corrvan would've been little more than a child."

"Aye. And when he grew to a man, he were determined to make Stratton pay. Been chasin' him, one way or t' other, ever since."

"But why? It can't only have been over damage to the ship." A pause. "Mr. Beals said something about his father."

"If you want to know more, you'll have to—"

"Ask the captain," she finished for him. "Yes, I know." With an exasperated sigh, she got to her feet and, by the sound, brushed herself off. He could too easily call up the image of her small, pale hands sweeping over the seat of those buckskin breeches. "Well, he may have a feud with Captain Stratton, but I don't see how he can expect all of you to go along with him. Isn't anyone ever tempted to—?"

"I know what you been about these last days, Miss Holderin," Bewick spoke over her question. "It's dangerous business, tryin' to persuade sailors to go against their captain. Best give it up. The *Colleen*'s crew ain't got no cause to complain."

"I'm not so sure, Mr. Bewick. Because instead of chasing the *Justice*, now the *Justice* is chasing us."

Bewick hesitated for a moment before simply saying, "Aye."

Another not-so-soft sigh of exasperation. "I suppose I'll say good night, Mr. Bewick."

"G'night, miss."

Andrew waited until the sound of her footsteps had disappeared before ascending the ladder the rest of the way. On deck, the gloom of evening had begun to gather as the last rays of the sun left the sky. The brilliant blue of the Caribbean Sea had long since given way to the colder gray waters of the Atlantic.

Although he had moved silently, Bewick seemed to have sensed his presence. "Wondered when you was comin' up."

"You knew I was there?"

"Aye." After a moment, he added, "T' bottom rung squeaks. Allus has."

"Why did you tell her?" Andrew asked after a moment.

"She'd a right t' know. An' if you let her go on askin' questions, there's no knowin' what she'll hear. Or do. Women on board ship are a danger, I've allus said."

"Yes, well, having that one aboard means you'll get home again—and with enough money to stay there, if you please."

Bewick appeared to consider this. "Who'd look after the *Colleen* then?"

Andrew mustered a humorless laugh—it was an old joke, always told at his expense. "There's a card game in Fleming's cabin. I left them shorthanded when I came up to relieve you."

Jeremiah Bewick's knobby hands made no move to relinquish the wheel, steadfast as always. Would that they had never given it up.

"But I find I must ask you to stay at your post a bit longer," Andrew continued. "I've some business to attend to first."

"Aye, Cap'n."

With a nod, Andrew strode toward the quarterdeck.

After almost a fortnight of avoiding the inevitable confrontation, the undeniable temptation, it was high time he returned to his cabin.

With Caliban at her heels, she descended the short flight of steps to the captain's cabin. Before she could even cross the floor to light the lamp, Caliban exhaled in a deep *woof* and curled into a ball. In another moment, he was snoring softly. So much for companionship.

The lamp cast its stippled glow around the room, making the sky outside look comparatively dark. In a few moments, the bells would sound, signaling a change of watch. Perhaps she ought to have waited for Captain Corrvan to arrive on deck. But what good would that have done? He would never tell her the truth.

With a muffled cry of frustration, she slapped her hands onto the paper-strewn desktop. The motion dislodged a heavy book, which slid onto the floor, narrowly missing her toes. The volume of Shakespeare. Certainly not in the mood for reading, she was on the point of returning it to its crevice in the bookcase, when the corner of a folded sheet of paper peeked from between its pages and caught her eye. After a moment's hesitation, she laid the book on the desk, slid her nail between the edge of that folded sheet and the pages surrounding it, and flipped open the book to reveal a letter that bore no direction, only a name.

With the fingertips of one hand she held the book open while lifting the letter with the other. *Andrew* was written on the outside in a delicate, surely feminine, script. Whatever the missive's contents, they had certainly been of interest to the captain, for the paper had been folded and refolded so many times that its edges were like the book's, soft and worn. What words had he been compelled to read again and again and again . . . ?

"Find something interesting, Miss Holderin?"

She was surrounded, suddenly, by Andrew's heat, the hard length of his body behind her, pinning her to the desk. She had been too absorbed by the book and the letter to hear him enter, and of course Caliban had sounded no alarm.

One broad, calloused hand slapped onto the desktop, rattling the instruments, while the other hand came forward to twitch the letter from her grasp.

"Just what the hell do you think you're doing?" Despite the biting anger of his words, his voice was dangerously soft. Behind them, the cabin door clicked shut.

For a long moment, neither one moved. Tempest closed her eyes. She could hear his breathing over the furious tattoo of her own heart. Then the low, ominous rumble of a growl.

"*Et tu*, Caliban?" Andrew laughed wryly.

But he took a step backward, all the same. Once free, she darted across the cabin, putting a half-dozen strides, the table, and the dog between them. Briefly, she considered fleeing the cabin altogether. He made no other movement, gave no sign that he would try to prevent her, but his apparent indifference offered little comfort. They both knew she had nowhere to go.

"I d-did not intend to p-pry," Tempest stammered, suddenly desperate to fill the silence.

"Ah, but you did. You've been asking questions of every member of my crew." She felt her eyes widen, and he seemed to find amusement in her surprise. "Nothing happens on this ship without my knowledge, Miss Holderin."

With his head cocked to one side, Caliban looked from one to the other, as if watching a fencing match between skilled opponents.

Restoring the note to its place in the volume of Shakespeare, Andrew turned from the desk. Then, with one booted toe, he drew out a chair and slung himself into it, as if she required further proof he was no gentleman. "So here's your chance," he said, tossing the book onto the table and gesturing for her to take up the chair opposite. "Ask me. If you're certain you're ready for the answers."

Andrew tipped back in his chair and propped his heels on the table's edge, ankles crossed, as if he were perfectly at ease.

Tempest, for her part, looked as if she had taken his caveat to heart. If she had been wearing a skirt, she would have been arranging it nervously around her as she sat down in the chair he had indicated. Caliban, the faithless cur, came and nuzzled his head into the narrow gap between the backs of her breeches-clad knees and the chair, a gesture that somehow seemed to bolster her resolve, for in the next moment, she raised her eyes to his face and said, "Mr. Beals told me, and Mr. Bewick confirmed, that you and this Captain Stratton have some sort of history."

"That's not a question, Miss Holderin," he pointed out, forcing a lopsided smile. No, he should never have invited her to plumb his depths, to churn up the foul darkness that was buried there. "But, aye. We've that."

He expected some sharp retort, but none came. Instead, she looked wary, and he felt a sudden stab of regret for frightening her. Not as much as he regretted the discovery that her hair smelled of jasmine, however. How was it possible, after more than two weeks at sea? Had the sweet scents of the islands simply become a part of her blood?

"My father was a ship builder," he said at last. Best to start at the beginning. "In Cork. The *Fair Colleen* was, as it turned out, his last ship. The company who'd commissioned her asked my da to sail out with her, to bring her to London. I'll never forget standing on the dock, waving him off on a grand adventure, just the sort he'd long been craving." His father had never truly settled, despite his marriage. And Patrick Corrvan's son was unlikely to end up any different. Would Tempest understand the warning in his words?

She didn't strike him as the sort to heed it, even if she did.

"In those days, Stratton still lurked in the North Atlantic. The English Channel." Andrew focused on the ripples in the supple leather of his boots, fighting the temptation to glance toward the sea. Or toward her. "He must've wanted the *Colleen* herself as his prize. She was carrying no cargo to speak of. There was a skirmish in the shallows off the coast of Cornwall. Enough damage to sink her, though she didn't sink. Most of the crew survived. But my father was killed."

A soft gasp. Of sympathy, he thought. But still she prodded, "What happened then?"

"After a time, the man who owned the ship came to Cork to pay his condolences. We were living with my grandfather."

"Alastor Mitchel."

He jerked his gaze to her face. "How did you—?" But she was staring at the book he had thrown onto the table, and his question was answered before it was asked.

"Despite the loss of my father, I had a good childhood. The man from the shipping company wrote a few times. I thought very little of it. Then . . ." Reaching for the volume of Shakespeare, he withdrew the letter, unfolded it, and handed it to her. "I woke one morning to find this note on my pillow."

He watched her eyes flicker over the paper that had piqued her curiosity mere moments ago. Did the contents of the letter disappoint? Its words were few enough, long ago committed to memory.

> *My dearest boy—*
> *Daniel and I are gone to London to be married. We shall send for you as soon as we possibly can.*
> *Your loving mama*

Her fingertips hovered over the faded ink, but she did not touch the words. "And did she? Send for you, I mean."

"Aye," he replied as he took up the letter without looking at it and folded it again. "Then shortly afterward, I was sent away to school." His chest ached as if the old loss, the terrible homesickness, were new wounds. Why hadn't he thrown away the letter years ago? Why had he read it, night upon night, after the other boys were sound asleep, as if a tattered piece of paper could somehow take him back to a place and a time before those words had been written?

Something in her expression caught his eye. "What is it, then?"

"Your voice. I have been thinking all this time that you really sound nothing like any Irishman I have ever known. But tonight . . ."

He gave a humorless laugh. "I expended a great deal of effort learning to sound nothing like an Irishman, Miss Holderin. English schoolboys can be quite cruel." There were moments, then and now, when he deliberately cast aside his carefully cultivated accent. Tonight, however, it had happened without thought. As if the mere memory of his origins could restore who and what he had once been. As if, with her, he could be his true self.

And what a foolish notion that was.

Horror mingled with pity in her face, but he brushed it aside and pressed on. "As soon as I was able, I claimed the *Colleen* for my own and ran away to sea. Bewick was her master by then, but he let me play at being captain. Still does—though God knows, he shouldn't. I was determined to avenge my father's death, single-minded in my pursuit of the *Justice*. I followed her across the Atlantic. I tried to engage Stratton more than once, but he always slipped away . . ."

He realized his voice had trailed off with the memory when she prompted, "And then?"

"And then . . . he didn't. We had trailed him to a spot on the coast of Montserrat and got caught out in the shallows, his favorite spot to hide. The *Justice*'s guns ripped a hole in the *Colleen* that Stratton might've sailed through, if he'd a mind to do it." Her blue-green eyes grew wide. "Two men died. Another lost both his legs. That was seven years ago."

In the silence that followed, he could hear her draw a steadying breath. "And you've been hunting him ever since?"

He swung his feet onto the floor and rocked his chair forward. Caliban gave an uncharacteristic yelp of surprise at the sound. "Aye."

Tempest leaned forward, too, meeting his gaze across the table. What glimmerings of fear he had once spotted in her eyes were gone. "Now you mean to fight Stratton again," she said, the words coming slowly, as if she were working out the terrible truth as she spoke. "You're luring him into deeper water." She jumped to her feet and strode back to his desk, the lamplight picking out golden sparks in her close-cropped curls, Timmy's breeches sliding provocatively over the curves of her backside. "Using me as bait."

Would the realization result in tearstained pleas? Or white-hot fury?

Instead, she offered sympathy. Of a sort.

"My mother died when I was only three." Her voice was low, as if she were not speaking to him. And perhaps she really was not. "My only memories of her are those that Papa's stories created. I lived for him, always. And I promised him I would do all that I could to make his dream become reality." She turned back to face him, her eyes hidden in darkness. "So I understand the powerful effect a father's life and death can have on his child. Truly, I do." Despite the shadow, he knew she was studying him, seeking the answer to some question she had yet to ask. "But what you're doing . . ." Shaking her head, she took one hesitant step forward. "It's selfish. Irresponsible."

"I never claimed to be otherwise," he said, pushing to his feet. "But I suppose you believe you're selfless, living for someone else's dream?"

Her pointed little chin tipped upward in defiant acknowledgment of the truth of his words.

"Was it not 'irresponsible,' then, to get yourself trapped on a sailing ship with no means of getting back to the people who depend on you?" he challenged. "Not to mention bloody dangerous to go traipsing around wearing naught but boy's breeches and a smile, trying to persuade my crew to mutiny! Selfish? Irresponsible?" With each word, he stepped closer, until they stood face-to-face. Tempest showed no sign of backing down. "Aye," he whispered, dipping his head to bring his gaze level with hers. "The difference is, I'll own to it."

Her brow dove downward and her lips pursed together, an expression half scowl, half pout. And partly because he did not want to hear her retort, and partly because he had been wanting to do it almost since the moment he met her, he lowered his head farther and kissed her.

Whatever he had been expecting—resistance, rejection, a slap through the face—it certainly was not the feel of her hands sliding up his shirtfront, curling in the lapels of his coat, drawing him closer. Raising his hands to cradle her head, he brushed his fingertips along her jaw, and she opened to him easily, parting her lips so he could feel her soft heat when she moaned into his mouth.

No sooner had his tongue touched hers, than Caliban scurried from his place beneath the table, wedged himself between their legs, and sat, the breadth of his haunches pushing them apart. Reluctantly, Andrew broke the kiss and breathed in sharply through his nose to restore his equilibrium. Her scent filled his nostrils. *A proper English miss would smell of roses, not exotic island flowers.*

But Tempest Holderin was no proper English miss.

Resting his forehead against hers, he murmured, "That was . . ." . . . *tempting . . . teasing.*

"Unwise," she finished.

That, too.

Her hands slipped from his chest. "Caliban's instincts are true," she said. Having separated them, the dog was already on his feet again, pacing to the cabin door and back, as if seeking an escape from the tension between them. "You've as good as kidnapped me and now you're using me to draw a pirate into open water so you can kill him, sink his ship—"

"He'll take Delamere with him when he goes," Andrew reminded her.

"I ought to be railing at you, pleading with you . . . something,"

Tempest continued as if she had not heard him. With unsteady steps, she made her way to a chair and sank into it. "Not kissing you." She chanced a glance in his direction. "But I—"

He shook his head. Taking the seat opposite once again, he pulled the heavy book toward him. "Rail away, if you're so inclined. You're entitled. Just don't fret about the kiss, lass. One little misstep won't change our stories. They were written down too long ago."

She smiled uncertainly, as if trying to make out whether or not he was joking. "By Shakespeare, I suppose?"

"Certainly. Take yours, for instance. A wide-eyed girl grows up on an enchanted island with her magician father."

"My father wasn't a magician," she protested. "If he had been, my mother would never have died. *He* wouldn't have died."

"It's a strange little play, Tempest." She gave no sign either of pleasure or displeasure at his use of her given name. "Some unconventional elements, for a comedy."

The smile that had begun to lift her lips turned downward instead. "But a marriage in the end, nonetheless."

He lifted one shoulder. "To a prince. Not a monster."

"And which are you?" she asked, tilting her head and fixing him with one twinkling eye.

"Why, a prince, of course." He laughed. "But before you make any plans . . ." Skating his fingertips over the familiar pages, he found the play he sought and passed the book to her.

"Prince Hamlet?"

"Who else? Son attempts to avenge his father's murder. Fails again and again. Kills innocent men instead of guilty ones."

She closed the book and laid her hand on its cover, tracing the embossed leather with one slender fingertip, refusing to raise her eyes. "Hamlet dies in the end."

"Aye. But he takes the villain with him."

When the dog's next circuit carried him past the door, he stopped and began to bark, a high-pitched sound of distress that brought Andrew to his feet, breaking the quiet intimacy of the moment. "What is it, Cal?"

The barking stopped just long enough that he could hear the bell begin to ring on the deck. Not the signal to change the watch, but an alarm, jangling harshly, as if a frantic hand jerked the rope. Suddenly

he knew what the commotion signified. He had seen this sort of behavior from the dog before, and he could not quite believe he had
misunderstood its meaning now.

It seemed Bewick was right. A woman on board ship posed a dangerous distraction.

"What is it? An attack?" Tempest cried, jumping from her chair
only to drop to her knees and wrap her arms around the panting dog.

"No," said Andrew. "A storm."

Chapter 9

O nce Andrew had slipped into his oilskins and left, Tempest set about the small tasks he had assigned her, hoping it would make her feel better to be doing something.

Make sure everything that can move is secured.

She straightened the desk, placed the heavy brass instrument in a drawer, restored the battered old volume of Shakespeare to its spot on the shelf, then slid the doors of the bookcase closed and turned the tiny key in the lock. A place for everything and everything in its place. Even the chairs fitted into cleverly designed grooves underneath the table, she discovered. Too soon, all was as snug and tight and sound as it could be, and she had no further distraction from her restlessness.

Keep Caliban calm.

By far the harder job, since the dog had been desperate to follow Andrew onto the deck and alternated between scratching and whining at the cabin door and cowering awkwardly in the little cage of chairs' legs beneath the table. Eventually she persuaded him to join her in bed, pulling his ratty woolen blanket off the floor and smoothing it over the crisp linens, then patting it repeatedly to coax him up to lie, panting and anxious, beside her. Every gust of wind, every pitch of the ship, made them both stiffen and jerk with alarm.

And remember, stay put.

In truth, she had no desire to do otherwise. No stranger to the strength and unpredictability of tropical storms—on land, if not at sea—she knew worse, far worse, was yet to come. A glance at the rain-spattered window revealed nothing but night's blackness. Still, she could feel that the sea was rising. By morning light, the *Colleen* would be tossed like a cork on the ocean. If morning ever came.

She tried very hard not to think of Harper's Hill. Would this storm also touch them?

Was Omeah even now slipping into that trancelike state she inhabited when storm clouds appeared on the far horizon? Edward had speculated that she had survived a storm at sea on her voyage from Africa, but no one would ever know the truth, for Omeah, like most slaves, never spoke of that horrible passage.

Would strong winds damage the mill further, or delay its repair so that the harvest was suspended or people were endangered?

Would Edward regret having sent her into the unknown?

Finding her imagination worse company than her present fears, she sat up and looked around, disturbing the dog, who whimpered piteously and burrowed closer. Surely there was something else she could be doing. But Andrew had given her only one other order.

Don't fret about the kiss, lass.

And she stood far less chance of obeying that command than all the rest.

Without conscious thought, she pressed the fingertips of one hand to her lips, as if she expected still to feel the heat of Andrew's mouth on hers. A misstep, he had called it. She rather thought *madness* a more fitting word. But oh, what sweet madness it had been! How different from Edward's fumbling attempt, when she had been just fifteen and he old enough to know better.

Shortly thereafter, when her father had grown ill and died, and the marriage proposals had begun, she had made the vow never to wed. She would live independently for the sake of all those who were dependent upon her. She had sworn she did not need a man.

How lowering to discover she might still *want* one.

And to want such a one as him!

Prince Hamlet, indeed. She felt quite certain Shakespeare had not intended the play as a statement in support of revenge. No—the story was a tragedy, meant to demonstrate the futility of such behavior. Not that she lacked sympathy for Andrew's plight. She had spoken the truth when she had told him she understood the powerful pull of a father's dream on a child's destiny.

But if it was not unthinkable to want to avenge his father's death, certainly it was irresponsible to risk others' lives in the process. She was surprised by the loyalty his crew had shown him, under the circumstances. Why on earth did they not resist his plan? But maybe they had reasons not to. A man like Ford, for instance, would hardly be served by rebelling. It would only put him in another sort of peril. Perhaps she had been asking the wrong questions all along. Perhaps it was not what their captain had to hide, but the sailors' own pasts that shaped their decisions. Who could know what bound all of them to their service aboard the *Colleen*?

Perhaps they were inspired to risk their lives by his willingness to risk his own. It looked an awful lot like daring, even if there was a certain recklessness at its core.

And she could hardly fault them for falling under his spell. After all, on what foundation was her own attraction to him built? Not trust, certainly—he had been hired to kidnap her! Later he had argued that she must continue the journey to keep Lord Nathaniel on the hunt, when really, his own interests had been equally served by taking her across the sea. Could he have known from the first that having her aboard his ship would prove the surest way for him to lure his enemy out of hiding at last? No, too many pieces would have had to fall into place for it to have been a clear plan. Still, he seemed glad enough to reap the benefits.

It was not reasonable, the fascination she felt for this dark, dangerous man with a mysterious past and an even more uncertain future. Nor was it proper. Miss Wollstonecraft had many hard words for the human weakness of lust. Tempest knew a rational creature ought not to succumb to her animal nature.

But she had never quite mastered the art of behaving with perfect rationality. To say nothing of perfect propriety.

Could she satisfy the desire she felt without surrendering her dream? She had accepted that forgoing marriage would entail certain sacrifices . . . children, companionship. She had never worried about giving up passion, for that was pure emotion and something to be avoided. Physical curiosity, however, could be satisfied without involving her heart at all, could it not?

Her eyes darted around the small, ever-darkening room. Andrew's cabin. Andrew's things. Andrew's bed. Six weeks at sea without a chaperone in sight. She had courted scandal by coming aboard this ship. She was already ruined—at least, in the eyes of the world. And she had never cared much for what the world thought, anyway.

She was more than willing to live her life alone, if that was what duty required.

But would it be so wrong to have the memory of one night of pleasure with a scoundrel to keep her warm in the years to come?

If they survived to have one night together, that was. The *Colleen* heaved and Caliban groaned and shifted against her, having fallen at last into a restless sleep. Tempest doubted she would be so lucky. The storm raging outside would make sleep impossible.

To say nothing of the one roiling within.

Sailors were a notoriously godless lot. So Andrew knew things were bad when he found Hackett kneeling on the aft deck, his hands uplifted in prayer.

The darkness was thick, almost palpable, as Andrew struggled against the wind to make his way to the helm, where Bewick stood with his pipe still clenched between his teeth, although the rain had long since put it out.

"Where did you last see the *Justice*?" Andrew asked. The last thing he wanted was to come up against another ship under these conditions. If the storm didn't take them, a shipwreck surely would, and all Edward Cary's money would not buy back the *Colleen* from the murky depths of the Atlantic.

"A league or so off t'starboard and makin' way."

"Before the storm came up, or after?"

Bewick looked thoughtful. "Weather changed so fast, it's hard t'say. Before, if I had t' guess."

So Stratton had slipped past them, presumably with the idea of turning back to challenge them head-to-head. And he was out there now, in the blackness of a rough sea, much closer than Andrew would have liked. It was not the report he had hoped to hear.

He laid a hand on the wheel. "Get some rest. I'll need you, come daybreak." As wild as the wind already seemed, he knew the storm would only strengthen with the rising sun.

Bewick looked for a moment as if he intended to protest, then nodded and took his leave.

Through the night Andrew battled against an enemy he could not see, not to keep the *Colleen* on course, for there was nothing to chart by. Simply to keep her afloat. And his whole body screamed with the effort.

When dawn began to lighten the sky, he found himself longing for darkness again. Better not to see those waves that rose like mountains and threatened to tumble over them. Better not to see the panic on the faces of his crew. In ten years, he had known nothing to equal the power of this storm.

Although he was not a superstitious man, it was difficult not to wonder whether he had brought this on them all. He had bid his crew risk their lives for a justice—and a *Justice*—that might never be served. Perhaps this was the end of their journey. What sort of man went to sea with a woman whose very name invoked storm and shipwreck?

The sort, apparently, who also took comfort in the knowledge that if the *Colleen* went down, at least he would die with Tempest's kiss on his lips.

With practiced eyes Andrew studied the seam between sea and sky, which was neither blue, nor gray, nor green, but somehow all three at once—the ineffable color Thomas Holderin had seen in his daughter's eyes and yet had seen fit to name.

Oh, he was cursed, all right. He would be surrounded by that stormy shade until his final hours. He would never be able to forget those eyes—or the woman to whom they belonged.

After three days—or thereabouts, for in this mix of dark mornings and swirling nights, who could say how many days had passed?—Tempest was ready to join Caliban in clawing at the door, desperate for news, fresh air, and fresh water ... and not necessarily in that order.

With every window shut tight, the cabin had grown stale with a mixture of odors, both human and canine, scents she would rather not untangle. She was not hungry, at least. The pitching sea had taken care of that. Her body felt heavy with the strange sort of exhaustion that came from lack of sleep and enforced inactivity. When the gray view of a ragged sea grew too much, she drew the curtains and tried not to wonder whether she and the dog were the lone survivors of this terrible storm, tossed about in an abandoned ship on the vast, inhospitable ocean.

And then on the fourth day, in the afternoon—or so she called it, anyway, for the sky was yellow—a sort of lull fell over the sea. Kneeling on the bench to peek between the drapes, she studied the rise and fall of water that only a week ago she would have called rough, but now felt eerily calm. Was the storm relenting at last? Or had it merely paused to draw its breath before whipping itself into a frenzy once again?

She glanced over her shoulder at the cabin door. The unlocked cabin door.

Remember, stay put.

But he would never even know she had defied him. Just a breath of fresh air. Just a glimpse of another human soul.

Fearing that Caliban would make a break for it when the door was opened, but incapable of denying the dog a momentary reprieve from the confines of the cabin, she rummaged everywhere for something that could be used as a leash. When she could find nothing like rope, not even twine, she settled on one of Andrew's cravats and tied one end of the length of linen around the dog's neck, wrapped the other around her wrist, and prayed that the fabric was sturdy.

"We stop at the top of the stairs, Caliban. Do you hear me?" The dog wagged his tail in acknowledgment, if not necessarily agreement, then looked expectantly at the door. Tempest's fingers lingered over the latch. What would she find on its other side?

From the bottom of the open stairwell, she could see nothing of the deck. Still, she paused and looked up at the sky, welcoming the wash of rain over her face, swallowing its sweetness with the gusto of a parched man wandering in the desert.

Caliban was content to lick the water from the bottom stair for a moment, and then tugged mightily to be allowed to ascend. With a sturdy grip on his makeshift leash, and a sturdier one on the railing, Tempest followed him up the few steps.

Only a step or two into the climb, she could see that the deck was not empty . . . of people, at any rate. But everything that had not been anchored, and even some things that had, were gone, swept overboard by the waves that still buffeted the ship, clawing their way up its sides and spilling their salty froth over the planking. The section of damaged railing Ford had been attempting to repair had entirely disappeared.

A handful of sailors, so soaked as to be indistinguishable from one another, were working to capture the rope of a sail that had broken loose. Andrew was at the helm, she thought—at least, she felt certain the man muffled in oilcloth and holding the wheel wasn't the shorter Mr. Bewick.

As she watched, the rope jerked free of the hands of the half-dozen men trying to secure it and whipped across the deck like a snake about to strike, catching on the main mast and snapping back again, throwing off at last a tenacious straggler, the one man who had been unwilling or unable to release his grip on the rope. The man slid across the water-slick wood, scrabbling for purchase and finding none.

And she realized, as she looked on, that it was not a man. It was a boy.

Timmy Madcombe's mouth was open in a shriek of panic, but the wind and the waves swallowed the sound. As he sped toward the jagged gap in the ship's railing, Tempest dropped Caliban's leash and clasped her hands over her mouth. There was nothing now between the boy and the sea but a few yards of empty deck.

Afterward, she could not be certain who reached Timmy first, Andrew or his dog. Both sank iron grips into his clothing and around his limbs, Caliban lowering his body and digging his claws into the soft, wet wood, Andrew holding on for dear life to a remaining fragment of the rail. All three hung suspended, fighting the greedy, grasping fingers of the sea in a desperate tug-of-war over the boy's life.

The *Colleen* lurched, knocking Tempest to her knees, and when she looked up again, a wash of foam was retreating over the edge of the ship. Hands gripped the captain's ankle, the last link in a chain of men that had suddenly sprung into being, extending from the mast to the disaster, while Andrew's hands now grasped Caliban's improvised leash. Although she searched frantically, squinting through the rain, Timmy was nowhere to be seen. The powerful Atlantic had won the struggle and claimed its prize: a boy's life.

The ship pitched back, slinging the captain and his dog away from the railing and back toward the mast, where they collided with the others in a gasping heap. Andrew hugged the dog to him and buried his face in the wet, gray fur, his hands still tangled in the now-ragged linen leash. He glanced down at the strip of fabric, then looked up sharply, as if some realization had suddenly struck him.

Scanning the deck, his eyes stopped when they found Tempest, who still knelt at the top of the small flight of stairs, her hands over her mouth, her cheeks wet with salt water that had not all come from the sea. When he saw her there, his face contorted in a mask of anguish as much as anger, and he shouted at her—words that were lost, thankfully, to the elements. But she knew their import. With a jerk, she struggled to her feet and darted back into the cabin, the surge of bile in her throat unable to make its way past her heart, which felt as if it had been lodged there permanently.

She stayed in the cabin, alone, for the next day—or was it two?—until the storm really had died down and the ship rocked more smoothly and the sun rose once again over the gray waters of the Atlantic. Though the brightness seemed a betrayal, anathema to her grief, she opened the windows to let in the sweet air and was just wondering how she might reach the skylight when she heard the door latch rattle.

As she turned toward the door, it swung open to admit Caliban, who sprayed the cabin's interior with a vigorous shake of his damp fur. Andrew stood dripping on the threshold.

She hurried to him because she could not do otherwise. "Is everything—everyone—everyone else all right?" she asked, stumbling over a question that required more courage than she had anticipated. His cheeks were gaunt and pale beneath his dark beard, and heavy lines of fatigue etched his face. "Are *you* all right?"

"Aye," he said as he staggered past her toward the bedroom, stripping off his sodden suit of oilcloth as he went, and collapsed onto his bed. His next words were muffled by the pillow, but she had no doubt of what he had said.

"The *Justice* went down in the storm."

Chapter 10

Tempest awoke stiff and sore, surprised to find she had slept at all. Fear stabbed through her at the sight of the darkening sky. *Night-fall*, she told herself, pushing down her rising panic. *Not another storm.* Stretching, she rose from the padded bench beneath the window and then chanced a peek into the other room. Andrew's oilcloth suit lay in a puddle on the floor and he lay in a similarly damp heap on the bed, sprawled facedown, showing no sign of having moved for hours.

Wagging a finger at Caliban, who would have pushed past her and gone to wake him, she pulled the door closed with silent caution and in a few steps emerged onto the empty deck. A steady breeze, still tropically warm but without the oppressive weight of the storm, ruffled her short curls as she drew greedy lungfuls of its fresh goodness. The sun was just dipping below the horizon, and already she could see stars winking in the sky above. Like a ghost ship awaiting its haunted crew, the ship sat still, its sails tightly furled, its decks swept clean by the storm. The sudden isolation was more than a little frightening, like finding oneself a sole survivor on a deserted island. Caliban's snuffling exploration of every abandoned nook and cranny, broken only by stops to relieve himself on the masts, called to mind the heart-wrenching description of Robinson Crusoe cast away with only a dog for company.

Her eyes searched the horizon, a last line of light against a black-ening sky, but it remained as inscrutable as it always had. Some-where out there, a ship called *Swift Justice* was still sinking into the depths, taking its crew—and Lord Nathaniel Delamere—to a watery grave. A finger of night air caressed her neck and traveled down her spine. She shivered. It would be a terrible way to die.

A terrible death for a terrible man.

But knowing that other men, and at least one innocent boy, had died that same terrible death made it impossible for her to celebrate her unexpected release from Lord Nathaniel's clutches. What other losses might have been sustained during the storm?

"Caliban, where is everyone?"

For answer, the dog put his nose down and scented his way to the fore, stopping at the steep stairs that descended into the ship's depths. A good portion of the crew could be found in much the same state as their captain, collapsed in unruly heaps, the lucky ones in hammocks strung along the passageway, many others on the floor. In the galley, she found the handful of souls who weren't dead to the world: the cook, Greaves, putting the tools of his trade to rights; Ford, nursing a deep cut in his hand; and Caesar, who sat at the near end of a long table, one elbow resting on its surface, his chin propped up by his hand, apparently sound asleep although his eyes were open.

At the far end Mr. Bewick and Mr. Beals were hidden in half darkness, their heads tipped together, almost, but not quite, touching. Mr. Bewick's body turned toward the surgeon, one arm across the back of the chair in which he sat, looking almost as if he had been about to whisper something in the other man's ear, although neither spoke. Despite the fact that they were not alone, their posture was so private, so intimate, Tempest dropped her gaze.

All of a sudden, an overheard, offhand remark about the captain bunking in the empty surgeon's quarters made perfect sense. The surgeon slept . . . well . . . *elsewhere.* And the captain knew and accepted the fact, as did, she suspected, the rest of the crew. Certainly the two men were currently making no effort to hide, their raw honesty born of deep fatigue and the sense of euphoria that comes with survival.

An ache stirred at the back of her throat. Perhaps it ought to have been caused by disgust. She knew such a relationship was considered a sin, of course. Even young ladies sometimes heard words like *abomination* and *unnatural* tossed about in scandalized whispers.

At the moment, however, she was keenly aware of her own isolation, just as if she were still standing on the empty deck. When she looked at the two men, she felt only envy, a potent emotion made more so by her never having felt it before. Was that what love looked like? The sight of a quiet moment of affection between two people pushed her to acknowledge what she had tried for so long to deny: It would be nice to have someone for whom she could care in that way, someone on whom she could lean, occasionally, for support.

But could she ever lean against a man without wondering every moment if she were about to be smothered—whether through good intentions or ill?

"Summat t' eat, miss?" The cook's offer roused the attention of the others around the table—all but Caesar, whose eyes had at last drooped closed and whose head was beginning to slide from its perch on his fist. Tempest's eyes rebelled at the basket of hard biscuits and a platter piled with some sort of unidentifiable dried meat, but her stomach growled out its own answer.

"Yes, thank you." She took up one of the biscuits and cautiously nibbled an edge, keeping a lookout for weevils. "And would it be entirely frivolous to ask for some hot water? To freshen up?"

Beals laughed and reached for a piece of leathery jerky. "You're asking the wrong man, Miss Holderin. Sailors are a crusty sort—and I mean that quite literally," he said as he chewed. "But no one can expect a lady to adopt *all* our salty ways." He gave her a wink and nodded toward her clothes. *Timmy's clothes*, she remembered with a fresh stab of grief.

With an uncertain smile, she accepted the bucket of water Greaves ladled up. "T'aint hot, though," he said. "No fire 'til we makes sail."

"Oh. Of course." A little water sloshed over the side as she rested the bucket on the table to finish her biscuit.

"Give t' lad a nudge," Mr. Bewick urged. "You can't carry that."

Tempest shook her head sharply. "I assure you I am perfectly capable of doing things for myself." For however long the storm had raged, she had felt helpless, and helplessness was not a feeling she relished. "Besides, Caesar needs his rest. You all do," she added, looking around the table at the faces lined with fatigue. "I'll come back shortly and fetch a tray for Captain Corrvan, if that's all right. He's still asleep."

Greaves grunted his assent and returned to the task of hanging pots and stacking trenchers. Mr. Beals said only, "He's earned it." Bewick nodded in agreement, his faraway look tinged with something like pride. She felt a twinge of regret for ever having called Andrew irresponsible.

"How the captain kept the *Colleen* from going under, I'll never know," Ford confessed with a wave of his injured hand. "When the *Justice* began to take water, I thought that was the end for us, too. She'd been pushed right into our path. But neat as you please, Cap'n slipped us right past the wreckage, without so much as a coat of paint to spare . . ." His words trailed off with a low whistle and a shake of his head. The awe in his voice was reflected in the other men's faces. The undercurrent of doubt in the crew's behavior toward their captain had been invisible to her until it had been erased.

Survival tended to alter one's perspective like that. It was almost enough to tempt her to trust him herself.

Ah, who was she kidding? She was tempted to do far more than trust.

Dusting the crumbs of the biscuit from her fingers, she lifted the bucket with both hands, determined not to spill another drop. "I'll be back shortly." Caliban, who had curled up near the empty kitchen hearth in anticipation, lifted his head to look at her but made no move to follow. It was just as well. She didn't need a witness, not even a canine one, to her awkward ascent of the stairs or her lopsided shuffle across the deck.

Once inside the cabin's great room, she set the bucket on the floor and made a few tentative circles with her aching shoulder. But after so many days of sitting and waiting, it was a good ache. A quick peek into the bedchamber showed that while Captain Corrvan had at last stirred himself into a slightly different position, he looked no closer to waking than he had when she'd left.

As she rummaged in the near-darkness for a towel, her fingers tangled with an unexpected fabric. Muslin. Fashioned into a dress. *Her* dress, she confirmed when she pulled it into the light. Not cut into rags, but washed and pressed and carefully mended—by whose hands, she did not dare to guess.

After bathing and dressing and running damp fingers through her short curls, she walked back to the galley, welcoming the breeze as it tangled her skirts. The other clothes had been infinitely more practical. Another day, she might return to them. But right now, it felt too much like disrespect for Timmy.

The ship was returning to life. Mr. Bewick was at the helm, and Mr. Fleming was directing the repair of rigging and tattered sails.

They were moving again, carefully, easing into the wind like the belle of the ball with a twisted ankle.

During her absence, Greaves had lit a fire and managed to put together something slightly better than biscuits and jerky for the captain. The smell of hot coffee and fried salt pork nearly had Tempest salivating over the tray. But she hoisted it with a smile and carried it back with her, swallowing against her still-unappeased hunger. Maybe Andrew wouldn't miss a bite or two?

Pushing her hip against the door, she wedged her way into the cabin with the laden tray and froze on the threshold when she heard that familiar off-key whistle—although this evening it was more dirge than jig.

It seemed the captain had awakened at last.

She stepped to the door between the rooms. Because his back was to her, she could watch unobserved as he grasped his shirttails and stripped off the stained and wrinkled garment in one smooth motion. Then, without hesitation, he slipped free the buttons of his breeches and dropped them to the floor. Every inch of skin she could see was bronzed, and the fine linen of his drawers left little to the imagination.

The child of a hot climate where hard physical labor was done, she had often seen men in various stages of undress—bare arms, backs, chests, even legs were nothing new to her. But she could not remember ever wanting to stand and stare before. If his daring exploits during the storm had not been proof enough of his strength, she could hardly argue with the evidence on display before her now: muscles that rippled and bunched as he sponged himself clean with what water she had left in the bucket. Even in the dim lamplight, she caught glimpses of a few old scars and at least one fresh bruise where something had struck him across the shoulders. Somehow, those imperfections only increased his appeal. They were signs of a flesh-and-blood man, not some picture-perfect gentleman.

Contemplatively, he scrubbed his hand over his beard, then paused. "Was there something in particular you were hoping to see, Miss Holderin?"

Uncertain what had betrayed her—the clumsy rattle of crockery, or a sharply drawn breath—she made no answer, just retreated back into the great room to deposit the tray on the table. And waited. For what, exactly, she could not say.

When he joined her a few minutes later, he was dressed again—after a fashion. His lean calves were bare beneath his breeches and his shirt hung open at the neck, revealing the muscled curve of his chest. Those snatches of tanned skin and the sprinkling of dark, crisp hair that covered them were somehow even more distracting than all that had been revealed by his earlier state of undress. When combined with his shadowed jaw, the effect was somehow unsettling. There was a wildness about him that would only ever be half-tamed, despite his fine English education. Her gaze darted away, uncertain.

She waited for him to speak, to tease her, to scold her. But when he said nothing, she at last worked up the courage to raise her eyes and her heated cheeks to his face. Despite hours of uninterrupted sleep, shadows still lurked beneath his normally sharp eyes. A sign of exhaustion, yes, but also something else. She had expected to see triumph written on his face. After all, he had saved his ship and vanquished his enemy.

But she saw only his terrible sense of guilt.

He brushed past her on his way to the cupboard at the far side of the room, the one Mr. Beals had opened on the night of her arrival. Withdrawing the decanter and a single glass, he carried them both to the table, then pulled up a chair, pushed the untouched tray of food aside, and poured himself a drink.

"You cannot blame yourself for what happened to Timmy." She spoke firmly as she came to stand before him.

He took a single swallow of whiskey before meeting her gaze. "Who is to blame, if not I?"

"Perhaps no one should be blamed," she ventured. "No one could have anticipated a storm of that strength, so late in the year . . ."

"This *No One* sounds like a capital fellow. Careless. Good-for-nothing. I rather think we'd get on." The familiar cynicism had crept into his expression and his voice. "Why was the boy even on my ship?" With the toss of his hand, he finished off the contents of the tumbler before answering his own question. "Because I found him on the street, and I arrogantly assumed he would be better off somewhere else. I stuffed his head with rousing stories of sea life no lad could resist." He paused to refill the glass, but when the neck of the decanter rattled against its rim, as if his hands were unsteady, he returned it to the table instead, leaving the glass empty. "I caused that child's death as surely as if—as if I had—"

"As if you'd abandoned him on the streets of Kingston?" She had never seen the place, but she could imagine what a grim future Timmy would have had if he'd stayed. Few orphans enjoyed Edward's good fortune.

Andrew's head jerked up, and he settled his gaze on her, as if surprised to find her so close. "And why are *you* on my ship?" he whispered as his hand leapt out and snagged her wrist.

The strength of his grip did not surprise her. What she did not expect was his gentleness. Or the tingle of longing she would feel when his calloused fingers slid along the delicate skin of her inner wrist.

"Because you wanted me here," she reminded him.

"So I did," he agreed, drawing her closer, pulling her downward, until there was nowhere to go but into his arms.

Andrew brought his free hand to the back of her head, capturing her mouth with his, holding nothing back. Lips, teeth, tongue—he was not gentle. *Unwise*, she had called their first kiss. Let her see that a second was pure folly.

He felt the heat of her palm against the clenched muscles of his abdomen. That hand should have meant she had come to her senses and was pushing him away.

Instead, it felt like a claiming.

Falling forward, she tumbled into his lap, her skirts billowing around them. The fingers of her other hand came up to curl and twist in his hair. With open mouth, she met his kiss, snagging a tooth against his lip in her eagerness, then sliding her tongue anxiously over the nick.

Did women feel it, too, then, that deep hunger for life in the face of death? The urge to couple, to ensure that the struggle to survive had not been for naught? Nature was a bit mad, he had often thought, the way it made a man who had just come through some mortal peril want to bury himself inside a woman. Tempest hitched herself against him as if she could read his thoughts, as if she feared she might be denied.

But he was in no mood to deny her anything.

Releasing her wrist, he let his hand roam. From her knee, he traveled over her hip to settle for a moment at the indentation of her waist before rising still higher to cup her breast. Beneath the thin fabric of her dress, he felt her nipple peak, and when he plucked it with his finger-tips, she groaned into his mouth. For answer, he did it again.

Neither of them spoke, for really, what was there to say?

That he wanted her?

Given how the curve of her backside fitted against his groin, she must already know it.

That he needed her?

True though it might be, he was hardly prepared to admit *that*—even to himself.

After a time, he managed, somehow, to rein himself in enough to remember where they were. If they were going to tup—and what, short of another hurricane, would stop them?—it would not be in a chair. Not even on the table, although the vision of her spread there before him, beneath the swaying, speckled lamplight, almost undid him.

Shifting her weight, he rose with her in his arms, carried her easily into the other room, and laid her on his bed. In some dark recess of his brain, a part of him urged caution. If she had still been wearing breeches, perhaps those extra layers, that heavier fabric, would have given him pause, would have brought him to his senses.

But the voice of reason was drowned out by the pounding of blood in his ears, as he plucked at the tie to her dress, exposing her, inch by inch, to his eyes. By the flickering light of a single candle, he gazed upon her naked flesh—dotted here and there with freckles, but soft and white as buttermilk and almost certainly as sweet.

She blushed beneath his regard but did not hide, and her own eyes were wide and dark with desire as she reached up to help him shed his own clothes. When her hands moved to the tie of his drawers, he stayed her fingertips with kisses and joined her on the bed instead, unwilling to allow her too-eager touch to deprive him of greater plea-sures yet to come.

Slight of stature as she was, he had not expected to find her so voluptuous, and his hands swept greedily along the same path they had taken earlier—over the flare of her hips, up the soft slope of her belly, to weigh the fullness of her breast. God, how he wanted to nip and kiss and lick his way from her toes to her earlobes, with a lengthy detour at the midpoint, to taste the sweetness hidden by a thatch of coppery-brown hair. But this was not the moment for languorous love-making, so he contented himself with swirling his tongue around her navel before lifting his head to draw a nipple into his mouth.

He feasted on that pert, ripe berry until she began to arch against him, and a whimper of need bubbled from her throat. As he shifted his lips to the other breast, he slid his hand between them and cupped her mound, easing his fingers into her curls, teasing her, stroking her, until they were both coated with her wetness.

"Tempest," he breathed as he rose higher against her, nestling his lips in her hair. Part question, part plea, his whisper was answered when she opened beneath him and canted her hips, inviting him to enter her.

In another moment, he had stripped off his drawers and then knelt on the bed between her spread thighs. When he hesitated, she reached for him, sliding her hand up the arm that supported his weight, pulling him closer, until he could feel the press of her nipples against his chest and she whispered against his ear. "Please."

That single word was his undoing. With his other hand, he set the head of his cock against the slick opening of her body and pressed slowly into her. Too slowly for her liking, it seemed, but oh, she was tight, as tight as a—

His body knew the truth before his mind would admit it. Because it had aligned with his own base needs, he had allowed himself to imagine that her disdain for convention, her admiration for Wollstonecraft—hell, even her surfeit of eager suitors—meant that this boundary must long ago have been crossed. She had been all eagerness, meeting him kiss for kiss, touch for touch. For all her boldness, though, Tempest Holderin was still an innocent.

He *could* have drawn back, *would* have drawn back—he had sufficient strength for that. But only just.

Then she clawed at his arms, pressing herself closer when he tried to pull away. "Please," she whispered again, sapping his resistance. Trailing his hand over her hip, he sought and found that little nub of nerve endings and circled it with his thumb, relentlessly building her pleasure until she was shuddering beneath him. When he at last slid in fully, a gasp burst from each of them—his of relief, hers of . . . shock, he hoped, more than pain.

"Kiss me," he murmured, holding himself as still as he could until she began to relax around him. His thrusts, slow and shallow, soon ratcheted up her need, and in a few strokes she was meeting them, straining against him, panting. So he quickened the pace, the swirl of his thumb keeping time with the plunge of his cock, until she shattered with a cry and reached for his buttocks, pulling him deeper yet, spurring his release. He could no more have pulled out of the slick heat of her body than he could have stopped the tides.

He came, and for one bright moment, all was peace.

"*That*, my dear, was unwise," he said after a time. He rolled off her, onto his side, and pulled her close to him, her back against his chest. When his own breathing had returned to something like normal, and her pulse had begun to slow, he traced her collarbone with an idle finger and ventured a quiet question. "Why didn't you tell me?"

"I was afraid you would stop."

"I *should* have stopped."

For a moment, she did not answer. "I wanted it," she said at last. "And I was already ruined anyway."

As explanations went, its logic was rather faulty, but he thought he knew what she meant. He had once said something similar to Cary. If she would as well be hung for a sheep as a lamb, he supposed he could not blame her. "Still . . ." he began.

"Oh, do not say you must marry me now," she cut across him, twisting slightly against his hold. "I have already told you, I mean never to wed."

"What if there are . . . consequences?"

She swallowed hard and shook her head, her silky, bright curls tickling his shoulder. "There won't be."

Hoisting himself onto one elbow, he turned her toward him so that he could meet her eyes. "There might, and for that, I blame myself. But if you are carrying my child, Tempest, we *will* marry." He might be an irresponsible scoundrel, but even he had his limits. "That is that."

She struggled into a sitting position, clutching the sheet around her chest in a sudden show of modesty. "We will do no such thing."

He understood the reasons for her resistance to marriage in general. He even respected her reluctance in this particular case. After all, except perhaps for in bed, they did not seem particularly well-suited. *The reformer and the rogue.* It sounded rather like the title of one of those tawdry novels Beals picked up in every port. The book always made its rounds through the crew until it somehow wound up—worn and tattered, much like its misguided heroine—in his own hands. Tempest could be forgiven for wishing to avoid such a fate.

Nevertheless, he wanted to argue with her about the matter. Wanted to watch her temper flare, see her cheeks warm, feel her pulse rise. Wanted to steal her breath, her words with kisses, until defiance was the last thing on her mind.

And precisely because it was *not* what he wanted to do, he got up and began to dress. She watched him in openmouthed shock, her brows driven down into a sharp V. When he went into the other room, she followed, the bedsheet-turned-gown trailing behind her. "You cannot simply walk away. Our conversation is not finished."

"Oh yes, it is," he countered, shrugging into his coat. "Because if I stay, I'll be tempted to do far more than talk."

A flush rose high on her cheekbones. "You needn't worry about that," she insisted. "It won't happen again. I would not take such a risk."

"Liar," he whispered, moving one step closer.

As if to prove his point, she shifted slightly, putting the corner of the table between them. "Let me ask one question. Where are we bound now?"

"London," he said simply. "What do you imagine has changed?"

"Well, the *Justice* has sunk and Lord Nathaniel is dead," she pointed out. "The danger you claimed to be avoiding is gone. So you have no excuse not to return to Antigua."

"No excuse?" He scoffed. "Ought I to risk sailing into the back side of that storm, then?"

Her eyes sparked—mostly anger, perhaps a glimmer of fear. "I will see you a wealthy man if you take me back."

"I'll be a wealthy man if I don't, my dear," he said, only half-thinking of Cary's promise to double what he had already paid once Tempest had been delivered to her grandfather. "Besides, the *Colleen* needs repairs, and London is the best place to make them. Thanks to those winds, we're better than halfway there."

He didn't add that it would be best—or at least necessary—to stay close together until they knew whether she was with child.

And perhaps he didn't need to make that point. Although she tipped her chin and gave a rebellious scowl, for once she didn't argue with him. Perhaps she was beginning to grasp the ramifications of what they'd so rashly done.

Fishing in his pocket, he withdrew a brass key and tossed it onto the table with a clatter. It slid across the polished surface and struck the empty whiskey glass with a *ping*. "For the door," he said.

Something flickered across her eyes too quickly for him to identify. Selfishly, he hoped it was regret at discovering he did not mean to return to her bed.

With a nod, he stepped into the night air and closed the door behind him.

But he waited until he heard the key grate in the lock before he walked away.

Chapter 11

Snatching up the key from the table, she was to the door almost before it had latched behind him, fitting the key to the lock and twisting until she heard a reassuring *snick*.

It seemed more than slightly ridiculous to take comfort in the action. Shutting the stable door after the horse had bolted, and all that. Was she locking him out? Or locking herself in?

She rather feared it might take more than a few stout oak planks to keep her from committing further folly.

As she passed the table, she picked up a morsel of the captain's untouched supper and put it to her lips. But the food was cold and her appetite had flown.

Wandering back into the bedchamber instead, she almost stumbled over the sheet tangled around her ankles. The candle had guttered, but the room was still lit by a bright swath of moonlight spilling across the bed. When she let the sheet drop to the floor, her pale skin glowed under those luminous beams.

Did she look different somehow? If she closed her eyes, she could still feel his lips on her breasts, the rough scrape of his jaw, the brush of his calloused fingertips. And the unfamiliar ache between her legs, the lingering slickness of his possession. She clung to every scrap of memory, storing away every sensation. One night of pleasure to carry her through the lonely years ahead.

She had gotten what she wanted, had she not? And perhaps a bit more besides.

When she opened her eyes, her gaze was drawn to a spattering of dark spots on the center of the bed. By morning light they would be crimson, but under the moon's deceiving rays, they looked black. It was not much blood, really. She had not known what to expect. With the cool water remaining in the washbasin, she carefully sponged between her legs and then picked up her shift from the floor and drew it on over her head.

Consequences, he had said.

It seemed to her as if the shedding of blood once should be consequence enough. She ought not to have to wait in a state of panic until she bled again. She scrambled to recall every word Omeah had ever spoken on such matters, but those conversations had been few and far between, and Tempest had never been prone to listening. She had last bled a few days before this grand adventure began. It was mid-November now, or later, meaning almost a month had already gone by. At least she shouldn't be kept in suspense for long . . .

When she climbed onto the mattress, she folded the stained sheet over itself so it would not mark her garments. Oh, how could she have allowed a momentary fantasy to eclipse her good sense? She might have harsh reality for her bedfellow for all eternity now.

Andrew's insistence on doing the honorable thing surprised her. After all, he had proudly proclaimed more than once that he was no gentleman. And having been as good as kidnapped by him, she had had little cause to doubt it.

She couldn't—wouldn't—marry him, of course, but she found it even more difficult to believe that he would be willing to marry her. What was it he had said about marriage? That he was a man "ill-suited to such responsibilities."

He had also said that a marriage ought to offer affection, even love.

She suffered no illusions about what had just passed between them. It had nothing to do with love. And as foundation for a lifelong match, heedless passion seemed to fall rather wide of the mark.

Then, of course, there was the matter of "economic security," as he had phrased it. What if . . . ? *Oh God.* Despite the warm night, a chill chased down her limbs. What was it he had said about getting more money if he didn't let her go? What if he only really wanted from her what everyone had always wanted—Harper's Hill and her father's fortune?

No, no, no, she reassured herself, clutching her ribs as if she were trying to hold herself together. She had fallen into his arms because she wanted him, and she had returned kisses that had made her believe he wanted her, too. Had he known she was still a virgin, he would not have made love to her, of that she felt certain. And when he discovered it, he would have stopped—if she would have let him. That was not the behavior of a man who intended to force a marriage. She could say that with some authority, familiar as she was with the type.

Besides, he was the captain of a merchant ship in a very wealthy part of the world. If he were out solely for gain, he had numerous avenues by which to acquire it. And he must have enjoyed some success, for his clothes, his books, his personal effects all bespoke a man of some means. She scoured her memory, trying to piece together what she knew of his life before he went to sea. His father had been a ship builder—not a mere carpenter, but a man of such skill and sufficient status that he had been allowed to name his creation and invited to sail with it to London, where the man who would later become Andrew's stepfather, presumably a successful merchant, had commissioned the ship. Andrew came from respectable, well-to-do people, and that must count for something.

Of course, he had also told her he had "claimed" the *Fair Colleen*—what if that had merely been a polite euphemism for taking something that had not been his to take? And what had he been doing with it all these years? In all her investigations, had she ever heard talk of lawful cargo, of regular routes, of reasonable profits? No. Only kidnapping, an outlaw crew, and revenge.

Money was, presumably, the reason he had accepted Edward's bribe. Revenge no doubt paid very poorly. After ten years, he might be in desperate straits indeed. Perhaps, in the wake of Stratton's demise, Andrew had hit upon the perfect scheme to make up for lost fortune and lost time.

What would Miss Wollstonecraft do?

Ludicrous as it seemed to imagine the serious-minded writer in the clutches of a pirate, Tempest nonetheless applied herself to a question that had always brought her some comfort before. Miss Wollstonecraft would not despair, that was certain. She would think quite rationally about the future: In a fortnight or so, they would be in London, one of the largest ports in the world, filled with ships sailing to every part of the globe. Tempest had found her way across that terrifying sea once; surely she could find her way home.

Miss Wollstonecraft did not strike her as the sort of person who wasted her energy on regret. What was done, was done. Tempest had enjoyed the experience of making love with Andrew, and if there was a price to be paid for her actions, she would pay it—any price short of marriage, that was.

As she settled into the bed and tried to make herself comfortable, the scent of him—the scent of *them*—surrounded her, and the memory of his touch washed over her with all the force of a storm-tossed wave. Suddenly, her shift felt rough against her peaked nipples, and the throbbing between her thighs had nothing to do with discomfort.

She had known the mechanics of the act, of course. Innocence— or at least ignorance—was difficult to maintain in her world. But the knowing and the doing were such different things.

When Lord Nathaniel had first begun to cast lascivious glances in Tempest's direction, Omeah had warned her about the things a man might do to a woman. But she had never said—perhaps had not known, given her plight before coming to Harper's Hill—that a woman might long to do such things with an intensity that was almost painful, or that a gentle, generous man might give as much pleasure as he got.

With a strange sort of hesitation, she reached out for the key Andrew had given her. Moonlight gleamed along it on the small bedside table. As she curled her fingers around it and drew it across the table-top toward her, she thought about why he had given it to her now, of all times. When she had first come aboard, he had not trusted her. Now, it seemed, he did not entirely trust himself.

If she returned the key to him, might he return to her?

Oh, but that was a dangerous thing to wonder. Beneath the pillow, she gripped the cool metal until the bit dug into her flesh, hoping the prickle of discomfort would bring her to her senses. She had allowed herself one night, and that one night might end up costing her dearly. She was going to have to content herself with nothing more than the memories of passion.

Some might counsel her not to indulge in even those.

But on that point at least, Tempest declined to consult Miss Wollstonecraft's otherwise sage advice.

It seemed that every member of the *Colleen*'s crew, even those who were on duty and ought to be tending to other tasks, was pressed against the railing as the ship slipped into the wide mouth of the Thames and sailed past Gravesend on its way to the Pool of London.

The only face missing from the eager crowd was Tempest's.

Andrew had hardly seen her since that ill-advised interlude after the storm. He had continued to make himself scarce on deck during the daylight hours, but she had made herself scarce altogether. For the final portion of their voyage, she had stayed within his cabin with the door securely locked from the inside—as at least a part of him had intended she should.

No doubt she supposed the locked door had given her privacy, but in his capacity as captain he had access to far more information about her habits than she would have liked. He knew what she ate—or more accurately, what she didn't. He knew she must be sleeping poorly, for she had gone through a larger than usual number of candles.

And he knew he might yet have to make good on his promise—or had it been a threat?—to marry her.

With a nod to Bewick to take up the helm, he drew in a sharp breath and strode toward his cabin. As their destination neared, it was time for rapprochement. She was going to have to come out, and he would rather avoid having to go in after her.

"Miss Holderin," he called as he rapped on the door. "I thought you should know we will be in London in a few hours' time. Make yourself ready to go ashore."

To his surprise, the door swung open and she faced him across the threshold, clad once more in Timmy's waistcoat and breeches, with the addition of a wool cap over her ragged curls. It might draw fewer eyes than a dress, he supposed, but no one who truly looked would mistake her for a boy. "I am ready," she declared quietly as she picked up a small bundle—her own clothes, he supposed—from the floor.

"Come up," he suggested. "See the sights."

With a hesitant nod, she agreed and stepped out of the cabin. A gust of raw early December air swirled past him, taking her breath. "Oh," she gasped. Before he could offer his coat, she retreated inside once again and emerged with a rough wool blanket pulled tightly around her shoulders. At his feet, Caliban snuffled the air and cocked his head suspiciously, and at once Andrew recognized her makeshift shawl as the dog's bed.

He opened his mouth, not to laugh, but to offer . . . well, what? If she had wanted something of his to wear instead, she could have taken it. And if she was stubborn enough to wear an old blanket covered in dog hair rather than don one of his coats, any words of his weren't likely to change her mind.

"You'll grow accustomed to the cold," he said instead, although after so much time in warmer climes, it cut through him, too, with the keenness of a freshly whetted blade.

"I don't intend to stay here long enough for that," she replied as she brushed past him.

Resisting the temptation to argue, he lifted the bundle from her hand and tossed it back into his cabin before closing the door. "I'll have someone fetch your things once we're docked."

She looked as if she wanted to protest, but in the end she allowed herself to be led to the railing and ensconced in a place where she could watch the great city as it grew on the horizon. With a surreptitious word to one of the crew to keep an eye on her, Andrew returned to his post at the wheel.

Would it be his last time guiding the *Colleen* into port? He had little excuse to return to the sea now. Stratton and the *Justice* were gone. He'd reached his goal, after a fashion, but had he really gotten what he wanted? Truth be told, he felt more adrift now than he'd ever felt while sailing the Atlantic.

It was not that he had imagined Stratton's death would somehow restore his father's life. Oh, perhaps once upon a time, such a notion had formed a part of the childish fantasy that had first sent him to sea. But he had seen too much in the intervening years to cling to the kind of magical thinking his gran's stories had encouraged.

No, this was a different sort of grief, a different sort of emptiness altogether. He had never considered that the celebration over an evil man's demise might be tempered by mourning for an innocent boy. He had not expected to feel guilt—for leaving, for returning, for everything in between. He had neglected to consider that success might leave a gaping void in his soul, one made worse by the fact that the storm had denied him the chance to deal the final blow to his enemy. Something new would have to be found to dwell in the space once occupied by the quest for vengeance.

Had he sought out Tempest's arms, her soft lips, her welcoming body, hoping she might somehow fill that emptiness? Not consciously—but he could not deny that for a moment, at least, she had. For a moment, he had allowed himself to imagine her filling it far longer than one night. But in the clearer light of day he had recognized the danger. They were not for one another, and the hole a man like him would rip in her life would prove the more devastating wound.

So. Someone else, then. Some*thing* else. If the sea no longer lured him as it once had, no doubt the landlocked future that had loomed before him at seventeen was still out there, waiting to be taken up. But as he scanned the shoreline pressing in from either side, he wondered: Could such a life ever hold sufficient appeal for him?

A hollow homecoming, to be sure.

He glanced around at the faces of his crew: the distant longing in Bewick's eyes, as he stood with Geoffrey Beals's hand on his shoulder. Fleming, red-faced in the wind and beaming from ear to ear. Ford's jaw set, his fists clenched, his expression determined. He couldn't imagine what sort of reception awaited any of them, but they were nonetheless eager to land.

Only Tempest seemed to share his reservation. She sat with her back to the panorama unfolding behind her, trying to coax the dog into her lap—for the added warmth, if he had to guess.

Before he could put a name to her expression, he felt a tug on his coat sleeve. He looked down into Caesar's newly plump face. "Beg pardon, Cap'n"—the boy spoke through chattering teeth—"but I did wonder—"

"What was going to become of you?" Andrew finished for him. Caesar nodded, a little uncertainly, and Andrew smiled to reassure him. "You must decide whether you prefer life on land or life at sea, young man, and choose accordingly."

"I wish to stay wit' you, sir. An' the *Colleen*."

"The *Colleen* will be in port for quite some time."

"You'll captain 'nother ship, then?"

"I, well—" *God, what a question.* "The truth is, Caesar, I don't know. But I'll need a personal servant, wherever I go. Would that suit you?"

"Yes, sir!"

Andrew suspected Caesar had little idea of what such a job would entail. Neither did Andrew, precisely, but under that guise he could pay the boy well and see that he learned some skills he could use to make his own way at a later date. Most important, he could keep him from being stolen back into a world of slavery. "You may begin by going to my cabin and seeing that all my things are packed and ready to be taken off the ship." Caesar set off eagerly, but Andrew called him back. "Include anything of Miss Holderin's that you find as well."

After that, all was a flurry of activity that afforded him no time for watching faces or studying the scenery. Only when the ship was at last docked, and most of the crew dismissed, did he have leisure to look around him again.

Remarkably, Tempest had not moved from the spot where he had left her. At some point, Caesar had come to sit beside her and slept there now, leaning heavily against her shoulder. Caliban was still curled in her lap.

"Come," he said, striding toward her. The word roused the dog, and Andrew bent to lift the drowsy boy into his arms, allowing Tempest to rise.

"Where are you taking him?"

Andrew hesitated. The most likely destination was also the one he was most reluctant to visit. "The same place I am taking you," he said.

At least it would be only temporary. As soon as arrangements could be made, he would complete the journey he had begun six weeks ago and take her to Sir Barton Harper as he had agreed to do.

If he allowed himself to recall what Tempest had said of her grandfather, doubt about the plan began to creep in, but he was going to have to overcome his reservations. For a short time longer, at least, such a trip would keep her under his watchful eye. And if nothing else, there was Cary's promise of a great deal more money when the job was done.

"In that, sir, you are mistaken." Tempest crossed her arms over her chest. "I see no need for me to travel any farther than the next ship. Surely I can find one nearby that's bound for the West Indies."

He ought to have expected such an answer. Still, he felt his heart rate tick upward in a mixture of anger and alarm. He knew better than to think she wouldn't do it. "Look about, Tempest." The river was filled with ships of every size, their masts rising from the sluggish water like so many needles in a pincushion. "Which of them ought you to choose?"

"I—I don't—"

"Come now. Which are honest merchants' ships? Which have

more nefarious voyages in mind? Which of them have men aboard ordered to shoot anyone who comes near?"

"I think I have sense enough not to go sneaking aboard some dangerous ship," she snapped. Andrew raised one brow and she darted her eyes away. "Surely there is a place where one may bespeak a passage on a suitable vessel?" she said, more quietly.

"Shipping offices galore," he replied, waving his hand in the direction of a row of buildings along the riverbank. "To say nothing of the pubs and other dens of iniquity where sailors congregate. And I daresay you'll find more than one captain who's willing to take on a likely looking lad such as yourself."

Tempest glanced down at her clothing as if surprised to find herself dressed as a boy.

"Really, the only question is whether he'll be glad or disappointed to find there's a lass underneath those clothes."

"What could he do to me that you've not already done?" she retorted with a sniff and a toss of her head.

"A great deal, my dear," he said, his voice low and rougher than he had intended. "And you ought not to expect a proposal of marriage afterward."

Those words succeeded at last in cowing her. *Good*, he thought savagely as he turned to leave and felt her following in his shadow.

Onshore, the mighty heart of the city seemed to throb with the shouts of men and the rattle of carriages. Farther off, one determined ray of afternoon sun pierced the fog and set the golden dome of St Paul's afire.

Andrew signaled for a hack. "Where to, guv?" the cabby called down. When he heard the direction, the driver's eyes widened a bit, but he readily nodded his agreement; it would mean a substantial fare.

Once Andrew had handed Tempest in, the dog scrambled up after her. Andrew laid a sleepy Caesar on the bench opposite Tempest. Reluctantly, she shooed Caliban onto the floor of the carriage and slid over to make room for Andrew to sit beside her. As the hack jostled its way through the streets, the occasional brush of his leg against hers was impossible to avoid. At first she stiffened and drew back at every touch, but after a while, she seemed to decide that ignoring him was a more suitable punishment. He tried not to relish the feel of the curve of her thigh where it rested alongside his.

If she were still curious about their destination, she asked nothing more. Instead, she sat with her head leaning drowsily against the window, still huddled under the ratty old blanket. But even in the coach's dim interior, he could see that her eyes were open, taking in everything they passed. He wondered what about the unfamiliar scene most caught her attention—the press of carriages, the soot-stained architecture?

"I have never in my life seen so many white faces together in one place," she whispered to him at last, then her brow wrinkled in fascination as she watched the words puff from her body in little clouds of steam.

Without waiting for a reply, she returned to the glass.

When the carriage rolled to a stop, he roused the boy before descending himself. As he handed Tempest to the curb, her eyes scanned the house in front of them. "What is this place?" she asked as her gaze rose up the terraced brownstone façade.

"The home of the Honorable Mr. Daniel Beauchamp, younger son of Viscount Renfrew," he said, for those were the credentials that mattered most in this part of town.

"Daniel Beauchamp," she echoed, as if she could not have heard correctly. "The shipping magnate?"

"Aye," said Andrew, leading her up the steps. "That, too."

When the door swung open, he could see that very little had changed since he had seen the house last. The entryway still gleamed with cold marble, and Williams, the butler, still ruled over it with stiff disapproval.

"Is the family at home?" Andrew asked, almost grateful not to be recognized.

Williams frowned and began to deny them, when they all heard lighter footsteps hurrying down the stairs. Before the butler could speak or Andrew could react, a woman had enveloped him, pulling him into the light of the hall. "Andrew! Is it really you? At last!"

It was as if some otherworldly sense had alerted her to his arrival. Or perhaps she had been keeping watch all this time. As she sobbed in his arms, he looked down at her and saw that her once-chestnut hair was now liberally streaked with gray. After a moment, she composed herself enough to take his hands in hers and draw him over to the stairway. Stepping onto the second stair, so that they stood almost on a level, she studied him thoroughly with hazel eyes that still sparkled with unshed tears.

"Thank God," she whispered, then freed one hand and dealt him a cracking slap across the face.

Out of the corner of his eye, he saw Tempest's hand fly up to cover her mouth. He half-suspected her of hiding a grin. Even his own lips lifted at one corner, although his cheek stung mightily.

"I suppose I deserved that," he acknowledged, stepping back and gesturing toward Tempest. "Now, may I introduce Miss Holderin? Mrs. Emily Beauchamp. My mother."

Neither woman seemed to know what to do with the introduction. While his mother took in Tempest's appearance, Tempest stared at Andrew and stammered, "Y-your m—?" then stumbled through a curtsy that might better have been a bow, given her clothes. "You have a lovely home, Mrs. Beauchamp," she said once she had composed herself.

"Goodness, child," his mother effused in a voice that had never been expected to temper its Irishness, "thank you. And it's very welcome you are to it. But 'tisn't really mine," she insisted with a little shake of her head as she glanced back at him. "It's Andrew's."

It would have been difficult to say whose shock was greater, for Tempest's jaw actually dropped open, while Andrew could feel his own expression turn to stone. "Mine?"

"Why, yes, dear. I would have written to tell you, if I'd known where to send a letter," she scolded gently as she smoothed a hand down her dove-gray skirts. "Daniel has been gone for almost two years now. In his will, he left everything to you."

Chapter 12

When she felt Emily Beauchamp take her arm in her own and begin to lead her up the stately, curving staircase of polished mahogany, Tempest knew she must have missed the rest of the conversation between Andrew and his mother. But she was still trying to make sense of the portion she *had* heard.

Andrew Corrvan, the man she had lately been thinking of as a money-hungry pirate, was, in fact, heir to a fortune that must nearly match her own.

Not, of course, that the two identities were mutually exclusive. She rather imagined, given what she knew of Beauchamp Shipping Company, that Andrew's stepfather had had a bit of piracy in him as well. She had heard both her father and Edward mention the name of Beauchamp with a certain amount of awe, if not precisely approval. The company's private fleet rivaled His Majesty's, and there were few harbors in the world into which those ships had not sailed.

In the apartments to which Mrs. Beauchamp conducted her, lavish gold and green bed hangings replaced the mosquito netting to which Tempest was more accustomed, and heavy velvet curtains framed unshuttered windows, admitting a pale, wintry light.

"I'll ring for a hot bath, my dear," Mrs. Beauchamp said. "And then you'll join Andrew and me for dinner."

"No," Tempest demurred. "I cannot stay."

"Don't be ridiculous," Mrs. Beauchamp said as she strode to the bellpull. "Wherever would you go?"

"I must find a way to return to Antigua. As soon as possible."

"You'll not go back to the docks tonight, to be sure."

For the first time in her life, Tempest did not bristle at the tone of command. Perhaps because it was softened by a woman's touch. Or perhaps because the way back to the shipyard was far from clear to her. They had traveled a great distance across the city, a journey that had lasted almost as long as a trip across the entire island of Antigua.

Mostly, though, she could not quite shake the sense of alarm that had come over her at Andrew's last warning aboard the ship, try as she might. It could not have been more clear that she was no longer in English Harbour—and that had been a dangerous enough place for a woman alone. She had grown accustomed to thinking of Lord Nathaniel as the greatest threat she faced; he might be gone now, but she ought not to forget she was still, regrettably, vulnerable.

She was used to dismissing fear as an irrational, emotional response. Sometimes, however, there might be reason in it, too. It would be foolish to risk her life unnecessarily. What good could she do in Antigua if she were dead?

But was the alternative to stay *here* until she could arrange her passage home? After all that had happened between them, Andrew was the very last person she ought to be trusting to keep her safe.

"And you certainly can't travel dressed as you are," Mrs. Beauchamp added, her hazel eyes darting over what had once been poor Timmy's best clothes. "I suppose such garments were practical at sea. But you'll wish to wait for your own things to arrive from the ship, I'll be bound."

"I haven't—that is, there isn't much . . ." Tempest's words trailed off, interrupted by the arrival of a parade of footmen carrying steaming ewers of water to fill a hip bath that had been placed near the fire, which a maid was assiduously lighting. Without meaning to, Tempest wandered toward the copper tub and trailed the fingertips of one hand in the water, shivering at the welcome heat.

Once the footmen were gone, Mrs. Beauchamp stepped forward and pried the old blanket from her grasp. Tempest watched, slightly horrified, as a cloud of dog hair surrounded them, some of it clinging to Mrs. Beauchamp's simple but elegant dress, while the rest drifted down to the carpet. "I'm certain I can find something better for you to wear while you wait." In another moment, she had deposited the blanket and Timmy's clothes in the arms of the rather alarmed-looking maid. "Go on, dear," she prompted Tempest, nodding toward the tub.

Tempest sank into the bath, feeling rather as if she had drunk another mug of Greaves's special tea and her actions were not quite her own. Whatever it was, she did not feel equal to arguing against being warm and clean once again.

"Antigua," Mrs. Beauchamp said when she was settled in the water. "That's quite a journey for a young woman, all alone."

"I never meant to come to London, Mrs. Beauchamp. There was a—a misunderstanding between me and . . . your son."

"A misunderstanding." Mrs. Beauchamp looked thoughtful. "I see."

"Not that I—that he—I would not wish to give the impression that we—" The sudden flush on her cheeks had nothing to do with the temperature of the bath. Unable to push the lie past her teeth, Tempest wished the water were deep enough for her to slide entirely beneath its surface instead.

With a shake of her head, Mrs. Beauchamp held up a staying hand. "Not another word, child. You cannot say anything about Andrew worse than has already been said—occasionally by me. He's always been a bit of a scoundrel." But on her lips, and with that twinkle in her eyes, the word was not entirely a criticism.

Strangely, Tempest felt she understood Mrs. Beauchamp's equivocation. The woman had been waiting for her son for years. Her husband had evidently expected he would return to take up the reins of the family business. In abandoning his responsibility to them, Andrew had behaved unconscionably, but was not that behavior at least somewhat tempered by the commitment he had shown to his father's memory? In the end, she could not fault his mother for greeting her long-absent son with both an embrace and a resounding slap across the face.

If only Tempest had given in to the desire to slap him, instead of embracing him, she might still be free.

She longed to press for more details about Andrew's past, but before she could frame an innocent-sounding question, Mrs. Beauchamp had bustled toward the door. "I'll send Hannah back to help you dress and show you down to supper," she called over her shoulder, leaving Tempest no wiser than she had been before.

In a house as flush with servants as this one, what could possibly be the delay in bringing up his trunk or fetching hot water for a wash and a shave? Restless, Andrew paced across the room that had been his when he was a young man. Very little had changed about the spacious, ostentatious chamber; its dark, heavy furnishings and draperies seemed to suck the fading light from the room, making him wish he had called for a lamp as well.

At a knock, he went to the door and found himself facing the petite but undeniably formidable figure of his mother, who stood at the threshold, arms crossed and brows knit together in a frown.

"Andrew!"

Although he towered over her, the force of her glare set him back on his heels and made his cheek tingle afresh. "Come in, Mama," he said, bowing his head slightly to shield himself from a repetition of the greeting he had received earlier. Caliban, who had accompanied her up the stairs, edged past her and set about inspecting the room. "I suppose I can guess why you're here."

But her reply was not at all what he had expected. "I have just been talking with Miss Holderin."

He hesitated. "She's been telling tales, I take it?"

"She has not," his mother said, refusing a chair. "But I don't doubt she has a tale to tell. There's a 'misunderstanding' between you, she says. She never wanted to come to London. So why is she here?"

"Because I was paid to bring her here, Mama." When that answer proved unsatisfactory, he explained. "Miss Holderin was in danger, the seriousness of which she refused to acknowledge. So a certain person arranged for her to leave the island until the danger had passed."

"An *interested* person."

Andrew was forced to stifle a smirk at such a description of Edward Cary. "Yes. Very much so."

"And you are certain she really was in danger?"

A memory of Lord Nathaniel Delamere's actions in Gillingham's pub flashed in his mind's eye. "I am."

"Even so, she seems eager to return. She would've gone back to Wapping tonight if I'd let her."

"Yes, I know." Andrew strode to the window and tugged back the drapery with one curled finger. Having completed his inspection, Caliban trotted over and stood with his paws on the ledge to see what his master spied. Although it was not yet evening, lamps had already been lit along the street, brighter smudges against a yellow fog. "She can be rather . . . impetuous."

His mother appeared to take in the significance of that word. "Has she family here?"

"A grandfather, with whom she has had no contact for some time, as I understand it." He said nothing of his intention to take her to him, nor of Tempest's reluctance to visit the man. Yorkshire must be their destination, whatever her wishes. Or his.

"I see," she said after a moment. "Well, I never like to hear of a young person in trouble, but as she has been the cause of bringing you home at last, I cannot help but be grateful."

"*Home?*" he repeated, finally turning away from the window. "Daniel ought to have left this house to you. You know very well, Mama, that this life is not mine."

"Oh, and what is?" she countered. "A cramped, musty cabin? Scurvy? Storms? Surely you do not mean to tell me you are going back to sea, back to chasing after—"

"That pirate Stratton is lying at the bottom of the Atlantic," he cut across her, "with his ship beside him."

Her sharp intake of breath was loud in the quiet room, underscored by the thump of Caliban's tail against the patterned wool carpet. "I will not pretend that this news does not make me glad," she said after a moment, lifting her gaze and meeting his with surprising composure. "But I hope, for the sake of your soul, yours was not the hand that put him there."

Although he could easily have reassured her, he did not. The hand of God had intervened at the last, it was true. But had it not, Andrew would have been only too glad to have raised his own to deal the deathblow. His mother ought to suffer no illusions about that.

She laid her fingertips along his arm. "I have worried about you more than you can know, Andrew." Beneath her gentle, maternal touch, he longed to soften. God, how he had missed her, worried about her, all these years. Instead, however, he held himself stiff against the words he feared were coming.

When she spoke again, however, she dealt a sharper strike than he had expected. "You are my son," she said, "and I will always love you. But when I hear that lust for revenge in your voice, or learn you have been involved in what sounds suspiciously like a kidnapping . . . I do not think I like what you have become."

"I was little more than a boy when I left," he reminded her. "Ten years at sea were bound to change me. They made me a man."

"Perhaps," she acknowledged. "I had hopes, however, that with your grandfather's early influence and Daniel's efforts, you might grow to become a *gentle*man."

He stepped away so her hand slipped from his sleeve. "Would you ignore my father's influence entirely, ma'am?" he asked, not bothering to mute the sardonic edge in his voice.

"If I could," she admitted, although the moment of hesitation between when the word was formed and when the sound of it left her lips made him certain it was not what she had started to say.

Before either of them could speak again, a pair of footmen staggered into the dressing room under the weight of his sea chest, while another bore the long-awaited hot water. The servants' arrival would not have had to end their conversation, but his mother took the opportunity to excuse herself. "You will wish to freshen up before dinner," she said and quickly left.

With a sigh, Andrew crossed to a chair near the empty fireplace and sat, his elbows propped up on his knees, his head dropped into his hands.

"I love you, too, Mama," he whispered after she had closed the door behind her.

He had often regretted their long separation, repented the concern he knew he was causing her. But he had also suspected that she understood why his voyage had been necessary. The wash of relief across her features when he told her Stratton was dead had confirmed it.

In all his reflections over the course of those ten years, however, he had never imagined he was leaving her alone. Daniel Beauchamp had always seemed like such an unstoppable force. Now, to know he had been gone for nearly two years . . .

The dog nudged against him and licked his damp cheeks, as if trying to rouse him from his mourning. When Andrew could muster no more attention for him than an absentminded pat on the head, he lay down at his master's feet with a sigh.

Andrew and his stepfather had not always gotten on—and was not that an understatement?—but he knew he would miss the man, and not just for his mother's sake. Daniel had been a kind and generous stepfather, and in truth, Andrew had never resented his mother's remarriage—or at least, no more than any boy of seven or eight might. What he *had* resented had been the attempts, both overt and covert, to remake him in his stepfather's image when it was so clear to anyone who so much as glanced his way that he had been cut from the same cloth as his father.

After so much time, he could call up no very distinct memory of his father's face. He knew, of course, that they shared the same dark hair and green eyes. Sometimes, when he stared into a glass, Andrew fancied it was his father looking back. But it was not so much the resemblance in physical appearance but in character that mattered.

Strange to think that he was now almost the age his father had been when he died. He could still remember how his da had spoken longingly of the life Andrew had gone on to live in his place. Danger. Adventure. Nothing to tie him down.

Only after his father had been gone for many years had Andrew really begun to understand what the man's fascination with the sea had put the family through. Risky investments. Near ruin. His wanderlust had touched every part of their lives. And he had been unfaithful in every sense of the word, leaving his wife and child with nothing. Those idyllic months living with his mother's parents had, in fact, been borne of cold necessity.

For his mother, the only bright spots in the year or so after his father's death had been first the visit and then the letters from Daniel Beauchamp, although Andrew could also recall how the happiness of the letters' arrival had been tinged with worry over the expense of the postage. When his mother had written to tell him the correspondence must end, Daniel had brought her to England and married her instead.

How could a son resent someone who had at last given his mother the life she deserved?

Still, Daniel had been serious and sober, everything his father had not been. Could a man really own a fleet of ships that sailed the world over and have no desire to see any of those places for himself? For ten years, his stepfather had smoothed every pathway, forged every connection Andrew could possibly need for success on land. And for ten years, Andrew had done whatever he could to prove he was not cut out for life behind a ledger.

Selfish. Irresponsible.

No, Tempest had not been the first to accuse him thus.

Now, as if those years had taught him nothing, Daniel was trying from beyond the grave to shape his stepson into a man of business. But Andrew was no more to be trusted with such responsibility than his father had been. Men—and a boy—had died under his command. The ship he captained had nearly sunk. Twice. Beauchamp Shipping, this house, this life—it was not a generous bequest. It was a millstone around his neck, and if he did not find a way to shed it, many others would drown right alongside him.

Pushing himself up from the chair, he strode into the dressing room, where the remaining footman was striving to make everything neat. "Good evening, sir," the young man said with a bow that did not quite hide a darting glance of curiosity at the new master and the rough-coated dog at his feet.

Andrew scowled. "What took so long?"

"Mrs. Beauchamp ordered water for the young lady first, sir."

Ah, yes. Tempest. Proof incarnate—if further proof were required—that he was not to be trusted. Not with life. Not with wealth. And certainly not with virtue, for thanks to the footman's dutiful reply, Andrew's mind was now filled with an image of a copper-haired sprite rising, sleek and damp and beautifully bare, from a steaming bath.

"Begging your pardon, sir," the footman interrupted, scattering the mental fantasy to the wind, "but Mr. Williams wanted me to ask what you meant to be done with the Negro boy."

Andrew looked around the dressing room to confirm the presence of a valet's cot on which Caesar could sleep. "Send him to me."

He hardly noted the footman's departure, for his attention had been drawn to something else that had been revealed by his quick sweep of the space. All his possessions had been unpacked, hung up, laid out. Almost as if he had come home to stay. Almost as if he had never left.

Only a rather limp dress of brownish-green muslin, looking sorely out of place, reminded him of how much had changed.

Beauchamp Shipping. This household. His widowed mother. A vulnerable serving boy. His responsibilities were racking up by the moment.

And if Tempest were as unlucky as he, he could soon add a wife and child to the list.

Feeling suddenly as if the walls of the already tiny room were contracting, he would gladly have taken refuge in the contents of his father's flask. But among the neat rows and stacks of this new life that was being built up around him, he no longer knew where to find it.

* * *

Reluctantly, Tempest submitted to Mrs. Beauchamp's hospitality, coming down to dinner in a dress that belonged to Hannah, Mrs. Beauchamp's maid, who was of a similar build but several inches taller. The skirt hems dragged along the carpet.

Inside the dining room, Andrew turned from the sideboard to observe her entrance. One dark brow rose, but thankfully, he did not laugh. "Well, it makes a change from buckskin breeches, at least," he said with a twitch of a smile as he showed her to her chair.

By contrast, he was more elegantly dressed than she had ever seen him, in a coat of dark green superfine paired with crisp white linen. His hair was tied neatly at the nape of his neck, revealing the sharp angle of his freshly shaven jaw. For perhaps the first time in their acquaintance she was not struck by the disparity between his appearance and his manner, for when he bowed and offered his arm, he looked every inch the gentleman. *And why not?* she thought, as she glanced around a room whose tasteful appointments had been purchased with profits from the trade in silk and spices, sugar and slaves. His stepfather had been a gentleman, and wealthy enough to buy his stepson's entrance into those exalted ranks as well.

"I half-expected to be told that you had run from the house at the first opportunity," he said.

"I might have done," she admitted, then lifted her skirts just enough to reveal her feet, bare but for a pair of borrowed stockings, "if I had been provided with shoes."

"A footman took your own to be cleaned and polished—and, as it turned out, repaired," Mrs. Beauchamp explained. She had entered behind them, unnoticed. "And Hannah's would have been far too large." Unlikely though it seemed, Tempest might have accepted the excuse, if not for the glance that darted between mother and son.

Why did either of them care whether she left or not? Despite his rash proposal, she had expected that Andrew would prove only too eager to be rid of her the moment they docked. Instead, he seemed determined to keep her under his guard indefinitely. What on earth was he waiting for?

But she knew the answer, of course, because she was waiting for it, too. Proof that she was not carrying his child. Proof that seemed alarmingly slow in coming, given how predictable her courses had always been. Not that she would allow herself to do anything so unreasonable as worry, since her plan for the future was already decided. Still, at the thought that his mother might suspect what they had done, a blush spread from Tempest's cheeks down her breast, clashing most dreadfully with Hannah's pink gown.

"Well, never mind it," Mrs. Beauchamp said as the soup was served on delicate china plates. "It gives us the perfect excuse to do a little shopping on the morrow."

"As if ladies have ever required an excuse to go shopping," said Andrew, and the mocking note in his voice was not entirely good-natured.

"While I'm sure an outing would be delightful," Tempest replied, struggling to maintain her composure, "I fail to see how I am to go about the streets of London in winter without shoes."

Mrs. Beauchamp, who had no future on the stage, attempted to appear struck by the incongruity as she fingered the chain of a heavy locket she wore around her neck. "A very good point, Miss Holderin. I shall ask my *modiste* to come to us instead."

For Tempest, who had been denied very little in her life, these past weeks of powerlessness had been more frustrating than frightening. At least on board the ship, there had been movement. There had been the illusion of doing *something*. To be trapped in this house, however grand, might just drive her mad. Not that the cold, crowded city outside offered much in the way of recourse, however.

"I thank you, but I'm afraid I have nothing with which to pay for her services."

Mrs. Beauchamp considered this newest dilemma. "I'm quite sure your grandfather will make good on the bill. He will not wish to see his granddaughter looking like an urchin."

"My—!" Tempest began but was forced to pause to collect herself. What had Andrew told her? What was he about? "I fear there has been another misunderstanding. I have no dealings with my grandfather and certainly no expectation of seeing him."

"You'd best begin to adjust your expectations, Miss Holderin," Andrew said. "I was hired to take you to Sir Barton Harper, and that's what I intend to do."

Tempest dipped her spoon into her soup with no particular desire to taste it, but rather because she was struck by a sudden need to be doing something with her hands. Something other than cheerfully strangling him, that was. "If you take me against my will, Captain

Corrvan, that would be kidnapping," she said once the mouthful of soup had scalded its way down her throat.

Kidnapping. The word had the desired effect on Andrew. He set his jaw hard, while his mother's eyes flared in alarm.

"I intend," Tempest continued, more evenly, "to return immediately to Antigua."

Andrew waved for his dish to be taken away and turned his attention squarely to her. "But you've just said you have no money. How then do you propose paying for your passage?"

He could easily lend her the money needed, of course, but the point was moot if he refused to do so.

"That's one problem easily solved," his mother proclaimed as the fish course replaced the soup. "She can travel on a Beauchamp ship. If I have not misunderstood the case, Andrew owes you at least that much."

Seeing the displeasure dart across Andrew's face at his mother's suggestion, Tempest felt no little satisfaction. Perhaps Mrs. Beauchamp would prove more of an ally than she had first expected, or than any of the men on the *Fair Colleen* had been. She would find a private moment in which to explain the reasons for her reluctance to travel to Yorkshire and persuade Mrs. Beauchamp to arrange her passage home first thing. "I would be most grateful for your assistance," she said, remembering with a pang the days in which she had never needed to ask for another's help.

"Excellent. I shall send 'round a note to Mr. Farrow in the morning and enquire."

"Farrow? A familiar name. I am relieved to hear he is still in charge," said Andrew.

His mother smiled and nodded as she chewed. "Oh yes," she said after she had swallowed and dabbed at the corner of her mouth with her napkin. "Well, not precisely *in charge*. I would not go quite so far."

"No? Then, who is?"

"I am," she answered before popping another bite into her mouth, delaying any further reply. Suddenly interested, Tempest laid aside her own fork.

Andrew, by contrast, allowed his to clatter onto his plate. "How's that?"

"As you know, Mr. Beauchamp fully expected you would take up the concerns of the business," his mother reminded him with a smile that seemed to Tempest to contain a bit of ice. "But as the date of your return was . . . *uncertain*, he specified in his will that I was to serve as de facto head of the company until you were able to do so. Mr. Farrow handles a great deal of the day-to-day operations, but I have been meeting with investors and the company's directors, and making decisions that could not be put off."

"That cannot have been easy," Tempest remarked.

"Indeed, it wasn't," agreed Mrs. Beauchamp, turning toward her. "Many gentlemen are reluctant to allow a woman to be heard on certain matters."

Thinking of her exchange with Mr. Whelan regarding the repair of the mill at Harper's Hill, Tempest gave a knowing nod.

"Which matters?" Andrew asked, sounding wary.

"The construction of new docks, in particular. The West India Merchants, of which Mr. Beauchamp was a member of long standing," she added by way of explanation to Tempest before returning her attention to Andrew, "has concocted a plan, under the leadership of a Jamaican planter, Mr. Milligan, to establish separate docks for the off-loading of our ships returning from Caribbean ports. The river is crowded, as you no doubt observed, and the loss of cargo has been quite shocking. Theft, spoilage." She shook her head. "The plan is sensible, on the surface. Still, it is a risky undertaking, and I have my reservations about its success without more support. When I attempted to express those reservations, however—"

"You were met with resistance," suggested Tempest.

"I was met with derision," Mrs. Beauchamp corrected. "Mr. Hibbert, the chairman, all but told me to go home to my needle, and I do believe Mr. Milligan would have patted me on the head had I been seated closer to him at the time."

"Why not send Farrow to voice these concerns on your behalf?" asked Andrew.

"With all due respect," his mother replied in a lofty tone, "Mr. Farrow is not a member of the West India Merchants. The head of Beauchamp Shipping is. I had every right to be heard."

Unexpected admiration for the woman's acumen and persistence flared in Tempest's chest. "You did, indeed," she concurred. Here was a woman of whom Miss Wollstonecraft would undoubtedly approve. Under any other circumstances, Tempest felt she and Mrs. Beauchamp might have been friends.

Her reply lit a spark of green fire in Andrew's eyes. "This is a family matter, Miss Holderin."

"I am glad to hear you say so," his mother interjected. "I take it from your reaction you will be only too willing to study the matter and take up the interests of Beauchamp Shipping at the Merchants' next meeting?"

Remembering Andrew's characterization of himself as unsuited to responsibility, Tempest joined Mrs. Beauchamp in leveling a steady gaze on him as they awaited his reply.

But it seemed the wait would be longer than they had expected.

"Excuse me," he said, pushing away from the table and rising to his feet. "I find I have lost my appetite." And without another word, he strode from the room.

Chapter 13

Andrew was still stewing over the exchange the next morning when he set off for Beauchamp Shipping to oversee the payment of his crew. Unfortunately, the long carriage ride from his stepfather's—God, *his*—house in the West End to the offices in Mincing Lane only gave him more time to think.

Neither his mother nor Daniel had ever been much given to subtlety. It was not in his mother's exuberant nature, and Daniel would have dismissed it as a waste of time. But really, to attempt to decide a man's future over ill-prepared sturgeon was worse than he had learned to anticipate, even from them.

Inside the offices, he identified himself as captain of the *Fair Colleen* and was greeted with furtive glances and ill-disguised whispers, as old hands explained to new ones what his arrival might mean. After some conversation held behind a closed door, he was shown by one of them into a room and given a ledger in which to record his ship's business.

Cramped by an overlarge and empty desk, the barren room seemed to suggest that the clerks had decided amongst themselves that the prodigal stepson of Daniel Beauchamp had not yet earned much in the way of preferential treatment. Morning sun passed through a grime-streaked window, picking out dust motes yet somehow failing to provide much in the way of light. Andrew settled into the rickety chair behind the desk to wait.

Fleming was the first in, eager to catch a northbound stage. Greaves soon followed, already clutching his next assignment in one beefy hand. At midmorning, he glanced up from his absent sketching in the margin of the ledger page to find Ford on the threshold, looking . . .

well, Ford always looked angry—with cause, Andrew knew—but these lines of frustration on his face appeared to be fresh.

"Where to now, Mr. Ford?" Andrew asked, counting out the carpenter's money.

Ford's shoulders lifted, the movement too tight to be called a shrug. "Can't say, sir."

"How are you finding your first taste of real freedom?" He bent his head over the ledger. "All you'd hoped?"

"Seems I've the freedom to starve, anyway," Ford replied, pocketing his pay.

So the man had spent his morning seeking work and being turned away? Andrew wished he could say he was surprised. "I'm in need of a man to head up the *Colleen*'s repairs," he said, not quite offering a job he felt certain Ford under any other circumstances would have been glad of the chance to decline. The man's general dislike of his captain, of almost everyone with any authority over him, had been well known.

Ford paused, considering. "I wouldn't have thought you in a position to hire. On land, and all," he pointed out, folding his arms across his chest. The pose wasn't quite defiance, although Andrew recognized the challenge in it. Here, on this soil, they met as equals.

At least, until Farrow entered the room behind him. "So it's true," Farrow exclaimed, obviously debating whether he should offer his hand or bow.

Andrew stood and stretched across the desk for a handshake. "It is."

Ford watched the exchange with interest. "Mr. Farrow," Andrew said, "may I introduce Mr. Ford, one of the finest ship's carpenters I have had the pleasure of knowing. I'd like to see him put to work."

Farrow did not even need to glance Ford's way. "Of course. Whatever you say, Mr. Corrvan."

Mr. Corrvan. Just that quickly he had been stripped of one identity and given another, changed from a man not with dubious authority over one ship, but unquestioned authority over a fleet of them.

As if he could cast off those strangling moorings, he slammed shut the ledger and swept it from the desktop. But the gesture of protest went unseen by Farrow, who was already ushering Ford from the room.

His petulance did not escape notice entirely, however, for Jeremiah Bewick stood just outside, looking as amused as it was possible for a man with no very evident sense of humor to look.

Muttering an oath under his breath, Andrew snatched up the book from the floor. "And what are your plans, Mr. Bewick?" he asked as he dutifully recorded into the ledger the amount owed to the quartermaster.

"I mean to stay with the *Colleen*, if I may."

Andrew looked up. "It will be many months before she sails again."

"No matter to me. Geoff's got 'is heart set on seein' an English spring once more. Set out for the country first thing this morning. Says 'e means to rent us a little cottage in 'ampstead. With a rose garden."

"A rose garden?" Andrew echoed. "It's mid-December."

"Aye." The single word was gently spoken, accepting of behavior from Beals that Bewick would have called out as foolish in another man—the way one does with those about whom one cares the most.

As Bewick's gaze wandered toward the window, Andrew studied the weathered lines of the other man's face, how they had softened in that moment, despite the ochre-tinged afternoon light. So revealing, that look. "Be—" Andrew began.

Bewick's expression hardened again when the sound of Andrew's voice recalled his attention, as if he suspected what the next word would be.

Be careful, Andrew had been going to say, but Bewick and Beals must already understand the importance of discretion. At sea, men had largely turned a blind eye to their relationship, either out of indifference or grudging acceptance that such things sometimes happened among men who spent long months or even years without the company of women. Andrew knew that the bond between the two was far more than a shipboard convenience. But nosy busybodies in a country village were unlikely to see it as anything other than a sin and a crime.

"Beauchamp Shipping will be happy to have you both return, whenever you are ready," Andrew said instead.

Bewick nodded and stepped forward to accept his pay. "Like as not, folks are even happier to have you back."

Andrew hesitated. "I don't know that I mean to st—"

"Don't be a fool," Bewick interrupted, all shipboard hierarchies and formalities flown. Really, the marvel was that he had ever condescended to address Andrew as *sir* before the others. "Your pa weren't allus a bad fellow, I'll say that much for 'im. An' you look enough like him that none can suspect your ma of playing him for a fool—which is to say, you're 'is son, through an' through." Having sailed with the *Fair Colleen* from her maiden voyage, Bewick had some cause to know the character of both father and son. "But you've given 'im what you owed him, now. Isn't it time to do the same for the man who raised you?"

It was hard to argue with Bewick. Always had been. Which was probably why Andrew had done it so often—from the very first, when Andrew had announced he meant to captain what had by then been Bewick's ship, through the disastrous exchange with Stratton that had nearly cost them all their lives, until now.

And he meant to argue again, didn't he? Surely he had no intention of blithely following Bewick's advice. Not after all this time.

When Andrew made no reply, Bewick added one final twist of the knife. "An' for your ma?" Then he touched his finger to his cap in a sort of salute and was gone before Andrew could muster even a nod.

Alone again, his gaze fell on the open ledger, one of many identical books contained within this building, filled with the numbers on which rested the empire Daniel Beauchamp had built. Scanning his eyes down the column of figures he had added to that record, he came across the mindless sketch of a woman's heart-shaped face with which he had marred its margins. How in God's name had his stepfather ever imagined he was fit to do anything serious?

He closed the ledger, quietly this time, and tapped one finger against its green baize cover. The gesture called to his mind the neat stack of account books on Edward Cary's immaculate desk, incapable of being more than superficially disordered by a gust of wind.

Or even a Tempest.

Now, *there* was a responsible man. A respectable man. One willing to sacrifice his own desires for the betterment of others. If Andrew allowed Tempest to go back to Antigua instead of taking her to Yorkshire, she and Cary would find a way to work everything out for the best, even if it turned out she was with child. Meanwhile, Andrew could light out in the opposite direction. India, perhaps. Some destination that would put a few thousand miles between him and a woman with whom he had no business dallying. A woman who wanted her independence as badly as he did, and no doubt deserved it more.

Tempest Holderin was strong, determined, a fierce defender of freedom—others', as much as her own. He had known many men who respected those qualities in another man but who would have rejected them out of hand in a woman. Men who needed to be needed, he supposed. Well, this woman certainly did not need him.

It should have been a relief. He had never wanted to be needed. And yet . . .

He was needed here, or so his mother said. If he were looking for some excuse to keep himself apart from Tempest, he could simply stay in London and take up his duties at Beauchamp Shipping. That was what he *should* do, what he would do—if he were a responsible, respectable man.

Which, of course, he was not.

"Farrow!" he shouted as he pushed away from the desk, determined to find some way to shed his association with the place. "See that the other men from the *Colleen* are paid their due. I'm going—"

Damn it all. In a great city such as this, with numberless temptations to a man such as himself, he ought to have been pulled in six different directions. Why then was the next word on his tongue the last place he should want to be? The place that contained—or had when he'd left—the one person he ought to avoid?

He fumbled for some alternative, but in the end, the lure proved too strong.

"I'm going home."

"Ze red, I t'ink, definitely."

Tempest shivered, a reaction not entirely inspired by the dressmaker's abysmal faux-French accent. Mrs. Beauchamp had assured her of the woman's skill with a needle, but her abilities did not extend to acting the part of a French refugee with any credibility. Nevertheless, given the current demand for French *modistes*, Madame D'Arbay—Mrs. Derby, surely?—made every effort.

Tempest stood on a stool, clad only in a crisp new shift, as the dressmaker measured and chattered and held out samples of material for Mrs. Beauchamp's approval.

"It would be the perfect thing for Christmas," Andrew's mother agreed.

"And ze pastel coleurs do not suit her haf so well." The surrounding floor was a pale sea of rejected fabric, pinks and blues and greens that reminded Tempest of nothing so much as spring blossoms, struggling valiantly against the wintry blast.

Given the cold, Tempest could not blame herself for dreaming of an entirely new wardrobe of wool and fur and velvet. Why, she hardly even regretted the disappearance of her moss green muslin dress. The fashionable ladies of London had evidently abandoned their senses, however, favoring airy frocks that offered little protection against the freezing dampness of winter. She, who had never known what it was to miss the sun, was aware of the frequent aspersions cast on colonials, aspersions that centered on the perceived damage done to one's mind and morals by the heat of tropical climes. But she felt certain that incessant rain and fog had done little to clear the heads of those who inhabited the capital.

"I will be at sea by Christmas," she reminded Mrs. Beauchamp, "with no occasion to wear such a gown. A few, a *very* few, practical garments that can be done up quickly are the order of the day, I'm afraid," she explained to the *modiste*. Again.

With a sigh, Mrs. Beauchamp nodded her acquiescence and said to Madame D'Arbay, "I know it is not your custom, but perhaps you've something ready-made that will require only a little alteration?"

The corners of Madame D'Arbay's mouth turned down, but she spoke to her seamstress in a voluble mixture of bad French and Cockney, only the latter of which the seamstress seemed likely to understand. The girl shuffled through the contents of the fabric-filled trunk and withdrew a dress of heavy blue silk so dark it might nearly pass for black. Its funereal appearance was furthered by its severity of style; to fit Tempest's slight stature the scalloped hem would have to be cut off entirely, relieving the dress of its only ornament.

"Goodness, no," exclaimed Mrs. Beauchamp even as Tempest proclaimed it perfect.

Although she would have preferred wool, the sturdy weave would be practical, and the cut and color made it suitable for any occasion, even travel. Better yet, it looked as if the *modiste* had made it for a customer who had then declined to take it, meaning she would be likely to let it go for a reasonable price. Tempest had refused to have the bill sent to her grandfather, promising instead to repay Mrs. Beauchamp the moment she returned home. The better the bargain, the less guilty she would feel for being in Mrs. Beauchamp's debt.

"That will be all," she said once the seamstress had pinned and tucked and marked where the gown would be shortened. With pursed lips, Madame D'Arbay promised it would be done yet that day.

"For a young lady who arrived here with nothing?" Mrs. Beauchamp protested as the *modiste* and her seamstress packed the trunk. "Be reasonable. You must have more clothes."

Madame D'Arbay hesitated, hopeful, but Tempest remained firm. She had once been brave enough to march across the deck of a ship in nothing but her undergarments and Captain Corrvan's coat. For the return journey, one good dress, two shifts, and a nightrail would have to suffice.

Only after the other women had left did she observe a package lying on the floor near the bed. "Oh, Madame D'Arbay left behind a box," she said, on the point of going after her.

"That's for you," said Mrs. Beauchamp, staying her. "A gift. Something practical, I assure you," she added, forestalling Tempest's renewed protest. "Open it."

With uncertain fingers, Tempest lifted the lid from the box, pushed aside the paper, and slipped her fingers among folds of softest velvet: a cloak of deepest green, trimmed with fox fur around the hood and accompanied by a matching fur muff. She must refuse it, of course. Like a better angel on her shoulder, Miss Wollstonecraft's voice whispered that women were too easily seduced by fashion and furbelows. "The frippery of dress," she had written, "weakens the mind."

But what about the needs of the body? Tempest had dutifully turned down the perfectly impractical garnet brocade, but this, surely, was different. Had that noble authoress ever been forced to give up the Caribbean sun for a bone-chilling London winter?

In the end, the cloak's softness and warmth proved impossible to resist. Tempest wrapped it around her and whirled about the room in an impromptu dance. Only think! She need never again be bothered by this wretched cold. Would it be terribly inappropriate to wear it inside the house?

Mrs. Beauchamp laughed at Tempest's delighted surprise. Just then, there was a tap at the door. "This was just delivered by messenger, ma'am," Williams said as he entered and held out a letter on a salver to Mrs. Beauchamp. She took it and broke its seal while Williams bowed from the room.

"Bad news, I'm afraid," she said after scrutinizing the brief note.

At those words, Tempest came abruptly to a halt. The heavy cloak continued its dance for another beat, caught up in the momentum. Its weight as it swung against her frozen form almost knocked her off her feet.

"Mr. Farrow says no ship can take you until after the new year. Mid-January, at the earliest," she explained as she folded the letter and tucked it into her sleeve.

Betrayed, Tempest allowed the cloak to slip from her shoulders and drop to the floor. "I cannot wait better than a month to return."

"I am sorry. But at least now you will be at liberty to pay a visit to your grandfather, should you wish."

Tempest had never felt any pull toward her grandfather. The distance between them had always been too great. To cross that divide—smaller now, to be sure, but two hundred miles still sounded far away to her— only to be met with what? Disapproval? Disappointment?

"I do not wish."

She had nothing to say to a man who had all but ignored the management of his holdings in Antigua, who had cut her father, who had probably already sent word to have Edward removed from his post. The only possible pleasure such a trip could hold would be the pleasure of telling her grandfather that his bosom friend, Lord Nathaniel, was dead.

"Then you must consider yourself my guest while you wait, my dear," Mrs. Beauchamp offered.

Stepping carefully over the puddle of fabric around her feet, Tempest came to stand in front of her. Mrs. Beauchamp withdrew the letter and handed it to Tempest, as if she recognized there would be doubts over her claim about its contents. But the note said no more or less than had been reported.

Of course, that did not preclude some subterfuge involved in its composition. Tempest returned it to her. "I thought you of all people would understand why I need to go home. For many years now, since my father grew ill and died, I have been responsible for the oversight of our family business. Like you, I have been fortunate to have a reliable manager to assist me—as you know, a woman's opinion is not always heeded in such matters." With a chastened look, Mrs. Beauchamp nodded. "But I have been gone nearly two months already. A delay such as this will keep me from home for almost half a year. I cannot stay away so long."

"I do understand, my dear," Mrs. Beauchamp began. "Still, I—"

Her words were interrupted by a sudden flurry of barking in the corridor, to which Caliban had been relegated during the dressmaker's visit. From farther away came a deep rumble of greeting. So Andrew had returned from his jaunt into the City.

Tempest was not conscious of having turned toward the sound of his voice until she felt Mrs. Beauchamp's hand on her arm, reclaiming her attention. The glimmer of sympathy had not left the older woman's eyes, but it had shifted slightly, almost as if she realized that more than their business interests bonded them.

"Are you *sure* there's nothing to keep you here, my dear?" she asked. "Nothing at all?"

Was it so obvious, then, the way Tempest seemed to be as attuned to Andrew's presence and absence as the dog? Although his voice had been muffled by tight walls and heavy doors and plush carpets, it still had sent a spark of awareness along her skin and up her spine.

She had imagined herself prepared for the memory of his insistent touch, his wicked kiss. But she had *not* been prepared for the way those memories seemed determined to slip from her control. The way they came to her in her sleep, or in the last drowsy moments of the day, or on the edge of wakefulness just before dawn. When she was not quite mistress of her mind, her heart—or sometimes even her hands.

And she had been less prepared still for the way the memories of the passion they had shared seeped into every other encounter with him—how they inflected his roguish smile, or colored the expression in those sharp green eyes. How that one night together had changed the way she thought about his determination, his bravery. His grief. Her realization that she had been wrong about who he was—and her growing suspicion he might even be wrong about himself.

Now she might have four more weeks in his house. Four more weeks with him.

Her hand smoothed down the front of her dress, over her still-flat belly.

If she stayed that long, she might have to stay forever.

Pulling away from Mrs. Beauchamp, she forced herself to think instead of Harper's Hill, of Omeah and all the rest. It would not do to give in to temptation. How could she live with herself if she put her own desires above others' desperate need?

"No, there's nothing to keep me here," she insisted with a resolute shake of her head, then moved to pick up the velvet cloak from the floor. Despite its soft, seductive weight along her arm, she resisted the impulse to pet it.

If she had to, she would sell it and book her own passage back to the West Indies, where such a garment would, thankfully, never be needed.

Chapter 14

Andrew had never been one for confined spaces. Aboard ship, he had always preferred the open deck to the four walls of his cabin. But tonight, the library appealed to him. The butter-soft leather of the chairs, the scent of old books, the darkness. Dinner had ended hours ago, and when he had retreated to this silent place, the sky had still been streaked by the sunset. Now it was night, but he had not bothered to call for a lamp. The fire crackling in the hearth was enough. After all, he had not come here to read.

With one fingertip he traced the brim of the otherwise untouched glass that rested against his knee. He hadn't come to drown his sorrows, either. It would have been sullying the memory of his stepfather, whose private study this had always been. For that reason, he hoped his mother would hesitate to venture across its threshold. He doubted Tempest even knew the room existed. And so he had bought himself a few hours of quiet.

It would be a lie to call what he felt here *peace*, however.

At seventeen, with an enemy to best and the sea before him, it had seemed a simple thing to run away from this life, to reject everything for which Daniel Beauchamp had stood. At eight and twenty, he was finding it rather more difficult to persuade himself that he must leave. Not that he had any particular desire to divide the rest of his life between this room and the offices on Mincing Lane. But the comforts of this house were a strange sort of anchor to his soul.

Which was precisely the reason why he had to go. Staying would only make matters worse. Inevitably, he would run his stepfather's business into the ground and break his mother's heart. And then there was Tempest, whose proximity was about to shatter his sanity—

The squawk of the door opening brought his ruminations up short.

He wondered that Mrs. Long, or even Williams, had neglected the greasing of the hinge. But perhaps Daniel had wanted it that way? A sort of alarm if anyone invaded his sanctuary?

From his place by the fire, Andrew could not see the door, but he did not rise or even speak to whoever had entered. It could be only one of two people, after all, and he would know which in a moment. It was bad enough to catch himself hoping for one in particular.

Worse still when a spark of anticipation passed through him at the discovery his hopes had been realized.

Tempest crossed the corner of his vision on her way to the book-shelves lining the walls, oblivious to his presence. In the dim light, she was forced to lean close to peer at the titles, straining to make them out. The sight of her in breeches had had its own appeal, but it could not compete with what he felt as he watched her new gown skim her curves and cling to her hips as she climbed a few steps up the library ladder to reach the higher shelves, seeking something to read.

"You'll find very little with which to amuse yourself here, I'm afraid," he said.

Momentarily frozen, she clung to the ladder without turning to face him. "I am not so frivolous as to require nothing but *amusement*, Captain Corrvan," she replied after a moment when she had recovered from her surprise and picked her way carefully back to solid ground. "My father saw to it that my education was quite well-rounded."

"Of course he did," Andrew said, rising before she could move toward him. The last time he had been sitting in a chair and she had come to stand beside him, all manner of trouble had ensued. "And as a result you will no doubt fare better in this room than I ever have. I was forever hoping for adventure stories or books of travels. Imagine my disappointment." He pulled a random volume from a shelf near where she stood and held it out to her.

"*An Inquiry into the Nature and Causes of the Wealth of Nations* by Adam Smith. Volume the second. Fascinating, I'm sure," she said, taking it from him and returning it to its place. "But if I am to begin, it really ought to be with the first volume. I would not wish to lose the thread of the argument." Her hands and face were spots of light in the darkness of the room and against her gown.

When he had first seen her tonight, he had thought she wore mourning, perhaps one of his mother's old dresses made over to fit her. Under the blaze of candles in the dining room, however, the fabric had taken on a life of its own, shimmering and exotic, and he had recognized it for what it really was—not black, but the deep blue of a starless night sky stretched over a silent sea. Such a color ought to have rendered her wan, unappealing, almost invisible.

But it did not, of course. It darkened the blue of her eyes and made her pale skin glow like alabaster, and he caught ripples of warm ivory and cool blue as her chest rose and fell in the flickering firelight. When he looked back over all the circumstances under which he had seen her now, bedraggled and seasick and worse, he was forced to acknowledge to himself that nothing could ever make her unappealing to him.

"May I offer you a drink?" he asked, nodding toward his glass.

"Irish whiskey, I suppose?"

He lifted one corner of his lips in a sort of smile. "You are familiar with all my vices, it would seem."

"Mr. Beals gave me a sip of it aboard the *Fair Colleen*. To dull the pain in my hands."

"I see. And how did you enjoy your first taste of *uisce beatha*, the water of life, *mo cailín*?" The long-neglected language slipped over his tongue with surprising ease. "It *was* your first, I presume?"

"I think on the whole, Captain Corrvan," she said, studying his expression through those extraordinary eyes of hers, "I much prefer rum."

A bark of laughter escaped his lips before he could stop it. She had been aptly named, this one. She loved to trouble the waters.

"We're not at sea, Tempest. You needn't call me *captain*," he said, resting his glass on the mantel.

"What, then?"

He hesitated. How foolish to want to hear his name on her lips. How dangerous to encourage further intimacy between them.

When he did not answer, she said, "I suppose you must accustom yourself to no longer being called *captain* by anyone."

Almost of its own volition, the glass spun from his fingertips and rattled onto the stone. "What would make you say that?"

"Why, *this*," she replied with a glance into the dim corners of his stepfather's library—a room well suited to stand in for all he'd so unwillingly inherited from the man.

Against his better judgment, he stepped closer. "One thing only keeps me here, Tempest. And when I'm assured that you do not require the protection of my name, I shall return to sea." He spoke the last words with sudden confidence. As he'd left the office this morning, Farrow had reluctantly informed him of an eastbound route in need of a seasoned captain. Even given his prior misadventures, he felt certain he would do far less damage aboard that ship than if he stayed in London.

"The protection of your name?" A skeptical laugh burst from her lips. "Please do not postpone your plans on my behalf. The only assistance I require from you is in finding a ship to take me home as soon as possible." She returned to her study of the bookshelves, although he felt certain her eyes saw nothing of the titles over which they skimmed—not least because the fire's uncertain light made reading the embossed letters on the dark leather spines almost impossible. "Your mother tells me no Beauchamp ship is sailing to that part of the world for several weeks, and I will not brook such an unnecessary delay."

"Unnecessary?" He moved closer still, trapping her between his body and the bookcase; one forearm rested on the lowest shelf, almost but not quite touching her. "Are you certain of that, then?" he asked, dipping his head to breathe the words into her ear, wishing somehow he could make her share his sense that the bond between them was born of more than a mistake.

Ducking away from his lips, she slipped from his half embrace. "I am certain I can take care of myself."

He let her go. "I think you know that's not how this works."

"Why not? You once called yourself irresponsible. Though at the time I did not believe the label to be entirely apt, if you really intend to abandon your mother and the business your stepfather hoped you would manage, you have now proven it to my satisfaction." Her short curls gleamed gold in the firelight as she tossed her head to underscore her words. "I, on the other hand, mean to fulfill my responsibilities. *All* of them," she said, crossing her arms over her chest and lifting her chin. "Whatever they may be."

"You mark no difference, then, between the fate of a business and the fate of a child?" he countered.

"A business, be it shipping company or sugar plantation, is made up of people. People who depend on the guidance of a leader who truly cares for their well-being. In that, it is very little different from a family. If you are unwilling to take on the responsibility for one, do not ask me to believe you will take seriously your responsibilities toward the other. Why, for all I know, you might have left a string of—of *bastards*," her voice dropped to a whisper on that scandalous word, "in every Caribbean harbor."

"I—" he began, but to such a charge, what defense could he offer? He could not say there had been no other women. He would not claim he had always been careful. And he certainly should not confess that everything about his encounter with Tempest had been somehow different from any other in his rather checkered past.

"If you take me to my grandfather, aren't you afraid he'll demand you marry me?"

"Not as afraid as you seem to be," he tossed back, unwisely.

"Do you wish to know what I think?" she asked, but did not wait for his assent or denial. "You cannot bear to be tied down to Beauchamp Shipping Company, but you also cannot bear the thought of setting aside a fortune. So you have decided to get mine instead, imagining it will require less work on your part. You wish to take me to Yorkshire against my will because you're hoping my grandfather will force a marriage. You're no different from all the rest."

Although her voice was surprisingly calm, her words fell upon him as if she had picked up the fireplace tongs and tossed a hot coal in his direction.

Rounding the corner of his stepfather's massive mahogany desk, he jerked open the drawers until he found what he was looking for: a small metal cashbox, from which the household expenses and the servants' wages were paid. To his surprise and relief, the tiny brass key was still fitted to its lock. Fumbling with the catch, Andrew at last pried it open and scraped his fingers through the contents, pulling out a wad of banknotes whose denominations he could not read in the darkened room. Then he marched to stand before Tempest and, taking her hand in his free one, thrust the crumpled, jumbled mess of paper and coins into her palm.

"Go," he growled, knowing that if the firelight caught his face, she would see that a part of him was praying for her to rebel against his command, as she always had before.

Wide-eyed, she looked up at him, not down at her unexpected windfall. A few of the coins slipped through her grasp and tinkled onto the hearthstone. She seemed as if she might speak, then he heard the crinkle of paper as her fingers curled around the banknotes, and in another moment she was gone, darting from the room as if she feared he might change his mind.

So, it was done. He waited until he could hear her footsteps on the stairs before turning to leave himself. Caesar was likely already asleep. No matter. He could pack his own sea chest, had done it for years. He didn't know when that ship was bound for India, but no matter. By this time tomorrow, he would be off, one way or another.

He had not counted on meeting his mother on the threshold, however. "Oh, Andrew. What have you done?" she asked. There was a tremor in her soft voice, but no accusation. How much had she overheard?

"Not at all what I set out to do, Mama," he said, running a surprisingly shaky hand through his hair. "Not at all."

"You mean to say—or rather to avoid saying—that you ought to marry the girl, I suppose?" she asked.

He strode back toward the fireplace, dodging his mother's eye. "I think we might all be better served to hope and pray, as Miss Holderin herself obviously does, that a marriage will not prove absolutely necessary."

Despite the plush carpet, he could hear his mother's toe tapping. "You ought to insist."

"It cannot have escaped your notice that she is not terribly susceptible to *insistence*, Mama." Snatching his abandoned glass from the mantel, he tossed back its contents in a single swallow, forgetting that he had poured out the only thing he could find: Daniel's exquisite French brandy. To one craving the punishing burn of whiskey, its unexpected mellowness was regrettable. "Had I realized that from the first, I might have left her in Antigua, quite confident in her ability to fend off a most persistent suitor," he said, twisting the empty glass in his hands, watching the way the firelight gleamed through its faceted sides. "She is a great heiress, you see. Very much in demand."

His mother brushed aside his explanation. "I have some idea of who she is. But you have no need of her fortune. She ought to have no misgivings about you on that score."

"Perhaps not," Andrew said with a chary glance about the room. "Although her outlook on the matter is rather more sanguine than yours."

"How's that?"

"She believes me entirely motivated by money, but rightly doubts what you still believe: that I intend to accept my—this inheritance," he said, gesturing with the cut-crystal glass, a symbol of the wealth his stepfather had accrued. "If I had wanted any part of Beauchamp Shipping, I might have had it long ago. I mean to leave on the morrow."

"I see." She plucked the tumbler from his fingers and returned with it to the sideboard where the decanter sat, still unstoppered. He heard liquid slosh into the glass and watched in amazement as she raised it to her lips and swallowed. "You accused me once of ignoring your father's influence on your behavior, your character," she whispered, her voice roughened by the sear of the unaccustomed liquor in her throat. "But when you, too, desert those who most need you, I can hardly deny it."

The words stung far worse than the blow across his cheek had done, but they were no less deserved. "You will all be better off without me, I assure you."

Although her back was to him, he could see her head shake. "I will manage, as I have done all these years. Only this time, I will try not to waste my days praying for your return." She paused, and the crackle and hiss of the dying fire was loud in the stillness. "But what will become of Miss Holderin?"

"Has it not occurred to you that she wishes me gone almost as much as I wish to leave?"

"Frankly, no," she said, setting the glass down with a deliberate motion and turning to face him. "Not given the way she looks at you when she believes no one else sees."

"She—?" he began and then broke the sentence off abruptly, hearing the ridiculous note of hope in his voice. Had she not just called him careless, concerned only with himself? "Nonsense, Mama," he said instead, although his heart was not quite in the denial. "Her misgivings are well-founded. We are ill-suited in every conceivable way."

"Yes." Her skirts whispered as she walked toward him, hand outstretched. "And no."

Reluctantly, he took her icy fingers in his. "You have the look of a woman hatching a plan. What is it?"

"Her grandfather is in England, you say?"

"Yorkshire, yes. But—"

She raised her free hand to interrupt him. "If she could be persuaded to visit him, then perhaps . . . It is nearly Christmas, after all."

Once, he had imagined that such a trip would buy him a few more weeks with her—time that would tell for certain whether she was to bear his child, time in which he could . . . In which he could *what*, exactly? She had made it perfectly clear that England was the last place she wanted to be, and he was the very last man she wanted to be with.

"I cannot force her, Mama, and she will never go willingly with me. She suspects my motives for making such a journey."

"I said nothing of *force*, Andrew," she scolded, "nor of her traveling anywhere with you. I daresay I shall make a more fitting chaperone, if not a more . . . *engaging* companion."

Andrew was familiar with his mother's powers of persuasion. For that reason, he had left her a letter all those years ago, expressing in writing his intention of going to sea, rather than confronting her face-to-face. Otherwise, he might never have screwed up the courage to leave. But could she do this? Could she convince Tempest to do what she did not want to do?

"She will never agree to it," he said flatly.

His mother conceded that possibility with a slight tilt of her head. "But if she does, then you must promise to do one thing for me in return."

He did not ask. He did not need to.

"Stay here and manage Beauchamp Shipping in your place," he said, every muscle in his body tense with the effort of fighting his natural impulse to run.

"Precisely," she said with a small smile. "Only for a few weeks, of course."

"Of course." A few weeks that would mean throwing away a perfect opportunity to sail away from his troubles. A few weeks that she no doubt hoped would stretch into forever.

At least the trip to Yorkshire would set some distance between him and Tempest, distance he had always known to be necessary—for his peace of mind as much as hers. And it would complete his bargain with Cary, although the money seemed rather beside the point now.

"Perhaps the holiday will work its magic, its miracle, as it has been known to do before," his mother said, her hazel eyes bright with anticipation.

Although he had more than a sneaking suspicion they would each be praying for a different miracle, he jerked his head in a stiff nod, just as he had done the last time he had been presented with a devil's bargain.

"All right, Mama," he said.

With so little to her name, Tempest's packing was complete in a matter of moments. Into a small valise she had found in the bottom of the armoire, she placed the nightrail and spare shift, a pair of Hannah's stockings, and a silver-backed hairbrush from the dressing table. And of course the money Andrew had thrust into her hands with such fervor. She was past caring what was and wasn't hers to take. When she was home again, and mistress of her own purse, she would find a way to make things right.

Only the velvet mantle gave her pause, but in the end, she could not bring herself to step out into the night air without it. She wrapped herself in its softness, raised the hood, and slipped down the stairs on silent feet. At this late hour, the hall was empty. One sconce remained lit, but its flickering candle served only to cast the corners of the room into further darkness. The butler had long since retired to his own room; now not even a footman remained. As she laid a hand on the door, wondering if she would find it locked, she heard a sound behind her, beside her. She jerked back her fingers when they encountered something cold and wet.

"Caliban," she scolded in a whisper. "Stay." The dog sat as ordered, squarely between her and the door. In the stillness she could hear him pant, could picture his doggy grin, the eager sweep of his feathery tail across the marble tile. "You mustn't try to follow me. Go on, Caliban. Back to your master." Only her first command seemed to have any effect, for Caliban interpreted her second as an invitation to lie down. "Shoo," she tried again, but was answered only with a soft groan.

Then a voice spoke from the shadows.

"Miss Holderin."

Her pulse sped and her heart sank simultaneously. Mrs. Beauchamp's voice, not Andrew's.

"So you are determined to be off at once."

Tempest's answering nod barely stirred the fur trim of the hood.

"I cannot blame you."

Those were not the words Tempest had expected to hear. Her eyes sought the woman's figure, still hidden in the deep well of the door to the receiving room, invisible but for the occasional shimmer sent up when the candlelight caught the golden chain of her locket. "Still, you intend to stop me."

"You must be allowed to make your own decisions. It is not for me to say whether you stay or go."

"You mean to claim you had no hand in the disappearance of my clothes? Or my shoes? That you did not discourage your Mr. Farrow from looking too hard for a ship that was leaving sooner?"

"Ah," came the answer on a breath of quiet laughter. "Guilty as charged, I'm afraid. I confess I wanted to know what could possibly hurry you away so quickly. I wondered what it was you were fleeing."

"But now you have found your answer?"

A pause, loud in the late-night silence of the house. "I have." With a rustle of skirts and a tap of shoes, she crossed to the door, reaching out and lifting Tempest's hand from the knob.

"I cannot stay here," Tempest said, her voice the merest whisper despite her determination.

"I understand. But it is not necessary to leave in the dead of night, I do assure you," Mrs. Beauchamp insisted, turning her away from the door. Caliban looked up with interest and rose when Mrs. Beauchamp tried to lead her up the stairs once more. This time, Tempest did not follow. "Andrew tells me your grandfather lives in Yorkshire."

What else had Andrew said? "So I have been told, yes."

"It is to be regretted that you have been unable to know one another."

"If there is regret to be felt in the matter, it must be felt by him. I am not the one who has kept us apart."

"No," Mrs. Beauchamp agreed. "At least, not until now."

Pushing away the pang of guilt she knew those words had been designed to produce, Tempest asked, "What is it that you want, Mrs. Beauchamp?"

The older woman appeared to consider the question. "Miss Holderin, have you any other family?"

"No."

A cluck of the tongue. "And you so young. Your only living relative, and this your first—and likely last—chance to meet him."

"As I said, I have no desire to—"

"Forgive me for speaking out of turn," Mrs. Beauchamp interrupted. "It's just that, having been separated from my only child for

so many years, knowing that pain, I worry that you will wish someday that you had known him—when it is too late to satisfy that desire." When Tempest began to shake her head, she held up a finger to
stay her. "Mothers know these things."

Did they? Although she felt very little curiosity about her grandfather, she knew that a few days' journey would also take her to the
place where her mother, the mother she had never really known, had
been born. Unbidden, her mind called up the flyleaf of Andrew's
book, his grandfather's faded name, his own scrawled beneath it.
What would it feel like to find some similar treasure bearing her
mother's girlish hand?

Resolute, she shook off the mental image. "I thank you for your
concern, ma'am. But my mind is made up. Your son has provided me
with the means to leave forthwith, and I intend to seize the opportunity, before it is snatched from me once again."

Unexpectedly, Mrs. Beauchamp wrapped her arms around Tempest
and pressed her cheek against hers. "Then I wish you a safe journey, my
dear," she said, turning and walking up the stairs, all liveliness gone
from her step, all music gone from her voice. Caliban followed, paus-
ing only to glance behind him once with an expression Tempest
would have sworn was a frown.

"Mrs. Beauchamp, wait," she called after her, resting her satchel
on the bottom stair. "Tell me one thing: Did your son ask you to persuade me to stay?"

The woman hesitated between two steps. "He did not."

Tempest lifted her bag again. "I had hoped you would be honest
with me."

"I am telling the truth, child," she promised. As she spoke, she sank
heavily down to sit on a stair. Caliban whimpered and Tempest was at
her side in a moment, her hurry to be gone temporarily forgotten.

"Are you all right, Mrs. Beauchamp?"

"It will pass," she replied, laying a hand across her breast. "Leastways, it always has before. I just have to accustom myself to the
ache."

"Your heart?"

She drew a steadying breath. "He agreed that if I would take you
to Yorkshire he would . . . look after things while I was gone. I confess I had hoped that a taste of the business—"

"Might tempt him to stay for good." Despite having no memory of her own mother, Tempest had known enough grieving women, slaves separated from their children, to recognize Mrs. Beauchamp's pain.

She nodded. "It was wrong to tease you into going. I had no right. I know how you long to go home. Can you forgive me?"

Tempest took the woman's hand in her own, surprised by its warmth. "Of course."

Mrs. Beauchamp gave a hopeful smile, as if waiting for Tempest to say more.

But no. She could not stay. She was needed elsewhere. It would be madness to agree to go to Yorkshire merely to give Andrew a chance to prove he was a better man than any of them believed him to be.

Not nearly as mad as haring through London alone in the middle of the night, however. And was she not always reminding herself of the need to think rationally, to act reasonably?

By acquiescing to Emily's plan, she could acquaint herself with more of the country of her parents' birth and her own citizenship, even if it would never be her home. She could try to forge a relationship with her grandfather, who might then be persuaded to improve things at Harper's Hill immediately, rather than requiring her to wait grimly for his death. She could also repay the kindness of a woman whose strength she had come to admire over the last few days.

Any one of those reasons for going had more sense in it than the truth: She simply could not trust herself to stay here, with Andrew, another moment.

If she ran to the docks tonight, she would be acting with her heart, trying to shield it from the sort of ache to which Mrs. Beauchamp's had already succumbed.

She needed, more than ever now, to act with her head.

"All right. We will leave for Yorkshire first thing tomorrow morning, Mrs. Beauchamp. Just you and I."

"*Och*, thank you, child," she exclaimed, squeezing her fingers with unexpected strength. "But make it the next day. I've a few things I must do first."

"Very well. But we must return in time for me to make that ship to the West Indies, Mrs. Beauchamp," Tempest insisted. "I will go home when it sails."

"Of course," she readily agreed. "Now, please, if we are to be traveling companions, you must call me Emily."

"And I am Tempest," she offered, returning the press of Emily's fingertips.

"*Tempest*. How unusual." Seeing the surprise on the other woman's face, Tempest prepared to launch into the oft-rehearsed explanation, but Emily kept speaking. "I like it." With a twinkle in her eye, she rose from the step without difficulty, wrapped Tempest's arm through hers, and walked with her briskly up the stairs. "It suits you, my dear."

Did it? The name connoted power and strength, her father had always said, qualities he had believed she possessed. But a tempest was also unpredictable and disastrous, and sometimes she wondered whether she had not allowed her unusual name to become an excuse for rash behavior. Had Papa's choice been blessing or curse?

Either way, she knew she had just witnessed proof that when it came to shaking a stubborn oak, sometimes a gentle breeze was more effective than a gale.

Chapter 15

As Emily Beauchamp stepped into the carriage, Tempest peered past her. Beyond the coachman and the stable boy, however, not another soul was in sight—except Caliban, sitting beside the kitchen door, watching the goings-on in the mews with interest. Andrew and his mother must have exchanged a private good-bye.

Just as the carriage door was closing, the dog bounded forward, leaped into the carriage without touching his paws to the steps, and wound between the two women's legs.

"Now, Caliban," Tempest began to chide, glancing back toward the house, expecting someone—Andrew—to retrieve him.

"It *would* be a comfort to have him along on the journey," Emily countered, reaching down to scratch the dog's head. "An extra set of ears to stay alert to mischief."

While she didn't have much faith in Caliban's abilities as a guard dog, Tempest could already feel how having the animal curled between them warmed the carriage's interior a few more degrees. "I suppose," she agreed, "but won't Captain Corrvan—"

"Oh, Andrew will be too busy in the City even to care properly for the poor dog. Besides, our need is greater," his mother said, settling the matter with a firm nod.

Given everything that had happened over the last two days, Tempest was left only to wonder that the gentlemen of the West India Merchants had not immediately acceded to Mrs. Beauchamp's wishes in the matter of the construction of a new dock, or whatever other plans she might have had in mind. Clearly, the woman was unaccustomed to being gainsaid. If Andrew could be persuaded to take up his duties at Beauchamp Shipping, even temporarily, what hope had Tempest ever had of resisting this trip to Yorkshire?

Why, she was even wearing another new dress. Mrs. Beauchamp had swept into her room this morning as she was dressing and snatched up the blue silk, muttered something about how it would be ruined by three days in a carriage, and swept out again. In its place she had left a traveling dress of tobacco-brown wool—trimmed about the bodice with apple-green ribbon, but otherwise as simple and plain as Tempest could have demanded if she had been allowed to place the order herself. Given how well it fit, she could only guess that Madame D'Arbay had made it according to the measurements she had taken during her visit. Wanting to protest—at Mrs. Beauchamp's duplicity, at the shocking expense of having another new dress made up so quickly—Tempest had nevertheless put it on, fearing the alternative would be to make the trip in her shift and petticoats. If she had understood Hannah's chatter correctly, where they were headed it was likely to be even colder.

Despite the wool dress and the heavy cloak, the morning air took her breath away, leaving in its place those peculiar little clouds of steam that no one else seemed even to notice. The groom and the stable boy had been talking and laughing with one another, oblivious to the haze surrounding them. Even the horses made smoky puffs of breath when they snorted. Good heavens, what if they were all indifferent to the sight of their frozen breath because they had never known any different? What if it were *always* this cold in England?

No, no, that could not be so. Her father had often spoken of bright spring days and warmer summer ones, and Edward had learned to swim as a boy in England. One could not swim if the water were always solid, as it looked to be now.

As the horses' hooves broke through thin layers of ice on the puddles, muddy water splashed up and starred the windows, but Tempest did not turn away. The fog had finally lifted and the rising sun turned everything they passed into a diamond-crusted wonder. The carriage wheels squeaked over cobblestones that were coated with a fuzzy sort of rime—*frost*, Mrs. Beauchamp had explained when Tempest had reached out uncertainly to touch the similarly afflicted lamppost and found that the fur was cold but melted away under the relative warmth of her fingertip. It was a strangely beautiful world, nothing she ever could have imagined.

And she felt as if she had it all to herself. Mrs. Beauchamp and

Caliban dozed contentedly, indifferent to the swaying of the carriage that reminded Tempest of those uncomfortable first days at sea. The streets were still mostly bare on this early morning, and they passed quickly through town. After a while, she caught her first glimpse of the famed English countryside, its rolling hills and leafless trees all painted with Jack Frost's silvery brush. Straining her eyes, she sought any sign of coastline, of water—was this not an island?—but the sun sparkling against the landscape blinded her and she was forced to give it up. At least two days, probably three, to get to their destination. A somewhat larger island, then, than the one to which she was accustomed.

At midmorning they stopped to change horses, and as they dismounted to take refreshment at the inn, Tempest approached Hannah to persuade her to join them inside the coach, unable to bear the thought of leaving the young woman outside in the freezing air any longer.

"Yes, miss?" Hannah curtsied as she approached, turning laughingly away from some remark the coachman had made. Framed by her hood and long woolen scarf, her pink cheeks and twinkling eyes did not suggest discomfort. And the air did not seem quite so bitter as it had at first light. Aware, suddenly, that she would be depriving the maid of other sources of comfort—the coachman's witty, flirtatious banter, and whatever it was in the flask he had tucked into his coat as Tempest had approached—she swallowed her offer for the time being and passed off her interruption with some nonsensical question about their route.

When the journey resumed, Mrs. Beauchamp was wide awake and eager to make up for the morning's silence. "Henry says last night's hard freeze was really quite a blessing, for without it the road would have been shockingly muddy. Though, of course, we have the frost to thank for the ruts and bumps, I suppose," she said as she climbed in and settled a blanket around their laps and a hot brick at their feet. Caliban burrowed his way into the tent created by their knees. "And the innkeeper's wife thinks it far too cold to snow now—too clear, you know, which I'll own is a bit of a disappointment. Ah well, it's for the best. So pretty, but not to be borne in a carriage. I'll wager we won't escape it entirely at this time of year. Though it really never does snow at Christmas in London. It always waits until January, when it's merely a nuisance and can't be enjoyed.

But I remember some of our Christmases with Mr. Beauchamp's family in Shropshire, sleighing and sledding and even snowball fights. The children began it, of course, but the adults were never slow to—"

Into this merry monologue, Tempest ventured a single, uncertain word. "Snow?"

"Yes, dear. Snow. Why surely you've—?"

But Tempest could only shake her head. She had heard the word before, and read it, too, but it might as well have been a word in a language she did not speak. Having nothing to associate with it, its meaning, its significance had eluded her grasp.

"Of course you wouldn't know. How silly of me! Well, snow is . . . not rain, but little flakes—"

"Like dust?" Tempest suggested. "Or ash?" Digging through her memory, she recalled Edward once telling her the drifts of white sand along the beaches put him in mind of snow—she must have filed the comparison away without fully understanding it.

"Much prettier. And colder, of course." Emily shook her head and folded her hands in her lap. "I think you'll just have to see it for yourself. Though I'm almost never at a loss for words, I frequently find myself without the right ones."

To that, Tempest could not concur. One heard stories of the Irish gift for gab, as well as their propensity for making bulls, of course—those characteristic errors that struck an English ear as comical. For all her bustling, fumbling manner, however, Emily Beauchamp was, in fact, quite silver-tongued. How else to explain that she had managed to talk both her son and Tempest into doing exactly what each had said they would never do?

Tempest had already forgiven her for that slightly duplicitous scene on the stairs. An apoplexy might not be imminent, but she knew the woman's heartache was real enough. Oh, how she wished that Andrew would live up to his mother's hopes for him. But she feared it was a wish destined to remain unfulfilled.

It was far more likely that Sir Barton Harper would grant her request to free his slaves. And *that*, as she very well knew, was not likely at all.

"What ought I to expect of Christmas in Yorkshire, do you suppose?" Tempest asked, no longer thinking of the weather.

Emily considered the question for a moment. "Is it a large family or small?"

"Oh, small. My mother was Sir Barton Harper's only child. A distant cousin is to inherit the baronetcy."

"And your grandfather's health?"

"Quite poor, I believe," she said, recalling Lord Nathaniel's oft-expressed concerns. "Certainly, he is no longer a young man."

"Nevertheless, I suspect he will be delighted to see you," insisted Emily, "to know you. I am sure he has felt the separation from his family keenly."

Beneath the weight of her heavy cloak, Tempest shifted her shoulders. "If he has, he must know he has only himself to blame."

"There was some cause other than distance for the estrangement between your parents and your grandfather, then?" Emily ventured after a moment.

"My father always ascribed it to Sir Barton's foolish pride," Tempest replied honestly. "Papa and Mama met at a performance of *A Midsummer Night's Dream* in Drury Lane and fell head over heels in love—at least, so Papa told the story to me. Both knew her father would disapprove of her marrying someone whose fortune had been made in trade. When Sir Barton refused his consent, they were not to be dissuaded, however."

"How romantic," cried Emily. " 'The course of true love never did run smooth.' "

Tempest managed a slight smile. "No, I suppose not."

"How did they end up in the West Indies?"

"Some months after they eloped, a circumstance arose in Antigua that required Sir Barton's personal attention, but he was reluctant to go. My father offered to go in his place, and his proposal was eagerly accepted—at least, until my mother announced she meant to go with him." The rumble of the carriage muffled her sigh. "Mama died four years later, never having returned home."

That part of the story earned a *tsk* of sympathy from Emily.

"My grandfather had been content enough to allow Papa to manage his business affairs, but he had never really forgiven him for taking his daughter away. He cut off all communication," Tempest continued, determined to see out the story to its end. "Many years later, when Papa grew ill, he wrote and told my grandfather he had named him my guardian, but even that was insufficient to earn his lasting attention. I had a letter from him, nothing more. As I never intended to visit England, I accepted that I would never know him."

"Yet, now you will. And who knows?" The usual twinkle had returned to Emily's hazel eyes. "You may learn that something else entirely lay behind the rift. Perhaps his grief made him ill, or there were other letters that were written but never made their way to you. Perhaps he has been pining for his granddaughter all these years."

"Perhaps. Or perhaps I shall find him exactly as he has been painted—difficult, callous, and proud." With a sigh, Tempest turned back toward the window, studying a landscape that no longer sparkled with frost but whose colors had been leached by its passing. To her eye, everything seemed gray and faded, so different from the intense blues and greens of home that she began to wonder if her memory could be trusted. Antigua was such a long way away. "I ought not to have allowed you to persuade me to this journey against my better judgment," she murmured, hardly even aware she had spoken the words aloud.

"What worries you so, my dear?"

Tempest turned her gazing from the passing scenery. "I worry most about those I have left behind. Their futures depend on me. What if something happens while I am gone, some disaster that my presence might have averted?" she suggested, imagining all sorts of grim possibilities, especially if, in fact, Edward was no longer at his post. "Or what if I have jeopardized their happiness by coming here? What if . . . what if my grandfather is displeased with me and decides to alter his will?"

A frown wrinkled Emily's brow. "I don't understand. What would make him do such a thing?"

"I promised Papa that when I inherited Harper's Hill, I would free the slaves. It was his dying wish," she explained, seeing Emily's surprise, "but beyond that, I believe it is the right thing to do. It may ruin the value of the estate. It may, as the plantation manager has warned me, put me at personal risk. But I cannot stand by and see human lives destroyed just so we may put rum in our punch and sugar in our tea."

Emily reached across the carriage and took Tempest's hand in hers. "And you fear that if your grandfather learns this, he will think better of his decision to leave the plantation to you?"

Not trusting herself to speak, Tempest nodded.

"Then the less said, the better," Emily advised. "You are under no obligation to tell him your plans. 'Discretion is the better part of valor,'" she quoted.

The words were surprisingly calming, reminding her of the way Papa had invoked Shakespeare at every opportunity. "I do sometimes find it difficult to hold my tongue about the matter," Tempest confessed.

"I have noticed a tendency to be forthcoming," said Emily, diplomatically. "You are very firm in your opinions for such a young person."

Tempest smiled. "Stubborn, you mean. Yes, I suppose I am."

"It would seem to be a family characteristic."

"In more families than one, I dare say."

Emily looked momentarily taken aback, then laughed. "I blame my first husband for the stubborn streak you have observed in my son . . ."

"I was not thinking of him," Tempest demurred, somewhat dishonestly. "I was thinking of the admirable determination you have shown in managing Beauchamp Shipping."

"If I have been determined, it has always been on Andrew's behalf," she insisted.

Tempest wished suddenly she had not encouraged the conversation in this direction. Her mind and her heart were full enough already.

"He left home—ran away—at seventeen," Emily said, a faraway look in her eye, "convinced he could never follow in his stepfather's footsteps, determined to seek justice for his father." A pause. "Mr. Beauchamp would have, could have, put a stop to it. The ship was his, after all. I hardly knew which was the right course of action. In the end . . . I let him go, believing he would find his way back to me."

"And he has."

"You must think me impossibly naïve for believing he will stay now, merely because I wish it."

"I think you have proved yourself remarkably adept at making others dance to your tune," she said with another small smile, unable quite to deny Emily's words. It was not naïveté, exactly, but rather faith in the power of love to change another's character, and Tempest could not share her faith.

"To be perfectly honest, my recent successes are unprecedented. I am far more accustomed to find that no one is listening."

"You must wonder how you persuaded me, then," Tempest said, dredging up a self-deprecating laugh from somewhere deep inside. The carriage rattled over a particularly deep rut, and Caliban gave a groan of disapproval when the women's knees knocked together. Weary suddenly of his blanket fortress, he rose, shook off his covering, and set his chin on her knees, nudging her hand for attention.

Emily watched with interest, her head tilted to one side. "No," she said finally, and Tempest felt herself blush beneath her scrutiny. "I believe I have some idea of what tipped the balance."

"Caliban!"

Andrew paused, listening for the sound of claws ticking across the entryway. Hearing nothing, he thundered down the stairs and shouted again. Where had the dog gotten to?

When a search of the house turned up nothing, he stepped into the back garden and gave another call. It would be just like Williams, who had been looking along his fastidious nose at the dog ever since their arrival, to have put Cal out on the coldest night of the year. If he found the dog tied in the stables, the man would be lucky not to spend the next week there himself.

"He's g-gone, sir."

Andrew whipped around, seeking the source of the voice. Caesar stood in the doorway behind him, shivering.

"Gone? Gone where?" Suddenly aware of the biting cold, he ushered the boy back inside and down the steps into the kitchen, where a blast of welcome heat greeted them both. "Did he run off? Or did someone take him?" he asked, eyeing the staff. Every face but Williams's bore traces of alarm. The butler merely looked affronted at the intrusion.

"Missy Tempest took 'im. I saw it all from this window," Caesar piped up, motioning to the clouded glass through which one could just glimpse the mews.

"*Took* him?"

"Well, she didn't *call* 'im," Caesar corrected, "he just—"

"Followed her," Andrew finished from between clenched teeth, a sound that sent most of the servants scurrying to their duties, or in search of a place to hide. "Damn it all."

"Sir!" cried Williams, looking even more injured, if such a thing were possible.

"Call for a cab," Andrew ordered.

Williams did not move, but Caesar leapt to attention, his dark eyes bright. "You goin' after 'im?"

"His duty lies in the City," the butler reminded archly, making Andrew wonder if his stepfather's will had stipulated a sinecure for the man, or if he was allowed to send him packing.

"That may be, Williams, but this morning, I am bound for... Hampstead," he said, naming the first place he could think of that was neither where he should be nor where he wanted to be.

"Hampstead, sir?"

"Aye," Andrew confirmed, somewhat reluctantly. What on earth had inspired him to say it?

Mumbling the destination repeatedly under his breath so as not to forget it, Caesar left in search of a cab.

As the hack carried him away from the house, Andrew realized he had no more specific direction to give, really no more specific direction in mind. When the village drew in sight, however, he called for the driver to stop and simply wandered until he found an overgrown rose garden, which Jeremiah Bewick was attempting to tame in his shirtsleeves, despite the cold.

If Bewick were not such a familiar figure, Andrew would have imagined he had found the wrong cottage. The idea of the grizzled quartermaster contentedly—or at least willingly—gardening in a bucolic country village was comical. Or would have been, once upon a time. Now, however, it struck Andrew with all the force of his mother's slap across the face. It had always seemed to him that love demanded great sacrifices—expected him to do what he did not want to do, be a man he could never be. But perhaps, when one loved, some of those things ceased to be sacrifices. Maybe love helped a person become his better self.

"Never expected to see you in this neck of the woods," Bewick said before Andrew could speak. He laid his clippers aside and stepped to open the garden gate. "Summat I can do for you?"

Andrew could not ever remember having sought out advice before. But he desperately needed some now. "I think," he said, ducking his head beneath the wrought-iron trellis, "I think it's more a question for Beals."

"Ah," replied Bewick, sounding ever so slightly disappointed at being deprived of an excuse to abandon his task. He picked up the clippers once more and gestured with them as he spoke. "Go in through the back, then. First door on your right. Geoff's fixed 'imself a laboratory. Best knock first, though."

Picturing smoking vials or jars of pickled specimens, Andrew was relieved when his knock was answered by a bespectacled Beals, dressed much as he always had been and carrying nothing more alarming than a thick book. Bewick might call it a laboratory, but the room looked to him very little different than a smaller, snugger version of his stepfather's library.

"Why, what a pleasant surprise. What brings you here, Cap'n?"

Andrew didn't correct him; it was almost a relief to hear the old form of address again. "I wanted . . ." he began, then stopped. How to put his question into words?

He had known it was necessary to put distance between himself and Tempest, whatever the cost. But as the carriage had rolled away this morning, he had realized that those two hundred miles or so would be at once too far and not far enough.

Far enough to fray the tie that ensnared them. Not far enough to snap it cleanly in two.

Could the constant pull he already felt do some sort of internal damage? Tear his heart right out of his chest?

And she had even had the temerity to take his dog . . .

"I wanted to see how you and Bewick had situated yourselves," Andrew said instead. "I'm glad to see you've put him to work."

Beals smiled. "It was time for a break from the sea. Wears a man down, after a time. Changes him, and not always for the better."

"Ye-es," Andrew acknowledged, hesitation stretching the word. Was it possible Bewick had grown as weary of chasing Stratton as he? "Though he tells me he plans to sail with the *Colleen* again when she's fit."

"We'll see." Beals gave a thoughtful nod. "Sometimes a man changes his mind. For instance, Jeremiah tells me you've agreed to take up the helm of Beauchamp Shipping rather than another of its ships." Outside the window, the gossiping quartermaster was back at work. Andrew watched Bewick for a moment, feeling Beals's eyes on him all the while.

"I'm sure he claimed that rose garden was for me," Beals continued. "But I knew he couldn't bear to be idle. And it gives me a chance to work on that paper about yellow fever. Likely naught'll come from it, since I'm a mere surgeon, no one for the physicians and Royal Society chaps to heed. But I mean to give it my best."

"Your experience will do you credit," Andrew insisted. "In fact, it is your medical expertise I've come to consult."

"Sit, then. Sit," Beals said, gesturing toward a chair already drawn close to a cozy fire.

As Andrew settled into the comfortably worn cushions, the scent of Bewick's tobacco rose from them, and he felt suddenly ashamed of intruding on the two men's sanctuary, merely because he could not bear to be alone with himself.

"And how is the boy, Caesar?" Beals asked, seating himself opposite.

"Well, very well. I had thoughts of training him as a valet, but I think his true calling is in the kitchen. At least, I find him there more often than not."

"'Tis bound to be the warmest room in the house," Beals said with a laugh. "What of Miss Holderin? Already on her way back to the West Indies, I suppose?"

Andrew drummed his fingers on the arm of the chair, then wished he could snatch the betraying gesture back. "She is . . . also well. She and my mother are on their way to Yorkshire this very morning, a Christmas visit to Miss Holderin's grandfather."

"Oh?" Beals raised a brow. "I understood she meant to return home immediately."

"I—that is, she—we—"

"Say no more." Beals laughed again and raised a staying hand. "A perfectly understandable change of plans, under the circumstances."

"And which circumstances would those be?" snapped Andrew.

"Why, proximity, for one," Beals replied, unruffled. "Even if she did not mean to be in this part of the world, she's here now and likely won't be again for some time. And some folks think of Christmas as a time for family, setting aside old differences, that sort of thing."

"Yes, of course," Andrew agreed, relieved. "I imagined you meant—no matter."

They sat together in silence for several minutes after that, until Beals cleared his throat and prompted, "A medical matter, you say? *You* are well, I trust?"

"Well enough."

"And your mother? She must have been overjoyed at your return. I hope it wasn't too much for her heart."

"She seems strong enough," Andrew said, not conscious he had raised his hand to his face until he felt the chill of his own fingers against his cheek. "Though I suppose it might be difficult to tell . . ." His voice trailed off and he finally shrugged and muttered under his breath, "delicate condition."

The phrase startled Beals into a more upright position. He took off his spectacles, polished them against his waistcoat, then threaded them over his ears once more, as if a smudge on one of the lenses had somehow interfered with his hearing. "Did you say 'delicate condition'? I believe I must've misunderstood you, Cap'n. Surely you didn't mean to suggest that your mother is—er—? That is, she can no longer be a *young* woman, beggin' your pardon."

"My mother? In a delicate—? No. Good God, man. I was speaking of the sex in more general terms. Fragile. Prone to mysterious maladies."

Beals's lips appeared to try out several replies before his voice joined in. "Er—yes. I—I gather that's true. Never had many female patients, myself."

"Oh." As if disappointment were a physical weight, Andrew slid further down in the chair. "No. Of course you haven't."

"Still," Beals said, studying his posture with one raised brow, "I rather think I know enough to answer a simple question or two, if something is preying on your mind, lad. Some worry about your mother, or . . . well, any other lady of your acquaintance."

He must know. And Bewick, too. Likely the whole crew of the *Fair Colleen* knew. Or if they did not *know*, they surely suspected. They would've been fools *not* to suspect. And Andrew had never made a habit of sailing with fools.

Pushing himself out of the chair, Andrew stood and began to pace. "How soon does one know for certain if a woman is with child?" he asked when he paused before the window, feigning interest in the frost-coated shrubbery. Bewick had disappeared from sight.

"Your . . . your sister you're worrying about, is it?" Beals asked.

Andrew turned sharply. "Sister? I haven't any—" he began and then stopped. The man surely knew he had no sister, and a single glance confirmed it. They stared at one another for a long moment, until Andrew tipped his chin instead and muttered, "Aye."

"Then your concern is understandable. Understandable. Well, now, confirming a pregnancy can be a tricky case. The quickening—

when the babe begins to move—is the surest sign, although many a woman will say she knows much sooner."

"When her courses cease."

Beals looked surprised by his knowledge. "That is one symptom, yes."

"So, within a very few weeks, even a month or so, a woman may begin to suspect—" His voice was rising, in spite of himself. Seeking a distraction, he picked up a glass specimen case containing a half-dozen mosquitos, fat with blood.

"She may," Beals interjected, calm as always, "but there are other conditions that may disrupt her usual cycle. A strain on the body, lack of proper nutrition, an illness—"

"Seasickness?" he asked, forgetting for a moment his determination to be discreet.

"If the case were severe enough, perhaps," he admitted. "Such as Miss Holderin experienced, for instance . . ."

"Who said anything of Miss Holderin?"

"I meant nothing by it, lad," Beals said soothingly, shaking his balding head as he lifted the fragile box from Andrew's fingers and replaced it safely on a shelf. "Just a—a familiar case, I suppose you'd say. A point of reference. In a situation where a young woman has undergone something stressful, some brief disruption of her courses is normal and no cause to assume a pregnancy. Have I answered your question?"

Before Andrew could reply, the door swung open and Bewick entered, carrying a tea tray and wearing—*good God*—an apron over his clothes. His eyes met Andrew's on the far side of the room, but neither one spoke, as if they had come to some prior agreement that comments about Bewick's unaccustomed domesticity were off-limits. Which, of course, they were. After so many years, Andrew had imagined he knew these two men—that they were rebels and rogues like himself. As they all stood together in a cozy room in a rose-covered cottage in Hampstead, however, such labels no longer seemed fitting. Perhaps they never had been.

"Join us for a cup?" Beals offered, indicating the chair Andrew had vacated, the one that was so obviously Jeremiah Bewick's usual place of repose.

"I cannot," he demurred, stepping toward the door as Bewick moved further into the room. "I have taken up enough of your time."

"An' he's got a business to run," Bewick added, setting down the tray with a clatter.

Andrew nodded absently. He had been assuming his fate was already decided, but Beals had given him reason to believe that Tempest might not be carrying his child after all. And if he were not to be bound to her, he supposed he need not be tied to a desk in Mincing Lane, either.

"For the time being, at any rate," he agreed with a nod as he let himself out.

All the way home, the surgeon's words swirled in his brain, producing an occasional twinge—of relief, he told himself, not regret.

No, certainly not regret.

Chapter 16

By the time they reached Yorkshire, the weather had changed dramatically. Not colder, as had been promised, but warmer—warm enough that Emily had thrown off her share of the lap blanket, Tempest had been persuaded to put down her hood, and the sound of mud sucking at the carriage wheels filled their nervous ears. Hannah had long since abandoned her perch beside the coachman in favor of a place inside, her visions of romance sullied by the droplets of mud being flung up by the horses' hooves, spattering her clothes, her face, and her hair.

So it was that all three women sat crowded together in the carriage—along with a regrettably dirty Caliban, who had managed to break free of Tempest's hold at their last stop to chase the innkeeper's cat—when the coach turned and made its way along the narrow lane that ended at Crosslands Park.

Once London-born Hannah had turned up her nose at the square-built stone manor house surrounded by moorland, she abandoned her position at the window to Tempest, who was left to imagine what kind of life her grandfather lived in what looked to her to be an entirely lifeless place. Emily had written to warn of their arrival, but Tempest had been unwilling to wait for a reply, and she suddenly wondered whether they would even find him at home. Only a thin wraith of smoke winding its way from the central chimney block indicated the house was inhabited at all.

But when the carriage wheels crunched across the gravel sweep and rolled to a stop in front of the pillared portico, a groom trotted out from somewhere to assist the coachman with the horses while a dark-suited butler opened one of the double doors and bowed them into the house.

"I will let Sir Barton know you have arrived."

While he went on his errand, a footman took their wraps, and a maid materialized to show Hannah to the rooms that had been assigned to them. Tempest hardly noticed the disappearances. Her attention was entirely taken up with searching the paneled entry hall for some sign of her grandfather. Only when Emily laid a hand on her arm and indicated with a nod that the butler had returned and they were to follow him upstairs, did she understand he did not mean to come to welcome them.

Although the man shared Williams's unapproachably erect carriage and serious expression, Tempest nonetheless ventured a question. "My grandfather is . . . well?"

"His health is what it ever has been, ma'am," was all the butler's reply before they stopped at a paneled door, which he opened with the words, "Miss Holderin and Mrs. Beauchamp, sir," and left them.

Tempest closed her eyes and steeled herself for a very old man, dour, an invalid perhaps, confined to a chair near the fire. When she had gathered sufficient courage to look into the room, she found she had been right in one respect. He *was* beside the hearth. Hanging above him was a life-sized portrait in oils, the baronet in tweeds with his gun over his shoulder and a pack of leggy pointers milling around his knees. The painting was not recent, but one glance lower confirmed that very little had changed.

Her grandfather stood with one arm leaning against the elegantly carved mantelpiece, although anyone could see he did not require the support. He reminded her of no one so much as the *Fair Colleen*'s quartermaster, Mr. Bewick—just as wiry, if somewhat less weathered, with white hair that might once have been ginger.

As if he were unaccustomed to company, or at least uncertain how to greet these particular guests, he waited until Emily and Tempest had made their way to the center of the room before coming forward a few steps to meet them.

"Mrs. Beauchamp," he said with a bow, and Emily dipped a curtsy.

"Grandfather," Tempest said, stretching out her hands.

He did not immediately take them. Instead he studied her features by the wintry afternoon light spilling into the room from a pair of tall windows. "So very like my Angela," he murmured, almost to himself. For a moment, she imagined he might embrace her. When he instead took a step backward, she dropped her arms to her sides, embarrassed by her impulsive gesture. "Why, it's as if Thomas Holderin contributed no part of you," he added after further scrutiny, a note of relief in his voice. "Except, of course, that ridiculous name."

The breath she had been holding whooshed from her lungs, leaving her momentarily light-headed. "Yes, Grandfather. I am Tempest," she said and curtsied.

"I hope our arrival has not come as a shock to you," Emily said, diverting his attention.

"No," he said with an expression that hinted at displeasure. "I received your letter. Although I had already been alerted to your intentions a week or so ago by a piece of correspondence from Mr. Cary."

"Edward wrote to you?"

Her grandfather's eyes snapped back to her face, disapproval—perhaps at her familiar form of address for an employee—now etched into his features. "He did." Without shifting his gaze, he reached into the breast of his coat and withdrew a folded paper. "His letter also enclosed this. For you."

Tempest did not know her hand was trembling until she touched the paper and made it flutter. Were her grandfather's fingers cold or warm? She did not reach forward far enough to find out. "Thank you."

"How long do you plan to stay?"

Before she could answer with anything like the truth—that she could be gone as soon as the carriage could be made ready—Caliban burst into the room, indifferent to the butler's shout and easily eluding the arm that grabbed through the doorway to stop him. Paws and belly coated with mud, mostly dried, he scouted out the room, sniffing here and there before making his way not to Tempest's side, but to her grandfather's. Stopping before the man, he sat abruptly, raised one paw, and gave a sharp bark of greeting.

"Caliban!" she and Emily gasped in unison.

But Sir Barton looked more curious than perturbed. "And who is this fine fellow?" He leaned forward to shake the offered paw, ignoring the dirt. Though his face was partly hidden from view, Tempest could have sworn he smiled. Flicking her gaze from the man and dog standing before her to the portrait above the fire and back again, she felt amazement give way to understanding—and perhaps just a hint of envy. If only her arrival had inspired such a warm welcome.

Emily, however, seized the unexpected discovery of Sir Barton's soft spot as an opportunity. "We mean to stay through Christmas, Sir Barton," she interjected in her coaxing, musical voice. "If it's quite convenient. Your granddaughter is looking forward to getting to know you."

"You are Irish," he said, turning his head toward her without rising, disregarding her words in favor of the accent with which they had been spoken. Tempest could not decide whether there was a criticism implicit in the observation. Emily merely dipped her head in assent.

"Mrs. Beauchamp's son captained the ship on which I sailed from Antigua," Tempest explained, hoping the connection would satisfy him and preclude any awkward questions about her chaperone for the voyage.

Sir Barton considered this piece of information before at last returning Emily's bob with one of his own. "Then I suppose I am in his debt," he said, straightening at last, though his hand still rested on the dog's ears. "You must wish to rest after your long journey. Porter will show you to your rooms."

Accepting his instructions as dismissal, Tempest turned to leave. Caliban's ears pricked up and his warm brown eyes followed her to the door, though his body did not. As her foot crossed the threshold, her grandfather spoke again, and she hesitated, though she could not face him. "We keep country hours," he added unapologetically. "Dinner will be served promptly at four." With a sharp nod of acknowledgment, she threaded her arm through Emily's and nearly dragged her through the door.

Porter, the butler, was waiting outside the room for them and led them silently to an upper floor. From the doorway, Tempest took stock of the first room he showed them. Painted a soft blue and trimmed in ivory, Emily's suite overlooked the front of the house, the gravel sweep, and the double line of bare-limbed trees that marched out of sight, to the place where the drive met the road. Hannah was already there, unpacking.

When Porter gestured to a door on the opposite side of the corridor, Tempest hesitated. "Go on, then," Emily said with a smile. "You must want a moment to yourself. To read your letter." She nodded toward the crumpled paper Tempest had forgotten she still held in her hand.

"Yes, of course," Tempest lied and turned to follow the butler's lead.

Porter opened the door on a chamber somewhat larger than the one that had been given to Mrs. Beauchamp, decorated in a cheery floral motif, with painted sprays of violets, smiling pansies, and bright primroses adorning the papered walls. The frosty air of the room, however, threatened to nip the bloom from those buds. A fire had been lit, but too recently to have driven away the chill and the damp of disuse.

As soon as she was alone, she hurried to the fireplace and sank down beside it—not in one of the curving chairs upholstered with damask roses that framed it so pleasantly, but right on the hearthstone, craving the heat.

She ought never to have come. This cold house, that cold man—there was nothing for her here. The memory of her mother she carried in her face had only served to remind him of his hatred of her dear papa. Twenty years of bitterness had not made him weak and ill, as she had always imagined. They had merely hardened his heart.

Wishing she could crawl past the fire irons and into the flame like a salamander, she drew her knees against her chest instead and heard once more the crinkle of paper as her fingers curled around Edward's letter. She did not know whether she could bear to read his words, could stomach whatever paltry excuse he would offer for sending her to this terrible place.

To her surprise, the letter was still sealed. Even curiosity did not melt her grandfather's stern reserve, it seemed. Opposite the seal, *Miss Holderin* was written in the same neat hand that filled the account books of Harper's Hill. Its formality made her hesitate.

But when she had slid her nail under the wafer of wax and unfolded a single sheet dense with ink, the first words to greet her were more familiar:

> *My dear Tempest—*
> *If this letter has reached you, you are at Crosslands Park and under the care of your grandfather, so I shall pretend an ease I do not yet feel and write as if you are safe at long last. I hope that rascal Corrvan took good care of the precious cargo with which he was entrusted.*
> *I know I cannot expect, perhaps do not deserve, your forgiveness for disregarding your wishes and arranging for you*

to be taken away. Yet I cannot count myself entirely in the wrong. I did what I believed your blessed father would have wanted done.

Two hot tears spilled over her lashes and spattered the paper, smearing words she had yet to read. Ridiculous, really, to talk of forgiveness. Dear Edward was too honorable ever to do anything that he did not think was best. Of course she would forgive him. Eventually. But forgiveness would not erase her fury. He should certainly expect to feel her anger when he saw her again.

She would not nurse her anger until it made her as cold and unfeeling as her grandfather, however. Dashing unshed tears from her eyes, she returned to the letter.

> *Believe me, my dearest friend—my more than sister—I could never have borne to send you off if I did not believe the danger here was real, and graver than you seemed capable of imagining. If past experience is any predictor, you will even now be plotting your return to Antigua. I must urge you not to be rash. With you in England, under watchful eyes, Lord Nathaniel will find it impossible to force a marriage, impossible to connive and deprive you of the inheritance that must come into your hands, your gentle hands, and none other's.*

In that way, at least, she was better off than Edward could have hoped. Here she sat in Yorkshire—safe, to be sure, but sound? Little could Edward have imagined how the trip he had laid out would threaten her peace of mind. The warmth of which her oldest friend had deprived her by sending her on this voyage had very little to do with the change in climate.

But that was not entirely fair. She had known warmth in the weeks since leaving Antigua. Which had only added to her problems. Heat still pooled in secret places and flared in her cheeks whenever she thought of Andrew's touch.

It was to that forbidden warmth she owed her greatest anxiety. Every day that ticked by made it more difficult to ignore the very real possibility that she might be carrying Andrew's child. By itself, the idea did not frighten her as much as it probably ought. If necessary, she would find a way to manage without a husband, even if it meant fabricating one who had died on the journey back to Antigua. Only a faux marriage would protect the inheritance that, as Edward warned, must come into her hands and no one else's. Even Andrew was a risk: She could not tie herself to a man who would inevitably resent being tied down.

Then again, if there were a child, that tie would exist between them, whether they had solemnized it or not.

Oh, how foolish to parse the future in that way. The tie was already there, with or without a child. No matter if it *should* be so. And because of it, she who had lived her life to ensure the freedom of others would never be free again.

No, Edward decidedly would *not* approve of the way the captain had handled the cargo with which he had been entrusted.

Before she could resume reading, Hannah entered from the dressing room. Reluctantly, Tempest rose from the floor, folded the half-finished letter, and tucked it away in a little writing desk a few steps from the hearth. "I suppose it is time to dress for dinner?"

"Yes, miss," replied the maid with a rather saucy bob. "Only I didn't know which dress you'd like."

"Which dress?" Tempest glanced down at the skirt of her traveling dress, speckled with mud and thick with dog hair. "I cannot wear this. That leaves only one other."

"Didn't Mrs. Beauchamp tell you, miss? Come and see."

Tempest followed Hannah into the dressing room and saw a gown of dark red brocade picked out with gold thread that shimmered and sparked like wine in a crystal goblet. As her eyes darted from hem to bodice, she felt Hannah watching her, waiting for her reaction. The maid no doubt expected tears of joy, but Tempest felt on the verge of shedding tears of frustration.

"The blue, please." Each word was as expressionless as she could make it, the terseness itself coloring her answer more than she had intended.

Hannah looked as if she would like to argue, but she managed to swallow her disappointment and helped her to wash and dress. Although Hannah had trimmed her cropped hair into something slightly more stylish, it required little attention, so Tempest was ready and waiting when Mrs. Beauchamp came to walk with her to dinner.

She expected Emily to offer some words of wisdom about dealing with her grandfather, or to ask after the contents of Edward's letter.

Instead she said, with a contrite, nervous smile, "Can you forgive me? About the dress, I mean."

"You shouldn't have," Tempest began to scold. Had she had even an inkling of Emily's plan, she would never have countenanced such an expense or indulged herself in such a fashion. When Emily's face fell, however, Tempest's heart sank with it. Today ought to have taught her a lesson about implacability. "But it *is* lovely," she whispered and squeezed her friend's hand.

Together, they made their way to the dining room and stopped to wait for the footman to open the door. Sir Barton's voice could be heard within, although to whom he spoke was not immediately clear. Not a servant. Her grandfather did not seem the sort who entertained his neighbors. Who could be joining them, then? At first the thought of a stranger at dinner irritated her. But really, was her grandfather any less a stranger to her? Perhaps a fourth would help smooth the conversation.

With a firm grip on Emily's arm and a smile stretched across her lips, she stepped across the threshold, her eyes seeking her grandfather. The room was large, stately, with bronze-colored draperies, sparkling chandeliers, and a table that might seat twenty. At last she spotted him on the far end of the table's polished mahogany length, standing near the sideboard, handing a glass of bloodred wine to his guest. As she followed the movement of the goblet to its destination, her knees buckled.

"Why, Miss Holderin, is something the matter?" Emily gasped, plying her other arm around her waist to steady her.

Tempest straightened and shook her head, as if she could wish away what she saw. Surely, her eyes must be playing tricks on her. Fatigue. Or the false glow of too few candles.

Because it looked from here for all the world as if Lord Nathaniel Delamere had come back from the dead.

If all had gone according to schedule, they were in Yorkshire. At this very moment, Tempest might be in her grandfather's welcoming embrace, rethinking her decision to fly away at the first opportunity. Perhaps, even now, the miracle his mother had promised was beginning to take shape . . .

Thud.

Farrow dropped another stack of ledgers on the center of the desk, turning an already tottering pile into an avalanche.

Andrew lifted one brow. "Mrs. Beauchamp read all these, did she, before talking with Milligan about the West India docks project?"

"Not all at once, sir," Farrow explained with a sniff of disapproval that made Andrew wonder whether he and Williams were somehow related. "She had some years with which to familiarize herself with their contents."

"Ah."

Choosing a volume at random, Andrew thumbed through its pages. Each book was a chapter in an ongoing saga of profit and loss, and truth be told, the story interested him more than he had imagined it would. He'd already looked at the maps, walked to the suggested site one damp morning, read Milligan's proposal to the board. The case for the new docks was clear and convincing, but like his mother, Andrew still felt some niggling doubt. If the plan failed, investors like Beauchamp Shipping stood to lose far more than they gained. With public support for the project, however, the risk could be dispersed among all those who stood to benefit from better access to the goods brought from corners of the globe to the pounding heart of Britain's economy.

While he chewed over the likelihood of securing such support, he heard a commotion in the outer office. In another moment, the doorway was filled by the broad-shouldered frame of Frederick Clarkson, admiral in His Majesty's Navy.

"Now, that's a sight I never thought I'd see," boomed Clarkson in his laughing baritone, stepping forward to take Andrew's outstretched hand.

"A sight a great many men never thought they'd see," Andrew conceded. "Myself included."

Suddenly embarrassed by the disorder in front of him and wishing for some distraction, he began to stack the ledgers. Farrow clucked and immediately began rearranging Andrew's feeble efforts according to some other organizational scheme.

"What's all this?" Clarkson asked, his eye drawn to the desktop by their movements.

"The West India Merchants have it in mind to build a new dock for ships coming in from the Caribbean. I've been weighing the strengths and weaknesses of such a scheme."

"Well, you're well-suited to the task, I'd say. Some of those chaps have never even set foot on a merchant ship, I'll wager. You've done a sight more than that."

"Aye," Andrew acknowledged absently.

"You can set 'em straight as to what would work for their ships and what wouldn't, what the real risks would be. They're too used to dealing with numbers on paper, rather than dealing with people," he said, folding his arms behind him and rocking back slightly on his heels. "'Course, most of them are men of property. Planters. Their motives might be rather different from yours. It'd be ideal if some of your adventures had parlayed into real connections in the islands, some arrangement that would make an overseer or a manager inclined to do business with Beauchamp alone. Then the others would sit up and take notice."

Andrew's first thought was of Tempest. He tried and failed to imagine them as mere business partners, tried and failed to imagine Cary agreeing on her behalf to the sort of contract Clarkson proposed.

Once his mind had been given permission to wander in her direction, of course, he had the devil's own luck trying to rein it in. He would like to witness firsthand her triumph at Harper's Hill. He would like, just once more, to see her in her native environment. Those copper curls under a Caribbean sun, the scent of jasmine in the air, on her skin.

Could doing his duty by Beauchamp Shipping give him an excuse to maintain some connection with her even after she returned to Antigua? And if it did, should he?

"I've been thinking a great deal about the slave trade of late," he said after a moment. "Or, more accurately, the abolition of it. Will it happen, do you think?" He had been pleased to discover, in his perusal of the books, that Daniel's ethics had kept Beauchamp Shipping out of the trade, despite its profitability.

Clarkson scratched his chin and considered the matter. "It'd be deuced hard to enforce—keep my boys busy, no doubt. And Wilberforce has been beaten back more than once." Andrew gave a reluctant nod of acknowledgment. The West India lobby, of which he must now consider himself a reluctant part, had proved powerful, while Parliament had been regrettably weak, despite the efforts of staunch abolitionists like William Wilberforce. "But his side's not out of it entirely," the admiral added. "It'll happen, I think. One day."

"That would change everything," Farrow interjected, a squeak of something like alarm in his voice.

"That it would," agreed Andrew. "That it would. Well, but you didn't come to talk business," he said to the admiral, rousing himself. "What brings you here?" he asked his unexpected visitor as he stepped away from the desk and left Farrow to his work.

"Merely hoping to see that the rumors were true," Clarkson replied, clapping Andrew on the shoulder the way he had done when Andrew was a boy, although he had to reach up to do it now.

It was on the tip of Andrew's tongue to caution him against hope, to explain that the arrangement was merely temporary, but the broad grin on the face of the man who had been one of his stepfather's dearest friends silenced his protest.

Then Clarkson's face sobered. "A pity Daniel isn't here to crow about it."

"A great pity."

"Not that he wasn't proud of you," Clarkson insisted. " 'My brave boy,' he used to say. He understood your desire to see the world. Well, of course he did. He shared it."

Genuinely taken back, Andrew could not speak.

"Why, when we were boys at school," Clarkson reminisced, "Daniel and I had grand plans to join the navy together. 'Course my future had already been decided, but he felt certain the sea was in his blood, too. He even asked his father to buy him a pair of colors. In the end, though, his mother forbade it. Said the risk was too great." His voice was tinged with regret. "Can't blame her, of course," he conceded, shaking off that long-ago disappointment. "It's a mother's duty to worry."

Andrew's head was spinning with the revelation. Was it possible Daniel had shared his father's wanderlust without indulging it? Was it possible that stern exterior had masked a face Andrew would otherwise have recognized in an instant, like looking in a mirror?

"He might have gone anyway," he pointed out when the answers to his inner questions proved uncomfortable.

"No," Clarkson demurred. "He started Beauchamp Shipping instead. Every shore leave I got, I knew I could find him right here, staring at that wall with a gleam in his eye," he said, gesturing toward the map of the world that filled one side of the office, dotted with red and blue and green pins marking the route of every Beauchamp ship. "Watched every ship that sailed off, every ship that returned. Fretted over those that didn't."

"Like the *Colleen*?" Andrew asked, speaking around a sudden ache in his throat.

"For one." Thankfully, Clarkson did not move his gaze from the map. "I hear she was shaken up a bit in her last voyage. Nasty storm, by all accounts."

"Aye." A fellow sailor would understand his taciturn response.

Indeed, the single word seemed to convey more to the admiral than any lengthy description could have done. "Well, you survived it," he said easily, after a moment. Another might have taken his tone for dismissive. "Part and parcel of your legend now."

Andrew swore he could actually hear Farrow's ears prick up with interest. "Leave the account books, if you please," he said, nodding toward the door with a gesture of dismissal for the manager. Although obviously disappointed, Farrow bowed and left, closing the door behind him. "My reputation has not preceded me into this office," Andrew said, turning back to Clarkson, "and I would prefer to keep it that way."

"Can't think why," Clarkson said, spurning Andrew's offer of a chair in favor of standing in a sailor's customary spread-legged stance, a position that many years had made more comfortable to him than sitting. "Say the word and I'll see that His Highness hears about your assistance in running all those Caribbean pirates to ground. Why, if you hadn't alerted us to their ships and their plans, think of the merchant vessels that might have been lost. Think of the risks you spared my men by telling us what you saw." After a slow shake of his head, he lifted his brows and added encouragingly, "There might be a knighthood in it, you know."

Andrew scoffed. "I doubt the king likes to hear an Irish name preceded by 'Sir.' Besides, you know my motives were hardly pure. It was all to find Stratton."

"If that were true, you would never have bothered with the rest."

Andrew balked. Certainly he had never thought of it that way. The discoveries had been incidental, their revelation a matter of dropping a word or two into the right ear in some dockside pub or an alley behind the wharves. Most often, the lips from which those words had dropped had not even belonged to Andrew. How the informing had been traced back to him was something of a mystery. Only Jeremiah Bewick had known it all, and he was as tight-lipped an old tar as any—

"*Damn* him," Andrew muttered under his breath.

The curse seemed a matter of perfect indifference to Clarkson. Or perhaps he had not even heard it, for he continued as if uninterrupted. "A pity you did not succeed."

"How's that?" Andrew snapped to attention, retracing the conversation. "Stratton is dead," he insisted. "The *Justice* went down in that storm. I watched it with my own eyes."

The admiral pressed his lips together and gave a compassionate nod. "It did that. But the *Vernon* picked up a couple of survivors from that wreck. Found 'em floating on a spar. Half-dead, to be sure. But not entirely."

"And was one of them Stratton?" Andrew demanded, taking a restless step toward the door.

Suddenly Admiral Clarkson's stiff authority gave way to sheepishness. He shrugged. "I can't say for certain, but based on the description I heard, old Lazarus had another resurrection up his sleeve. 'Course, he gave a false name, and the boys on the *Vernon* didn't recognize him. When they landed in Portsmouth, he disappeared."

"When?"

"A week ago."

A tremor started deep in Andrew's gut. Anger? Fear? Almost certainly some of both. "He might be anywhere by now."

"He might," Clarkson conceded. "But I have a theory."

"What's that?"

"What really brought you here?" the other man asked with a tip of his head toward the laden desktop.

The indirection caught Andrew off guard, and it took all his considerable strength to keep his hands at his sides, not to grab the admiral's gold-trimmed lapels and send him into the wall in an attempt to bring him back to the point. "Family ties," he ground out when he had found sufficient self-control to produce the words.

Love, his conscience whispered.

He had learned something about duty in the last few weeks. He had come here for his stepfather. For his mother. To see for himself if he could do this thing.

For Tempest.

"Just so," agreed Clarkson. "There's usually something that calls a man home after so long away. A wife. A child. Something draws a man back to his roots."

"You'd have me believe that Lazarus Stratton has a family somewhere?" Somehow Andrew had always imagined him having sprung from the murky depths, like some mythical sea beast.

"He does," the admiral insisted. "Or did, at least. In Hull."

"Hull. In Yorkshire."

"Don't know of another."

"Farrow!"

The bellow seemed to startle Clarkson. "You're not thinking of going after him?"

"No."

"Good, good," he said, visibly relieved. "It's only a theory. Might lead you on a wild goose chase. And by the looks of things, you're wanted here."

Farrow must have been standing quite near the door, because he was through it before the admiral had finished speaking. "Yes, sir?"

"Call for a hack. And send a message to Milligan telling him something's come up. I'll meet with him when I return." Something in Andrew's tone must have conveyed the seriousness of the matter. Farrow showed no sign of arguing, but turned around immediately and sent a clerk scurrying to the street for a cab.

"Just a minute, now," Clarkson cautioned. "You've just said you weren't thinking of going after him."

"I'm not *thinking* of it," Andrew said, shrugging into his greatcoat. "I'm doing it."

"See reason, my boy," the admiral urged. "Daniel Beauchamp—"

"This isn't about Daniel," Andrew cut across him. "Or my father," he added before Clarkson could. "This is for me. Now if you'll excuse me, sir," he said, brushing past him without waiting for a reply.

Still, he felt a hint of hesitation about the decision.

Yorkshire, he thought as he threw himself onto the hackney coach's worn seat. *Why did it have to be Yorkshire?*

Chapter 17

From across the dining room, Lord Nathaniel studied her. When he bowed in greeting, she pulled herself free from Emily's support and answered with a curtsy. If not recovered from her shock, she was nevertheless unwilling to supply him with further evidence of it. She had never fainted before. She did not intend to start now.

Slowly, she crossed the room with Emily and stopped before them. "Good evening, Grandfather."

"Lord Nathaniel arrived just yesterday," he explained. "When I told him you were expected, he insisted that I say nothing. It is a pleasant surprise to see an old family friend here, I trust?"

"It is a surprise," Tempest replied with a thin smile. Now that he was only a few feet from her, she could see that while he had indeed survived the storm, he had not escaped from his ordeal at sea entirely unharmed. A deep cut at his hairline was still healing, and when he took a step forward, he moved stiffly, with the slightest hint of a limp.

"You weren't worried, I hope?" Lord Nathaniel said.

"Indeed not."

"Won't you introduce me to your companion?"

Suddenly Tempest wished she had not revealed Mrs. Beauchamp's full identity to her grandfather. The last person she wanted to involve in this conversation was the captain of the *Fair Colleen*. "Of course. This is Mrs. Emily Beauchamp. Mrs. Beauchamp, Lord Nathaniel Delamere."

"A pleasure, my lord," Emily said with another curtsy.

"*Beauchamp*," Lord Nathaniel echoed thoughtfully. "Any relation to the Shropshire Beauchamps?"

"My late husband was brother to Lord Renfrew, yes."

Lord Nathaniel nodded approvingly, and Tempest breathed an inward sigh of relief. Then he asked, "And how do you know Miss Holderin?"

"Well—" Emily began.

"You might also recognize the name Beauchamp from the family shipping line," Tempest spoke over her. "I sailed from Antigua on a Beauchamp ship."

"Yes, I know. Word of your—departure spread quickly through English Harbour."

No one in the room knew Lord Nathaniel Delamere well enough to recognize the warmth in his eyes and his voice as anger. No one, that was, but Tempest. She forced herself to take a step closer to him. "I did not know you also had plans to travel," she said. "I hope you did not do so out of concern for me. As you can see, I was always perfectly safe."

A muscle spasmed in his cheek as he clenched his jaw. "You were perfectly safe in Antigua."

"Now, there I would have to disagree," said Sir Barton. "Deuced unhealthy. Wicked, too. Not a proper place for a young lady to live."

How would you *know?* she wanted to object.

But Emily did her one better. "Have you been to the West Indies, then, Sir Barton?" she asked in that soft, musical, deceptively gentle voice of hers. "I was under the impression you had not."

"Well, I—"

"I will vouch for Sir Barton's opinion," said Lord Nathaniel. "What a blessed relief to find myself on English soil once more."

"It sounds as if you intend to stay," Tempest said, unable to keep the note of hope from her voice.

Before he could answer, Porter announced that dinner was served. Lord Nathaniel proffered his arm, and she had little choice but to take it. Her grandfather escorted Mrs. Beauchamp to a chair on his right, while Lord Nathaniel led Tempest to the foot of the table. She realized she was to be seated opposite her grandfather, separated from Mrs. Beauchamp by half a dozen chairs. Lord Nathaniel, on the other hand, took the place beside Tempest, perfectly positioned for intimate conversation.

Beneath the scrape of chairs and the clatter of service, he whispered to her, "I intend to stay right by your side, my dear. But I suspect you knew that already."

He reached for her hand as he spoke, but she snatched it away under the pretense of taking up her goblet.

In his letter, Edward had insisted that she would be safer in England, where Lord Nathaniel's power would be checked by rules and customs that were less susceptible to corruption. Perhaps that was true. But she certainly was not free here, whatever Lord Mansfield had claimed. What a terrible mistake she had made in coming to Yorkshire. What a mistake to allow anything so irrational as sentiment to guide her choices.

"Did you find your room to your liking?" her grandfather called from the other end of the table.

"Yes, thank you."

"It was your dear mama's when she was a girl," he explained. "So like her—bright and cheerful."

"That she was," Lord Nathaniel agreed. "A perfect angel."

"That was her namesake, you remember. *Angela*."

"Indeed I do."

There was a wistful note in Lord Nathaniel's voice that Tempest did not think she had ever heard there. Oh, she had listened to him talk of her mother many times, often with the intent of scolding her into better behavior. The sound of her name on his lips always brought with it a prickle of jealousy. Only an unjust God would keep a child from knowing her mother but grant such a man the privilege.

But something about the way he spoke now suggested a different sort of intimacy. Tempest had always understood the acquaintance had first been formed in Antigua, through her father, after her parents' marriage. Was it possible Lord Nathaniel had known her as Angela Harper, known her here?

A more long-standing connection would go some way toward explaining his decision to come first to Yorkshire rather than seek Tempest out elsewhere.

"What can you tell us of the Christmas festivities in the neighborhood, Sir Barton?" Emily asked. Tempest shot her a grateful glance for the attempt to turn the conversation, although she could muster no enthusiasm for the particular subject. It was only another reminder that she was expected to stay through the holiday. Those few days would feel like forever.

"Festivities? You will no doubt find them sadly lacking, Mrs. Beauchamp. The neighborhood is quiet, the number of families small."

"I was struck by the remoteness of Crosslands' situation when we arrived," Emily confessed. "Not terribly conducive to wassailing parties or the like, although with a carriage or two, or even a sleigh, people might . . ."

Her sentence trailed away when Lord Nathaniel cleared his throat. "Do they go in for such frivolities in the village?" he asked disdainfully. "I'm sure our host takes no particular pleasure in the thought of being descending upon by a horde of strangers, singing off-key and demanding a bowl of punch for their trouble."

"Well, a quiet family party is often pleasantest," Emily acknowledged, only slightly daunted. "When shall we decorate the house?"

"Decorate?" Sir Barton sputtered. "The house?"

"With boughs of greenery? Holly and such? Bows and bells?"

With each suggestion her grandfather's eyebrows rose, as if Emily were speaking words in a foreign tongue and he suspected her of spouting profanities.

"Forgive me, sir," she said at last. "I only imagined you would wish to show Miss Holderin a bit of holiday cheer. It is her first English Christmas."

"But not, it is to be hoped, her last," said Lord Nathaniel.

Tempest narrowly suppressed a shudder, but her grandfather nodded approvingly, Lord Nathaniel's voice drawing his eye. He squinted along the length of the table, as if trying to bring the two of them into sharper focus. "Do you know, at this distance, I could almost persuade myself that a twenty-five-year-old wish had at last been granted."

Mrs. Beauchamp soon recaptured her grandfather's attention by suggesting further ways of imbuing Crosslands Park with the Christmas spirit. Distracted, Tempest caught only pieces of the conversation, but the gradually increasing slump of Sir Barton's shoulders suggested Emily was wearing him down.

"You look perplexed, my dear." Lord Nathaniel spoke low, so that only Tempest could hear.

"What did my grandfather mean by it? What wish?"

"Can it be that your sainted father never told you?" he asked sardonically. "I suppose I should not be surprised. It was hardly his favorite memory—although his distaste for the truth did not make it any less true." Triumph gleamed in his dark eyes. "Your dear mama and I were betrothed when she met that shopkeeper Thomas Holderin and decided to run away with him instead."

"Betrothed?"

"With Sir Barton Harper's blessing. I fancy he looked forward to hearing his daughter addressed as 'my lady.'"

Despite the horror of Lord Nathaniel's revelation, Tempest forced herself to remain calm. What was past was past, and Sir Barton's wishes for his daughter need have no bearing on her future.

Yet she could not make herself drink. Or eat.

When the last dish was cleared, she pushed her chair back and stood before a footman could come to her aid. Emily rose, too. "If you will excuse us, Grandfather. We will leave you to your port," she said and left.

But she did not retreat into the drawing room for tea. Instead she climbed the stairs with carefully measured steps.

Once more in her bedchamber, her mother's bedchamber, she looked around at the springlike décor and tried to summon some memory, some spirit of the woman. What had been a pretty but unremarkable room, filled with flowers only familiar to Tempest from pictures in books, suddenly acquired new interest. She tried to imagine her mother surrounding herself with warmth and color and perpetual summer, antidotes to the cold, gray world in which she actually lived. Had Mama *wanted* to marry Lord Nathaniel? Or had she merely acceded to her father's wishes until the promise of eternal summer was within her grasp?

"Back so soon, miss?" Hannah said, coming from the dressing room. Caliban trotted behind her, freshly washed. With pursed lips and a little frown, Hannah shooed him toward the fire, where he shook from head to toe before curling up to dry his fur.

"The journey fatigued me more than I realized," Tempest made excuse. "I think I'll retire. I'm certain a good night's sleep will restore me to myself."

"Yes, miss."

Hannah had only just begun to help with the fastenings of her dress when Emily tapped at the door and entered without waiting for an invitation. For the first time, Tempest realized there was no lock. "Are you all right, dear?"

188 • *Susanna Craig*

"She's just tuckered out, ma'am," Hannah supplied helpfully, but Tempest knew the answer would not satisfy Mrs. Beauchamp.

"I fear I have caused you distress. My insistence on your making this journey—"

"No, indeed," Tempest said, not entirely truthfully.

"But this Lord Nathaniel person—forgive me." She stopped herself, a note of indecision in her voice. "My son spoke of some persistent suitor you were forced to flee. I feared he might be the man."

A single nod confirmed Emily's suspicion. "Lord Nathaniel Delamere was most determined to marry me—the reason, I suppose, it was believed I should leave Antigua. But left to my own devices, I would have stayed. Lord Nathaniel is vile, but he doesn't frighten me."

"Left to your own devices," Emily echoed warily. "That hints at coercion, force. Did Andrew—did my son have some hand in taking you away against your will?"

Tempest opened her mouth to reply, then darted a quick glance at Hannah, who was humming as she went about the work of brushing and hanging Tempest's dress, paying no attention to their conversation. "Not exactly," she said and briefly told the story of how she had come to find herself aboard the *Fair Colleen*. "So it was not, strictly speaking, kidnapping." She narrowed her gaze as she studied the relief spreading over Emily's features. "Could you believe it of him?"

Emily hesitated. "Once, no. After so many years, though, I could not be sure."

"Gracious, miss," Hannah exclaimed, drawing their attention. She had been peeling apart layers of undergarments and was frowning over a rusty mark. "Didn't you know your courses had begun?"

Tempest stared for a long moment at the reddish-brown stain on the linen in Hannah's outstretched hands, the sign she had been praying for, respite from the lapse in judgment that had been torturing her for weeks.

So why were there tears welling in her eyes and stinging the back of her throat?

"Oh," she breathed, wrapping her arms around her waist to fight the trembling that threatened to overtake her. "Oh no."

A shadow of concern crossed Emily's face. "Are you all right, dear?"

Hannah bustled about, cleaning her up and helping her into a fresh nightgown. "Now, don't you fret, miss. I'll fetch you a clout and then just take all this down to the kitchen and put it to soak. No harm done."

Tempest hardly heard the maid's chatter. How could she suddenly find herself mourning the loss of something she ought never to have had, something that had never really existed? Had she really been *hoping* for something so unutterably foolish? A child—a girl with her mother's eyes and a sweet, heart-shaped face . . . framed with raven hair.

"I'm fine," Tempest said, shaking off both the mental image and Emily's assistance in getting into bed. "Never better. I can't think what came over me just now."

Birdlike, Emily tipped her head to one side and studied her. "Oh?"

"I assure you, Mrs. Beauchamp, I am never ill," she insisted, attempting to hide her secret, her shame, behind the more formal address, although she had little hope Emily would not see through the mask with those bright eyes of hers.

"I've no doubt that's true, dear." Emily paused, evidently waiting for Hannah's departure. "Nonetheless," she continued when the door had closed behind the girl, "I thought you might welcome the excuse for a day or so in bed. It would give you a bit of time to think. And a little space to breathe."

"True," Tempest conceded. A day without having to speak with either her grandfather or Lord Nathaniel would be most welcome right now.

As Emily leaned forward to tuck in the blankets around Tempest's sides, her heavy locket swung forward and caught the light. Tempest watched it settle into the hollow of her bosom once more when she sat back on the edge of the bed. "Emily, what's in that locket? I don't believe I've ever seen you without it."

"This?" Her fingers curled reflexively around it. Flicking the clasp, she displayed the contents to Tempest: an oval portrait of a man—Daniel Beauchamp, she presumed—stern-faced and bewigged, in a style popular a decade or more ago. Facing it, behind a bubble of glass, lay a lock of dark hair, braided and coiled.

"A memento of your husband," Tempest murmured, suddenly embarrassed at having pried.

"Both my husbands," Emily corrected. "The portrait is a likeness of Mr. Beauchamp, though not a very good one, I'm afraid. Makes it look as if he had the toothache," she said, staring at the picture, her own features soft and fond, as if she could coax an answering smile from oil and vellum. "The love lock came from Patrick Corrvan, when we were courting. 'Twas all the gift he could afford."

"Captain Corrvan is very like his father, I suppose?" Tempest ventured after a moment, wishing there were a picture of Emily's first husband, merely so Andrew's face could be before her again.

Emily nodded, a faraway look in her eyes. "In looks, certainly. Both too handsome for their own good." Tempest felt a blush rise to her cheeks. "But Andrew's steadier than his da ever was," she insisted, "whatever he chooses to believe of himself."

"Ah." She could think of nothing else to say as she watched Emily restore the locket to its customary place, tucked into the bodice of her dress, close to her heart.

"Daniel knew I kept it, if that's what you're wondering," she said with a small smile, seeing the direction of her gaze. "Patrick's memory was no threat to Daniel. I loved them both, each in his own way. No question Daniel was the better provider. But without Patrick . . . well, there'd be no Andrew."

"You have no regrets, then? Even though—" *Even though they broke your heart?*

She stopped herself before the words could pass her lips. Her earliest memory had been of Papa mourning her mother's death. In truth, he had mourned her until his dying day. Tempest had tried, over the years, to persuade herself that his devotion ought to have given her a favorable notion of love and marriage, a counterpoint as it were to the marriages founded on nothing more than wealth or status. She had no doubt that her father had loved her mother.

But she had never been able to fathom giving up a part of herself only to be rewarded with pain.

"Even though they died and left me alone?" Emily finished for her. "Yes. I have been sad, at times. But I have also been so very, very happy. Grief cannot take that away. You'll understand, someday. When you marry."

"I'll never marry."

Emily's brows curved inward. "Never?"

"What is there in marriage to benefit me? I am not poor, so I do not require another's support or security. I need not fear spinsterhood for that reason, certainly."

"Mightn't you be lonely, dear?"

"May not a single lady of fortune travel, correspond, call and be called upon by her friends?" Tempest countered. "Miss Wollstonecraft says that a proper education allows a woman 'to support a single life with dignity,' and Papa certainly gave me that."

"Miss Wollstonecraft? The radical author?"

"It pleases people to call her so, but I for one find her principles quite sensible."

"I confess I have not read her works. I know that she is said to be sympathetic to those terrible French republicans."

"It would be more accurate to say that she is sympathetic to cries for liberty, from whatever corner they may come."

Emily nodded. "I can understand how her ideas might offer support for your plans regarding your grandfather's plantation, but why should those same principles require one to fight such a difficult battle alone?"

"Because marriage is simply another form of slavery. It would only be granting power to another—power over my actions, my fortune, even my body."

"It sounds, forgive me," Emily said in that soft voice that Tempest had learned was really made of steel, "as if this Miss Wollstonecraft can have had no very good model of a happy marriage in her life. What about love?"

Tempest could not help but recall Andrew's expression when he had asked her the same question. Not wry, for once. She might almost have called it genuine.

"'Love, from its very nature, must be transitory,'" she quoted.

Emily's hand went to the heavy oval locket at her throat. "No," she insisted. "Not always."

Somewhat chastened, Tempest conceded that it might not always be the case. "But you cannot deny that love values the heart over the head. I strive for perfect rationality. I know I have not always achieved it, of course, but I cannot afford to indulge in sentiment. By marrying, I would place my inheritance in another's hands. I would be giving up not only my own freedom, but everyone else's, too."

"Surely there must be a man who can be trusted to be led by your wishes in the matter?" Emily suggested.

Was she thinking of Andrew? Andrew, who was proud to claim

his irresponsibility, his selfishness? Emily might be content to trust him with the future of Beauchamp Shipping, but Tempest could not trust him with Harper's Hill—to say nothing of herself.

She shook her head, half-closed her eyes, and nestled into the pillows, feigning drowsiness.

His attention drawn by the movement, Caliban stood and stretched before the fire, then trotted over to the other side of the bed. Tempest patted the downy coverlet with her palm, and the dog did not hesitate to accept the invitation.

Emily leaned forward again and pressed cool lips to Tempest's forehead, a maternal gesture she had not even known she craved. "Sometimes we're drawn to a thing we ought not to have. But not everything that looks like a mistake really is. Sometimes your heart is smarter than your head," she said, scratching behind Caliban's ears before she rose and went to the door. "I think your Miss Wollstonecraft has that to learn, yet. Good night, dear."

At least an hour later, realizing that sleep was not likely to come, Tempest abandoned the warmth of the bed, ignoring Caliban's groan of protest. After she had relit the candle Emily had extinguished on her departure, she retrieved Edward's letter from the little writing desk, hoping its contents would distract her from what the evening had revealed. When she returned with it to the shelter of the blankets, Caliban grudgingly made room for her beside him once more.

She forced herself to read again the words about Lord Nathaniel. Dear Edward had often been critical of Sir Barton, but he never could have foreseen that he might prove to be her enemy in this case. She must find a way to help her grandfather see Lord Nathaniel's true character. If he knew the depravities of which the man was capable, he would not continue to open his home to him, would he?

Skipping ahead to the still-unread portion of the letter, she tried to distract herself with Edward's plans for Harper's Hill during the time she was gone, his hope that Regis could soon be restored to his duties, that Whalen's crew would get to work on the mill shortly, that the harvest would not disappoint. His descriptions of familiar people and places and activities brought very little in the way of comfort, though—or diversion.

Instead, she was reminded of where she ought to be, of the people she ought never to have left. If only she had never listened to Andrew or Mrs. Beauchamp. If only she had found another ship the very moment of her arrival in London. She might be halfway home right now, leaving Lord Nathaniel to wonder what had become of her.

As she allowed her eyes to wander over the remainder of the letter, she was brought up short by a final few lines, added in a hand that lacked Edward's usual care. Two sentences had been begun and then crossed out, as if he had been unsure of his words—blots he normally would never have allowed another person to see, blots she was almost shocked to discover him capable of making. The packet must have been on the point of sailing for London, or he would have insisted on taking the time to recopy the entire letter rather than send it in this state.

> ~~Not knowing when, or even if, I shall ever see you again, I find myself~~
> ~~You must allow me to tell you XXX~~

The last word had been scored through so many times it was illegible. When he had begun again, the words had to be cramped into the remaining space, making them even more difficult to decipher.

> *With so many miles between us now, I feel free to speak—this once, but never, should you wish my silence in the matter, again. I know that you have sworn, for the sake of your inheritance, never to marry, a sacrifice I have always respected. Yet I fear I may have inadvertently sent you into dangerous waters, in which your reputation, even your person, may now require the protection you so adamantly oppose. Should such a circumstance arise, I ask only that you think of me. You who have known me for so many years cannot be a stranger either to my temperament or to my feelings, both for Harper's Hill and for you, my dear, dear Tempest.*
> *Yours, always.*
> *E*

She read the passage through twice to be sure of it, then folded the letter, tucked it beneath her pillow, and blew out the candle so that she could not be tempted to read it again.

Edward *would* be a perfect partner in the future she envisioned for herself. He shared her commitment to freeing the plantation's slaves and would never value a few pounds' profit over peoples' lives. His manner was always calm and serious, a useful antidote to her more . . . *animated* nature. Without a doubt, she esteemed him, and Miss Wollstonecraft repeatedly insisted that if a woman was determined to wed, friendship and esteem were the only proper foundations on which to build a marriage, for passion would inevitably fade.

And yet, she had never given more than a moment's thought to Edward as an eligible match.

Well, she would be remiss not to think of him now. His proposal had much to recommend itself. She had always trusted Edward implicitly. He would forgive her for her . . . *indiscretions*. And she could never doubt his affection for her. If she chose, she might go down on the morrow and announce her engagement. It might even free her from Lord Nathaniel's unwanted attention, since she could hardly be expected to marry him if she were betrothed to someone else, as Omeah had pointed out all those weeks ago.

But she would not do it. She could not marry Edward. Even if she had changed her resolution about marriage—and she had not—a part of her had always known that esteem would never be enough. If she ever were to marry, she would demand more. But *more* was dangerous. *More* meant dependence and, inevitably, disappointment. So she had foresworn marriage, favoring the cool dictates of reason over the heat of a broken heart.

And look where that had gotten her.

With trembling fingers, she stroked Caliban's rough gray fur. Sleepily and without opening his eyes, Caliban thumped his tail against the bed. She was reminded of the first time she had petted the dog, her introduction to his master.

Despite her resolutions, her heart was in the possession of someone with whom she ought never to have trusted any part of herself. She, who would never have left home, given the choice; he, who wanted to be forever on the move. She, bound by duty to fulfill her family's responsibilities; he, who had abandoned his. The two of them ought never to have come together.

Yet they had. A spark had jumped from his skin to hers the first time they touched, each time they touched, the current growing ever stronger. If there were a next time, the spark would grow to a fire and burn her to a cinder. But like a moth, she could not resist the flame.

Much as she hated to admit it, Lord Nathaniel had been right. Denying a truth didn't make it less true.

She was in love with Andrew Corrvan.

Chapter 18

Four days. Four days to get from London to Hull, as if he were an elderly lady out for a quiet airing, stopping at every coaching inn for a cup of tea. Having grown accustomed to the vagaries of sailing, Andrew could never have imagined that travel over smooth, straight roads on dry land could be so prone to delays and difficulties. Of course, the land hadn't exactly been dry, and therein lay the problem. Mud. So much mud. Mired in it axle-deep on more than one occasion, wheels clogged, a horse lamed. And every minute, every mile, he could envision Lazarus Stratton slipping away from him once more.

Better, perhaps, than imagining his mother's face when she discovered he had run from his responsibilities at Beauchamp Shipping with all the speed his current mode of transport denied him. Well, he *had* warned her that her faith in him would be misplaced . . .

Mostly, he tried to avoid thinking about his proximity to Tempest. Crosslands Park was at best sixty miles from Hull. He had asked an hostler along the way. Half a day's ride, when conditions were right.

Well, he could be thankful for the mud, then. It was the surest antidote to temptation he knew.

The crooked, narrow streets of Hull stank with mud—and rotten fish and coal smoke and shit. Heavy with dampness, the air moved along in foggy waves, turning midday into dusk and making every alley blind. When the coachman refused to go one foot farther, fearing for the remaining paint on his battered conveyance, Andrew roused Caesar by grasping one of his small shoulders and shaking it gently.

The boy had insisted on accompanying him on this cold, dull, and likely pointless journey. When Andrew had asked him why, Caesar's answer had been a punch in the gut.

"Because I'm safest with you."

Good God, had anyone ever said such an absurd thing to him in his life?

Unable to bear the thought of leaving a child in Williams's hard hands, however, he had nodded his reluctant assent, realizing it would only be wasting precious minutes to argue.

"Let's see if our tip was a good one," he said as Caesar emerged from beneath three layers of blankets, although the temperature was quite mild for December, especially in Yorkshire.

But as he helped the boy from the coach, he felt again the horror of Timmy Madcombe's hand slipping from his grasp, saw once more the blank terror in that boy's eyes as the sea came up to meet him. One more ghost to haunt his every footstep.

And here he was, inviting disaster, risking the addition of another to their number.

They had no real information, no confirmed sighting of Stratton. Just the name of a street and the number of a room once occupied by the wife of a sailor rumored to have turned pirate and disappeared. It was devilishly little to go on, and Andrew alternated between feeling apprehensive and feeling a fool.

Once they had found the street, a series of sharp slaps with the heel of his hand against the proper door brought him face-to-face with an older woman wearing a black dress and a surprisingly crisp mobcap. "Canna he'p 'e?" she said, turning her narrow-eyed gaze on each of them in turn.

"I'm looking for a Mrs. Stratton. I was told she lived here."

When the landlady at last pulled her eyes away from the curiosity that was Caesar, she nodded. "Aye. Onc'it."

"You mean she's gone?"

"Aye."

Andrew waited, but it seemed no further information was forth-coming. Still, the woman had not slammed the door in his face. Per-haps she had more to say, with the right encouragement. Fishing in his waistcoat pocket, he withdrew a shilling and offered it to her.

"She left last quarter day," she said after inspecting the coin and then tucking it into her bosom. "Couldna pay t' rent. 'er man had gone t' sea many a long year ago and hadna been seen for nigh on ten year. When 'er lass took sick an' died, she packed up 'er things, and I ne'er saw 'er again."

Last quarter day. Michaelmas. As recently as September, Stratton's wife had still been here waiting for him. If he had come here and learned of her departure, would he have searched for her?

"Do you have any idea where she might have gone?"

"Naw," she said finally when he produced another coin. "Folks do say she took up wit' another sailor, but I ne'er saw t' like hangin' around 'ere."

"Thank you," Andrew said, touching one finger to the brim of his hat and turning away from the door. A dead end.

"Curious," she muttered, rubbing the second shilling between the tips of her fingers, bare below her carefully darned mitts.

He froze. "I beg your pardon? What's 'curious'?"

"In all those years, I canna put my mind on a caller. Now she's gone, 'tis twa in a fortnight."

"Someone else has been asking about Mrs. Stratton? What can you tell me about him?"

He reached for his pocket again, but she shook her head, as if gossip were suddenly a more palatable sin than greed. "Man o' the sea. Like yourself," she said, fixing his face with those shrewd eyes. "But he's an' old tar. Not so 'ansome as 'e," she added with a wink.

Swallowing his shock, Andrew dredged up his wickedest, most flirtatious grin. "Oh?"

And with a few more words, she began to conjure Lazarus Stratton.

"So he left disappointed when he learned the woman was no longer here," Andrew said when she finished describing the man.

"Dunno if'n 'e were disappointed. Didna seem t' care much, one way or t' other," she said. "Leastways, 'e didna leave. T' room were empty yet, so 'e took it."

Andrew shot a glance at Caesar, who had been taking in the whole conversation with wide eyes and a frown of confusion. But the woman's last words at least had been clear to the boy, despite her thick Northern accent.

"He's *here*?" Caesar cried.

The woman jumped, evidently startled to find the boy capable of speech. "Not just at present," she insisted, drawing back slightly as if to close the door.

"Where?" demanded Andrew.

Something in his look, or in his voice, must have conveyed his desperation even more clearly than those shillings, for she scuttled farther into her dark house. "Like as not, you'll find 'im at t' Dog," she said, nodding down the alleyway before slamming the door and bolting it.

Through the swirling miasma of fog, he could just glimpse a shingle hanging above a doorway at the far end of the street. Upon investigation, he found that the sign belonged to a seaman's pub whimsically called the Golden Hind. The artist's rather clumsily rendered picture of a deer, perhaps combined with its patrons' illiteracy, made "The Dog" as likely a name for the establishment as any.

Unsure whether it was more dangerous to leave Caesar in the alley or bring him into the unknown, Andrew looked up and down the deserted street before instructing the boy to hide himself in the vacant doorway opposite.

The ancient pub was empty of patrons. Near the meager fire, a tankard stood on a battered tabletop, as if someone had recently abandoned the seat. Or perhaps, given the pub's general air of disuse and decay, the mug had been left there weeks ago.

Behind the bar, a man watched his arrival with dull eyes but did not speak.

"I'm looking for Stratton," Andrew said, sliding half-a-crown across the worn slab of wood that separated them.

For reply, the man snatched up the coin and jerked his chin toward a steep set of stairs in the back.

Andrew nodded his thanks and moved into the darkness, pulling his knife from his boot as he climbed.

Two doors faced one another across a narrow, low-ceilinged corridor. From behind one came a few grunts and groans; behind the other, all was silence. Raising one foot, Andrew kicked open the first door, then paused on the threshold, blinking against the room's comparative brightness. The small chamber's amenities were few: a filthy window with one limp, tattered curtain drawn halfway across it, a broken chair in one corner over which a man's coat had been tossed, and a chamber pot that needed to be emptied. In the middle of the room stood a sagging rope bed.

And in the middle of that bed knelt Lazarus Stratton, driving himself into a woman.

Either out of eagerness, laziness, or more likely, practicality, neither one had bothered to undress. The woman had simply rucked up her skirts, while the hollow cheeks of Stratton's arse jiggled with his effort, supported by a pair of spindly legs that disappeared into breeches shoved down around his knees. He had not even removed his muddy boots. The woman's fingers curled in the hems of his shirt, baring his scarred, pale flesh and a few knobby ribs that must once have been broken.

Neither seemed at first to have noticed Andrew's arrival. Then Stratton grunted, "Can't a fellow have a toss in peace? Give over."

"Get up."

Stratton laughed and kept rutting. "So you caught up with me at last, bog trotter. Well, send me off, then," he challenged. "There's worse ways to go. Unless you'd rather join us?"

The woman, however, seemed to have lost whatever enthusiasm she had had for the deed, and pushed against Stratton until she could wriggle her way free.

"This doesn't concern you," Andrew said to her, averting his gaze while she righted her skirts. "Leave us."

"'Tis my room," she insisted with a toss of her head as she rose. Then a feeble shaft of afternoon light touched the blade of Andrew's knife and its gleam caught her eye. "Lor' bless us," she said. "Don' want no part o' that." As she slipped warily past him to the door, he saw her face clearly for the first time. Lank brown hair, big eyes in a sallow face. A striking resemblance to the barkeep—his sister, perhaps. Or his daughter. She was barely more than a girl. "Wait for me outside," he ordered. She gasped, then nodded her understanding, gnawing her lip in a well-practiced, if not proficient, gesture of seduction.

As she sashayed her way out of the room in an unmistakable invitation, a shudder of revulsion went through him—not at her, but at the circumstances that compelled a mere child to make such an offer.

Stratton had buttoned up his breeches and pulled his braces over his shoulders, but his shirt still hung open almost to his waist, and when Andrew stepped toward him, he laughed again, showing off a mouthful of rotting teeth. "Go on, then," he said, jabbing at his chest with his middle finger, for his index finger was missing on that hand. "Right here. It's your chance at last. I ain't armed."

Andrew fingered the handle of his knife, weighing it, as if considering where to land the blow. But the shock of meeting Stratton face-to-face tempered the bloodlust that pounded in his ears. Had he really wasted ten years of his life chasing after this worthless specimen? What his mind had built up as fierce adversary, the dingy light of this room revealed to be a feeble old man. Not that he spared him any pity. But suddenly he was no longer certain that the satisfaction of justice at long last was worth the price of bloodying his hands—further than they had already been bloodied, that was.

At Andrew's hesitation, Stratton snorted his disbelief. "Thought the Irish had spirit," he said as he turned to pick up his coat from the chair.

Andrew watched him slip his arms into bedraggled red sleeves. "Where did you get that coat?"

"This?" Stratton brushed off one shoulder as if flicking a speck of lint from superfine rather than fleas from a rag. "Why, it b'longed to that nob what paid me to come after you. Wore it to the bitter end, 'e did."

"Until he drowned, you mean."

"Drowned? Naw." Stratton shook his head. "Somehow in all the twistin' and turnin' after that storm, the two of us ended up floatin' free. Mighty glad to be alive, I was, but I don' know how much longer we coulda lasted if'n 'is Majesty's boys hadn't hied into view. When we got on board, t' lieutenant said he'd never have seen us if'n it weren't for this 'ere red coat. That nob was all set to toss it in the rag bin, but I snatched it right up. Kinda took a fancy to it, I guess you'd say, since it saved my life an' all. 'Sides, I ain't got nuthin' left after t' old bitch sank."

Andrew heard very little of the account after the point at which Stratton had revealed that Delamere had survived the wreck. "He's alive? Where?"

"Delamere? Said he had business in t' North. 'llowed me to ride along. Decent enough fellow, for a nob."

"Which is to say, not decent at all."

My God, the man was in Yorkshire. When Tempest had arrived at Sir Barton Harper's, Delamere had likely met her at the door.

And Andrew had been the one to send her to him. Had insisted she must go. For his own peace of mind.

Well, what little peace their separation had bought him had certainly flown when Stratton had begun to speak.

Andrew sheathed his knife and turned toward the door. He could be at Crosslands tonight if he left immediately. If he were not already too late . . .

"I allus knew you was a coward, Corrvan. You'd have had me years ago if you weren't. Always runnin' off jus' when things got interestin'."

"You might be right, Stratton," he said, glancing back over his shoulder. "But I'm not running now."

With a swift lunge, he drove his right fist into the man's gut, then cut upward with his left to break the man's jaw and send him crashing into the wall. Stratton slid down and collapsed onto the floor in a groaning, immobile heap.

"It's not enough," Andrew said, shaking out his hand as he walked away. "But it will have to do."

On the other side of the door, the girl still waited, her eyes wide with shock as she attempted to peer past him into the room.

"I need you to do something for me," he said to her, reaching into his pocket as he spoke.

Warily, she watched his hand. "What's that?"

"Grab your cloak, if you've got one. Go and fetch the constable and tell him there's a wanted criminal, a pirate named Stratton, in that room. And then," he said, thrusting a number of crisply folded banknotes into her hand, gripping her fingers to keep them in place, "keep going. Don't come back here."

"But I—" She glanced down, bewildered by his gift.

"Promise me. There's enough there to keep you in a better life than this."

Mutely, she nodded and slipped down the stairs. He followed close enough behind that he saw her pluck a filthy mantle from a hook and sling it around her shoulders. "Goin' out, Pa," she called over her shoulder.

The man at the bar grunted in acknowledgment. With the luxury of more time, Andrew might have served him as he had Stratton. Instead, he paused and fixed the man with a fierce glare that seemed for once to capture his full attention.

"Have you another daughter?" Andrew asked.

The man looked taken aback by the question but shook his head. "Naw. Jus' Nell there."

Despite himself, Andrew felt one corner of his mouth lift. "Good."

Caesar was not waiting where he had left him. Instead the boy was running breathlessly toward him, having just rounded the corner of the cross street. With a shake of his head that would have to serve for a scold, Andrew hoisted the boy onto his shoulders and set off in the direction from which they had come, winding through cramped streets in a swirling fog that seemed to turn them around and send them in the wrong direction more than once. The air was turning sharply colder; every breath pierced his lungs and clouded his vision further.

At last he saw the carriage ahead. "Crosslands Park," Andrew ordered breathlessly, lifting Caesar inside. "As fast as you can travel. I'll double your usual fare," he vowed, conveniently ignoring the fact he had given the barman's daughter, Nell, most of the money he had brought on the journey.

"Did you find 'im?" Caesar asked eagerly, almost knocked onto the floor as the coach jerked, then lumbered away.

"I did."

"I knew you would! That's why, when I saw those officers, I went after 'em."

A few questions produced a clearer explanation. Suspecting that Stratton was within and fearing for Andrew's safety, Caesar had kept an eye open for help and gone after a party of militiamen when he saw them. Two had gone around to the back of the pub to keep Stratton from escaping, while a third had gone after their commanding officer to get more assistance. By now, Stratton would be under watchful eyes, perhaps those of the constable himself. When Admiral Clarkson's information about Stratton's activities in the West Indies came to light, he would be swinging at the end of a rope before his jaw had a chance to heal.

"Thank you, Caesar," Andrew said, laying his hand on the boy's shoulder.

But the boy brushed aside the gesture of gratitude. "Somethin' still wrong?"

"Aye," he admitted reluctantly, watching as the afternoon light faded from the sky, leaving the gray world gloomier yet. "Miss Holderin is in grave danger. And I have put her there."

Caesar appeared thoughtful for a moment, then gave a sharp nod as if he had reached some conclusion. "Then we save her, too."

Chapter 19

When the mantel clock chimed twelve, Tempest started, roused from her book as if from the depths of slumber. Why, more than two hours must have passed since Emily had announced her intention to retire. She looked for Caliban, but even he had abandoned her. She was alone but for the footman by the door, whom she caught struggling to stifle a yawn when she glanced around the room.

Christmas Eve.

She had not meant to stay up so late. Well, she was likely not the first to have been kept awake by one of Mrs. Radcliffe's books. Tempest had really never had much interest in gothic tales. Such novels were precisely the sort of frivolous reading Miss Wollstonecraft cautioned against.

But as Tempest had lain resting in her room on the morning after her arrival—on Emily's advice but for reasons quite other than her health—her grandfather had knocked on the door and entered bearing a small armful of books, the volumes of Mrs. Radcliffe's *Mysteries of Udolpho*. "Your father once wrote me saying you were a great reader," he had explained, looking rather uncertain. The revelation—not that Papa had written, but that her grandfather had read, and remembered, his letters—startled her into accepting the gift eagerly despite her general disdain for such books. Perhaps a show of enthusiasm might encourage a longer visit, perhaps even a real conversation. But he had stayed only a few moments, his eyes darting uncomfortably around the room the entire time, leaving her wondering when he had last visited his late daughter's chambers.

Mysteries of Udolpho, despite its popularity, had a number of flaws as far as Tempest was concerned. Its pages and pages of description did not transport her to some ancient alpine castle; she had no difficulty remembering she was sitting in a comfortably modern and improved manor house in the north of England, one now tastefully decorated for Christmas at Emily's gentle insistence. The heroine of the story she found insipid, too perfect by half, and the hero—to the extent he could be said to deserve the title—too prone to fainting. Only the villain, the wicked uncle, seemed to her to have been drawn from life. At least, it required no great stretch of imagination for her to believe there were men who would threaten and imprison a young woman to get their hands on her fortune.

Still, beggars could not be choosers, and the book gave her an excuse to closet herself away at all hours to read, a place to stick her nose when she did not wish to be drawn into conversation. Thanks to Mrs. Radcliffe, she had enjoyed several days not of terror and excitement, but of peace and quiet.

Once her courses had come and gone, her head felt somehow clearer. The strain of worry must have befuddled her senses. By the light of day, even Edward's letter had looked unremarkable. Nothing of a marriage proposal in it at all, just some hurried words assuring her of his steadfastness and brotherly affection, ending as he had begun. Even Lord Nathaniel had been making himself scarce.

And as to that other late-night realization? No doubt as much a figment of her imagination as the rest. Why, all afternoon, she had given at best half an ear to Emily's tales of Andrew's boyhood mischief-making—hardly the mark of a woman in love.

Her fears, her feelings on that night, had merely been an outburst of irrationality, such as women were unfortunately sometimes prone to experience. She was capable once more of behaving with sense, of using reason to apprehend the world around her.

Frowning at the clock, she marked her place in her book, stretched and inhaled the spicy sent of pine boughs, then shivered. Despite the fire, there was a chill in the room. Wind moaned past the windows. The weather must be turning colder. She needed no better excuse to retire, to lose herself under the weight of wool blankets and down-filled quilts. Though perhaps, once upstairs, she would indulge in just a few more pages before she extinguished the lamp . . .

A stream of light leaked beneath her bedchamber door into the corridor. Hannah must have left a candle lit for her. Mentally imagining what lay in store in the final chapters of her book, Tempest's eyes went first to the writing desk where the candle glowed.

A figure stood there, back to the door, between her and the flame. For a moment, she tried to persuade herself it must be Hannah, although one glance had made it clear her midnight visitor was a man. But no—it simply was not possible. A puff of air left Tempest's lips in a gasp.

"What are you doing here?" she demanded.

As Andrew turned toward her and the light limned his profile, she could see he had been frowning over some scrap of paper, which he now laid aside. His features eased. "Tempest. Thank God."

"What are you doing here?" she asked again as she stepped toward him.

"I've been in Hull. A few days ago, an old friend told me Stratton had survived the storm, was believed to be in Yorkshire. So I came after him." He paused and searched her eyes, as if expecting condemnation. He was meant to be in London, after all.

But the fate of Beauchamp Shipping was the last thing on her mind.

"Did you find him?"

"I did."

"Did you kill him?"

Again that hesitation, as if he were torn between telling her the truth and trying to divine what she would most want to hear. "I did not."

She had not known whether she wanted him to say yes or no, until the denial passed his lips and relief swept through her. "I know you wanted justice for your father, but his life is not worth your own."

"My life is inconsequential," he insisted. "Believe me—when he revealed that Delamere was also still alive, and in Yorkshire, my only concern was for you." If the intensity of his green gaze had not confirmed it, everything else about his appearance made it clear that he had come to her with all possible haste. He looked almost as he had aboard the *Fair Colleen* after the storm, his clothing damp and mud-spattered, his face lined with fatigue, his cheeks hollow and unshaven. It must have been a terrible journey. "Is he here?"

"Yes."

"Are you all right? Has he—has he hurt you?" He sounded almost as if he were reluctant to hear her answer.

Without conscious thought, she clutched her book tighter to her chest. "I am fine."

"Where is he now?"

"Gone to bed, I daresay."

"Good God, why didn't you leave the moment you found him here?" His cat's eyes gleamed in the flickering light of the candle.

"I—" she began. What reasonable excuse could she offer? She had considered it, of course. But her options had been limited. Without a coin to her name or a ship to sail on, leaving Crosslands would have meant returning to London, returning to Andrew's house, where she faced an entirely different sort of danger. In some ways, Lord Nathaniel's presence seemed far less threatening. She cared nothing for him, so he could never hurt her the way Andrew might.

Unable to explain herself, she shrugged.

"Well, you're safe now." His hand slid up her arm, and she allowed herself to be pulled into his protective embrace, although she knew she should not want it. It was a violation of all her principles to lean on someone else. But, oh, the relief of allowing him to bear her weight, bear her worries for just a moment. It would not last for long—he had his own burdens to carry.

"I'd take you away this instant," he said, "but the roads were nigh impassible in the daylight. Impossible after dark. We'd be risking our necks to try it now."

What do I risk if I stay? she wondered. "If the roads are that bad, how did you get here?" she asked instead, her voice muffled by the capes of his greatcoat.

"The luck of the Irish, I suppose you could say." The note of humor in his voice was entirely self-deprecating. "And I walked the last three miles or so."

She shivered. That explained the cold radiating from his clothing. "And how did you find your way here, to this room?"

"Mama's abigail, Hannah, happened to be below, and as she is technically in my employ, I was able to persuade her to assist me. Although she *was* reluctant to escort a man to the bedchamber of a young lady. It seems she had recently overheard *someone* brand me a kidnapper."

He paused, and Tempest glanced up in time to see something of the old devilry gleaming in his eyes. "And you said I was safe with you here."

His smile faded. "You are," he said, all seriousness, releasing her and stepping back to shrug out of his coat. "If you've a blanket to spare,

I'll make my bed in the corridor, right outside your—where is Caliban, anyway?" he asked sharply as he glanced toward the door.

"I don't know. Probably with your mother." *Or with Sir Barton,* she added silently. The dog had taken a great liking to her grandfather, but she did not think Andrew would appreciate hearing further proof of his canine companion's unfaithfulness. "You cannot really believe I am in any danger tonight. Let me ring for someone to make up a room for you."

"No danger? Cary was right," he snapped, tugging off his gloves and tossing them onto the chair along with his coat. "You're too stubborn to know what's best. Too blind to see what's right in front of you. Are you trusting in Delamere's honor to keep you safe in your bed?"

"If all he wanted was to force himself on me, he has had ample opportunity to do so," she said, tired of mincing words. "If not here, then in Antigua. He has always been determined to have some legal hold over me first. But at that he cannot succeed. As long as there is breath in my body to say no, to scream it if I must, he will never have my consent. He would have to kill me first, and I do believe that would defeat his purpose." Folding her arms across her chest, she met Andrew's stare. "Now, would you care to tell me exactly what it is I fail to see?"

"This," he said as he lowered his mouth to hers.

At first, his lips felt chill against hers, but after that first brush the familiar spark passed between them, heating them both. As she stretched onto her toes, reaching for a taste of him, his arms came around her, lifting her against his chest. Her own hands, trapped between them, scrabbled up his shirtfront to clasp his neck.

Despite the eagerness of their hands, the rough scrape of his beard against her cheek, the kiss was tentative. Seeking, finding, their tongues danced and retreated as they learned one another once more. Beneath the ordinary smells of horse and sweat and starch, she caught a hint of salt air, and she inhaled greedily, eager for that scent that was uniquely his, the scent that reminded her of home.

The longer he held her, the deeper the kiss, the more she wished he might never let her go. Nervous fingers tangled in the dark hair that fell over his collar. To the nibble of her lips, the tentative swipe of her tongue, he replied by hitching her higher against his hard body, one arm around her hips, the other cupping the back of her head, stilling her to his plunder.

Only when a moan of surrender bubbled from her did he break the kiss and release her.

"This?" she echoed breathlessly as she slid back down to earth. "This can never be." The denial rose to her lips automatically, even as every fiber of her being, those traitorous lips included, still vibrated with Andrew's touch. "I think you know that."

"Do you mean to accept him, then?"

"Lord Nathaniel? Can you even ask—?" Before she could finish her question, however, he glanced toward the writing desk and her eyes followed his. Edward's letter lay there, almost where she had dropped it after her last perusal. That must have been the piece of paper Andrew had been scrutinizing when she entered.

"How dare you?" She twisted to face Andrew. "That's private correspondence."

"Well?" he demanded, ignoring her protest.

How fitting that jealousy was sometimes called a green-eyed monster. But if Andrew were jealous of Edward, then that would mean . . . "You know I don't intend to marry anyone," she said, her voice quieter. "I don't—there is absolutely no need, now, for me to marry at all."

She lowered her gaze so as not to be burned by the intensity of his own. Had that been a flicker of disappointment that crossed his face? Or relief?

"Despite Edward's worries, I'll be fine on my own," she said, the reassurance falling somewhat hollow. "I do not need a man."

"So you've said." One hand came up to cradle her face. With warm fingertips, he traced the shell of her ear, along her jaw, down her throat, stopping at the place where her pulse beat. A sudden rush of blood surged to flush her skin when she realized he could feel her heart race. And those eyes! He could not help but see. See her thoughts, her fears. Her desires.

"Show me." When he tipped his chin toward the bed as he spoke, the heat in his voice sent a quiver through her that had nothing to do with fear.

"I—I don't know what you mean," she lied. Despite the chill in the air and the layers of fabric between them, she could feel the evidence of his arousal where it pressed into her belly. After that kiss, she could feel her own, too, pooling between her thighs.

"There are some young ladies of whom I might believe it," he murmured, turning her away from him as his fingers went to the row of buttons down her back. "But you are not one of them. You're a woman of passion, Tempest." With each word, another button slipped free, and she could feel the whisper of his breath across her skin. "For some time I suspected Cary of stoking those fires—"

"Edward never—"

Andrew's lips brushed along the turn of her neck, across the top of her shoulder. "The more fool he." She offered no resistance as he pushed the blue silk down her arms, over her hips, onto the floor, where it formed an inky puddle around her ankles. Her shift soon followed. "You're no stranger to your body's needs, no stranger to pleasure. Such knowledge can only be acquired in certain ways. If not at another's hands, then your own. So," he said, stepping away from her, forcing her to stand on her own two feet, giving her the independence she had always claimed to want, "show me."

Did he really mean for her to pleasure herself? While he watched?

The darkness in his expression, the way his breath rose and fell, left little doubt in her mind.

Could she really do such a thing? No, of course not! Although . . . it *would* go some way toward proving to them both that she was mistress of her destiny.

With a catch of breath, she scampered to the relative safety of the bed, settling herself among the pillows, pulling the sheets up to her chin, the linen cool against skin that felt almost too warm.

"Shy, Tempest?" He lifted the fragile chair away from the desk and placed it at the foot of the bed, straddling it and leaning forward, intent on the spectacle she was to provide. Behind him, the candle flickered in a draft, and she took some comfort in the way his body blocked the light once more, leaving her robed in shadow. Until, that was, he reached behind him and moved it, casting its glow across the slopes and valleys of the bed. "Go ahead. There's no shame in it. Or have you forgotten how much I've already seen?"

With those words, he dispelled the cold Yorkshire night, replacing it with a memory of the sticky heat of the tropics. As her eyes closed, sensation almost overwhelmed her. Once more the rocking of the ship merged with the thrust of his body into hers. She smelled the spicy scent of his skin, felt the sure stroke of his fingers against her breast.

But it was her own hand that swept over her body now, plucking and pinching an already peaked nipple, then sliding lower, beneath the sheets, to cup her mound. Just one quick press, the heel of her hand against her nub, something to dispel the forbidden ache. No, she could not do this, not while he watched. What must he be thinking?

From some wicked, wayward corner of her mind came another image, his strong hand stealing to the bulge in his breeches, mirroring her movement.

With a gasp, she reached lower and dipped her fingers into her wetness. *Ah.* Had the groan escaped her lips, or his? No matter. She had indulged her desire for Andrew once, knowing that someday it would come to this—reliving that memory in the dark, lonely hours when she had no touch but her own to ease the terrible throbbing.

The slick stroke of her fingers became her only focus. She opened her eyes once more, but she saw nothing. She might almost have forgotten he watched if, some moments later, he had not twitched the blankets impatiently aside, baring her to a gaze that heated what the night air cooled. The mattress dipped when he settled beside her, and she felt his naked body stretched along hers, though he did not lay a hand on her.

Better, perhaps, if he had. Her nerves felt suddenly frayed, divided between their awareness of him and the demands of her own body. The muscles of her abdomen clenched as she hungered for release.

"Shhhh," he soothed, and the sound, the heat of his breath, pulsed through her. "Don't chase it. Let it come to you."

"I—I can't do it." Her fretful voice seemed loud in the stillness.

"You must."

Had he spoken? The dark demand seemed to come from somewhere deep inside her.

At last, though, he took pity on her, one long finger moving to trace the delicate bones of her hand where it slipped between her thighs. She could almost, *almost* imagine his fingertip stroking her straining clitoris.

When she whimpered in frustration at the light brush of his hand, he laughed, low and slightly cruel. "I thought you didn't need a man for this, Tempest?"

"I—I—" Her short curls scrubbed against the pillow as she shook her head. She didn't. *She didn't.*

Still, when he lifted his hand from hers, she cried out at the deprivation. It was not simply *need*, it was . . . oh, she had no word for it. Desperation, perhaps.

Andrew slid his palm over her hip, down her thigh, coaxing her legs farther apart. She opened to him on a sigh of relief. *Yes. Let him— let him—*The pulse beneath her fingertips took up the rhythm of her unspoken chant. Expecting him to brush her hand aside, to ease one finger, perhaps two, into her slick channel, she knew a new torment when he merely circled the opening to her body with the pad of his thumb, the pressure firm but still teasing. *Not enough, not enough, not—*

The explosion took her entirely by surprise, seeming to come not only from the bundle of nerves she stroked, but the place where he touched her, some deep recess she could not quite reach herself.

A soft cry caught in her throat, parting her lips but producing no sound, as if she were trying to hold this moment within her. When the crisis had passed, she watched as Andrew drew his hand up her body, trailing her wetness in his wake, until his fingers caressed her face and he circled her lips with his thumb. Her eyes widened in shock and flew to his, which were heavy-lidded with desire. Not allowing herself to reason her way into a denial, she darted out her tongue and tasted. More salt than sweet. Heat flared in his pupils as she drew his thumb into her mouth and suckled, satisfaction curling her lips when she felt his erection jerk against her hip in response.

"You greedy minx." He replaced his thumb with his mouth, jealously nibbling her lips for some taste of what she had enjoyed. When that failed to satisfy his appetite, he moved down her body, following the path of his fingers, licking and laving, leaving a string of love bites behind. How could something that ought to sting produce so much pleasure?

Boneless, she offered no resistance as he rolled her onto her belly and kissed over one shoulder blade and along her spine. Only when he covered her body with his own, enveloping her in his heat, branding her with his arousal, did she stiffen, feeling an answering tremor stir within her once more.

"Tell me, Tempest." The words were a mere breath against her ear, stirring her hair. Her scalp tingled. "Do you want this?" he asked, and she felt his sex brush the entrance to her body. "Do you want—me?"

She should say no. She *could* say no—he was giving her the choice. But that *no* would be a lie.

Although she shouldn't, she wanted him, wanted this. One night together had most definitely not been enough. And somewhere at the back of her mind, a doubt niggled at her. What if she were not always free to make this choice—to choose him?

"I want you," she said, canting her pelvis, inviting him to enter her.

He surged forward on a groan, an invasion that was part conquest, part caress. The pressure at this angle was exquisite, and as soon as he began to thrust, another orgasm rippled through her—or perhaps it was merely an extension of the first, which seemed still to pulse under her skin.

"I need you."

The confession escaped her lips on a sigh of breath. A dangerous admission for a woman who had never craved a man's possession, could never imagine reveling in what she once would have called powerlessness.

No sooner had the thought crossed her mind, however, than she realized she was far from helpless. Catching his rhythm, she pressed her buttocks against his groin, lifting her hips as much as she could to meet his thrusts and clenching her inner muscles around his hardness. A low grunt of pleasure rumbled in his chest.

No, not powerless at all.

He countered by catching her hands in his and stretching her arms upward, pressing her into the downy softness of the bed, blanketing her with his weight. Pinned beneath him, able to do little more than receive the pleasure he was intent on giving her, she surrendered to sensation. *Yes.* She needed him. She did not think she would ever stop needing him. He rode her mercilessly, then. As another climax racked her body, she muffled her cry in the pillow. She was lost, utterly unmoored, floating through space.

I love you.

The words echoed inside her head. Had she spoken them aloud? Behind her, Andrew stilled, and she held her breath, waiting, as if expecting some reply.

Abruptly he withdrew. Liquid heat spilled onto the sheets and across her skin before he collapsed atop her, breathless, sinking her still further into the snowy depths of the warm featherbed.

She should be grateful he had thought to spare her the burden of worrying once more over possible consequences. Or at least had thought to spare himself.

So why did she feel inexplicably like weeping?

Chapter 20

Andrew awoke to the sound of a pistol being cocked beside his ear.

He should never have allowed himself to fall asleep, but after four days—and three nights—on the road, exhaustion had overtaken him. Nor should he have made love to Tempest again. But in both cases, her body had been warm and gloriously soft, the darkness so inviting . . .

Once more, he had let his base needs trump the terrible risks to her. He had promised her safety, and left her more vulnerable than ever.

Selfish. Irresponsible.

"Get up!" Delamere growled, pressing cold steel against the base of Andrew's skull.

Beneath him, Tempest stirred. Andrew squeezed her shoulder, silently willing her to stay put, snugging the blankets around her as he rose, shielding her bare skin from Delamere's prying eyes.

I love you.

He should have told her weeks ago, if only he had been willing to admit it to himself. Would it be cruel to tell her now, when he was about to die? His death had never before been much cause for regret to anyone, except perhaps his mother.

Now he found himself wondering if Tempest, too, would mourn.

"That's right, Corrvan." Delamere nodded as Andrew came to his feet beside the bed. His dark eyes glittered in the feeble light cast by the dying embers of the fire. The candle must have long since guttered. Beyond the window, the first streaks of a gray dawn were brightening the sky. "Now, put some clothes on, for God's sake—I won't have it look as if I came too late to rescue this innocent girl from some marauding rapist."

As Andrew bent to snatch his breeches from the pile of discarded clothing on the floor, his mind whirled. Where were his boots? His knife? He had to save Tempest from Delamere somehow, whatever the cost to himself.

"Stand over there against the wall," Delamere hissed, gesturing toward the corner with the pistol. "I have a premonition I'm about to shoot an intruder."

"Just what do you think you're doing?"

The eyes of both men snapped to Tempest. As soon as she had been freed of the weight of Andrew's body, she had risen up on her knees in the center of the bed, drawing the coverlet over her as she moved, thinly disguising her own nudity. As Delamere paused to devour the sight of her naked and kneeling before him, Andrew tried not to imagine how long the man had fantasized about just such a moment.

When Andrew took a single step toward him, however, hoping to use the man's distraction to his advantage, Delamere turned back and leveled the pistol, sighting along its barrel. Though his eyes remained focused on Andrew, when he spoke, his words were for Tempest.

"You have been adept at denying me a private moment to make my suit, my dear. But I am not above creating opportunities when I must."

"I have already heard—and rejected—your suit," she said, rising from the bed and wrapping the sheet securely around her. As she spoke, she moved closer to Delamere. Andrew did not know whether to admire her courage or despair of her good sense. "You needn't have come four thousand miles to make it again."

His free hand shot out and caught her wrist in a vise-like grip. "Did you really think I would just let you leave?"

"*Why*, my lord?" she whispered. The light of the fire behind her made every curve, every tremor, visible. "Why are you so determined to marry me?"

Delamere gave a sardonic laugh. "Haven't you figured that out by now?"

"My fortune, I suppose, but—"

"Revenge."

"Revenge?" Both Tempest and Andrew echoed Delamere's answer, she in shock, he in horror at the discovery he shared the man's bloodlust, as well as his obsession with a woman who would never be his.

"I ought never to have followed her to Antigua," Delamere said, sounding far away. The gun shifted, drooped in his hand. Stretching out one leg, Andrew slowly drew his discarded boot closer, almost within reach. The knife hilt poked from its hidden sheath.

"My mother." Tempest's voice was flat with shock.

"You cannot imagine the torture of watching your beloved's belly swell with another man's child, to know his hands have . . ." His gaze wandered over the tangled bed linens. "What makes a woman turn down an alliance with good breeding, pure blood, in favor of dallying with someone so—unrefined? It's like choosing muscovado when you might sweeten your tea with sugar instead. Though it does seem that certain women are drawn to the darkness," he said, shooting a glance toward Andrew, a murderous gleam in his eyes' depths, before focusing once more on Tempest. "In any case, when you were born and grew to be as lovely as your mother, I began to see a way to make your father understand his error, a way to make him pay."

Tempest swallowed hard, visibly struggling to regain her composure before she spoke. "You intended to use me to punish my father?"

Delamere tilted his head in acknowledgment. "And though he did not live to see his judgment," he said, gesturing with the gun as if waving away a matter of little consequence, "I shall still enjoy every minute of dispensing it. I was in the village earlier. It's all arranged. Our nuptials will be solemnized this morning."

"That's not possible."

"Oh, but it is," he said softly, and Andrew could see her wince as the man tightened his grip. With agonizing care not to catch Delamere's eye, Andrew lowered himself, his fingertips straining for the weapon secreted in his boot. Why in God's name hadn't he driven a blade into Delamere when he'd first had the chance?

"I purchased a special license when I passed through London," explained Delamere. "Being the son of a duke, even a disgraced one, does have its advantages."

"You may have a license, but a legal marriage also requires a willing bride," said Tempest, "and that you'll never have."

"Don't be so sure, my dear," Delamere whispered, pulling her closer until his body was flush against hers, pressing his lips against her ear. "Besides, as I told you once before, resistance has its own appeal. I enjoy watching you struggle almost as much as I'll enjoy seeing you succumb at last."

"You beast," she spat out, striking a stinging blow across his sneering face with her other hand.

Despite the slap, the man did not flinch. "Ah, love, come tomorrow, you'll pay for that," he murmured, sounding almost pleased. "Tit for tat."

With Delamere's dark eyes focused squarely on Tempest, Andrew took a chance, grabbing for his knife, his fingers brushing against the leather of his boot.

"Drop it, Corrvan," Delamere said, never turning from Tempest, although the pistol found Andrew nonetheless. "And back up a bit. I'd hate for your blood to spatter my bride."

"Your bride," Tempest repeated, as if testing the words with her tongue. She no longer twisted against his hold. "Was it never about Harper's Hill, then?"

"Your inheritance was never my *primary* motive," Delamere agreed, "but I cannot say that it has not added a certain spice to my desire." One brow lifted suggestively. "My own fortune is regrettably small. I always knew I would have to marry well. I thought I had formed just such a match once. I won't let a second slip through my grasp."

Tempest eyed the gun but did not look at Andrew. "All right," she whispered. "I'll do it. I'll marry you, my lord—"

"Tempest, no!" shouted Andrew.

But she ignored him, hurrying on before he could interrupt. "On one condition."

Delamere laughed mirthlessly. "You may save your breath, Tempest, if that condition concerns a certain shanty-Irish sailor."

Andrew's gut clenched. She had earned the right to choose her fate, but he could not allow her to do this, certainly not for him.

But Tempest, it seemed, had something else in mind.

"It—it does not," she said, and he tried to take some comfort in the obvious difficulty with which those words passed her lips. "Not exactly, anyway. You've no reason to harm him. What's done is done."

"Well?" Delamere sounded intrigued. "What, then?"

"I will marry you if you'll first sign papers agreeing to keep Edward on as manager at Harper's Hill and promising to free the slaves there once I've inherited."

Delamere laughed. "Not more of Holderin's abolitionist nonsense."

"Do it, and I will willingly give myself to you. Or—or—" Her head jerked away and Andrew saw tears glistening on her cheeks. "Or unwillingly, if you wish it that way."

"No," Andrew snarled, surging forward. "I'll see you in hell before I'll let her sacrifice herself to you, Delamere."

With a twisted smile, Delamere thrust Tempest away from him and welcomed the attack. His eyes narrowed as he took aim at Andrew's chest and his finger twitched against the trigger. "You go first."

Andrew felt as if he were watching the events unfold in slow motion while looking through the wrong end of a spyglass. Sound, sight, time—all perception was distorted.

Out of the corner of his eye he saw the door to the bedchamber swing open, and a blur of gray flew through the air with a savage growl. A flash of fire, a puff of smoke as Caliban sank his teeth into Delamere's raised forearm.

Where had the dog come from? How had he known? His lunging attack must have sent Delamere's shot wide of its mark. Caliban had saved his life. The sickening crunch of bone was loud in the room as Cal worried his prey.

Good dog.

But somewhere, Tempest was screaming his name. He had to get to her. If only the damned cloud of smoke would clear. If only he could fight his way free of whatever rooted his feet to this spot. Bewildered, he looked down to see blood, his own blood, dripping from his fingertips and staining the carpet a lurid shade.

Andrew struggled back to consciousness to find sunlight flooding the room, picking out brighter hues all around him—pinks, reds, yellows, greens. He closed his eyes against the glare. Heaven? No, that was surely not where he had been headed when Delamere pulled the trigger . . .

This time his eyes popped open, and the splotches of color formed into flowers. Flowers on the walls, the draperies, the furniture. A bed-chamber. A lady's bedchamber.

"Tempest?" he croaked from between parched lips.

A white-haired man stepped between him and the light pouring through the windows. "Awake at last, Captain Corrvan? Miss Holderin is with your mother."

Andrew blinked to bring the speaker into focus. "You are Sir Barton?"

"That's right." The baronet's arms were folded across his chest, and he wore a scowl. "And I find myself in the unenviable position of insisting that you marry my granddaughter."

Andrew struggled to sit up. A deep groan emanated from some-where near his feet, and he looked to see Caliban, lying on a folded counterpane draped across his legs. Although the dog's eyes did not open, he thumped his tail once against the bed in admonishment.

"Settle yourself," Sir Barton said, raising a hand. "If that wound opens again, you have very little blood to spare."

Blood? Wound? One downward glance clarified the meaning of the baronet's words. A crimson-stained bandage was wound around his left arm, near his shoulder. Strips of linen crossed his bare chest and strapped the injured arm against his side. Andrew closed his eyes and licked cracked lips with a tongue that felt numb and heavy. He tasted something bitter—laudanum, if he did not miss his guess. It held his pain at bay, but did not erase it entirely.

Someone brought a cup of water to his mouth and tipped it slightly, raising another hand to the back of his head. The cup clat-tered against his teeth, but he drank deeply and gratefully, then opened his eyes to see Caesar's small black hand lowering the cup. He tried to turn to look at the boy, but his body refused to comply. Good God, but his head ached. "What happened?" he whispered when the cup was taken away.

"I'm not perfectly sure," said the baronet. "I awakened last night to the sound of a gunshot, hurried down the corridor, and found my guest being mauled by a wild dog while my granddaughter had ap-parently removed her nightdress to stanch the wounds of a perfect stranger."

Sir Barton painted a vivid picture. Unable to meet the man's eye, Andrew allowed his gaze to drift to the spot where he had been standing when Delamere fired. The carpet had been rolled up and taken away. He tried not to imagine it soaked with his own blood.

"It seems Lord Nathaniel Delamere did his best to put a bullet through your heart," concluded Sir Barton gruffly. "After what appears to have happened here last night"—his eyes scanned the room, then settled on Andrew—"I for one can understand the temptation to shoot you. But I suppose I should be grateful that his aim went awry."

"Caliban save you," piped Caesar's voice from his post near the head of the bed. "When Jackson get the wheel fixed, we come with the coach, an' I find him tied up in the barn. I don' like to see no living thing in chains. I turn him loose and he make for the house like a shot. I don' know how he knew, Cap'n, but he found you right quick." As the boy spoke, he leaned into Andrew's field of vision and beamed. "Broke the man's arm, too."

Two more thumps of Caliban's tail, evidently acknowledging Caesar's words of praise.

"That's right," confirmed Sir Barton. "Along with his skull. Bring your master some hot water and something to eat," he ordered, pulling the boy's wide-eyed gaze to himself. "And his razor, while you're about it," he added with a disparaging glance at Andrew's scruffy jaw. "He has a marriage proposal to make."

After a moment's hesitation, the boy nodded, found Andrew's shaving kit, delivered it to Sir Barton, then left for the kitchen, casting one nervous look behind him.

"Where is Delamere now?" Andrew demanded as soon as the door closed and he had gathered enough strength to push himself upward in the bed despite the dire warnings.

"In a room just down the corridor, under the watchful care of my personal physician," Sir Barton said. While Andrew's head still spun with the exertion of sitting up, he could not read the other man's tone. "Dying."

Leaning back against the cushioned headboard, he closed his eyes and prayed the laudanum was not making him hear things.

"When the dog jumped, Lord Nathaniel fell and struck his head on the mantelpiece." Above the now-empty hearth, a stretch of carved marble gleamed. "I called on the magistrate at first light and explained the situation," Sir Barton continued, shifting the case from hand to hand as if uncertain what to do with it. Finally, he tucked it beneath one arm. "He's prepared to say it was an accident. Otherwise, you know, the dog might have to be put down."

Was there a note of sympathy in his voice? Andrew glanced back at the sleeping dog draped over his feet. Caliban lifted one ear but appeared otherwise indifferent to the conversation. Sir Barton reached out a hand and scratched the dog's head.

"What of Delamere's family?"

"Gave him up for lost years ago. I've sent word to his brother, the duke, but I doubt he'll care one way or the other. You're a lucky man."

"It's Tempest who's the fortunate one," Andrew said. "Delamere is a sick bastard who hurts and humiliates others for his pleasure. Yet your granddaughter was prepared to marry him."

"To save your miserable hide, I suppose?"

"No." He tried to dismiss the sour taste in his mouth as the effect of the drug. "To save the people of Harper's Hill."

Sir Barton made a scoffing sound in the back of his throat. "He told me of her father's scheme to turn slaves into tenant farmers. Do you mean to say she really intends to go through with that madness?"

"She does. Whatever the cost." The image of her standing there, offering herself to Delamere, rose in his mind. "I'm certain Delamere meant to prevent her. If she had died at his hand after they wed, her inheritance would have been his, and no one the wiser. It was that outcome your plantation manager, Cary, hoped to avoid by sending her here."

"Lord Nathaniel claimed he had brought my granddaughter home. But she tells me it was really you." He gave Andrew another hard stare, then jerked his chin in a nod. "For that, sir, I thank you. Now, however, it's your duty to make her stay."

"Make her—?"

"Marry the girl and keep her *here*." To Andrew's shock, Sir Barton's voice broke on a muffled sob. "I drove my daughter away. I thought a match with a duke's son would be a fine thing for her. But she wanted no part of it. I all but pushed her into Thomas Holderin's arms. And he took her to Antigua. I *won't* have my granddaughter return to that godforsaken island. I won't have her leave *this* island, in point of fact!" Sir Barton said, masking his fear with fury.

"What will become of Harper's Hill if she does not go back?"

"That sugar plantation has been a scab on my conscience for

years, though God knows I've endeavored mightily not to pick at it. Who gives a damn what becomes of it now?"

"Tempest does," Andrew said. "And she is determined to go home."

"Home?"

"Antigua is the only home she's ever known."

"This is her true home. She's all I have now. I cannot let her leave . . ."

Andrew felt a surprising surge of sympathy as he watched pained emotions flit across the older man's face. "I've got it," the baronet exclaimed after a few moments' reflection. "Why, I'll give her Harper's Hill. As soon as my solicitor can be made to draft the papers, it will be hers, and she can do with it as she likes." A pause. "So long as she agrees not to go back there herself."

Andrew's heart knocked in his chest. Would she take that bargain? A little encouragement, a word in Sir Barton's ear, and he might never have to tell her good-bye.

"No," he said. There might be little to choose between two blackguards bent on revenge, but he would be damned before he would coerce her as Delamere had done. "No conditions. Do it because it's the right thing to do, or not at all."

"Then she'll be on the next ship bound for the West Indies." Sir Barton scowled. "And I suppose you mean to be at the helm."

Yes, he wanted to say. *Yes. Even if I actually have to kidnap her this time.*

"I have commitments here, Sir Barton," Andrew said instead. "Commitments to my mother and to Beauchamp Shipping. I will be returning to London as soon as I am able."

"London." Sir Barton's white head wagged. "Two hundred miles off. Well, it could be worse. You'll marry here first, though. No need for the banns to be called," he said, the plan developing in a rush. "I'll arrange a license from the bishop. Although . . . you're a bloody papist, I suppose?" Before Andrew could reply, he added, "Not that it matters, of course. After what I saw last night, were you the veriest Hindu, Corrvan, I would still have to insist on a wedding."

"You may set your mind at ease, Sir Barton," Andrew replied, his eyes dropping shut. Damn, but his arm ached. "I am not a Hindu." Sir Barton gave a rumble of disapproval, but Andrew did not open his eyes. "Nor, as it happens, am I a Catholic. In fact, my mother's father was a clergyman in the Church of Ireland."

"That's something," Sir Barton reluctantly admitted.

"Aye," Andrew gritted. "Something." When he had first come to England and entered school, the fact had smoothed his way. It had also made it all the easier to strip him of his Irishness.

"Well, then." Sir Barton's voice was still gruff, but some of the bluster had gone out of him. "You can marry her without delay."

"Nothing would give me greater pleasure," Andrew answered honestly, though a part of him—the better part, certainly—insisted that Tempest's desires must be paramount, that she deserved the liberty of choice, even if polite society, led by her grandfather, would say that she had already made her choice and must now live with the consequences. "But you should know that your granddaughter has firm views on marriage. She has made it abundantly clear she means never to wed."

Sir Barton waved off the protest. "Nonsense. She cannot escape it now. Anyway, she was only trying to protect her inheritance. Once she has Harper's Hill, she will have no further objections."

Andrew wished he could agree.

"Well," the baronet said, reaching beneath his arm and proffering Andrew's shaving kit, "I'll leave you with this. You look like a bloody pirate."

Andrew glanced once more at his bandaged shoulder and the arm bound to his side. "I'm left-handed."

Sir Barton muttered something under his breath that sounded suspiciously like *Irish devil*. "Your boy will be back in a moment."

"Caesar's a fine lad, but no valet." Was he really inviting Tempest's grandfather to hold a razor to his throat?

With a grumble, Sir Barton opened the case.

"She may yet refuse me, you know," Andrew said, listening to the rhythmic *thwack-thwock* of the razor being stropped. "It cannot have escaped your notice that your granddaughter has a mind of her own."

Sir Barton gave a weary nod and reached for the shaving soap. "Like her mother. But I've learned my lesson there. I cannot force her hand, so it will be up to you to convince her."

Andrew closed his eyes, bared his neck to the blade, and tried not to imagine what would happen if he failed.

Chapter 21

When her grandfather entered Mrs. Beauchamp's sitting room, Tempest was on her feet and at his side in a moment.

Nevertheless, Emily beat her there. "My son? Is he all right?"

"Yes, Mrs. Beauchamp. Yes. The physician left before he had fully recovered consciousness, but I stayed with him. He is awake now, and talking sense—for the most part. The physician said that the wound itself should heal without incident, once Corrvan recovers from the loss of blood."

"Thank God! I must—I must go to him," Emily insisted, squeezing Tempest's hand and darting past Sir Barton and across the corridor.

How Tempest longed to go after her. As if he could read her intentions, however, her grandfather stepped between her and the door. So far as propriety was concerned, at least, Andrew was nothing to her. She could have nothing to do at the bedside of a man to whom she was not related—even if the whole household must be buzzing with the knowledge that he had been *in* her bed the night before.

Sir Barton cleared his throat. Tempest did not know whether she was expected to invite him to sit down or not. They had had very little in the way of private conversation since her arrival. To her surprise, her grandfather took up her hand and patted it consolingly. "Do not worry, my dear. He will be all right."

She had expected a scolding, a lecture, an order. *You will marry the man without delay.* Had those been her grandfather's words, would she have readily agreed? Or would she have bristled against another's command, as always?

Drawing him over to the chairs by the fire, she sat and invited him to do the same. By the still-gray light of midday and after an almost sleepless night, he looked every minute of his seventy-odd years. "You need your rest, Grandfather."

"I will be fine. It is you for whom I worry." Given his expression, she wondered if she did not look almost as harrowed as he.

"There is no need, I assure you. I am perfectly fine."

"I imagine Captain Corrvan's injuries will delay your return to London. Mrs. Beauchamp will not want to leave until he can travel."

"I—yes. I suppose you are right." Absently, she twisted the handkerchief she had forgotten she was holding. "A short delay will not signify. The ship on which I have booked passage does not leave for the West Indies until the middle of the month."

"Ah." Pairing the interjection with a nod of understanding, he rose to his feet and paced in front of the fireplace before his restless thoughts seemed to require a wider scope. He strode to the window and stared down the drive as he spoke—to himself, more than to her. "How can I ask it?"

"I beg your pardon?" She leaned forward, perched on the very edge of the chair, the better to see and hear him. But she would not allow herself to rise.

"I would like . . . I wish you to stay," he said in a rush. "I would like to know my granddaughter."

The handkerchief dropped from her suddenly nerveless fingertips. "Excuse my surprise, sir," she said stiffly, squaring her shoulders. "You have shown so little interest until now."

"Can you forgive me—Tempest?" he asked, turning away from the window to face her as her name passed his lips. "I have been a fool. When my Angela left, I allowed what I believed to be righteous anger to color my behavior toward her . . . and your father. When she died, my grief became my excuse. When . . . when *he* died, I should have come for you—come *to* you. But by then I had persuaded myself that I was not needed. That I would not be welcome. Like the idle king in some fairy tale, I sat here, waiting for you to come to me instead."

"So I have."

"Eventually, and most unwillingly, I know. But I am glad, nonetheless." He hesitated. "Now, emboldened by my good fortune, I ask you to stay longer where you never wished to be. Is that not the epitome of a selfish old man?"

Tempest could not answer that question honestly without giving offense, but the one she asked instead was hardly more politic. "Did you really intend for my mother to marry Lord Nathaniel?"

He shook his head, but his words soon made clear that the gesture was self-recrimination, rather than a denial. "God forgive me. I saw little beyond his family connections—my daughter married to the son of a duke."

She recalled his words about the fulfillment of a twenty-five-year-old wish. "Did you mean for *me* to marry him in her place?" Fatigue and uncertainty combined to reduce her voice to a rough whisper.

A stricken look passed over his face. "No," he insisted. "I have thought a great deal, then, and"—he glanced toward the door—"more recently, about the price of my obstinacy in such matters. And I could not like his manner, his determination to succeed with you, although I had no suspicion until last night, or rather this morning, what he truly was—what he had become. I suspect the West Indies was the worst sort of place for a man such as he. Little need there to check one's . . . appetites."

"I firmly believe the people make the place what it is," she countered, unwilling to accept the familiar slander, "and not the other way 'round. My father—"

"Was a good man," he finished, much to her surprise. "I know that now, even if I did not want to see the truth all those years ago."

After a long, silent moment, Tempest suggested, "You might come with me."

Her grandfather gave a bark of surprise. "I? No. I should have nothing to do in Antigua."

"Nothing to do?" She could feel her color rising with her temper. "Do you imagine estates in other parts of the world manage themselves, that absenteeism is no scourge there—?"

"I imagine nothing of the sort," he spoke over her, holding up a hand to halt the flow of bitter invectives. "I meant only that my presence would be superfluous. Harper's Hill is yours to do with as you see fit. From this moment, if you wish it," he said, waving his hand as if he were granting a wish. "The very least I can do to make up for so many years of neglect."

"I—" Tempest began and then stopped, pressing her lips together. She must have misunderstood.

She found herself on her feet, although she did not remember standing. Could her grandfather really be offering her the chance to realize Papa's dream, the chance to right what her heart had always told her was a great wrong? And if so, at what price?

"You will grant me my inheritance now . . . if I stay here with you?"

How could she refuse the bargain he offered? He was giving her everything she wanted. The promise of her inheritance, the chance for a family. *Everything.*

Even an excuse not to leave. If she wanted one.

His reply was slow in coming as he wrestled with himself. "Or if you go," he said finally. "It's up to you."

"Thank you, Grandfather," she cried, throwing her arms around him.

The embrace clearly caught him off guard, but he did not hold himself rigid for long. In a moment, his hand was patting her back, and she felt something suspiciously like tears against her neck. "Thank *you*, child. Thank you."

Though the words were muffled, she heard a note of hesitation in them. He was waiting, hoping for her to say more. To tell him that she would not hurry back to Antigua.

"I condemned myself to misery twenty-five years ago. Now I would like to become acquainted with my granddaughter, in whatever time is left to me," he said, pulling away enough that he could look her in the eye. "But I can offer very little to tempt you to stay, I'm afraid. A cold house, and a dull old man for company. I suppose we might arrange to pay a call on Mr. Wilberforce, if the weather permits."

"*William* Wilberforce, the abolitionist? You know him?"

"Oh yes. He is MP for the county. I understand you and he have a common interest."

Tempest could only nod.

For as long as she could remember, she had been dreaming of the day when the slaves at Harper's Hill would be free. Once that goal had been met, she had told herself, she would be content. But she knew their emancipation was only a drop in the bucket—a "grand gesture," as Andrew had told her, that would in the end have little impact. Leaders like Wilberforce were working to change things on a much larger scale: first, by ending the slave trade, then eventually putting an end to slavery. It would be an honor to meet someone doing such noble, necessary work.

Enough of an honor to tip the balance in favor of extending her visit here, if only for a little while?

"Or perhaps you can think of better reasons to stay than just to satisfy an old man?" Her grandfather's rather misty gaze darted once more toward the door, toward the patient recovering in the room across the way.

Andrew. The anchor to which her heart was tied. The temptation she had so little will to resist. The very reason she ought to go.

Ah, there it was. The age-old contest between head and heart—which was, in her case, a marked tendency to claim to act with the former while being led entirely by the latter. For weeks now, her impulsive actions had put her at risk. That was how she had wound up aboard the *Fair Colleen* in the first place. How she had wound up in Andrew's arms.

And how she had almost wound up losing him forever.

It was time to do what she had promised Papa. It was time to behave like a rational creature.

"It is not a decision to be made lightly, Grandfather. I will have to think about it."

"Another horrid novel, Tempest?"

The sound of Andrew's voice jerked her into the present moment, and she clutched automatically at the book in her lap before it could slide off her silk-covered knees and onto the floor. Although it felt inappropriately festive, Hannah had insisted on the dark red dress. *For Christmas*, she had said.

At her feet lay Caliban, as he had done since having been shooed from the sickroom by Mrs. Beauchamp earlier in the afternoon. Now, however, his ears were perked forward and he looked alert, awaiting permission to move.

Andrew stood just inside the door to the library, devouring her with his eyes, and suddenly she could not resent Emily's or Hannah's interference in the matter of her wardrobe. His uninjured shoulder was propped against the jamb—a characteristically devil-may-care pose, except that this time, she suspected he could really do with the support. How long had he been watching her?

"Not *another*," she corrected as she rose and laid the book aside, remembering how he had once teased her about such reading. Taking her movement as consent for his own, Caliban went immediately to Andrew. "My first. *Udolpho*."

"Oh?" Andrew shook his head laughingly, whether at her or at the dog she was not sure. "I thought it was meant to be exhilarating, but I haven't seen you turn a page for a quarter of an hour at least."

"I—" As before, she had picked up the book, hoping for a reprieve, a distraction from her conflicted thoughts, but her eyes had passed over the words without seeing them. While her mind had wandered, the room had grown dark, far too dark now to read. "I've had quite enough of villainy and bloodshed for a while. Shouldn't you be in bed?"

Her heart would willingly have carried her to his side if her feet had not seemed to be frozen in place. After a night of terror and a day of worrying, to have him now standing before her as if nothing had happened . . . Despite the dog's confirmation, she still half-feared Andrew was an apparition, and if she touched him, he might disappear.

"My mother has spent the afternoon pouring beef tea down my throat. For strength, she says. I do believe I'm as strong as I'm going to get." He managed a wry sort of grimace, but his face was pale. "I could do with a bit of fresh air now. Will you walk with me?" he asked, straightening and holding out his good arm, over which was draped her velvet cloak.

"If we must talk, cannot we sit here, where you can rest? I will call for a lamp," she insisted, moving closer and reaching for the bellpull near the door.

"Please."

The whisper alone would have been enough to stay her, but his hand touched her arm, and she took some reassurance from its warmth. With a catch in her throat, she nodded and let the tasseled silk cord slip through her fingertips.

The brighter light from the sconces in the entry hall did nothing to improve his pallor, and above his cravat, along the edge of his jaw, she glimpsed a fresh-looking cut.

As if feeling her eyes on it, he brought his fingers to the collar of his greatcoat and hitched it higher. "A shaving mishap. What do you have on your feet?"

Embarrassed, Tempest raised her skirts enough to show him the worn toes of her half-boots, the ones she had been wearing when she left Antigua, now scuffed and salt-stained and patched. In her hurry, Emily had managed dresses, underthings, everything but shoes.

"They'll do." Andrew smiled. "I half-expected to see them bare."

As she slipped the cloak around her shoulders, he reached to raise her hood, fumbling a bit as he worked one-handed. Caliban wove himself between their knees. At Andrew's nod, a footman opened the door, and a gust of cold air swept in, taking Tempest's breath with it. "Are you sure this is wise?" she asked.

"I'm quite sure it isn't."

But the wind seemed to brace him, invigorate him. How galling it must be for a man accustomed to going where he wanted and doing what he would, to find himself confined—to a sickbed, to a house, to a desk in a London shipping office. And what was it that he was bringing her out here to say? After last night, did he feel forced to tie himself to her, too?

Offering her a surprisingly steady arm, he led her out into the twilight.

"Oh."

The world around them was blanketed in white; downy flakes still fell silently from the darkening sky. After only a moment, they coated the capes of Andrew's greatcoat, caught and sparkled in the fur trim of her hood. Nothing like ash, nothing like dust. Cold. But beautiful, so beautiful.

Caliban was first down the steps, barking in celebration and snapping at the snowflakes. The noise startled a hare from beneath a snow-covered bush, and the dog readily gave chase.

"He's earned it," Andrew said, watching him run.

"Yes."

The reminder of Lord Nathaniel's grim fate recalled to her mind the evening aboard the *Fair Colleen*, after the storm. Then as now, she had felt somber at the thought of the death of another human being. But also a deep sense of relief. She could not mourn him.

Cautiously, she released Andrew's arm and walked down the few steps, shuffling her feet through the snow. When she turned back toward the house, he was watching her.

"I saw it start more than an hour ago. I hoped you had not noticed. I wanted—I wanted to be the one to show you."

"*Thank you*," she mouthed, not wanting to disturb the stillness.

Little eddies of snow swirled around his feet as he strode toward her. "It will be a memory to take with you to Antigua."

Why should those words stab her to the quick? He spoke only the truth. She meant to return to the West Indies, did she not?

But she would never forget this night. Nor any other she had spent with him.

"Yes."

When he stopped beside her, he did not reach for her hand or offer his arm again.

"My grandfather has made me a gift of Harper's Hill," she said after a moment of watching the snow fall. Her feet were growing cold. "As soon as the paperwork can be drawn up, I will be able to do what I have wanted, what I have waited to do all my life."

In the half light, she could not read his expression, but the news did not seem to surprise him. "You will be off as soon as possible, then."

It was not a question, so she did not attempt an answer. "And you? Will you strike out for the sea once more when you are able?"

"No. My sailing days are behind me. At least," he added after a moment, "I shall not captain another voyage."

"What will become of the *Fair Colleen*?" she asked. "Mr. Bewick will take her out, I suppose."

"I don't know about that. The air in Hampstead seems to agree with him, at least for now. But there will be someone right for the job, someone eager for profit and adventure on the high seas." He lifted his shoulders in a shrug and then winced, as if he had forgotten his injuries for a moment. "I am going to manage Beauchamp Shipping. Important changes are coming. Key decisions must be made, and my stepfather wanted me to make them." He sounded certain, but far from happy.

"Oh. Yes. Of course." It was what she had wanted for him, was it not? "Will you never go back to the West Indies, then?"

"Perhaps," he said after a moment, his eyes scanning the horizon. "Someday. There is an argument for maintaining my connections in that part of the world. But for now, I am needed in London."

"Then that is where you should be, doing the work you have to do." How easy it was to make rational decisions for others!

"As you must do yours."

"Yes."

Snow capped the balustrade, made strange figures of the topi-
aries in the garden, coated the bare tree limbs. A landscape with
which she hardly had had time to become familiar grew more alien
with each passing moment. "So, a journey that began under tropical
skies ends here," she said, studying the feathery pattern made by the
hem of her cloak against the snow. "Soon it will be as if we never
met."

She heard him inhale sharply through his nose, as if something
gave him pain. The cold settling into his wound, perhaps. Surely not
her words.

Then he said, "I brought you out here thinking to propose."

"Because my grandfather wishes it?"

A humorless laugh burst from his lips. "*Wishes* it? I believe it
would be more accurate to say Sir Barton sees our union as a necessary evil, something to paper over a scandal." Before she could speak
again, he stepped in front of her, so close that she had to look up to
see his face. "But in any case, I would not marry to make him happy.
I would only marry because I was in love."

Overhead, the sky began to clear, giving way to a rising moon.
The heavy snowfall slowed. All around them the world lay at peace.
Only the pounding of her heart threatened to disturb it.

"You . . . you love me?"

Did two people ever mean the same thing when they uttered those
words? She had never doubted Andrew was capable of passion, of
strong attachment. But love was more than that. It was also sacrifice
and heartache.

Wasn't it?

"I do," he said. "And if I thought there were a way to teach you to
need me the way I need you, Tempest Holderin, I would never let you
leave my side, shipping companies and sugar plantations be damned."

Suddenly in need of something on which to steady herself, she laid
her palms against his chest and wondered at the easy rhythm of his
heart. Her own thudded against her ribs as if determined to escape.

"Marriage . . ." she began, then stopped, no longer certain what
she had been about to say.

"I know your mind where matrimony is concerned." He spoke
quickly, as if to reassure her. As if loath to hear what she might say.
"Your feelings about marriage stand between us, even if every other
barrier to our being together could somehow be overcome. So, be-

cause I love you, I won't ask you to marry me." He took a step backward, then another, until her hand slid down his shirtfront and he slipped from her reach. "And because I love you, I never will."

Her arm was still outstretched, exposing her wrist to the cold air, to the moonlight. A phalanx of oval bruises bloomed on her pale skin where Lord Nathaniel had grabbed her. Andrew's fingertips, encased in cool, supple leather, brushed across them, his touch feather light. "You should never have told Delamere you would marry him, either. Nothing could be worth that particular sacrifice."

"I had to do something."

"To save the people of Harper's Hill?"

She gave the tiniest shake of her head. "No. Well, yes. That too. But mostly to divert his attention from you. I realize now it was a reckless thing to do—one of many reckless, foolish things I have done. But you were in danger. And I—I told myself he couldn't hurt me." A derisive noise escaped Andrew's lips, but she spoke over it. "I'm not naïve. Physical pain is not the only thing that matters, you know." She drew her arm back so her cloak fell forward, covering the marks. "I always believed that if I never gave my heart away, I would keep my dreams, keep *myself*, safe. So I convinced myself I was never in any real danger from him. How could I be hurt by someone I cared nothing for?" She glanced past him, across the snowy landscape. "The far greater risk was letting myself fall in love with you."

His hand came up and brushed back her hood so that she could not avoid meeting his gaze. Despite the cold, despite his pain, there was heat in his eyes. "Still, you want to return to Antigua," he pointed out soberly. "And I am needed here. What sort of future can we have together?"

"There must be some way—"

"We cannot be in two places at once," he pointed out.

"No. You are right. So I propose," she said, holding out one hand and then the other, palms upward, as she spoke, "that you do just as you have suggested: Stay in London, but travel occasionally to the West Indies, in the interests of Beauchamp Shipping. And for myself, I—I propose taking an active role in the work being done by the abolitionists. Here, where the laws are made. In short—" Her voice broke and she drew her hands inward, clutching them to her chest. "I propose."

"Tempest." Andrew's dark brows knit together, shadowing his eyes. "What are you saying?"

Grabbing his hand for balance, she lowered herself to the ground, indifferent to the fate of garnet silk and green velvet—although she could not help but shiver when her knee, covered only by her stocking, met the snow. "You have said you will not ask me. So it seems I must do the asking."

As he sank down to face her, one hand on her shoulder, his eyes searched hers, a question in their green depths. "Why are you doing this? Merely because it's expected? Merely to avoid censure?"

"I confess I have never worried much about what society says. I do what I think is best."

A huff of sound, not quite laughter, escaped him. "If you've made up your mind to marry, you might better accept Cary's offer," he said, and she could not be entirely certain he teased. "He's a far safer choice."

"And when," she asked, tilting her head, "have I ever done what's safe?"

His hand traveled across her shoulder to her throat and then rose to cup her ear. She rested her head easily against his palm. "Never."

The kiss seemed slow in coming, torturously slow, as he sank back on his haunches and then drew her toward him, never looking away, never allowing her to break his gaze, never letting her doubt his intentions. When his mouth finally met hers, she did not know whether to expect firmness or gentleness, a mere brush of his lips or a brand. Unwilling to wait to find out, she parted her lips and kissed him first, taking his breath for her own, sealing their bond in a way that felt more real than a ring ever could.

"And you are sure you can be satisfied with such an arrangement? Staying in England—with me? Returning to Antigua every few years, at best?"

"I suppose I have given you good reason to fear that I make only rash decisions I'll later regret," she whispered as she pulled back. "I swear that has not always been the case. I cannot promise never to be homesick. But coming here has made me see things differently. Home is—"

"Please tell me you are not about to say, 'home is where the heart is,'" he interrupted with a wry twist to his lips. "I did not have you pegged as a sentimentalist."

"Worse," she confessed with a wobbly smile. "I was going to say, 'Home is wherever you love.'" She fixed her gaze on the knot of his cravat, wondering absently who had tied it for him. "All my life, love has been linked with pain. Now I know it can be—"

"Pleasure?" he suggested in a tone that sent a bolt of heat through her core.

"I was not thinking of... That is, I..." She knew she blushed, for the few desultory snowflakes still wandering down from the sky stung her hot cheeks and melted away like tears. Slipping her arms beneath his greatcoat, she buried her face against his chest.

"Yes. Pleasure. And for the pleasure of being with you, I'll risk the pain." A pause, then the necessary question: "Andrew, will you marry me?"

He shifted slightly, perhaps to see her face, perhaps because kneeling on the frozen ground was far from comfortable. Whatever it was, her center of gravity followed his, and before she quite knew what had happened, the two of them had toppled into the snow, he on his back, she across his chest.

"Ooof."

Whether it was the sound or the movement or the little puff of snow that rose around them as they fell, she was not sure, but before she could recover, she realized Caliban's attention had been attracted to their predicament. He was loping toward them at full speed, hare forgotten, mouth wide in a doggy grin, and she could see on his face his eagerness to join their snowy scrum.

Andrew's anticipatory grimace of pain gave her a sudden vision of Caliban sailing through the air to land atop them. She did the only thing she could think to do.

"Caliban, stop."

It was not a shout, not a scream. She had learned from her dealings with Jasper the monkey that a firm tone required neither and usually got better results. Still, she held her breath, waiting for the order to travel from her lips to the dog's ears, wondering if he would heed.

Bewildered, Caliban braced his front legs and sat on his hind ones, plowing snow up before him as he skidded to a halt, stopping only inches away, quivering.

A breath of relief sighed from her lips. "Good dog."

"I should have known what I was in for that very first day," Andrew said, the rumble of his words traveling through his chest and into her own.

Startled to discover she was still sprawled across him, she tried to rise. But he was holding her tight, and she felt warm all over, despite the snow that had found its way beneath her skirts. "What do you mean?"

"The day I met you. The day Caliban stopped listening to my orders in favor of yours. The day he ceased to be my dog." There was laughter in his tone, she thought. If only she could see his face. "He knew before I did . . . as did Beals and Bewick and the rest."

"Knew what?"

"Who was really in command during the *Colleen*'s last voyage."

When he shifted beneath her, she understood that he wanted her to rise, so she pushed herself upright and scrambled to her feet. The dog danced around her ankles, rising up only once, forepaws at her waist, to be petted and praised for his good behavior, before allowing Andrew to make use of him to stand. As he got up, he brushed snow from her skirt, she from his shoulders, and in another moment she found herself bundled into his coat.

"What would Miss Wollstonecraft say?" he asked.

Darting her eyes to his face, she could not quite make out whether he teased only, or whether he *knew*. Had he been reading her heart all along? "She would not be entirely surprised. 'Suspense and difficulties exalt the affections,' she says, and we have certainly had our share of those."

His chin lifted in a nod of agreement. "What else?"

Would he know if she did not tell him the truth? But she could not lie. "Something about how the security of marriage makes the fever of love subside," she whispered.

"Hardly a ringing endorsement," he said. "And you're sure that's what you want?"

Her lip was between her teeth before she could stop herself, and she could only nod.

"This, from a rational creature." He laughed. "Then yes, my love, I'll marry you." Raising his hand, he dragged his thumb across her chin, tugging her lip free, then brushing his lips lightly across her mouth. "She's right enough about suspense and difficulties. But they do wear thin after a while." Another kiss, firmer. "They might even make one look forward to the calm after the storm." Nibbling, suckling. Her toes curled in her boots. "There's beauty in a glassy sea." Her lip between *his* teeth, now, and the last vestiges of her worry yielded to the flood of heat. "But I fear your Miss Wollstonecraft is wrong about the fever. At sea or on land, I'll always be a sailor at heart, and I feel quite certain a tempest will always make my pulse rise."

Despairing at last of their attention, Caliban snuffled away in search of other prey.

"I have seen endless proof that when people are tied or bound or chained, it only makes them yearn for freedom all the more," she said, when her lips were her own again. "They will do anything, risk anything to get free. But I never applied that lesson to my own heart. I thought that if I kept it under lock and key, it would always be under my command. I should have known eventually it would break away, it would fly. And it has flown. To you."

"Then I will guard it with my life," he said, his voice tinged with awe at the responsibility with which she was entrusting him. But he showed no sign of refusing it.

Moonlight turned the blanket of fresh snow into a crust of diamonds. Perfect stillness. Perfect peace. The crisp air carried the sound of church bells across the moor.

"Happy Christmas, my love," she whispered, laying her cheek against his chest.

For answer, his good arm tightened around her shoulders, a band of strength and support, and her heart knew true freedom at last.

Historical Note

The 1790s were a tumultuous decade for Great Britain. Even as Enlightenment ideals fostered demands for increased liberty, revolutionary fervor in France pushed Britain into war. Radical thinkers like Mary Wollstonecraft wrote in support of the Rights of Man (and Woman), while publishers of such works faced imprisonment for treason.

In those same years, the British slave trade reached its peak, carrying captives from Africa to places like Antigua, one of the Leeward Islands in the Caribbean Sea. Just twelve miles wide, Antigua was Britain's third-highest sugar-producing colony, after Jamaica and Barbados. In the late eighteenth century, it had a population of approximately fifty thousand people, 90 percent of whom were enslaved.

Not coincidentally, the movement to abolish slavery also had its origins in that era of conflict and change. Quakers led the charge, aided in their efforts by many individuals: Former slaves, such as Olaudah Equiano and Ottobah Cugoano, told their stories and captured public sympathy; William Wilberforce campaigned on the matter before Parliament; Granville Sharp helped to found Sierra Leone, an African settlement for free people of African descent who had been enslaved in the British colonies; Thomas Clarkson supported legislative action by conducting research into the horrors of the slave trade; and Josiah Wedgwood mass-produced popular cameos bearing an image of a slave in chains and the motto, "Am I not a Man and a Brother?"

The abolitionists' work eventually paid off. An 1807 Act of Parliament officially ended the slave trade in the British Empire. Despite the Royal Navy's enforcement of the act and heavy penalties for its violation, however, smugglers continued the trade on a smaller scale. When Parliament abolished slavery in Britain's colonies in 1833, they created provisions for gradual emancipation over the course of several years, and included £20 million for compensation to slave owners for their lost "property," but no reparations for the slaves themselves.

Keep reading for a sneak peek at
To Seduce a Stranger
On sale April 2017
And don't miss the first book in
The Runaway Desires series
To Kiss a Thief
Available now from
Lyrical Books

Chapter 1

Despite a gift for spinning stories and building castles in the clouds, Charlotte Blakemore had never gone so far as to imagine that her late husband would leave her a fortune.

It soon became clear that her stepson had not imagined it either.

Robert, the new Duke of Langerton, stepped forward and twitched the will from the bespectacled solicitor's hands, as if he suspected the man of fabricating. Neither of them actually said anything, however.

The incredulous squeak—*"Vraiment?"*—could have passed only Charlotte's lips.

"Yes, truly," said Langerton, lowering the parchment and fixing her with a hard stare.

It was not as if Langerton had been left nothing. As heir to the dukedom, with all its properties and a considerable income attached, Langerton was now one of the wealthiest men in England. Still, it was quite clear he objected to the fact that his father's substantial private fortune—whatever was not entailed or otherwise bequeathed—was to be divided among him, his sisters, and Charlotte. And not equally, either. Charlotte was to receive half.

Without saying anything more, Langerton returned the will to the solicitor and resumed his seat. A feeble ray of morning sun poked between the curtains covering the library window and picked out a few silver threads in his dark hair. Although he was not yet forty, the strain of the past few weeks, beginning with his vocal disapproval of his father's second bride, had aged him.

The remainder of the will's terms—gifts to the servants, sundry personal effects to those who would treasure them—passed by without comment. Charlotte hardly heard them. Sitting stiffly beside her, Langerton no doubt imagined she was calculating the interest on her inheritance. The thoughts flitting through her head were actually closer to a disjointed prayer of thanksgiving, however.

Thank God she would not have to return to her aunt.

Not that her father's sister, Baroness Penhurst, had been cruel, exactly. But no one who knew the woman would call her kind. *"Bad enough that James had to sow his wild oats with a Frenchwoman,"* Charlotte had overheard her sighing more than once. *"Did he have to saddle me with the baggage?"* "The Earl of Belmont's natural daughter," people called her when they were inclined to be polite. Which they rarely were.

"That's far more than you would be entitled to by dower rights alone." Langerton's voice broke through her ruminations. The solicitor was stuffing papers into his worn leather case. "You must be pleased."

Charlotte drew herself up. "Nothing about your dear father's death has brought me pleasure, Robert."

His lip curled. Did he really expect her to address her stepson as "Your Grace"? "Next you'll claim you were madly in love with him."

George Blakemore, fifth Duke of Langerton, had been gentle and caring, and Charlotte might honestly have answered *yes.* She *had* loved him, in the way one loves a sweet, grandfatherly man—fitting, since she was just four and twenty and he had been well past seventy when he had proposed. No one had been more taken aback by his offer than Charlotte, not even her aunt and uncle, who had done their best to dissuade their old friend from this act of madness—"*kindness,*" he had corrected when he and Charlotte were alone.

"Lady Penhurst always was a right dragon," George had told her with a laugh. *"No need for you to live under her thumb forever, Lottie."*

No one had negotiated marriage settlements on her behalf. Aunt Penhurst had refused to attend the ceremony. Perhaps it was an inauspicious beginning for wedded bliss—but bliss had been beyond Charlotte's expectation. It was enough that the exchange of vows in Bath Abbey just a few days after Easter had ushered in six weeks of the closest thing to peace she had ever known. Six weeks, broken by his heart seizure. Not the first he had suffered. Sadly, however, the last.

"Where will you go?" Robert asked, taking up the position behind the desk once the solicitor had vacated it.

"London." A note of wariness crept into her voice. "Your father's will—"

"Blakemore House is a residence of the Duke of Langerton." As he spoke, he began to rearrange various items—the inkstand, a paperweight, his father's seal—with a possessive hand. "And I do not intend to share it with the fortune-hunting daughter of a French whore."

Long years of practice had taught Charlotte how to disguise what she felt—fear, dismay. Even joy. Although her feet itched to fly from the room, away from her stepson's smirk, she refused to give him the satisfaction. "Fortunately for you, you needn't. Your father specified the house was to be mine."

"You have at best a *lifetime* interest in the property, to be clear," he corrected, crossing his arms behind his back and looking her up and down. "But if I were you, I would not put a great deal of faith in the promises of that particular piece of parchment."

Her hard-won composure deserted her. "You mean to—to—?" As sometimes happened when she was distressed, the English words flew from her head, leaving only French, and that she would not speak before him again.

"Fix my father's mistakes?" Robert supplied in a mocking attempt at helpfulness. "As best I can. There can be very little doubt that he was not thinking clearly when he married you. To say nothing of his state of mind when he rewrote his will."

Her lips parted on a gasp. "How can you be so . . . so *cruel*?"

"To you? Nothing so easy, ma'am," he said, making the last word sound like an insult.

"To your *father*," she corrected. "To the memory of a decent, generous man. You would have him called mad merely to serve your own selfish ends?"

A dismissive flick of one hand. "The damage is already done. Since your hasty marriage, he's known far and wide as a crazy old fool. The words are whispered behind every drawing room door in Mayfair, tossed about like dice in a gaming hell. How you must have plotted and connived to pull off that marriage," he said with a shake of his head, as if reluctantly impressed. "But the world knows it for a farce, Charlotte."

"A farce? How dare you suggest—?"

"I *suggest* nothing. You convinced a doddering old man to sign his name in a parish register. Can you prove he knew what he was about? No," he answered his own question. "Because he did not. Then you persuaded him to leave an exorbitant sum to some person he believed to be his wife," he continued. "But given his mental state, your marriage was invalid from the start. Now it's up to me to restore the natural order of things."

The natural order of things. Spiteful dukes and mean-spirited baronesses on top. The Charlottes of the world on the bottom.

"Such a ploy will only humiliate the family and tarnish your father's memory," she said, lifting her chin. No matter Robert's accusations, she *was* a duchess. "I will pray that time tempers your grief enough to make you see it for the foolishness it is."

He stepped within arm's length and fixed her with a narrow-eyed glare. A chill scuttled down her spine. She might have thought he meant her harm—if she could imagine him dirtying his hands with the effort. Should she call a footman? Or the butler? Would they dare to act against the Duke of Langerton if she did?

In the end, however, he waited only long enough to force her into betraying her own nervousness. She giggled. And when she attempted to stifle the sound, a satisfied smile curved his lips, and he slammed the library door in her face.

Then, and only then, did she allow herself to run—down the corridor, up the stairs, and to her bedchamber.

"Was it as bad as you'd feared, ma'am?" asked her maid, Jane, from the dressing room.

"Worse." Charlotte paced to the window and looked down on the garden. Just two weeks ago she had sat beside her husband on that very bench and admired the spring blooms. Now a few of them had already begun to fade.

"Never say His Grace left you with nothing?"

"If only he had, Jane, I might be better off. Instead he left me so much that his son grows vindictive. He means to forestall my claim to any inheritance by contesting the will . . . by contesting the validity of my marriage . . ." Without conscious thought, her eyes darted to the perfectly made tester bed in the center of the room.

The sight of it catapulted her back to her wedding night, when her new husband had stood beside her on the threshold to this room, patted her hand, and told her she had no cause to feel apprehensive. *"I will not disturb your rest, Lottie dear,"* he had told her. And he had not—not that night, nor any other.

She had not exactly been saddened by the discovery he did not intend to share her bed. Certainly nothing her aunt had told her had given her cause to look forward to what happened between husband and wife. And the late duke *had* been an old man, hardly the stuff of any girl's fantasy. Not that she permitted herself *those* sorts of fantasies.

Still, she had felt a pang of something—something for which she had no word, either in French or English—when he had brushed her knuckles with dry lips and wished her good night before retiring to his separate chambers. She had always been so very lonely, especially at night, when the house grew still but her mind did not.

She had let herself imagine that, perhaps, married life would be different.

Entering from the dressing room on silent feet, Jane must have caught the direction of Charlotte's gaze, for she said only "Oh," in a quiet, knowing way.

Jane knew how things had stood between her mistress and her husband, of course. Such matters could hardly be kept from one's personal servants. How many others suspected the truth? Could Robert somehow use it as evidence against her? The late duke's *mind* had been perfectly sound, but all in her marriage had *not* been as it should have.

"They won't do you as they did poor Lady Cleaves, will they?" Jane asked.

With fingertips suddenly turned to claws, Charlotte gripped the windowsill for support. She had forgotten all about the Cleaves affair, although it had been on everyone's tongue just over a year ago. Lord Cleaves had accused his wife of unfaithfulness and announced his intention of suing for a divorce. Lady Cleaves had countered with a petition for an annulment on the grounds of her husband's impotence, claiming their four-year marriage had never been consummated. Detailed accounts of the proceedings had been published in the papers and laughed over in none-too-hushed tones. Aunt Penhurst, for one, had enjoyed snickering over the stories of Lord Cleaves's failed attempts to demonstrate his capacity in front of the officers of the court. Meanwhile, Lady Cleaves had been forced to undergo physical examination by two midwives to prove she was . . . What had been the legal term bandied about? Ah, yes. *Virgo intacta.* Then, Charlotte had not been quite sure what it meant.

Now, however, she knew all too well.

Heat swept up from Charlotte's chest, across her cheeks, and settled in the tips of her ears, leaving her fingers cold.

The world could laugh at her if it chose. She was half-French, the daughter of a loose woman. She was used to derision, used to suspicion. She had never cared a jot for the world's good opinion, and she knew she had done nothing to earn its censure.

But she could not bear to think of anyone laughing at a man who had been so very, very kind.

As she stared down into the greenery, her eyes unfocused, a movement on the edge of the garden caught her attention. Someone in dark, nondescript clothes, neither servant nor gentleman, stood almost hidden by the stone pillar at the corner of the fence. Perfectly positioned to see both the house and the mews. A thief? But it was broad daylight.

"There's a man," she began, turning away from the window and gesturing behind her.

Jane nodded eagerly and came forward. "Now, that's the ticket, ma'am. A man. There must be some chap you took a fancy to, once upon a time. Someone you'd like to . . . That is, you might be a widow, but you're still just a bride at heart, and a bride has a right to look forward to—well, you know what I mean. No one would have to be any the wiser."

Charlotte's jaw had grown slack as understanding dawned, so that it was an effort to muster a sound. "Jane!" She giggled nervously once more—drat it all. Dropping her gaze to the carpet, she said, in what she hoped was a scolding tone, "Surely you aren't suggesting that I—that I indulge in—?"

"*Me*? Why, 'twas you who mentioned a man," said Jane, leaping to her own defense.

"Yes. A man. Standing just outside the garden gate." Charlotte nodded toward the window, still unable to raise her eyes. "I wonder what business he could have there?"

Jane hurried across the room to take a peek, then shook her head. "Not a soul about, ma'am. He must've moved on."

Charlotte looked again, but Crescent Lane was empty, just as Jane had said. She scoured every cranny she could see from the window before pushing away and turning back into the room. What foolishness. Robert's threat had made her jittery, that was all. She had nothing to fear from some poor fellow out for an afternoon stroll. Probably just the kitchen maid's new beau.

"We are going to London, Jane," she announced, forcing herself to straighten her shoulders. Duchesses did not slouch. To say nothing of giggle.

"Ma'am?" Jane spun away from the window and looked her up and down. "Now?"

"Now."

Fortunately, her trunk was ready. She had come to her marriage with only a few dresses, and those had been replaced too soon by a new wardrobe—of somber black crape, rather than the lavish spring gowns her husband had urged her to buy. The old dresses had already been packed away.

Into a valise Jane placed a few necessaries and a black gown almost identical to the one Charlotte was wearing. A second valise was soon filled with a similar set of items for Jane, all that would be needed for a night—or perhaps two, given the rapidly lowering sky—on the road.

To the first bag Charlotte added one final item: a battered volume of French poetry, found when she was a girl and which she chose to believe had belonged to her mother. That connection would have been enough to make it precious to her, of course, but of greater practical interest were the banknotes now tucked inside. Interleaving the book's thin pages was everything that remained of the pin money she had been granted on her wedding day. Six weeks ago it had seemed an exorbitant sum. Now, however, if Langerton had his way, it might be all that stood between her and an ignominious return to Aunt Penhurst.

If she would even be willing to take Charlotte back.

When the footman arrived to carry down the trunk, Charlotte placed her bonnet on her head, lowered its lacy black veil over her face, and strode from the house. Jane followed, a valise in each hand.

By the time the driver stopped to change horses at a coaching inn east of Chippenham, the fine morning had indeed turned to rain. The inn yard was a slurry of mud and worse, as travelers either hurried to depart before the weather got worse, or lingered in hopes of improvement. Charlotte and Jane picked their way to the door of the inn and were shown to a private parlor to wait.

From the window, Charlotte watched as people darted among the carriages, their faces hidden beneath umbrellas or the brims of hats, the brighter hues of servants' livery contrasting sharply with dull-colored, sensible travel garments. Everyone eager to get to the place they belonged.

All except Charlotte, who had never really belonged anywhere.

Under the eaves of the stable, one man stood apart, not hurrying to get out of the weather but looking up at the windows of the inn. A man in a dark, nondescript coat. Despite the blur of raindrops against the window and the distance between them, she felt certain it was the same man she had seen outside the garden that morning.

And he was watching her watch him. Her heart battering against her breastbone, she forced her suddenly frozen fingers to release the curtain. It swung back into place, leaving only a square of muslin where the reflection of her face had been.

An awful suspicion began to form in her mind. Had her stepson ordered her watched?

She shivered now as she had not allowed herself to shiver when Robert's cold eyes had skimmed over her in the library. He would stop at nothing to piece together a suit that might keep her from inheriting. Whatever information this stranger could gather might easily be twisted into evidence of her bad character, proof that she was not the sort of woman a duke would choose to wed. At least, not if the duke were in his right mind.

No. *Impossible.* Robert was not the sort to go about hiring spies. Aunt Penhurst had been right. She must stop letting her imagination run away with her.

But what if it weren't her imagination?

Her anxious gaze settled on Jane, pouring tea at a table nearer the hearth, clad in one of the better dresses Charlotte had given up for mourning. Jane was so similar in size and shape to Charlotte, the spotted cambric had required almost no alteration.

"I'll be glad to get back to London, Your Grace," Jane said. As Charlotte took the steaming cup she offered, the spoon rattled in the saucer. "Gracious, ma'am! You look as if you've seen a ghost."

"No." Charlotte clamped the silver against the china with her thumb.

"Not a ghost." She felt certain her vision had been all too real. "Have you a sweetheart in town, Jane?"

"No, ma'am." The girl reinforced the denial with a vigorous shake of her head, but a blush pinked the apples of her cheeks. "Not to say so."

"Family, then?"

A nod this time. "My sister. Married to a butcher in Clerkenwell."

It was not as if she were sending the girl into the abyss, Charlotte tried to reassure herself. Jane was eager to return home. Charlotte, on the other hand, had no real home to which she could return.

She stood and studied their paired reflection in the mirror above the mantelpiece. Jane was prettier than she, with her plump cheeks and upturned nose. The veil would hide those features, though, and the coif of nearly black hair behind might have been Charlotte's, but for its tendency to curl.

"Jane, I wish you to change dresses with me."

Dark brows shot up her forehead. "Ma'am?"

"I want you to go on to London, alone. We shall switch clothing before we return to the carriage, so anyone who saw us enter may think I am you, and you are I. Before the carriage leaves, I shall slip out and away."

Jane's eyes grew wider still. "Why on earth would you do such a thing, Your Grace?"

"Because I wish—" The answer was easy enough, really. Nothing more or less than she had always wished. Charlotte had often been lonely. But she had never been left alone. Widowhood, for all its sorrows, had held out the promise of independence to her. Langerton, and whatever mischief he planned, threatened to take even that away. A challenge to the will, scandalous aspersions heaped upon her, a watcher at every window—she would be little better than a fish in a bowl. "I wish some time out of the public eye. To—to grieve. And I hope in that time, the new duke will come to his senses."

"But where will you go?"

"I don't know." *North—a little cottage in the Lake District, perhaps? Or south, back to France?* The possibilities were limited only by the number of banknotes she had stashed away. "But even if I did, I would not tell you." When Jane looked offended, she explained,

"So if anyone asks, you may say honestly that you haven't any idea where I've gone."

Jane shrugged and began to unpin her dress. "If you wish it, ma'am," she said in a tone that quite clearly communicated her suspicion Charlotte had gone 'round the bend.

When the innkeeper announced that their carriage was ready, two women departed exactly as they had come: one all in black, drawing surreptitious glances of sympathy even as her own expression remained hidden behind her dark veil; and another, a servant, equally invisible to the eyes of the other travelers, carrying two small bags.

Once inside the carriage, Charlotte strained her ears to hear over the patter of rain on the carriage roof, waiting for the sounds of the postilion mounting, the rattle of the whip in its socket. Then she gave Jane's hand a squeeze, picked up her valise, and slipped out the door opposite just as the carriage rumbled into motion, intending to disappear into the anonymous bustle of the inn yard.

At almost the same moment, two other carriages started away, a lone rider arrived, and all was in chaos, but one sweeping glance revealed no sign of the man in the dark clothes. He must have fallen for their deception and followed the coach. Now she needed only to board the next stage, wherever it was bound. Any direction, that was, but the one in which the Duchess of Langerton was believed to be traveling.

With fumbling fingers, she tugged the hood of Jane's cloak more securely into place, then reached into her bag for the book, for her money. Nothing but fabric met her touch. She dug deeper, up to her elbow in the satchel's meager contents, before opening it wider and forcing herself to look, to confront the truth her fingertips had already revealed. No book. No black crape. Just her second and third best dresses and Jane's underthings.

In her haste to escape the coach, she had picked up the wrong valise.

Even as she groped frantically for her reticule, she remembered slipping it around Jane's wrist to complete the costume. She had nothing with which to complete her journey to a new life. No money for coach fare, not even a coin for dinner at the inn.

Growing wetter and colder by the moment, she stumbled blindly back in the direction of shelter. There would still be a way to go on, there *must* be a way, if she just took a moment to think—

She saw the valise fly up and heard the seam of her dress rip almost before she felt the hand on her arm jerk her to safety. A mail-coach thundered through the place where she had been standing a moment before, spraying her with mud and the driver's curses as it passed.

"Look sharp!" someone shouted from his place at the rear of the coach, and just as quickly as it had come, the danger was past.

"Are you harmed?"

A man's voice, low and close—accompanied by the realization that the wall against which she had been thrown was actually a man's chest, that the pounding in her ears was his heart hammering beneath her cheek.

Although her knees shook with the exertion, she forced herself upright and away from his support, determined not to draw more attention her way. "No," she said.

Or at least, that was what she had meant to say. But the word curved in her throat and left her lips as *"Non."*

In these days of revolution and war, most people seemed to be alarmed, even repelled by her French heritage, but on at least one memorable occasion, it had been an excuse for unwelcome familiarity. Would the strong hand still cupping her elbow drop away or grip her harder?

The stranger did neither. *"Vous êtes française,"* he merely said. *You are French.* It was not a question.

Something about his accent disoriented her. He did not speak French like an Englishman—at least, not like an English gentleman, one who had been tutored in the language from childhood, had spent time in Paris on the Grand Tour, and thought himself a fine fellow when he dropped a romantic phrase or two in some unsuspecting girl's ear.

Still less did he sound like a Frenchman, though.

She mustered the strength to take another step backward, to free herself from his touch, to look at him while she formulated a reply.

If she had imagined his voice unsettling, she was totally unprepared for his eyes, which were the soft, welcoming blue of a summer sky, startling in a deeply tanned face. He must have lost his hat during the rescue, for rain dripped from dark curls plastered to his forehead and ran in rivulets down his cheekbones and along his strong jaw.

His clothes offered no more enlightenment as to his status than had his voice: plain, well-tailored, but not elegant—even aside from being spattered with mud. No one would mistake him for a man of fashion. A merchant, perhaps. That might explain his having a few French words at his disposal. But he was as broad-shouldered and brown as a farmer.

Zut alors! Had she grown as snobbish as Robert? What bearing did the cut of the man's coat have on the fact that he had snatched her from almost certain death beneath the hooves of those horses? Even less did it matter how blue his eyes or how broad his shoulders. Although those shoulders, and the strong arms beneath them, certainly had played their part. And as for his eyes . . .

Even as she watched, a shadow flickered across them, and she found herself being looked at for the second time that day with a sort of curious frown.

Tugging off his glove, he raised his hand and brushed the pad of his thumb beneath her eye, flicking away a clump of mud. Beneath his surprisingly warm touch, her own skin felt cold. She shivered, then darted her gaze away from his face to discover her dress and Jane's cloak were all but ruined. Although the state of her clothes was the least of her worries, she found herself blinking away tears.

Shock. She drew her shoulders back and lifted her chin. "I must t'ank—*thank* you for saving my life," she said, marshaling every trick she had learned to make her English sound perfectly . . . well, *English*. And failing miserably.

Nevertheless, he paid her the compliment of replying in the same language. "I was simply in the right place at the right time. May I be of some further assistance, Miss . . . ?"

The hesitation at the end of his question begged for an introduction. "Lottie Blake—" she began, unthinkingly. *Blakemore*, she had been about to say, as if she could afford to go about revealing her real name to anyone who asked.

But it little mattered, because before she could finish, his brows dove downward. " 'Lottie'?" he echoed disapprovingly. "*Charlotte*, surely."

She had never really been fond of the nickname. Her aunt had begun it, disliking how *Charlotte* rolled off a French tongue. Before that, Charlotte could hardly remember having been called anything at all.

It felt doubly strange, then—doubly good?—to hear her given name now, even on the lips of a perfect stranger.

"Yes. Charlotte," she agreed, "Charlotte Blake." It was a comfortable alias, at least as fitting as *Her Grace, the Duchess of Langerton* had ever been. Although the muscles in her legs still quivered, she managed a curtsy. "Very pleased to make your acquaintance, sir."

"The pleasure is mine, Miss Blake." He bowed in return. "Edward Cary, at your service."

photo credit: Vicky Lea, Hueit Photography

A love affair with historical romances led **SUSANNA CRAIG** to a degree (okay, three degrees) in literature and a career as an English professor. When she's not teaching or writing academic essays about Jane Austen and her contemporaries, she enjoys putting her fascination with words and knowledge of the period to better use: writing Regency-era romances she hopes readers will find both smart and sexy. She makes her home among the rolling hills of Kentucky horse country, along with her historian husband, their unstoppable little girl, and a genuinely grumpy cat. Find her online at www.susannacraig.com.

To Kiss a Thief

**In this captivating new series set in Georgian England, a
disgraced woman hides from her marriage—for better
or worse . . .**

Sarah Pevensey had hoped her arranged marriage to St. John Sut-
liffe, Viscount Fairfax, could become something more. But almost
before it began, it ended in a scandal that shocked London society.
Accused of being a jewel thief, Sarah fled to a small fishing village
to rebuild her life.

The last time St. John saw his new wife, she was nestled in the lap
of a soldier, disheveled, and no longer in possession of his family's
heirloom sapphire necklace. Now, three years later, he has located
Sarah and is determined she pay for her crimes. But the woman he
finds is far from what he expected. Humble and hardworking, Sarah
has nothing to hide from her husband—or so it appears. Yet as he attempts to woo her to uncover her secrets, St. John soon realizes that
if he's not careful, she'll steal his heart . . .

SUSANNA
CRAIG

"A stunning, sensual storyteller,
Susanna Craig is an author to watch!"
—New York Times bestselling
author Jennifer McQuiston

TO KISS A THIEF

RUNAWAY DESIRES

CPSIA information can be obtained
at www.ICGtesting.com
Printed in the USA
LVOW03s1610090118
562393LV00002B/292/P